I MARRIED A MOB BOSS

A STANDALONE MAFIA ROMANCE

SHANDI BOYES

WANT TO STAY IN TOUCH?

Facebook: facebook.com/authorshandi

Instagram: instagram.com/authorshandi

Email: authorshandi@gmail.com

Reader's Group: bit.ly/ShandiBookBabes

Website: authorshandi.com

Newsletter: https://www.subscribepage.com/AuthorShandi

ALSO BY SHANDI BOYES

** Denotes Standalone Books*

Perception Series

Saving Noah *

Fighting Jacob *

Taming Nick *

Redeeming Slater *

Saving Emily

Wrapped Up with Rise Up

Protecting Nicole *

Enigma

Enigma

Unraveling an Enigma

Enigma The Mystery Unmasked

Enigma: The Final Chapter

Beneath The Secrets

Beneath The Sheets

Spy Thy Neighbor *

The Opposite Effect *

I Married a Mob Boss *

Second Shot *

The Way We Are

The Way We Were

<u>Sugar and Spice</u> *

<u>Lady In Waiting</u>

<u>Man in Queue</u>

<u>Couple on Hold</u>

<u>Enigma: The Wedding</u>

<u>Silent Vigilante</u>

<u>Hushed Guardian</u>

<u>Quiet Protector</u>

Enigma: An Isaac Retelling

Twisted Lies *

<u>Bound Series</u>

<u>Chains</u>

<u>Links</u>

<u>Bound</u>

<u>Restrain</u>

<u>The Misfits</u> *

Nanny Dispute *

<u>Russian Mob Chronicles</u>

<u>Nikolai: A Mafia Prince Romance</u>

<u>Nikolai: Taking Back What's Mine</u>

<u>Nikolai: What's Left of Me</u>

<u>Nikolai: Mine to Protect</u>

<u>Asher: My Russian Revenge</u> *

<u>Nikolai: Through the Devil's Eyes</u>

<u>Trey</u> *

The Italian Cartel

Dimitri

Roxanne

Reign

Mafia Ties (Novella)

Maddox

Demi

Ox

Rocco *

Clover *

Smith *

RomCom Standalones

Just Playin' *

Ain't Happenin' *

The Drop Zone *

Very Unlikely *

False Start *

Short Stories - Newsletter Downloads

Christmas Trio *

Falling For A Stranger *

One Night Only Series

Hotshot Boss *

Hotshot Neighbor *

The Bobrov Bratva Series

Wicked Intentions *

Sinful Intentions *

Devious Intentions *

Deadly Intentions *

COPYRIGHT

22/01/24

Editing: Mountains Wanted Publishing

Editing: Swish Design & Edits

Proofing: Lindsi La Bar

Cover: SSB Covers & Design

To Kelly,

Thanks for your message of support.
I appreciate the craziness you instill in my life.

Shandi xx

A gasp escapes my lips as I springboard into a half-seated position. While I rub the pain rocketing through my temples, I suck in big gulps of air, hopeful it will calm the panic scorching me from the inside out.

Goose bumps prickle my sweat-slicked skin when the coolness of air conditioning glides over my body.

Pure agony.

Gut-wrenching hell.

I'd rather die than open my eyelids is how I feel right now.

Someone, please tell me why the National School Board would ever think holding their annual conference in Las Vegas was a good idea. I swear, I only had a couple of drinks, at the very most a few, but there's no way I drank enough to suffer the side effects of a tunnel hole digger drilling through my skull.

I thought waking up the morning following my twenty-first birthday was wretched.

This is ten times worse.

After taking a few minutes to calm my pounding head, I reluctantly open my drooping eyelids. My lips quirk when I drink in the elaborate room. For a school district that can't afford to buy kindergarten students coloring pencils, the hotel they booked is extravagant. Monstrous vaulted ceilings, white wood-paneled walls, gorgeous dark wood furniture, and one of the largest beds I've ever seen confront me.

As I slide across crisp three-thousand thread count sheets, another confronting fact dawns on me.

I'm naked.

Not slightly nude.

Naked-*naked*.

Oh, Lord, what did I do?

I swing my eyes around the room while my sluggish brain struggles to gather my bearings. My heart wildly beats, matching the thumping between my legs when the typical Vegas lifestyle reflects back at me. Casino chips line the varnished wooden floor, my clothes are strewn from the door to the bed, and black polished dress shoes sit at the edge of a mattress that smells of hot, raunchy sex.

Nothing out of the ordinary here.

Not a single thing...

Wait a minute... black polished dress shoes?

After scampering off the bed, I fall to my knees next to the shoes. I assess them carefully like they're a bomb set to detonate in two point five seconds. The soles are well-scuffed, but the leather on the size thirteen shoes is so thoroughly polished I can see my disheveled appearance in them.

I cringe after taking in the travesty.

I don't recall using a spatula to apply my makeup last night.

Ignoring the fact I look like I've returned from a moonlighting job, I continue inspecting the shoes, seeking any sign of who their owner may be.

"Like grown men write their name on the soles of their shoes, Blaire," I mumble to myself.

Upon finding no signs of ownership, I stand from my kneeled position then drift my eyes around the vast space.

A silent squeal ripples from my parched mouth when a door creaking open booms through my ears not even two seconds later. I dive for the bed, only just making it beneath the scrumptiously thick covers when a female with a heavily wrinkled face enters my room.

While grumbling in a slurred accent, she retrieves my clothing from the floor and tosses it into a woven basket balancing on her ample hip.

"Oh... umm... excuse me. I didn't order housekeeping," I strangle out, my voice weak with embarrassment.

When the elderly lady's narrowed gaze connects with my light green eyes, I sink deeper into the mattress. Her nearly black gaze is fierce, and it has my heart pumping. "You no want me to clean your room?" From the depth of her accent and poor wording, it's easy for me to derive her first language isn't English.

After peeking my head out of the sheet I'm clutching for dear life, I shake my head.

"You want to live like pig?" Her words are spat out of her mouth in a malicious slur, right alongside some real-life spit.

Now I need housekeeping.

While muttering in a language I'm not familiar with, the silver-haired female scuffles to the door. I'm eager for her to leave, but she can't just yet.

I hold my hand in the air like my kindergarten students do when seeking my attention. When my efforts to secure her attention fail, I say, "Umm... excuse me." My voice is low, hindered by my pounding, hungover head.

The elderly lady's cotton skirt flares out when she spins around to face me. "Yes?"

The longer she stares at me, the more my heart palpitates. "Ah... I'm going to need my clothes." I point to the clothes she collected off the floor. "Unless you can get the concierge to bring up my suitcase?"

She glares at me with flaring nostrils and protruding veins in her chunky neck. "Concierge?" When I nod, she spits out, "You want *concierge* to bring your bag to your room?"

I arch my brow, shocked by the maliciousness in her tone, before nodding again. "Please?"

She smiles. It isn't a friendly grin. It is scary and life-threatening.

"I'll be sure to ask *concierge* to bring up your bag," she says in a heavily drawled accent.

"Th-thank you."

The wild beat of my heart weakens when she places the basket onto an antique dresser by the door. After issuing me a final reprimand solely using her eyes, she exits the room.

The instant the latch on the lock clicks into place, I slip out of bed and make a mad dash for the door.

Since my bare feet can't grip the overly polished floor, I crash into the door with an almighty thud. The winded rattle of my blow bellows up my chest before leaving my mouth with a huff.

After brushing an unruly strand of hair off my cheek, I secure the lock on the door, snag my clothing out of the basket, then make a beeline for the only other door in the room.

My quick speed slows to a snail's pace when I walk into an extravagant bathroom. I scan my eyes around the room, drinking in the black marble countertops, artisan glass sinks, and a ginormous clawfoot tub.

If I weren't concerned about receiving another visit from the Wicked Witch of the West, I'd be tempted to drown my hangover in that heavenly-looking tub. But since that is more a hope than a certainty, I ignore the pleas of my aching muscles and head for the double vanity to splash cold water on my inflamed face instead.

Confusion muddles my brain when sunshine bounces off my blonde locks. If the brightness beaming through the rooftop window is any indication, I only have mere hours until my scheduled flight home.

My first visit to Vegas was planned as a fly-in-and-out one-night affair. My odds of winning Teacher of the Year were small, but the privilege of being nominated saw me cashing in my parents' frequent flyer miles for a whirlwind weekend.

From the swirling of my stomach and thumping of my head, whirlwind is an extremely adequate word to describe my once-in-a-lifetime solo getaway.

While clutching the sparkling marble counter, I drag my heavy eyes over my reflection in the mirrored wall behind the vanity, eager to discover what has caused my muscles to be taut with the odd combination of agony and pleasure.

Deciding to start my assessment at a less risqué part of my body, I drop my eyes to my pastel yellow-painted toes. The fiery heat gifting my face with a pink hue hasn't extended to the lower extremities of my body. Other than my legs being bronzed with the effects of a desert sun, the lower half of my body is in the same condition it was before I arrived in Vegas.

I munch on my bottom lip while continuing my in-depth perusal. My scan doesn't get far, stopping mere inches from the lower half of my body when my eyes lock in on an accessory I didn't have Friday night.

Oh, sweet Jesus. What in the Lord's name is that?

As I stumble backward, I scrub the thick black ink scrawled across my right hip. My heart rate surges into dangerous territory as I scrub, scratch, and scour my skin.

Even with my hip on the verge of bleeding, nothing works.

The four-letter word scrawled across my skin won't budge.

"Who the hell is Rico? And why is his name tattooed on my hip?" I mumble to my wide-eyed reflection.

After planting my backside on the edge of a black marble tub, I bury my head in my hands. This is not me. I'm the safe friend. The good girl. I'm a kindergarten teacher, for crying out loud! I don't go to Vegas and get a man's name tattooed on my hip. I grade papers, hunt garage sales every Sunday for low-cost books for my students, and knit booties for the babies in the NICU at my local hospital. I don't get drunk and most definitely do *not* get tattoos.

Maybe I'm dreaming, and I haven't arrived at Vegas yet? Maybe those sleeping tablets I guzzled down with a wine spritzer while squeezed between a man whose body odor smelled like a cat's food bowl and the lady who had an extra toe are messing with my mind.

Yes! That makes perfect sense. This is all just a big bad dream.

Ouch!

Nope, I'm not sleeping.

Rubbing my leg, I soothe the sting of my pinch while I struggle to unscramble my confusion.

Minutes pass in silence as nothing but a sea of blackness greets me. There's one thing my over-fried brain can decipher—I need to get out of here.

After yanking my knee-length floral skirt up my thighs, I fasten my cotton push-up bra around my back. My movements are unsteady, inhibited by my thumping skull. Once I snag my dusty pink cotton blouse off the vanity, I sling it around my shoulders, then run my fingers through my ratted hair. The number of knots in my hair gives my usually straight design a bolder, much more risqué look.

"Ha! Who are you trying to kid? You look like you've just arrived home after starring in an eighties music clip for Bruce Springsteen," I mumble to my disheveled reflection.

While pretending I didn't wear any panties yesterday, I make my way back to the main part of my suite. The elderly maid found my clothes with ease since they were left where they fell, but my shoes are proving to be quite the challenge.

After searching every inch of the floor space, I drop to my knees and crawl under the bed. I inwardly gag when I find a strip of condoms stuck to the satin bed ruffle. My pounding temples drop several inches lower when I notice the three-strip of bare-skinned condoms is empty, then my heart rate kicks when the quickest memory filters through my brain.

I ripped open one of those condoms with my teeth while... while... *darn it!* My memories have converted back to black.

I flick the used condom packaging to the side before stretching my arm to reach for my orthopedic sandal wedged in the furthermost corner. Don't judge. Have you ever walked the entire strip of Vegas before? I did for three hours solid!

Comfortable shoes are not a recommendation.

They are a necessity.

I freeze before sucking in a big breath. That was my first recollection of arriving in Vegas. Other than recalling portions of the plane ride over, my memories of the last twenty-four hours are best described as hazy.

After snatching my second sandal from its hiding spot in the middle of the enormous bed, I fasten them to my feet then head for the door. Hazy memories, drunken mistakes, and googling how to have a tattoo removed without your parents finding out can wait until my feet are safely back on my home turf of Ravenshoe.

While exhaling a nerve-cleansing breath, I push down on the gold embossed handle and swing open the door. My brows hit my hairline when a second bout of elegance smacks into me. However, for an elegant hotel, they have a laid-back approach to security. None of the rooms have the swipe locks most hotel chains have, and not a peephole can be seen.

The more I take in the chandeliered hall, the more my heart restricts.

This isn't a hotel, is it?

Dammit!

My feet pad along the chunky woolen rug in silence as I make my way down the hallway. Renaissance paintings line the walls, and the aroma of garlic lingers in the air. The pounding of my pulse reaches deafening status when I hit the end of the hall. Two men with shoulders as wide as my height are at the stoop of the stairwell, talking to each other in a foreign language.

"Hello," I squeak out when my approach stifles their conversation.

While snubbing their imprudent stares, I race down the stairwell. The gallop of my heart matches the stomping of my feet as I charge through the massive unknown residence.

My tornado pace comes to a shrieking halt when a handful of women suddenly bombard me only seconds later. Lace and satin materials are shoved in my face as they fire a range of questions at me.

Well, I'm assuming they are questions because I don't understand a word they're saying.

Their approach reminds me of my backpacking adventures in Bali, Indonesia. If you haven't experienced the craziness of a street market in Bali, you haven't lived. It's the equivalent of shopping at Walmart high on crack.

That's another assumption, as I've never touched a drug in my life.

Not understanding a word the ladies are flinging at me, I spin on my heels and scuffle down a dark and dingy corridor on my right. Their hair-raising battering is left for dust when I creep deeper into the hall. My stomach gurgles when the women stop at the end of the hall and eyeball me with a snick of panic in their eyes.

Anyone would swear I just entered the gates of hell.

Taking no notice of their odd reaction—*and my brain pulverizing my skull*—I continue striding down the dark, dingy hall. Just like the hallway my room is in, this corridor is lined with doors, but unlike that hall, this corridor isn't elaborately decorated, and these rooms have locks—big clunky deadbolt locks.

I stop dead in my tracks and furrow my brows. *Why would there be locks on the outside of the doors?*

Oh, God.

My retreating steps out of the stuffy space halt when the faint murmur of voices tinkle down the bland corridor. When I slant my head to the side, I level my breathing and prick my ears. My regular breathing pattern returns when the distinct noise of men talking sounds into my ears.

Pretending the twisted feeling in my stomach is from my hangover drilling my skull into the next century and not fear, I pace toward the collection of deep, masculine voices.

My swirling stomach slackens when I catch the occasional sentence spoken in English between the heavily accented voices.

"If you just give me a chance..."

"As I said earlier..."

"It wasn't as your men are saying..."

After stopping outside the door the voices are coming from, I inhale a deep, calming breath. *"You can do this, Blaire,"* I chant to myself.

I clutch the handle for dear life before throwing open the heavily weighted door.

Just as it gives out a creak, pleading pummels my eardrums. "Please. No. I'm begging you. I have children. Small, precious little children."

With my heart clutched in fear, I float my eyes up from my feet. Men in midnight-colored suits are huddled around something in the middle of a poorly lit room. Just like the men in the hallway, they're tall, wide, and their snarling faces set my pulse racing.

I take a stumbling step backward when black smoke loiters through my nose. It burns my eyes and suffocates my throat. I try to hold in the cough the thick waft of smoke instigates. I try to smother it until I'm in the safety of the hall, but no matter how much I plead with my brain that now is not the time to protest about the disgusting habit of smoking, my efforts are fruitless.

The instant my measly cough splatters through my snapped-shut lips, the group of men shift their attention to me. I take another retreating step, alarmed by their fuming glares, and dread-induced chemicals pump through my body when my eyes zoom in on their original devotion.

A balding man in his mid-fifties is bound to a rickety chair in the middle of the room. A nasty gash across his right brow is trickling blood down his pale cheek, his eyes are wide and terrorized, and a wet patch goes from the crotch of his dark blue trousers until it joins a puddle sloshed around his shoeless and bloodied feet.

My pupils widen as my heart drops from my ribcage. I beg for my feet to move, but just like the man bound to the chair, I'm frozen in fear. The only remaining functioning part of my body—my eyes—swing to the side when a deep, rumbling voice vibrates through my chest. "Kitten?"

My head thumps for a completely different reason when my wide gaze is met with a dark, mysterious stranger in the corner of the room. He has thick black hair, bleak sable eyes, and a few days of stubble hiding a well-carved chin.

If I weren't immersed in a scary rendition of *The Godfather*, I would say he is handsome—perhaps even deliriously gorgeous—but since I'm on the verge of peeing my pants like the man bound to the chair, I harness my perving gaze for a more suitable occasion.

My pulse quickens when the dark-haired stranger stands from his chair. His aura demands my attention, and his stature alludes to his power. Even in a room filled with scary men, there's no doubt who the alpha of the room is.

It is him.

Unlike the other half a dozen men gawking at me in shocked anger, this handsome stranger looks at me with a sense of familiarity, and if I'm not mistaken, *ownership*.

Blinking to break the trance he has trapped me in, I squeak out, "Wrong room," before spinning on my heels and charging for the door.

Thick, accented voices yell for me to stop, but I barely hear a word over the mad beat of my heart. I race down the corridor remarkably fast for someone on the verge of wetting their pants.

Unfortunately, my fast-moving legs are not quite quick enough.

A window-shattering squeal rips from my throat when a broad arm wraps around my torso. His hold has my feet lifting from the floor and my heart smashing my ribs. I thrash and kick out wildly, fighting with all my might. After clawing the suit-covered arm with my nails, I attempt to bite the hand moving to cover my shrieking mouth while struggling to keep haunted memories buried.

My vicious attack only diminishes when my name comes barreling out of a deep voice, the same voice that called me Kitten mere seconds ago. "Calm down, Blaire, or you'll gain unwanted attention." Since I'm frozen in shock, he drags me into an unlocked room on our right without protest. "You're safe. No one will ever hurt you."

Air hisses through the small cracks of his hand covering my mouth as I battle to fill my heaving lungs with oxygen. With the fear of hyperventilating surfacing faster than my anger, I decrease my wails and shift my focus to breathing. The last thing I want to do is pass out in a house full of scary men and non-English-speaking females.

Upon realizing I'm no longer fighting, the stranger removes his hand from my mouth, dropping it to my neck. Every hair on my body bristles when he rubs his thumb over the dip in my collarbone. Now instead of suffering the crippling clutch of panic, I'm overcome by desire. Insanely, my nipples bud and my lips part, my body choosing its own response to the closeness of the spicy-scented stranger.

"That's it, Kitten. Nice big breaths."

The rasp of his tone tightens my insides even more. His voice is sophisticated and smooth, the type that could sell ice to Eskimos. It switches my heart rate from a frightened gallop to a leisured trot in an instant.

After a few more big breaths, my regular breathing pattern returns, and some normality takes hold. When the unnamed stranger places me on my feet, I run my sweaty hands down my skirt before swiveling around to face him.

My blood pressure skyrockets again. He's even more alluring up close—defined nose, dark, edgy eyes, and cheekbones any sculptor would love to carve. He's a true masterpiece.

I peer into his eyes, unable to look away for fear of missing something magical, while asking, "How do you know my name?" Not giving him the chance to reply, I add, "Have we met before? You seem so familiar." My words come out hoarse, strangled by both arousal and alarm.

The handsome stranger's eyes flare with a vast range of emotions before his lips tug high. The quickest flash of a smirk freezes my heart. My god this man is beautiful.

When he runs his hand across the scruff on his tanned face, a shimmer of platinum wrapped around his ring finger captures my attention.

"You're married!" I cringe when my nasally high voice bounces off the walls and jingles into my ears.

Since I'm locked in an enthralling daze of idiocy, I thought there was something greater than fear between us.

Obviously, I was wrong.

Masking my disappointment with a neutral look, I return the married stranger's rousing stare. "Is your wife here? Does she speak English?" I question when my inquisitiveness gets the better of me.

His brows knit, but he remains so quiet only my heart drumming against my ribs can be heard.

Astonishment and another unreadable glint brighten his nearly black eyes as he begins to speak, but before a syllable escapes his mouth, the door I was dragged through seconds ago flies open. The trance the sable-haired man's beauty placed on me lifts when a burly-looking thug in a full-length trench coat steps into the room. His hollow eyes bounce between the mysterious stranger and me for several heart-thrashing seconds before he locks them on the gentleman beside me.

Mimicking the direction of his gaze, I turn my eyes as well. My heart sinks into my stomach. The captivating specimen I was entranced by seconds ago has vanished, replaced with the man who confronted me in the room earlier. The same room with an injured man bound to a chair.

Oh, my God, I'm a terrible person.

I'm in a room eyeballing a man as if his body parts are on a dessert menu while another man sits helpless only doors up from me.

The despair digging a hole in my heart deepens when the man at the door says, "Rico, it's time." His voice is heavily drawled with an accent I don't immediately recognize.

"Do as requested. I do not need to be present," responds the handsome stranger next to me.

The gentleman at the door bows his head. "Yes, boss." He shuffles backward like a dog afraid of getting a newspaper whacked across his disobedient nose.

When he closes the door, I stand quiet for a minute, giving my scattered brain a chance to run the events from the past ten minutes through my blurry mind.

It's only when I reach the first half of the intruder's statement does my dazed state end.

While trying to ignore the room closing in on me, I stammer out, "You're Rico?"

Dizziness plagues my senses when Rico nods. I splay my hands across my hips and gulp in large breaths, shocked at discovering the stranger before me is Rico, the owner of the name tattooed on my hip.

When my swirling stomach becomes too much to handle, I slap my quivering hand over my mouth and battle to hold in the contents threatening to break free. The fiery heat scorching my veins unveils another discovery, a crisp coolness tingling on my parched lips.

Heavily panting, I pull my hand away from my mouth. Giddiness clusters in my head when my eyes zoom in on a sparkling platinum band wrapped around the third finger of my left hand. My twisting stomach extends to my heart when I realize its ruby and diamond design is an exact replica of the ring on Rico's hand.

I stumble backward as my pupils widen, and my heart falters.

Oh. My. Lord.

I married a mob boss.

3

White spots dance in front of my eyes as the room spins. This can't be happening. There must be a mistake. I'm a good girl. I wouldn't wake up married to a stranger, let alone a mob boss.

Stumbling, I make my way to a wooden chair similar to the one the gentleman three rooms over is bound to. Upon noticing my unsteady movements, Rico places his hand on my elbow. His touch is electric and it sends a surge of awareness over every inch of my body.

After plopping into the seat, I drop my head to my knees and draw in big breaths. My chest rattles as I battle the impulse to faint. The efforts of my heaving lungs double when a hand spreads across my back. My brain screams for me to yank away from Rico's touch, but my heart pleads for me to accept his comfort.

Unable to concentrate on anything but the panic havocking my body, I take the comfort he's offering with a grain of salt.

Over time, his heated hand soothes my shakes, and his smooth, gritty voice swallows the violent ringing in my ears. After giving myself a few moments to settle my crazy heart rate, I lift my head from between my knees.

Giddiness swamps my brain again. It isn't from my sudden incline. It's from the deliriously handsome specimen crouched in front of me.

"Are you all right?" Rico's tone is a unique mix of commanding and nurturing.

Unable to speak through my fire-scorched throat, I simply nod. He takes two retreating steps, then props his backside onto a wooden chest a few feet from me.

When his dark eyes run over my body, my shoulders instinctively roll, and I straighten my slouched posture. Unlike the chill I got when his eyes raked my body in the other room, this time, his perusal causes the temperature to become stifling.

I inhale a shaky breath when he returns his eyes to my face. His gaze is commanding, primitive, and strong, and it sets my pulse racing.

Upon spotting my heated cheeks, he smirks. "Did you not see the sign at the start of the hall, Kitten? Women are not allowed in this area. And where are the men stationed outside your room?"

My brows stitch, mindful of the authoritativeness in his voice. "Women aren't allowed down here?"

His powerful gaze burns into mine, charring my soul from the inside out before he nods.

"Was the sign in English?" I mumble, my voice incapable of hiding the insanity of the situation.

Rico smiles a lazy smirk that has my veins boiling. "No. It's in Russian."

My shocked eyes meet his. "Russian?" My pupils widen as reality dawns. "As in Russian, *Russian*?"

When he nods, the wooziness inflicting my head over the past twenty minutes travels to my stomach. I sit still in shock, watching him in silence, hopeful he'll fill in the gaps.

When he remains quiet, I stutter, "You're Russian?"

A mouthwatering smirk forms before he dips his chin. Even entranced by his lazy smile, I drop my head to my knees again before fighting through a second battle of keeping the contents of my stomach where they belong.

Unfortunately, my attempts this time are fruitless. Nothing can stop the uncontrollable swirls. Even certain my stomach is empty, I clamp my hand over my mouth and straighten my spine. "Is there a bathroom close by?" I ask Rico, mumbling through the cracks of my hand.

Blood on the cuff of his light blue business shirt becomes exposed when he gestures his hand to a door on my right. Seeing evidence of his corrupt life firsthand hinders any chance of containing my flipping stomach.

Springing to my feet, I bolt to the door as fast as my quaking legs can take me. I only just make it into the poorly designed bathroom when the slosh in my stomach makes its way into the world. My throbbing temples scream in pain as my back violently bends.

Despite the brutal heaves racking my body, I can't help but notice the way Rico's hand rubbing my back causes every fine hair on my body to bristle.

Once all the throat-burning contents of my stomach have been expelled, I lean back on my feet. Tears well, and my heart is a muddled mess of turmoil.

I've never engaged in a battle as vicious as the one my brain and heart are in right now.

How could one man incite such a contradictory set of emotions? My brain is begging me to leave this room before I walk so far into the darkness I'll never find my way out. But my heart is pleading with me to ignore the protests of my brain, and for once, let it have a chance to prove its decisions are as gripping as its astute counterpart.

Warmth engulfs me when a set of broad arms band around my body and hoist me from the floor. The stomach-calming smell of spices filters into my nose when Rico pulls me into his chest and strides out of the room. My first reaction is to repel from his grasp, but with my mind nothing but a hazy blur, my heart wins this battle.

When I press my cheek against Rico's well-formed chest, his wildly beating heart tames my pounding skull. If I closed my eyes, I could pretend I'm not in the midst of the scariest dream I've ever had.

Unfortunately, I lose any shot of normality when he strides past the room I scampered out of minutes ago. The door is only open a mere inch, but it's wide enough for me to see the immoral act playing out before my very eyes. I'm a kindergarten teacher, but I've seen enough Hollywood movies to recognize the weapon a man in the room is holding.

Like he can sense my snooping stare, the man clutching a black pistol with a silencer screwed on the end turns his gaze to me. His eyes are a vibrant icy blue, but they are lifeless and hollow.

With a conniving grin, he winks at me before swinging his gun to the now gagged and bound man I saw earlier.

I shoot my eyes to Rico just as quickly. "Are they... is he... are they going to..."

My words trail off when the faintest pfft of a silencer filters through my ears. It doesn't matter how much the manufacturer claims it's silent, there's no mistaking that sound. It's heart-shattering and devastating.

Dread strikes my heart as wetness floods my eyes. Rico doesn't flinch, balk, or even acknowledge he heard a thing. He continues moving through the vast residence without a single reaction crossing his face.

Who is this man I married? Only a monster could ignore the quiet screams of death.

Fighting my trembling muscles, I crawl out of his embrace just as we hit the door of my room. His eyes convey his protest to the loss of my contact, but his lips remain locked. My body is uncontrollably shaking with fear, but thankfully, my legs are in functioning order.

After entering the room, I force my eyes to lock with Rico's. "Did they kill him?" My words come out strained since they're coerced through the bile lodged in the back of my throat.

He holds my gaze, his eyes blazing with a range of emotions I can't read. "Don't ask questions you don't want the answer to, Kitten." Although his tone is clipped, the remorse concealed by his sharp eyes answers my question.

I throw my hand over my quivering lips. "Why? Why did they kill him?"

He slants his head to the side and stares at me with bleak, desolate eyes. "Why what? As far as anyone is concerned, you heard and saw nothing. Do you understand what I'm saying, Kitten?" My lungs become winded when he takes a step closer to me. "You saw nothing." His eyes relay the importance of his words. This isn't a request or a suggestion. This is a demand. "Tell me what you saw, Kitten?" His face is emotionless, his tone low.

Tremors rake through my body as I say, "Nothing. I saw nothing," through a sob. The indents lining his forehead smooth the instant the words seep from my lips.

No longer trusting my legs to keep me standing, I pace to the monstrous bed and sit on the edge. Rico's eyes track me, but his feet remain planted in their original position as he watches me with reserved silence.

Pain shreds through my heart when the man's pleas sound through my ears on repeat. Did he have small children like he said? Did Rico's men just make them orphans?

Several minutes pass in silence as I search his impassive face for answers to my inaudible questions. They are full of turmoil and despair. I don't know what's more disturbing, the fact I don't know the man in front of me, yet, he is my husband, or that I discovered him in a room with a man who was just killed. Rico nor I pulled the trigger, but we didn't stop it from happening either. Doesn't that make us just as callous as the man who did?

After running my hand under my nose, removing the contents spilling there, I return my eyes to Rico. A frown mars the space between his brows as he watches me like a hawk, but he has not spoken a syllable since he warned me to remain quiet.

"Can I go home?" My voice is rickety but full of silent begs. "I want to go home."

Rico's brows scrunch as the quickest flash of antagonism fills his eyes.

Even with the scent of fear plaguing our small gathering, I continue, "I shouldn't be here. I don't want to be here." My words fly out before I can stop them. "Please let me go home."

The small flare of anger in Rico's eyes expands to a raging tornado, but even rattled beyond comprehension, I hold his gaze as he spans the distance between us. He carries himself with a confident poise that not only demands respect but trust as well. And for some reason unbeknownst to me, I already trust him enough not to be scared of him.

His hand fills the side of my face when he places it on my jaw and peers into my watering eyes. For someone whose stern gaze alone could terrify any man, I find comfort in his gentle touch and glistening eyes.

"What do you remember about last night?" His tempestuous voice lowers to a more intimate tone.

My eyes bounce between his while I murmur, "Nothing."

His thick brows slant, his gaze searingly intense. "Nothing?"

Tears dribble when I nod, confirming his question.

He runs his thumbs over my cheeks to gather my tears before asking, "From when?"

Sick gloom spreads through me as I admit, "I don't remember stepping foot off the plane."

Rico yells a foreign word. From the harshness of his tone and the rage brewing in his eyes, I'm going to assume it was a Russian curse word. "You were sipping on a spritzer, Kitten. You had three at the most. How can you not remember anything?"

His deep timbre sends a shiver down my spine. Don't ask me if it's a good or bad shiver as I wouldn't be able to tell you.

When I fail to answer his question, he scrubs his stubbled chin before crouching down in front of me. I only just hold in my gasp when we meet eye to eye. His dark eyes are captivating from a distance, but up close, they're soul-stealing.

"You're my wife, Kitten. Do you understand that?"

When I nod, relief fills his eyes.

It's short-lived.

"But not because I remember marrying you. I put two and two together when I saw our matching wedding bands." *And my tattoo...* but I keep that snippet of information to myself.

With a furious storm raging in his eyes, he asks, "Do you regret marrying me?"

I balk, utterly shocked by his question. He can't be serious? He just walked me past a room where a man was murdered without a spark of remorse in his eyes. If I didn't regret meeting him, I'd be as much a monster as he is.

Furthermore, I don't know anything about the man standing before me. I don't even know if Rico is his full name or how old he is. I don't know him any better than the man who delivers my mail. He's a stranger. A scary stranger who can make my heart race in alarm and excitement, but still a stranger, nevertheless.

I can tell the exact moment Rico reads my silent response. The anger in his fear-provoking gaze grows, and his scruffy jaw can't hide its manic tic.

Standing from his crouched position, he extends to his full six-foot-plus height. With his eyes facing straight ahead, he says, "Collect your belongings. I'll have one of my men take you to the airport."

With that, he turns on his heels and stalks out of the room without a backward glance.

4

———

orty-five minutes later, a gentleman of medium build and short stature gathers my bag that was left dumped by the door within minutes of Rico fleeing it. Other than the clothes I'm wearing, I have no other personal stuff to collect, so I've spent the remaining forty-three minutes staring at the ceiling rose surrounding the crystal chandelier, silently pondering.

Forty-three minutes of reflecting only awarded me with forty-three minutes of blank memories and a lifetime of haunted ones.

Dozens of eyes track me when I follow the balding middle-aged man through the large residence. Unlike an hour ago, the women with thick accents don't accost me when I enter the main living area of the house. They eyeball me with curiosity, but remain quieter than the front row of churchgoers during Sunday mass.

My eyes shift sideways when the heat of an imprudent stare captures my attention. The man I spotted earlier with the icy blue eyes has his shoulder propped up on the curved wall of the corridor that saw me walking into the gates of hell. His hair is dark and slicked back, his eyes are mocking and full of evil, and his chin holds less stubble than Rico's.

When he issues me a conceited wink, I hold my head high and turn my gaze to the front, trying to display he doesn't scare me.

If only I could stop my knees from wobbling, then my attempts would be more believable.

The blue-eyed stranger's laughter shrills in my ears when I step out a set of double doors. The warm late afternoon Las Vegas sun reddens my cheeks when I stop on the front stoop of an elegant yet highly-guarded mansion.

I scan my eyes over the manicured grounds, absorbing the rolling turf that goes as far as the eye can see. A stream of elegant cars worth millions of dollars and beautiful floral displays make it feel like I'm not in the middle of a desert. If I could look past the heavily armed men in every corner, it would be a spectacular view.

Ignoring the gawking stares of the numerous men with guns strapped to their chests, I shadow the unnamed gentleman down the steps of the private residence. A thankful smirk curls on my lips when he holds open the back passenger door of a black Escalade.

"Thank you," I mumble while sliding into the car.

I balk when he unexpectedly slams the door shut.

After gathering my heart from the floor, I attempt to latch my seat belt. My fiddling with the uncooperative latch stops when the door opposite me swings open, and Rico slides inside. The veins in my neck twitch when he yanks my seat belt out of my grasp, then latches it into place in one swift motion.

I try to issue him my thanks, but just like the seat belt fastener, my mouth refuses to cooperate.

Once he has secured his belt, Rico turns his eyes to the window. I stare at him, gawking and confused. He said he'd have one of his men drive me to the airport, not himself.

When a gentleman in a cream checkered suit enters the escalade, Rico dips his chin in greeting before raising his eyes to the rearview mirror. Not speaking a peep, he signals to the driver to leave.

Confused and nursing a bruised ego, I keep my eyes rapt on Rico. If I were holding my breath waiting for him to acknowledge my presence, I would have been asphyxiated by now.

My eyes stray away from Rico when a deep voice calls my name.

"Sorry, were you talking to me?" I say to the gentleman across from me.

The corners of his lips tug high, exposing his perfectly straight teeth. "Yes, Blaire. My name is Erik Monstrateo, I'm Rico's lawyer." He offers me his hand to shake.

Masking my shock that he knows my name, I accept his handshake before shooting my eyes to Rico. From the way he keeps his gaze planted straight ahead and his subdued mood unwavering, anyone would swear he hasn't noticed my intrusive stare. Anyone but me. His scorching glare is burning a hole in my soul.

I drift my eyes back to Erik when he says, "Rico has been very generous with his settlement offer. Once the annulment forms are signed—"

I wave my hand through the air, stopping Erik mid-sentence. "Settlement offer?" I interrupt as my confused eyes bounce between Erik's light blue gaze.

Erik is a handsome man in his early thirties with sandy blond hair and sharp facial features, but just like Rico, he has a snip of danger in his eyes that sets me on edge.

Erik smiles. It's a warm smile in a callous and vindictive confrontation. "Yes. When you sign the annulment papers, a transfer of two million dollars will be wired into your account within twenty-four hours..." He continues speaking, but I don't hear a word he is saying. I'm too busy staring at Rico, slack-jawed and muted.

Throughout Erik's legal jargon on the terms of our annulment, Rico taps his finger on knee while his gaze remains fixated on the heavy flow of traffic whizzing by the window.

Anyone would swear he is being informed of the lunch specials at a fancy restaurant on the strip, not a life-altering decision.

The only time his attention is won is when I drift my eyes back to Erik and say, "I don't want Rico's money. All I want is to dissolve a drunken mistake and return to my normal life." My brows scrunch as bile crawls up my windpipe. "Well, as normal as it can be after what I've experienced this weekend."

A grin stretches across Erik's face as he scratches out the excessive monetary amount in the alimony section of our annulment documentation.

His smile is wiped right off his face when Rico commands, "Leave the figure as stated." He turns his hard-set eyes to me. "We had an agreement. The amount will remain. This is not negotiable."

"I don't want your money," I fire back, my voice surprisingly strong considering how fast my heart is racing.

"Then don't sign the annulment papers." Rico glares at me. "You either leave with the figure stated or remain married to me. Only you can decide which is the lesser of two evils."

When he returns his narrowed gaze to the window, I stare at him, blinking and confused. Why would he agree to hand over such an extravagant amount of money to a stranger? He has only known me for twenty-four hours. It honestly doesn't make any sense.

After adjusting the figure back to two million dollars, Erik hands the five-page document to me. I shift my eyes away from Rico to scan the densely worded form.

My heart squeezes when my eyes roam over Rico's full name—Enrique Julies Popov.

It's a beautiful name for a handsome but cold-hearted man.

My heart gets squashed for the second time when I spot the reason for our annulment. "Plaintiff lacked understanding of his/her actions to the extent that he/she was incapable of agreeing to the marriage because she was..."

"Severely inebriated," I read aloud.

Ignoring my twisting stomach, I snap my eyes to Rico. "I thought you said I only had a spritzer or three?"

He appears to be paying me no attention, but he can't fool me. I can feel the heat of his gaze on me. It's even more scorching than the blistering sun hanging in the sky. But no matter how long I glare at him, he never acknowledges my presence.

That hurts even more than a failed marriage under my belt before I turn twenty-five.

With my heart clutched with despair, I scribble my signature across the forms before passing them to Rico.

He doesn't read the document or pause for hesitation, he merely signs his name beside mine before handing the papers back to Erik.

I grit my teeth when tears prick in my eyes. I was married for less than twenty-four hours, so I have no clue why I'm being so dramatic. I guess, at the end of the day, I always thought when I married, it would be to a man I love, and it would last a lifetime. I never considered a quickie Vegas wedding.

While keeping my snivels to a bare minimum, I persevere with keeping my eyes locked on the scenery flying by. Famous Las Vegas landmarks stretch as far as the eye can see. It's a beautiful landscape, but nothing can ease the pain crippling me from the inside out.

It isn't just the freshness of an annulment maiming my heart or the coldness Rico is directing at me. It is the desolate look I saw in the eyes of the unnamed man bound to the chair shortly before his untimely death. He looked broken and defeated, similar to how I'm feeling now.

My eyes move away from the architectural wonder of Vegas when the Escalade suddenly stops at the side of the highway. Cars roar past the stationary vehicle, rattling the heavily tinted windows, and motorists beep their horns and yell obscenities, completely oblivious to who they're unleashing their vicious road rage on.

I bounce my dilated gaze between Erik and Rico when Rico demands he leave immediately.

Shocked and frozen in place, my brows hit my hairline when Erik exits the Escalade without a single protest. Warm, muggy air blasts into the car when he steps onto the road, adding to the outrage swirling in my stomach.

"It's a busy highway in the middle of a desert," I protest on Erik's behalf, my high voice conveying my utter disbelief.

I won't witness another untimely death without citing an objection.

Either not hearing a word I said—or continuing to ignore me—Rico signals for the driver to continue with our journey.

With my heart walloping my chest wall, I crank my neck back to Erik. He's standing at the side of the blistering asphalt with a cell phone attached to his ear and a complacent expression. Unlike me, he doesn't seem the slightest bit bothered by the one hundred-plus degree temperature beaming down on him.

Obviously, this is nothing new for him.

"One of my fleet drivers will collect him," Rico explains to my appalled expression, his tone deep and heart-clutching. He turns his blank eyes to me before asking in a more subdued tone, "Why are you crying, Kitten?"

The simplicity of his question causes a fresh batch of tears to trickle from my eyes. At a guess, I'd say he's a similar age to me, in his mid-twenties. So it makes me wonder how much darkness he's witnessed in his short life that knowing a man was killed has no affect on him whatsoever.

Rico is no doubt a handsome man, but as he's presents before me now, he's hideously ugly.

There's nothing uglier than a human being without compassion.

"Did that man have children like he said?" My words are brittle like cracked glass.

Rico adjusts his position so he faces me front-on. His thigh muscle twitches in sync with his jaw. "Does it matter?"

I nod. "Yes. He was a human being. How can you be so callous? You sit here demanding a woman you hardly know to take your money, but you can't have sympathy for a man who lost his life."

His dark eyes glare into mine, his gaze an odd mix of anger and interest. "I know you," he cites without a snick of hesitation. "And he was not a man. He was an errant coward who had to pay for his actions." His angry tone exposes a slight twang of a Russian accent.

"By death?" I blubber out.

He holds my gaze, his stern composure unyielding. "Yes. By any means I saw fit."

I balk, both flabbergasted and disgusted. "Who made you judge, jury, and executioner?"

"My birthright, my title, and my morals." His voice gets louder with every word he speaks. "You're convicting me, judging me, and sending me to execution all to defend a man you don't even know."

I run my hands across my cheeks, angrily removing the tears tracking down my face. Even knowing I'm waging a war against a man who clearly has no morals, I can't holster my campaign. I would have never married a soulless man, drunk or not, so I know there's more to this man than what I've witnessed this morning. My moral compass would have never blown so far off course.

"Nothing deserves a death sentence." I stare him dead set in the eyes. "*Nothing.*"

My breathing shallows to a wheezy pant when he asks, "Not even a child molester?"

My mouth falls open as a pain hits the middle of my chest. "W-what?"

"Or what about a murderer? Or the man who laced his drugs with cheap chemicals, resulting in the death of fourteen teens in one night? What punishment would you give them, Kitten? A slap on the wrist? A stern talking to?"

I return his stare, but I don't speak a word. I'm silenced by my heart sitting in my throat, and honestly, I don't know how to reply. I've never believed in the death penalty, but that was easy for me to preach when I wasn't confronted with a flurry of heinous crimes. Child molesters and murderers are the lowest of the low, but how does that give Rico the right to deliver justice?

"Two wrongs don't make a right." My softly spoken words point to the uncertainty of my reply. I'm at a loss on which direction I want to take our conversation.

"No, it doesn't. But justice isn't about what's right or wrong. It's about equitableness."

Our conversation comes to a shrieking halt when the Escalade pulls onto the curb of McCarran International Airport. When the driver exits the vehicle, Rico closes the small gap between us. Just like when we were together in the dingy bedroom, a vibrant, electric current fires between us. But it doesn't heal the damage my heart sustained in our volatile discussion. This man is technically a stranger. I've only known him for hours, but something deeper in my soul is telling me this isn't true.

My cheek twitches when Rico brushes away the leftover tears that slide down my face. His gentle touch and the cloud of sorrow in his eyes are a vast contradiction to the man debating who has the right to deliver justice mere seconds ago. It's like he is two completely different people. In front of others, he's a callous, cold-hearted monster who can dish out cruel punishments, but when he's with me alone, he's a man who appears caring—almost loving.

Once my tearstains have been removed, Rico connects his dark gaze with mine. "I'm the son of a monster, Kitten. Not a monster myself," he says like he can hear my internal dialogue.

My chance to reply is lost when the driver of the Escalade gathers my suitcase from the trunk and opens my door. Hot, muggy air streams into the cabin of the car, adding to my giddiness. The blaring desert heat of Las Vegas will always be stifling, but it's nothing compared to the roasting temperature building between Rico and me.

I curl out of the vehicle before my queasy stomach decides to act. My fast exit halts when a warm hand curls around mine. I sink deeper into my seat before swinging my eyes to Rico, discounting the way his simplest touch caused a shiver of euphoria to run the length of my spine.

The stern mask Rico was wearing earlier has slipped back into place, and his jaw is tense, but his eyes are still carrying the heaviness of remorse. "This is as far as I can go," he explains, his tone flat and brimmed with anger.

I swallow the brick in my throat. "Okay. Thanks for the lift." I catch my eye roll halfway. I met and married a man in less than twenty-four hours, yet I'm acting all modest and cordial.

My mother would be so pleased.

Overlooking the hammering of my heart, I kiss Rico's cheek. He twists his neck, forcing my kiss to land on his mouth instead of his cheek. I stop frozen with my lips attached to his. It isn't just the shock of excitement dashing through my veins that have my movements stiffening, it's the quickest snippet of a memory flashing through my mind...

"I want to kiss you, Enrique," I declare, peering into a pair of soul-capturing eyes.

My heart stops beating when the quickest flash of a smirk freezes time. "Nothing is stopping you, Blaire."

After closing my eyes, I rest my hands on his pecs and tilt my head to align our mouths better. Just as my lips brush, I open my eyes. His dark, beautiful gaze is staring dotingly into mine.

"You're supposed to close your eyes." My minty breath bounces off his lips and filters into my nose.

"I don't want to close my eyes," he replies as his heavy-hooded gaze dances between mine.

A grin curls on my lips. "Why?"

"Because I don't want to wake up and find out you were a dream." He runs the back of his hand down my flustered cheeks, causing every hair on my body to bristle.

I smile. "If it's a dream, it's the most beautiful dream I've ever had."

"Me too," Rico confesses, smiling a lazy grin that surges my heart into dangerous territory...

I pull back and peer into Rico's eyes. He's watching me with the same amount of intensity he bestowed on me in my memory, but his eyes are void of the tender spark that brightened his dark gaze last night until I mutter, "It was the most beautiful dream."

Not giving him the chance to react, I curl out of the car, snag my suitcase, and become lost in the heavy foot traffic on the terminal sidewalk.

In a muddled haze, I weave in and out of the bustling airport on my endeavor to reach my gate. The nicks in my heart enlarge with every step I take. My mind is scrambled, trying to recall any other events buried beneath the rubble of my drunken state while also ignoring the insane hope my statement might force a reaction from Rico.

I need to leave Vegas as soon as possible. This place is messing with my head. I only signed annulment papers twenty minutes ago, and now I'm praying my soon-to-be ex-husband will track me down and beg me not to leave.

Vegas doesn't just steal your morals, but your sanity too... and perhaps even your heart.

5

"Come on, Care Blaire, the water is beautiful," my best friend, Lacey, shouts while splashing me with the refreshing coolness of the inground swimming pool at our apartment complex. My skin is so sun-kissed, the water sizzles when it hits the skin high on my bare thigh.

Lacey cocks her brow and stares at me. "What's the deal? You've always been a water baby."

I rise from the daybed I'm lazing on, fling off my sunglasses, then gaze into her blue eyes. She is right. I've always loved the water, but after researching ways to have a tattoo inconspicuously removed, I discovered a range of new facts a tattoo virgin is naïve about. The most compelling, you can't swim in chlorinated water for two to three weeks after getting a tattoo. Considering my tattoo was only inked on my skin five days ago, I'm not willing to risk getting an infection on my newly open wound, even if I'm melting on a ninety-six-degree afternoon.

"I'm fine here," I lie, my tone as low as my hydration levels. "I thought I'd add a few more hours to my tan before school returns."

Lacey arches her brow into her drenched hairline. "Fine, but it's your loss."

I screw up my nose and stick out my tongue. After returning my snicker, Lacey dives into the holy-looking water. People may construe our little banter as bickering, but there's no maliciousness in our exchange. Lacey is straight to the point and calls it how she sees it, but she doesn't have a malicious bone in her body. She's my very dear friend and my closest confidant. That's why I find it so shocking I've managed to hide my Vegas antics from her for the past five days.

Don't take my admission the wrong way. Lacey was on me like white on rice the instant my plane landed in Ravenshoe, but since I've always been the straight-laced friend, her interrogation never went further than asking what food was served at the conference and if there were any hot male teachers she could use to fulfill her naughty teacher slash student fantasy.

Her interest in the boring life of a kindergarten teacher only lasted as long as our ten-mile trip to our apartment building. By the time we walked into our two-bedroom unit, my adventures in Vegas were a forgotten memory to Lacey and, unfortunately, me too.

No matter how hard I try to unlock my memories, the only snippets I've unearthed the past five days are the quickest flashes of Rico's beautiful, tormented eyes and lazy smirk. The flashbacks are short enough to keep my Vegas memories hidden but long enough to tether my heart to a man I don't know.

This is incredulous for me to say, but I never thought it was possible to miss a man you only knew for hours. Rico defies that logic. Most of our time together is lost in the background of my mind, but when I'm lying in bed, I miss him—the stranger I married.

I stop staring into space when Colt from Apartment 4A charges across the shimmery pool tiles and does a cannonball into the pool. "It's Friday, baby girl," he shouts at the top of his lungs before the pool water swamps his words.

His playful antics force a smile on my face while also saturating my one-piece swimsuit.

Leaping up from my sun chair, I snag a towel off the table next to me and pat my vibrant red one-piece swimsuit dry. Since I'm so immersed in drying my swimsuit, I don't notice Colt sneaking up on me until it's too late. Goose bumps prickle my forearms when he wraps his thick arms around my torso and hoists me off the ground. I squeal an ear-piercing protest. My pleas to be put down are barely heard over Lacey's boisterous giggle.

"Do it, Colt! Throw her in the water." Lacey yells through a barrage of laughter.

I scamper up Colt's torso—climbing him like a monkey climbs a tree—before locking my eyes with his mischief-filled gaze.

"Don't you dare," I warn, my voice low and crammed with false anger.

I've always been a sucker for Colt's mischief-filled eyes and cheeky grin. Normally, he just flashes me the quickest smirk, and I do anything he requests. But today is different. I'm not the same Blaire I was five days ago. *Not even close.*

"Don't you want to go for a swim, baby girl?" Colt smiles so broadly, the dimples in his bronzed cheeks become exposed.

"No." My reply is quick and resolute. "I'm happy tanning."

Colt stops striding when we hit the edge of the pool, then drops his gaze to me. The afternoon sun beaming off his blond locks shrouds him in a golden halo, making him look more angelic than his mischievous composure.

"Tanning?" His quick reply can't hide his laughter.

I return his sassy glare before nodding. Chlorinated skin, sunscreen, and the scent of a burly male filters through my nose when we face off in an intense, sweat-producing staredown. Lacey doesn't pay us any attention. This type of bantering is nothing out of the ordinary for Colt and me. Every time we're together, flirtatiousness hangs thick in the air. We've been flirting pretty heavily for the past seven months, but it's never gone any further than two friends toying around.

"What are you willing to give me not to throw you in the water?" Colt barters with his green eyes locked on me.

I narrow my eyes into thin slits, pretending I'm annoyed by his banter. "Nothing, because you're going to put me down as I'm requesting."

My grip on his biceps tightens when he dangles me over the water as if I'm a weightless child. This is no hard feat for Colt. He works as a personal trainer at the local gym. He can bench press two hundred and fifteen pounds, so my five-foot-six, one-hundred-twenty-pound frame is easy-peasy for him.

"Colt! Don't you dare," I squeal, praying to the Lord he doesn't dump me into the pool.

His smile broadens when I clamp his hips with my thighs. "Do you have your phone on you?" he asks, obviously recalling the time he threw me into the pool fully clothed while I had my cell phone in my pocket. His wages were stretched to the absolute limit when he replaced my phone with the latest model the very next day.

"Yes!" I lie. "I have my cell." I'll say anything if it saves me from being thrown into the deep end.

My lie is squashed when he turns his eyes to the lounge chair I was lying on and spots my cell phone on my beach towel.

"Nice try, baby girl." He chuckles, returning his blazing eyes to me.

I dig my nails into his biceps. "Please, Colt. I'm begging you."

This time, my voice comes out sounding like a plea instead of a demand. I'm not below getting down on my knees at this point.

"Three, two, one..." he counts down, ignoring my begging protests.

"I have a tattoo!" I scream when his shakes loosen my death-tight grip on his waist.

Colt freezes.

Time freezes.

Everything freezes.

Feeling an indiscreet stare burning a hole in the side of my head, I swing my eyes to my left. Lacey is staring at me, open-mouthed and wide-eyed. "No way. You'd never get a tattoo." The veins in my neck thrum when she scampers out of the pool and stands next to Colt in less than a heartbeat. "Bring her in. She has some explaining to do," she demands, her voice stern.

I gulp loudly.

Lacey only brings out her bossy boots during dire situations.

Obviously, she feels this is a dire situation.

Colt draws me away from the water's edge before placing me on my feet. A new type of awareness prickles my skin when every inch of his rock-hard body glides past mine in the process. Normally, his playfulness would have caused the pulse in my body to redirect to my pussy, but today his tease is less effective.

Don't construe my admission the wrong way. My nipples are budded, and euphoria has thickened my blood, but his appeal is nowhere near what I felt standing across from Rico in the dungeon-like room five days ago.

"Ms. Blaire Williams... cardigan-wearing, has never said a curse word in her life, kindergarten teacher got a tattoo? I knew there was a rebel hiding in there somewhere," Colt jests, lazily raking his eyes over my body. "What did you get? A cute little heart? A butterfly?" He locks his lust-filled eyes with mine. "Come on, baby girl. Are you going to show me? Or am I going to go on a treasure hunt?"

Lacey bumps my hip, her eyes wide, her jaw hanging. Even she can't miss Colt's innuendo-laced flirting. I'm not surprised. He has no trouble ruffling up any woman's interest. He just smirks, and they all flock to him. But this is different. Normally, our flirting is an acceptable notch over the friendship line, but this feels more like a gigantic leap.

After returning Lacey's hip bump, I cross my arms in front of my chest, ensuring my body's reaction to Colt's gawk remains concealed.

Unable to locate any ink on my scarcely covered body, Colt lifts and locks his eyes with me. "Where did you get it?" The waggling of his brows doesn't hide the eagerness in his words.

I tighten my arms under my chest, hoisting my moderate-size bosoms higher into the air. "Not in any place you'll ever see."

His smirk enlarges to a full-toothed smile, not believing a word I'm saying. He knows as well as I do, if given a chance, I'd climb him like a jungle gym.

Well, I would have before Vegas.

Now, I'm not so sure.

Colt's real name is Marshall, but we all call him Colt because... well... he's hung like a horse, that's why. And from the noises Lacey and I regularly hear bellowing from his apartment, he has no trouble bucking for hours.

Ignoring my flaming red cheeks, I say, "I'm... *leaving.*" After snatching my phone and towel off the chair, I bolt for the exit.

"But the fun is only beginning, baby girl," Colt jests, his tone low and tempting.

I've just hit the pool gate when Lacey catches up with me. "You have a lot of explaining to do, young lady." She weaves her arm around my elbow. "But I don't know where to begin. With the fire-sparking showdown I just witnessed? Or that you got a tattoo on an obviously *private* region of your body that you failed to update your best friend on?"

After guiding me into the elevator, Lacey snags the towel out and commences drying her light brown hair. The elevator ascends to our apartment in absolute silence. She doesn't need to speak. Her questioning eyes are more interrogating than her mouth ever could be. If the elevator car wasn't air-conditioned, I might have melted under her stifling gaze.

Her quiet approach lasts as long as it takes for us to walk into the front door of our modest apartment. "Spill. Now."

Throwing my house key onto the glass and wrought iron entry table, I pad into the living room. My steps are lazy, weighed down by the confusion still muddling my heart. I sit on a red wing-backed chair while Lacey props her backside on a stark white loveseat, not at all concerned her dripping wet two-piece bikini is soaking into the expensive material. She eyeballs me but has reverted to her silent stance, her gaze a unique mix of intrigue and shock.

"I got a tattoo in Vegas."

She huffs and rolls her eyes. "Duh."

The arch of her manicured brow increases when I blubber out, "And a husband."

Her mouth gapes as her eyes bulge. "Wait. What?" My admission has reduced a woman who can talk underwater to one-word sentences.

I gulp, washing away a lump in my throat. "I don't remember exactly how it transpired. All I remember is waking up with a wedding band on my finger and a man's name tattooed on my hip."

"Wow." She breathes out heavily, then scoots across the double-seated sofa to sit closer to me. "No half-baked Vegas experience for you. You went straight for the complete package."

I throw my hands over my eyes and slump into my chair. "That's not even the whole story."

Lacey gives herself a few moments to settle her shock before she sits on the edge of my chair and pries my hands away from my face. "Okay. We can handle this. First thing first... did you use protection? If not, there's a pharmacy half a block over. I can go get—"

"Yes," I interrupt, my words weak. "Although I have no recollection of the actual *deed,* empty condom wrappers were in my room."

Her lips quirk as a glint of curiosity fires in her expressive eyes. "*Wrappers?* How many are we talking exactly?"

I munch on my bottom lip before raising three fingers into the air. Her bugged-eyed expression grows, and the corners of her lips twitch, but she respectfully holds in her smile. Lacey knows me well enough to know the finger signal I'm holding in the air is the combined number of times I've done the *deed* the past two years, so to achieve that in one night is a record-breaking achievement for me.

"Okay. Good. Protection was used." Her voice is high with shock and excitement. "Second... was your husband still present the following morning, or did he do the Las Vegas hightail escape?"

Even in the intensity of the situation, her statement causes a smile to stretch across my face. Lacey can bring any girl down from the ledge, no matter how dire the situation may seem.

"He was still present."

I keep my reply short, deciding not to elaborate on where Rico was when I woke up.

"Huh. Must not be a Vegas local?" Lacey jests, her tone crammed with wit.

I laugh. It's laced with torment. "From what I witnessed, I'm fairly certain he's a local." *Judge, juror, and executioner local.*

Lacey takes a few moments to gather her bases. "So we have a name, a town, and a non-drunk description. Given to the right people, we should have enough info to track down your husband and file for an annulment," she advises, her mannerisms quickly reverting from life-long friend to third-year law student.

Her eyes rocket to mine when I mutter, "Already done."

"Tracking down your husband or the annulment?" Her words fly out of her mouth in quick succession.

"The annulment. Rico had his lawyer serve me papers during our trip to the airport."

She scoffs. "Wow! What a jerk. Did you seek alimony or request compensation for him being an asshole?"

"No." I shake my head.

Her eyes narrow into tiny slits. "It doesn't matter if you were married for two minutes or two years, Blaire. Alimony terms should have been included in your settlement."

"They were." I say anything to lessen her furious scowl burning into me. "Rico stipulated an amount he was willing to pay. Even though I didn't agree with the amount he was offering, I signed the forms."

She stands from her seated position and rests her hands on her tiny hips. "You never sign a legal document without having a lawyer present, Blaire. How many times have I stated this?" She crosses her arms over her chest and bores her eyes into mine. "What amount did you agree to?"

She falls back into her seat when I breathe out, "Two million dollars."

"Who the hell did you marry?" Her disbelieving eyes bounce between mine. "A prince from Saudi Arabia?"

"He seemed like a prince. Just not one from any fairy tales we've read."

6

———

The remainder of my weekend was spent holed up in my apartment. Although Lacey was apprehensive about my short replies to her grilling set of questions, she agreed that the dissolution of my Vegas wedding was handled in the best manner for both parties involved. It was quick and resolute, just like every Vegas wedding ends.

If only the nicks in my heart could be handled as swiftly.

After adjusting the heavy book satchel on my shoulder, I continue sauntering down the corridor of Ravenshoe Primary School. The chatter of little voices sounds through my ears, and the smell of dirty faces lingers in the air. I enjoyed summer break, but I can't wait to get back to work. This may sound a little geeky, but I missed seeing the smiles of students the past few weeks. There's nothing more beautiful than the innocence in a child's wide gaze.

My strides down the hallway slow when I notice Timothy Jamison in the doorway of his third-grade class. He's staring at me in a bemused, disarrayed type of way.

My heart rate quickens. I really hope I didn't make a fool out of myself in front of him last weekend. Timothy was nominated beside me for the Teacher of the Year award. We flew on the same flight to Vegas but were seated several rows away from each other. Due to my failing memory, I don't know whether to offer him my commiserations, congratulations, or an apology.

Deciding that avoidance is the best remedy for Las Vegas idiocy, I smile a greeting to Timothy before slipping into my classroom three doors up from his. Warmth blooms across my chest when I spot a large apple on my desk next to several hand-picked daisies from the school's front garden. I'm certain the children in my class this year will be absolute sweethearts. I'm always smitten with my class members. I don't care if I have to wipe smelly bottoms for the next sixty years, nothing beats seeing the smiles on my students' faces when they arrive for class every Monday morning.

My mom was a teacher for over thirty years. She loved each of her students as much as I do. Watching the way she nurtured her rebellious teenage students to become upstanding young adults made me want to be a teacher as well. But unlike my mom, I want to shape their minds before they are affected by outside influences.

Kindergarten students don't understand violence, hate, or racism. All they care about is whether Peter Rabbit is ever caught by Mr. McGregor and how many minutes remain until lunch. Seeing the innocence in a child's eyes is a truly magnificent sight, and I want them to hold on to that innocence for as long as possible.

I'm halfway through my first lesson of the day when the excitement on my students' faces grows exponentially. Smiling at their pleased reaction, I shift my eyes back to the book I'm reading them. My lips quirk. Although the story about the fluffy penguin seeking a new set of friends is riveting, I'm still surprised by my students' wide-mouthed responses.

Shrugging off their odd behavior as excitement for the upcoming lunch break, I continue reading. I lose sight of the words scribbled across the page when all twenty-three of my students crank their necks back to peer at something behind my shoulder.

After swallowing to relieve my parched throat, I place the book on my lap and twist my body around. My students' shocked expressions morph onto my face when I discover who's holding their interest. Rico has his backside propped on my desk, grasping my apple in his hand.

Despite the weather being considerably warm, he's decked out in a full suit and black trench coat. His face has been recently shaven, but his five o'clock shadow remains even though it's not even noon. His eyes are rapt on me, and he looks deliriously handsome and dangerous at the same time.

A handful of girls squeal when Rico takes a bite of my apple, sending a crunching sound bouncing around my class.

Clutching my chest to ensure my pounding heart doesn't escape my chest cavity, I shift my eyes to Mina, my teacher's aide. "Can you please continue reading the story to the children? I'll be right back."

Not waiting for her to reply, I scamper out of my seat, grasp Rico's hand in mine, and dash into the corridor. The children's eyes track Rico and me the entire time, their expressions a mixture of confusion and excitement.

The instant we step into the corridor, I release Rico's hand. From the throbbing ache between my legs, you'd swear I wasn't simply holding his hand. Just like last week, sparks of energy bounce between us, bristling the fine hairs on my nape and swelling my heart.

"What are you doing here, Rico?" I ask, incredulity heard in my tone.

He doesn't respond. He just runs his eyes over my outfit, absorbing my knee-length floral skirt, fitted lemon-colored blouse, and modest white sandals. If I didn't know he'd already seen me naked, I'd swear he was wondering what I'm trying to hide under my goody-two-shoes outfit. He wouldn't be the first man to accuse me of 'hiding my appeal with dowdy clothes.'

"Ah, Kitten, you're every teenage boy's naughty teacher fantasy."

My pulse quickens when his heavy-hooded gaze connects with mine. His eyes are dark and dangerous but innocent and beautiful at the same time. Don't ask me how that's even possible as I wouldn't be able to answer.

The throb between my legs intensifies when he says, "You look fuckable and sweet at the same time. Two complete contradictions."

"I could say the same thing about you," I reply before my brain has the chance to voice a protest.

A flash of excitement brightens his dark eyes and makes me hot and needy.

Striving to lead our conversation back into chartered waters, I say, "I meant the two contradictions part. Not that you look *fuckable*."

The excitement flaring in his eyes doesn't waver. He knows as well as I do there's no truth in my statement. He wouldn't wield the type of confidence he has without having the reputation to back it up. He knows he's so gorgeous, he merely needs to snap his fingers, and women would flock to his feet. That's why I find it somewhat surprising he's in the hallway outside my classroom, looking at me in a way I've only ever dreamed of—like I'm his savior.

Talking through a lump in my throat, I ask again, "What are you doing here, Rico?"

I can feel the heat of his tense gaze studying my profile before he answers, "I need you to come back to Vegas with me."

Speaking through the shockwaves rocketing around my body, I protest, "What? No! I can't... *why do you want me to come back*?" I roll my eyes when the last sentence comes with too much neediness clinging to my words.

"You witnessed an *event* last weekend." His eyes darken with every word he speaks. "In my industry, there are no witnesses."

I balk. "W-what d-do you mean there are no witnesses?"

I'm a stuttering idiot, but I can't help it. My heart was last seen somewhere in the region of my shoes, and even with my brain stuck in a lust-crazed haze, I felt the air shift between us. It's gone from steaming with yearning to roasting with danger.

My heavy breaths increase when he tilts in close to my side. Even frightened, I can't deny my body's signals. It's riveted by the man standing in front of me. In absolute awe.

My body's desire to overrule my astute brain flies out the window when Rico explains, "You either come back with me to Vegas as my wife, or they kill you." His words are straightforward and direct, ensuring there's no way I can misinterpret what he's saying.

"They?" I squeak out, my voice as high as the hairs on my forearms.

"My *family*," he replies, the timbre of his tone lowering.

When he lifts his eyes to peer past my shoulder, I follow his gaze. Two men in matching black suits stand side-by-side filling the double fire doors at the end of the corridor. The width of their combined shoulders is enough to block the late morning sun beaming into the hall.

I swing my eyes back to Rico. "If they're your *family*, why can't you call them off? Why can't you—"

"I've already tried." He glances at me with the same vivacity I saw in my flashback last week. "This is the only option I have left. If you're my wife, they won't touch you. But if you refuse to come with me, my hands will be tied."

My nose tingles as fresh tears prick into my eyes. Even if his eyes weren't relaying the truth, I've watched enough *True Crime America* to know I should believe him. Witnesses are the most critical element in any case. Without them, there's no case. But I can't just pack up and leave. I have commitments, a life... *an ex-husband.*

A thick cloud of despair hovers over my head. "We already signed the annulment papers. Your money was wired into my account first thing Monday morning. We're no longer married."

"The money was transferred, but the paperwork has not yet been filed."

I take a step back, flabbergasted. "Why didn't you file the paperwork?"

I try to keep excitement out of my voice. My attempts are borderline. My reaction can't be helped. With his eagerness to have our annulment papers signed, I assumed he would have filed them the very next morning.

His dark eyes dance between mine before he answers, "For the same reason you didn't let your *friend* throw you into the pool. If you were planning on having your tattoo removed, any concerns about it fading wouldn't have been an issue."

My heart beats triple time, equally shocked and excited. "You've been watching me?"

"I've been protecting you." A shiver runs down my spine from the edge of danger in his tone. He takes another step closer to me, engulfing my haywired senses with his delicious spicy scent. "I'm trying to keep you safe, Kitten, but this is as far as I can go. You either come back with me to Vegas or die. The choice is yours."

"What type of choice is that? I either go with a murderer or be murdered," I blubber out before I can stop my hurtful words.

When Rico's face lines with anger, I wish I could ram my callousness back down my throat.

"I'm sorry," I apologize, my tone sincere. "But you have to understand, this is all a little bit crazy. I'm a kindergarten teacher, and you're a..." My words trail off when I fail to find a word to explain who he is.

"If you want to live, as far as anyone is concerned, I'm your husband."

My stomach flips. I can't tell if it's from concern or because he's still my husband. I can barely breathe, let alone work out my body's crazy prompts.

"Are you sure there's no other viable option?" I ask, refusing to acknowledge the absurdity of my excitement.

Despair clouds his eyes before he shakes his head. Leaning against a stack of lockers on my right, I gulp in big breaths. My nostrils flare as they fight to fill my burning lungs. If I don't secure a full breath soon, I'm going to pass out.

I spread my hands across my hips and bend over. After saying something to the gentlemen at the end of the hall in Russian, Rico places his hand on my lower back and crouches down in front of me, meeting me eye to eye. Any chance of regaining my composure is lost when I look into his beautiful yet dangerous eyes.

"If I had any other choice, Kitten, I'd take it. I don't have any other option." His words are gruff, but his eyes relay the truth of his statement.

After sucking in a deep breath, I quickly mumble, "I understand, but I can't just pack up my life and leave with you. I have obligations, an apartment, my students."

"Everything has been taken care of." He removes a handkerchief from his pocket and hands it to me. I use it to soak up the sweat beading on my nape as he continues speaking, "Mr. Rodchester was happy to grant you an extended leave of absence. The rent for your apartment has been paid in full for a year, and your parents just discovered they were the fortunate winners of an all-expenses paid three-month tour of Europe."

My jaw muscle slackens as my heart rate skyrockets. "How did you get Mr. Rodchester to give me time off?"

The rest of his statement makes sense. They seem like an easy fix. But Mr. Rodchester governs Ravenshoe Primary with an iron fist. When I called in sick with the flu last semester, he couriered a mountain load of papers to my apartment for me to grade. He does not believe in sick days and never approves time off outside the standard school vacation schedule. He's such a stiff, I was only given a measly two hours off to attend my great aunt's funeral last year.

The swirling of my squishy stomach escalates when Rico replies, "My men are very persuasive."

I straighten my spine when he shifts his gaze sideways. The man at the end of the hall doesn't speak a peep, but his eyes must be forthcoming as Rico nods before turning his dark gaze back to me. I inhale a sharp breath, unnerved by the blackness filling his eyes.

"We have to leave now," he instructs, his monotone voice conveying the urgency of his statement.

I nod, giving in to the fact there's no other option. If I want to stay alive, I have to place my trust in a man who equally intrigues and intimidates me.

"Can I say goodbye to my class?" I ask Rico, my chin quivering.

His eyes drift between mine for several heart-clutching seconds before he nods. A sigh spills from my lips as I run my hands across my blemished cheeks. I don't want my students to see me upset.

The hum of young voices dulls to a slight buzz when I swing open my classroom door. My strides into the room fumble when my eyes lock in on Mr. Rodchester at the back of the room. His eyes are wide, his pupils massive, and his entire composure screams of nothing but fear. I would not normally condone an act of violence, but I'm glad to see karma finally caught up to Mr. Rodchester.

Overlooking the fact a man who typically shows no emotion looks like a frightened child, I lower my eyes to my students sitting on the carpet in front of my desk. Twenty-three tiny faces peer up at me, gawking and shocked. Like they can sense a change in my composure, they stand from their seated position and swarm around me.

A barrage of emotions slams into me as I bid farewell to each member of my class with a brief cuddle and an assuring word that I'll be back as soon as I can. My last embrace with a little boy named Jeremiah goes a bit longer than the ones before him. Jeremiah holds a special place in my heart after the rough year he had last year. His mom was arrested for conspiracy to commit a crime just after Christmas. Although her day in court has not yet happened, the events leading to her arrest have taken their toll on him.

"I'll be back soon, Jeremiah." I peer into his ocean blue eyes.

"Okay, Ms. Williams."

After running my finger over the dimple in the middle of his chin to remove a smudge of dirt, I stand from my crouched position. Rico has gathered my handbag and book satchel from the bottom drawer of my desk, so there's nothing left for me to do but walk out of my classroom.

Why does the simplest act have the greatest impact on my already pained heart?

he twenty-minute trip to my apartment is made in silence. The mask Rico wears in front of his crew members slipped into place the instant we entered the back of a black Escalade. The mood is somber, but there's still a weird crackling of energy in the air adding to the confusion of my pained heart.

The only good thing about the lack of ambiance is that it gives me plenty of time to study the man seated next to me. Taken out of the life-and-death situation I've been placed in, I can wholeheartedly under-stand my attraction to Rico. He has gloriously thick hair, a straight and defined nose, and lips that are too beautiful to ever spill the vicious words he has no doubt spoken in his short twenty-four years. And his eyes... *my goodness!* They are dark and beautiful but look like they are guarding a lifetime of secrets. He's night and day rolled into one strik-ingly handsome and complicated man.

When the Escalade pulls up to the curb of my apartment building, I run my hand down the front of my blouse. Two scantily dressed women with blown-out hair flock in close to the vehicle. They twist chewing gum around their fingers as they rake their sullied eyes down the length of Rico's body when he curls out of the Escalade's back seat.

After securing the button on his suit jacket, Rico offers me a hand out. His kind gesture reinforces what I already know deep down in my soul—there's something more to this man than just cloaked darkness.

The women stare at me, bitter and shocked when Rico ignores their propositions as he guides me into the lobby of my building. The way he moves with such animal arrogance, his allure demands the attention of every pair of eyes in the lobby, both male and female.

Snubbing the inquisitive stares rapt on him, Rico steers me into the elevator. The two men who have been shadowing us since we left my classroom move to the stairwell without a peep needing to be spilled from Rico's lips. Our ride in the elevator is made in silence, but a vibrant buzzing sensation infuses the air surrounding us.

When the elevator dings open on my floor, Rico directs me down the corridor without stopping to gather his bearings. With his splayed hand hovering near the curve of my lower back for the past five minutes, my body is achingly aware of the loss of his contact when he delves his hand into the breast pocket of his suit to produce a freshly-cut key.

Shoving the key into the front door of my apartment, Rico turns his gaze to me. "You have twenty minutes to pack."

"How did you get a key to my apartment?"

He removes the freshly-cut key from the lock and places it back into his pocket. "Nineteen minutes now, Kitten," he advises, rudely ignoring my interrogation. "Do you want to lose another minute?"

My body instinctively jumps to his command before my mind has time to object. Following the same routine I do every day, I gather the mail off the floor, place it on the entry table, and hit my answering machine button. While pacing into my bedroom, the mature voice of my dad sounds down the line.

"Blaire! You won't believe it. My raffles paid off. Your momma and I hit the jackpot! An all-expenses-paid holiday to Europe! Three months! Can you believe it?"

I roll my eyes. "No, I can't, and neither should you, Dad," I mutter under my breath.

"The only catch is we leave tomorrow. Your mother's gone crazy. She'll be lucky I don't take her out back and shoot her before we leave.

Anyway, darling, with your school schedule and our windfall, we won't see you before we leave."

A smile stretches across my face when my mom's voice chimes into the background. "Don't forget to tell her about the postcards, Norm."

"Postcards. Yes, yes, I'll tell her," my dad says. "We'll send you and your class postcards from each location we visit. We thought they could mark them on the big world map you have in your classroom like you did last term."

Heat creeps across my chest at the same time a stabbing pain hits my heart. Last term, my class spent the three months before summer vacation discussing which regions of the world we would like to visit the most. Surprisingly, the chosen locations varied significantly.

"All right, darling, I have to go and help your mother pack before she leaves without me. Talk soon, sweetie. Bye," my dad says before disconnecting the call.

My heart slithers into my gut. How long will it be until I see my parents again? Is this arrangement with Rico just temporary or permanent? Will I ever see my friends and family again?

"You will see them again, Kitten. I promise."

I jump, startled. Rico's movements are so agile I didn't notice him in the doorway of my room. Pushing off the doorjamb, he paces closer to me. I watch him cross the room, riveted just by the way he walks. Graceful yet authoritative.

"What can I do to help?" His tone is still commanding but not as gruff as it usually is.

You'd think my first thoughts would be to plead for my release, but for some strange reason, I hand him my empty cosmetics bag and point to the small washroom next to the entryway of my apartment.

"Anything marked with a B is mine."

Rico smiles a lazy grin that surges my pulse to the lower half of my body before entering the bathroom. Pretending I can't feel an odd pain twisting my heart, I grab a handful of my clothing off the overflowing racks in my closet and pace to my suitcase dumped on my bed. My brisk strides slow when the answering machine switches on, announcing it's about to record a new message.

After dumping my clothing into my open suitcase, I brace on the doorjamb of my room just as Colt's deep voice barrels out of the answering machine speakers. "Still trying to work out where you placed your new tattoo, baby girl. I haven't stopped thinking about it all weekend. Might need a private, in-depth search, starting at the cute little dip you have in your collarbone—"

The remainder of his message is lost when the answering machine sails across the room and smashes into a wall. It shatters into dozens of tiny pieces while also leaving a dent in the drywall of my living room.

With my heart hammering my ribs, I drift my eyes from the mangled remains of my answering machine to my entry table. Rico stares straight at me, unwavering and calm, a complete contradiction to the maniac who just demolished my retro answering machine in a rage of jealousy.

"What?" he asks, seemingly unaffected by my confounded stare.

When a trace of a smirk forms on his plump lips, the ache between my thighs has me grateful I'm leaning against a wall.

Is it wrong of me to say his aggressive nature turns me on? Even having no recollection of our time together in Vegas, I know it would have been better than anything I've ever experienced. You can't have his arrogance without skills to back it up, and the way he holds himself reveals he'd be exceptional in bed. I bet he has the type of control that would make even the most rational woman go wild to unleash it.

Wild enough they would marry him in a matter of hours.

My attention snaps back to the present when Rico says, "We only have fifteen minutes, Kitten, nowhere near enough time to work through your fiendish thoughts."

My cheeks heat from his bold words as my brows scrunch. I am in the process of packing my bags as I'm being forced to leave my home-town against my will, yet I am getting hot and bothered by the wicked smirk of a man who is the equivalent of a stranger to me.

While grumbling to myself about my newfound stupidity, I set back to work on packing my belongings. I've always been the cautious, safe-guarded member of my inner circle, but one glance into his dark gaze has me throwing caution to the wind. Even knowing I shouldn't be, I'm fascinated by him.

I should have heeded my grandmother's advice. Vegas made me lose my mind.

Ten minutes later, I hand my overflowing suitcase to a burly-looking man on my door stoop. When he exits my apartment, I scribble a quick note to Lacey, begging for her not to panic and that I'll call her as soon as possible.

After a final glance around the apartment I've lived in for the past two years, I shadow Rico outside. The instant I step onto the tiled floor, my regular breathing pattern turns into ragged pants. From the corner of my eye, I spot Colt emerging from his ground-floor apartment.

Sensing my snooping stare, he cranks his neck and locks his eyes with mine. My heart beats triple time when he smiles a roguish grin before he hotfoots it to the lobby.

I stop walking, muted and in fear. "I forgot something," I stammer out, saying any excuse I can to stop Colt and Rico from meeting.

With Rico's overreaction to Colt's playful message on my answering machine, I don't think a face-to-face meeting would come highly recommended. And considering there's no other viable exit from our building than to cross the lobby, I need to delay our departure.

"We need to go, Kitten. My men will collect anything you need later." Rico places his hand on my lower back and guides me into the open elevator two men are guarding.

Just like our first ride together, this one is infused with a shocking current—it isn't only filled with lust. I chew on my nails and fidget on the spot. My squirms make it look like I'm one of my students busting to use the bathroom.

When the elevator doors ding open, my eyes scan the room. I breathe a sigh of relief when Colt is nowhere to be seen.

My thankfulness is short-lived.

An unexpected squeal parts my lips when a set of arms wrap around my waist and hoist me off the floor, scaring the living bejesus out of me. Not just from Colt's sudden grabbing but from the livid glare that sparked in Rico's eyes the instant I was yanked away from him.

"Ready for round two, baby girl," Colt croons into my ear.

The temperature in the lobby becomes stifling when a deep, cavernous growl shreds through my ears. Like he can sense he's in imminent danger, Colt places me back onto my feet and drifts his eyes in the direction of the loud growl.

Rico glares at him, veins pumping, nostrils flaring. His eyes are black, haunted, and look like they could kill a man with only a stare.

Aiming to tame the beast, I stand next to Rico and sling my shaking arm around his waist, where I stop frozen, held captive by a sudden flashback...

Rico stares at me with blazing eyes, his attitude laid back, his smile lazy. "My beautiful Kitten. My light in a world full of darkness."

I roll over and balance my chin on his sweat-slicked chest. "Always. You'll not spend one more day living in blackness. Not while I'm by your side..."

Pain claws at my chest, leaving my heart open and exposed for all to see. That was one of the most beautiful memories I've ever had. Not just because of the words spoken but also from the loving gleam brightening Rico's dark gaze. He looked peaceful, and if I'm not mistaken, happy.

I snap back to reality when Rico's pulse surges through my arm wrapped around his waist. Pretending my spur-of-the-moment memory had no effect, I lock my eyes with Colt.

"Marshall, this is my... *husband*, Rico," I introduce, my words as uneasy as my facial expression.

Colt's brows become lost in his hairline. I don't know if his shock originates from calling him Marshall or my declaration that Rico is my husband.

"Rico, this is a friend of mine, Co... ah... Marshall."

Sweat forms on my top brow when the two men undertake a sweat-producing showdown. Colt's face is a mix of confused and amused. Rico's is nothing but blatant fury.

My heart recommences beating when Colt smiles hesitantly before offering his hand to Rico to shake. "It's a pleasure to meet you, Rico. I'd love to hear how you swooped in and stole Ravenshoe's most valuable asset." Colt's tone overflows with egotism. "As far as I was aware, baby girl was still on the market last week."

Rico growls. I'm not talking a slight rumble. I'm talking a full, pussy-quaking growl.

"I can assure you *Kitten* was not on the market last week." His gaze is as dangerous as his deep tone. "Unless this *market* you're referring to is my bed. Because that's where she was. *For hours.*"

My eyes bounce between Rico and Colt, beyond shocked two ridiculously handsome specimens are undertaking a pissing contest right in front of me—let alone *over* me.

The belligerent expression on Colt's face vanishes the instant Rico accepts his offer of a handshake. For every second that passes, the bronze coloring of Colt's face decreases, as does the size of his pupils.

When Colt's hand turns so white it looks like his fingers are about to drop off, I yank Rico's hand away from him. "We really must go."

I attempt to drag Rico toward the entry doors. My efforts are fruitless. His stance is so stable, a crane wouldn't budge him.

I peer up at his stern expression. "Come on, *honey*, we wouldn't want to miss our flight."

Colt's eyes snap to mine. "Flight? Where are you going?" The furious pace of Rico's pulse surging through his body wallops my hand when Colt takes a step closer to me. "What's going on, Blaire? Are you okay? *Are you safe?*" He whispers his last question.

My head rockets to Rico when he sneers. "She has never been safer, *Colt.*" He spits out his name like venom. "I can't make the same guarantee about you."

Spinning on his heels, Rico walks toward the double doors of my apartment building. His rough yank on my arm ensures I fall in step beside him. I briskly shake my head when Colt attempts to follow us out of the lobby. His exchange with Rico has already gained him the devoted attention of two of the men who have been flanking us for the past forty minutes. I don't want the spotlight to shine on him any more than it already has.

"I'm fine, Colt. I'll be back in a couple of weeks. Look after Lacey for me," I squeak out before Rico's fast speed has us hitting the sidewalk in under five seconds.

The two women who were roaming their gazes over Rico earlier hover in close the instant we step onto the cracked concrete sidewalk. I run my unclutched hand down the front of my blouse when their malicious words insult my already faltering composure.

"If you ever want a real woman, sugar, look me up."

"I thought trannie dressing was the latest fad, not grannie dressing."

"Bag it before you shag it, honey. Her head, not your cock."

Rico opens the back door of the Escalade and gestures for me to enter. When I slide across the cold leather seats, he turns his narrowed gaze to the gentleman manning the driver's door.

"Deal with them," he requests before sliding into the car next to me and slamming the door shut.

My heart rate climbs into dangerous territory when the man in the suit approaches the double doors of my building. I try to force words out of my mouth, but my fear has rendered me speechless. The blood pressure returns to a safe zone when Rico's goon stops upon reaching the two women who just insulted me. I suck in a grateful breath. I thought he was going after Colt.

With his hands clenched at his side, the man holds a conversation with the two women. Even though he's only speaking, the more he interacts with them, the more their expressions change from playful to scared.

After a few more silent words, the man in the suit gestures his head to the Escalade. My eyes dart between the two scantily clad women approaching the back-passenger side window Rico is sliding down.

With my heart in my throat, I tilt my head to the side and peer out the window.

"We're sorry if our words caused you any harm. We were only teasing," says the blonde wearing a hot pink sequin top.

Rico's furious growl rumbles through my chest.

"But we shouldn't have teased you. What we said was wrong and disrespectful, and we're very sorry." The brunette's words fire off her tongue before they have a chance to be fully developed.

Several seconds pass in uncomfortable silence before Rico's deep voice breaks the quiet. "Do you accept their apology, Kitten? Or should they be served a more severe punishment for their malicious jealousy?"

Two pairs of panicked eyes snap to mine, their expressions spooked and frozen.

They sigh loudly in sync when I shakily say, "I accept their apology."

With a wave of Rico's hand, the women are removed from the side of the Escalade. When the vehicle lurches into the dense flow of traffic that always impedes the streets of Ravenshoe, I glance back to my building. A pair of concerned green eyes reflect back at me.

"*I'm fine*," I mouth to Colt.

My words don't seem to reassure him, but they are all I have to offer.

Shocked—not only at the events that just transpired but the entirety of my day—I keep my eyes planted on the scenery whizzing by my window for the next ten minutes. It feels like I've emerged into a parallel universe. Everything looks identical, but somehow, it's all different.

My attention shifts from scenery gazing when Rico's low-timbre voice jingles through my ears. "Stop here," he demands to the driver.

I scan my eyes over the building we've pulled in front of. It's a night-club Lacey and I have frequented numerous times the past year called The Dungeon. It's owned by the same gentleman who is the landlord of my apartment building, Mr. Isaac Holt.

After scribbling a saying onto a blank square of cardboard, Rico swings open the back passenger door of the Escalade and walks toward a flashy-looking sedan parked at the side of the club. He twists his neck to the right before cranking it to the left. Happy he hasn't caught the attention of any curious eyes, he slips the card under the sedan's wind-shield before walking back to the Escalade and curling inside.

"Who was the note for?" I ask, incapable of harnessing my curiosity.

Rico turns his dark eyes to me before he answers, "My sister, Isabelle."

8

———

"**Y**our sister lives in Ravenshoe?"

Rico presses his index finger to my lips before he does a single nod.

"How did your sister leave your *family* without any repercussions?" I ask through his finger zapping my lips. I keep my voice calm even though my composure is anything but.

When Rico lifts his eyes to the rearview mirror, I follow his gaze. The driver doesn't hide the fact he's eyeballing us. I wouldn't be surprised if we veered off the road, considering his dark gaze is paying more attention to the rearview mirror than the heavy flow of traffic surrounding us.

A startled squeal rolls up my chest when Rico seizes my wrist and drags me across the dark leather seat. His endeavor of bridging the gap between us doesn't stop until I'm straddled in his lap. My eyes widen when his sudden movements cause the thickness in his trousers to brush the heat between my legs. I don't know if he's aroused, but try as I may, I can't ignore the... umm... girth of his... umm... penis.

Grow up, Blaire! You sound like one of your students!

Penis, penis, penis, I chant to myself as I struggle to settle the erratic beat of my heart. Once I've gained a small sense of composure, I drop

55

my eyes to Rico. He's staring straight at me, eyes blazing, heart thumping.

Any chance of calming my heart rate flies out the window when he says, "Undo the buttons on your blouse, Kitten."

I bounce my dilated eyes between his. "What?"

He runs his hand up my back, only stopping when he reaches the nape of my neck. His touch forces a breathless moan to ashamedly spill from my lips. From a man who is a stranger, he seems to know all the erogenous zones of my body. The most obvious, the portion of skin between my collarbone and neck.

He drags his thumb along my collarbone while asking, "Do you want to know how my sister left my family?"

I nod, a little overeagerly.

I can't help it.

Just the warmth of his hand on my neck has my usually noble persona weakening. When he's close to me, it's like I'm in a trance, stuck captive by his intoxicating eyes and alluring aura.

"Open your blouse, Kitten," he repeats, his words less demanding than earlier.

Ludicrously, I do as instructed without another protest spilling from my lips.

With teeth-shattering shakes impeding my hands, it takes a little longer than normal to undo the five buttons of my blouse. I'm wearing a fitted white cami beneath my shirt, but I feel naked when it drapes open at the front.

My unease has nothing to do with Rico drinking in every inch of my skin and everything to do with the driver's imprudent watch scorching a hole in the back of my head. The only way he could be more involved in our intimate gathering is if he placed himself in the small section of air left between Rico and me. That's how enthusiastic his spying is.

Keeping his captivating eyes planted on my flushed face, Rico cups one of my breasts in his hand, while the other draws me in close.

"Kiss me, Kitten," he murmurs against my lips. "I need your lips on mine."

I stare into his eyes, trying to force my mouth to cite a complaint to his request. Nothing comes out. So, operating purely on the desires of my heart, I cup his jaw and seal my mouth over his.

His lips move sweetly under mine, the strokes of his tongue controlled and gentle while his fingers send a jolt of pleasure down my spine when he firms his grip on my neck and strengthens our kiss. I part my lips more, surrendering my mouth to his mind-hazing talent. His kiss is sweet and tender while also dominating and controlling. He really is the equivalent of night and day, blackness and light... *enemy and lover*.

His five-o'clock shadow scratches the skin below my ear when he drags his lips down the side of my neck. "You can't trust anyone, Kitten. Even when they don't appear to be watching you, they are." I can only just hear his faint whisper over my pulse when he adds, "Especially me."

Suddenly, the reasoning behind his brash approach smashes into me. Because of our closeness, the driver can't hear a word spilling from Rico's lips. And since we look like every other newlywed couple who can't keep their hands off each other, he'll be none the wiser to the private conversation we are undertaking right under his snitching nose.

My heart rate climbs into coronary failure territory. I don't know if it's from Rico's admission that I can't trust anyone—not even him—or from the way his fingers have tweaked my nipple into a firm bud in mere seconds. For a man who can appear cold and heartless, his touch causes a burning heat to scorch every inch of my body.

I'm panting, wet, and waging one of the hardest battles I've ever fought not to rub myself against him like a crazed woman who can't control her libido. The only thing stopping me from carrying out my desire is when Rico continues talking. With how quiet he is, all my energy must be reserved for listening only.

As Rico nips, licks, and kisses my neckline, he tells me the story of how his oldest sister, Isabelle, was sold after the death of their mother. My heart squeezes when he informs me his sister was only six years old when she was placed on the black market. That's the age of half my students.

When Rico finishes his story, I take a second to gather my bearings.

It's no easy feat with every nerve in my body dedicated to Rico's lips still attached to my neck. But even with my brain muddled with fear and excitement, my conclusion about the information handed to me never alters. If the only way a blood descendant can leave Rico's family is by being sold, what happens to someone who doesn't have a drop of Popov blood running through their veins? What happens to people like me?

Like he can hear my private thoughts, Rico promises, "No one will *ever* hurt you, Kitten. Not while you're with me."

Before I can ask if his statement includes himself, the Escalade pulls into a private airstrip on the outskirts of Ravenshoe. After speaking to Rico in a foreign language, the driver climbs out of the car and stands guard at the side. The stern mask Rico wears in front of his crew slowly slides down his face as he adjusts my disheveled blouse back onto my shoulders and fastens the buttons.

Once I'm semi-respectable—*my outfit, not my mind*—Rico locks his dark gaze with mine. "Is Colt going to be a problem?"

My tongue grows thicker from the blackness forming in his sable eyes. "No." Strands of blonde locks fall into my eyes when I shake my head. "Colt has only ever been a friend." *Not through any choice of my own*, but I'll keep that snippet of information to myself.

Rico's Adam's apple bobs up and down. "Okay. Good. Because I don't share."

"Duly noted," I reply, my voice disgustingly chipper considering the circumstances of our exchange.

What the hell is wrong with me? I'm being forced to leave my hometown against my will, yet I'm pleased my husband is refusing to share me with another man.

Screw my mind. A lifetime of morals was lost the instant I stepped off the plane in Vegas.

I'm not the only one stunned by my reply. Rico stares at me, his face a cross between shocked and delighted. With a predatory smirk etched on his mouth, he curls out of the Escalade. Since I'm still on his lap, he takes me with him.

The vileness of my predicament smacks back into me when Rico sets me onto my feet and walks into a heavily manned airport hangar.

When I'm with him one-on-one, I forget he's shrouded by an impenetrable cloud of darkness. It's just me and him—the stranger I married.

While keeping my nosy glare hidden, I scan my eyes around the premises. At a quick guess, I'd say there are at least a dozen men with weapons strapped to their chests and another half a dozen dressed similarly to Rico. For a man more than capable of protecting himself, it seems a little dramatic for him to have so much excessive protection.

Rico stops at the end of a set of stairs that climb up to a private jet before cranking his neck back to face me. I almost swallow my tongue when he says, "The security detail is not for me, Kitten. They are here for you."

Ignoring my gaped mouth at the fact he read my mind twice in under a minute, he guides me onto the plane. As we enter the opulent space, my eyes shoot in all directions, unsure which fine feature to absorb first—the rich, opulent seating area that looks like it belongs in the middle of a mansion, not a plane, or the crystal and dark wood bar that's stocked with every bottle of alcohol you could imagine.

For men who live in the cloak of darkness, they sure have world-class standards.

Upon noticing the direction of my gaze, Rico asks, "Would you like a drink?"

My lips tug into a lewd smirk. "Why ask what I want when you can read my mind?"

While smirking a grin that sets my pulse racing, Rico gestures for me to sit in one of the two white leather chairs in the central area of the plane. Not trusting my thrumming-with-excitement legs, I plop into the closest leather seat.

Rico removes his suit jacket and throws it over the chair beside me before facing the pretty brunette flight attendant. I'm not at all surprised that her cheeks turn a vibrant hue of red when she's awarded his attention. "I'll have a double shot of whiskey, and Blaire will have a sparkling apple cider."

Huffing, I cross my arms over my chest before muttering, "Not even close."

Smiling, Rico slots his backside into the seat next to me. "I know it isn't what you wanted, Kitten. But considering what happened the last time you had a wine spritzer, I altered your request. Your drink will still have the apple flavor you're after, but without the alcohol content." When I stare at him with shock and disbelief tainting my face, he slouches back in his chair and rests his ankle on his opposite knee. "You did want an apple martini, didn't you?"

The smugness lining his face advises he's aware of my reply. He is one hundred percent correct. I pinch myself—hard. I must be dreaming. Otherwise, how would he have known that? There are millions of drinks in the world, so there's no way he could have known I was going to order *that* particular drink.

Rico accepts his double whiskey from the flight attendant before resting it on the table between us. I mutter a quick "Thank you" when she hands me an apple cider. After placing it on the table next to Rico's glass, I look back at him. It is the fight of my life not to clutch my chest when I discover he's watching me with a poignant stare, but I keep them fisted in my lap—barely.

After a heart-clutching staredown, Rico says, "You really don't remember anything about the night we got married, do you, Kitten?"

A range of emotions flare in his eyes when I shake my head. Relief. Confusion. Anger. It all pumps through his dark gaze. "I feel like I know you, I just... don't."

With knitted brows, he nods, then adjusts his position so he can peer out the arched window at his side, my confession ending our reunion on a somber note.

9

As soon as the plane is thirty-five thousand feet in the air, Rico unlatches his seat belt and stalks toward a varnished door at the back of the plane. He still walks with commanding power, but his shoulders hang a little lower.

Once he passes through the door, I lower my gaze to my lap. I've never been on a private jet before, but I'm fairly confident that's the bedroom. Considering I don't want a rerun of my response to his touch in the Escalade, I keep my backside planted in my seat and my hands flicking through a wide variety of magazines the flight attendant keeps handing me.

Two hours later, when my bladder's protests become too great for me to ignore, I dump a gossip magazine onto the table in front of me then head for the flight attendant who served me my drink earlier.

"Excuse me, where's the bathroom located?"

My heart sinks to my stomach when she points to the door Rico entered hours ago.

"Are you serious?" I gasp out in surprise.

After smiling to hide her shock, she bobs her chin. "The only bathroom in this jet is in the main bedroom, Mrs. Popov."

"Then where do you pee?" I blurt out before my brain can stop me or fathom that she just called me Mrs. Popov.

While staring me straight in the eyes, she mumbles, "I hold."

If her eyes weren't relaying the truth of her statement, I might have laughed. The flight is five hours long. No one can hold it that long. *Can they?*

When my bladder kicks up a stink about the delay, I smile a thank you before sauntering to the back of the plane, my steps hurried. I knock three times before opening the door. Rico is sitting behind a chunky wooden desk, speaking in a foreign language into the cell phone attached to his ear.

Upon noticing my presence, his head lifts, and his dark eyes connect with mine. I hook my thumb to the frosted glass door on my right, advising I need to use the restroom. His flow of conversation continues without pause as he nods, soundlessly granting my request.

I slip into the space, close the door behind me, then dash into the bathroom.

"Oh, Lord," I mumble under my breath when I enter the extravagant washroom. Such opulent surroundings shouldn't be reserved for peeing.

After doing my business, I wash my hands and exit the restroom. I freeze halfway out the door when I notice Rico is no longer behind the chunky desk. He's near the bed. His suit jacket has been removed, and the top two buttons of his crisp white shirt have been undone, exposing inches of his smooth, tanned torso.

Unlike when I entered the bathroom, his gloriously thick hair is rustled like he's been running his fingers through it, and his composure is a stark contrast to the man he was moments ago.

I'd be lying if I said his fierce gaze isn't scaring me.

"Come here, Kitten," Rico demands, his voice gritty. When my feet remained rooted in place, he releases a deep exhalation, infusing the space with his whiskey-scented breath before saying, "I'll *never* touch you against your will."

Even frightened, just like last week, my intuition tells me I can trust him. Furthermore, our time together has been an awkward dance routine—two steps forward, one step back—but I've always been a willing participant.

After unclenching my fists, I slowly step toward him. As I glide across the room, he shifts his head to the side and watches me in silence, categorizing every movement my body makes. The fear clutching my heart intensifies when I see nothing but anger clouding his beautiful irises, but then I remember the words I spoke to him last week.

You will not spend one more day in darkness. Not while I'm by your side.

Eager to keep my promise, I increase my speed. When I hit the edge of the bed, Rico lifts a single piece of A4 glossy paper I didn't notice he was holding until now. I was too focused on working out a way to lighten the darkness swamping his eyes to notice anything else.

"Do you know this man?"

When he hands the paper to me, my eyes widen while taking in the image. "That's Timothy Jamison. He's a teacher at my school."

It's a grainy surveillance camera image, but there's no mistaking Timothy's thick-rimmed glasses and wonky smile. I've also worked with him for two years, so I'm confident with my assessment.

"Was this taken in Las Vegas?" I ask upon seeing a bank of poker machines in the background of the highly pixilated photo.

When Rico nods, I gasp in a quick breath. I'm snitching on an acquaintance to a man who governs Las Vegas.

After raising my eyes from the photo, I ask, "Why do you want to know who Timothy is? He's a good person. He wouldn't have done anything illegal. He is a teacher at my school and a father. A well-respected—"

My blubbering halts when Rico announces, "He is the reason you can't remember your trip to Vegas."

I glare at him in shocked silence for a moment. "What! How?" I blurt out once my shock subsides.

"He drugged you," he replies like it's everyday news.

I take a step back, dazed and confused. "Why would he do that? He wouldn't do that. That doesn't make any sense."

Rico walks to a laptop in the middle of the desk. After hitting the space bar, a heavy flow of chatter booms out of his laptop speakers. Through wobbly legs, I move closer to the desk when the video on the monitor zooms in on a round table with a dozen people seated around it. Even having no recollection of my time in Vegas, I can tell this image is from the Teacher of the Year awards luncheon because I recognize a few faces around the table, drinking wine and laughing.

The most familiar face belongs to Timothy.

He's seated next to me.

Blood roars to the surface of my skin, illuminating it with a pink hue when Timothy drops a small pill into my drink as I stand from my seat to say goodbye to a lady I met at a joint school camp last year. After stirring my half-consumed wine spritzer with a butter knife from the table, he slouches low into his chair and joins a conversation with two gentlemen on his left.

I remain motionless as the unethical scene unfolds before my very eyes. After bidding farewell to Darlene, I retake my seat next to Timothy. He smiles before gesturing his head to the half-filled glass of spritzer in front of me, encouraging me to finish it.

Within five minutes of consuming the laced drink, I excuse myself from the table. Even watching the video from a bird's-eye view, I can see my eyes have a little more sheen than normal, and my mood is surprisingly chipper.

The camera angle shifts multiple times as it follows me through the facility where the event was held, but no matter which direction I take, Timothy is a few steps behind me in every frame.

When the image freezes upon me exiting a set of double doors, I snap my eyes to Rico. "What happened? Did he..." I can't force the words out of my mouth.

Luckily for me, Rico has no qualms filling in the gaps. "No, Kitten. He never got the chance," he replies, staring at me with angry eyes.

"How do you know that? How can you be so sure?" I ask while rubbing my chest, trying to erase the pain stabbing the middle of it.

"Because this happened."

Rico sits on the edge of the bed, seizes my wrist, then pulls me onto his lap. Before I can react, a hidden memory rushes to the surface of my muddled brain...

"Oh, I'm so sorry. The heel of my shoe caught the carpet pile," I apologize to the gentleman whose lap I just stumbled into.

Dark, beautiful eyes stare down at me, holding me captive by their unique beauty. The sable-haired stranger doesn't speak. He doesn't need to. His eyes share a lifetime of stories without a word spilling from his lips.

After giving myself a few moments to register every unique speckle in his mesmerizing eyes, I snap back to reality. I'm sitting in a stranger's lap after tumbling into his arms. Can anyone say, 'cliché?'

"Sorry about the intrusion."

Cringing at the weakness of my words, I continue my endeavor of locating a bathroom. Ever since I finished my wine spritzer ten minutes ago, my tummy has been unsettled and my mind woozy. I'd also like to say it is the cause of my inflamed cheeks, but unfortunately, that isn't the case. The blame for my blemished appearance solely belongs to the handsome stranger eyeballing me as I step away from him.

My pulse quickens when, in the corner of my eye, I catch sight of the dark-haired stranger throwing a casino chip into the middle of a poker table. After gesturing his head to a group of men dressed in black suits lounging at the side of the poker table, he races to catch up with me. His long, efficient strides have him reaching me in three captivating heartbeats.

A jolting spasm rockets up my arm when he places his hand on the crook of my elbow. Muted by my body's insane reaction to this mysterious stranger's touch, I allow him to guide me through the vast throng of people milling about the space without a word spilling from my lips...

When I lift my eyes to Rico, my heart squeezes from seeing the same dark, beautiful eyes from my memory staring back at me. "Where did we go?"

A grin curls on the edge of his lips, sending my heart rate skyrocketing. It's the first genuine smile I've seen, and it is nearly as striking as his dark eyes. "We went to the bathroom."

He tucks a strand of my hair behind my ear, stands from the bed, then places me on my feet. I try to hold in my disappointed groan, but it escapes my lips involuntarily.

"One memory at a time, Kitten," Rico responds to my whine, believing it was only based on my interest in unraveling my lost memories.

It wasn't.

The Rico standing before me intrigues me just as much as extracting my lost memories.

My brows scrunch when he strides to the bedroom door, opens it, and gestures with his head for me to leave. "I have some business to take care of before we land."

My heart smashes my ribs when the first half of our conversation dawns on me. I span the distance between us, my steps shaky, hindered by a pair of wobbly legs. "You're not going to do anything to Timothy, are you?"

"Don't ask questions you don't want an answer to, Kitten," Rico replies before slapping me on the backside, his spank so hard it pushes me into the central section of the private jet.

Defying my Jell-O legs, I pivot around to face him. Just like in my memory, his eyes relay his intentions without a word needing to flow from his plump lips.

My mouth twitches, dying to spill the objections my brain is screaming, but no matter how hard I fight, not a word escapes my parched lips.

Taking my silence as confirmation I want him to execute revenge on Timothy for drugging me, Rico winks before shutting the bedroom door.

Oh. My. Lord.

What did I just do?

10

Guilt consumes the next hour of our trip. Do I believe what Timothy did was wrong? Yes, without a doubt. Do I believe he should be punished for what he did? Yes, more to stop it from happening to another woman than anything else. Do I want that punishment issued by a member of the Las Vegas mob? No, not at all.

With my stomach twisted in knots, I stand from my seat and make my way back to the main bedroom of the private jet. My beliefs the past hour have never altered. It has merely taken me this long to build the courage to go against a man who equally frightens and intrigues me. However, I must do this. If I ever want the chance to rescue Rico from the blackness, I can't let him make heinous decisions no man has the right to make.

Timothy will one day meet his maker, but until then, there are legal ways justice can be served.

Not bothering to knock, I enter the room. Rico is back behind the desk, speaking into his cell phone. Even not understanding a word he's saying, I can tell his temper is short-fused. The veins in his thick biceps are bulging, his jaw is clenched, and his entire composure screams blatant fury. My hesitation to approach him only lasts as long as it takes for me to recall Timothy's youngest son only turned two last month. He's a baby.

Just like earlier, Rico's eyes follow me as I cross the room to stand in front of him, except this time, his eyes aren't filled with anger. They're brimming with downright fury.

Overlooking the feverish agitation beaming out of him in invisible waves, I remove the cell phone from his grasp, disconnect his call, then toss his phone onto a stack of papers on his desk.

The furious tick impinging his jaw amplifies when I lower onto my knees and peer up into his eyes. "Please, I'm begging you, Enrique. Don't do this. I may not remember you, but my heart does. It knows there's more to you than this lifestyle. It knows you're a good man. Don't break its confidence."

If I thought his eyes were violent before, it's nothing compared to how they look now. I don't know if his anger originates from me pleading to him on my knees or from the fact I called him Enrique for the first time.

"You're willing to fall to your knees and beg for mercy for the man who drugged you?" he snarls out, his voice the most malicious I've heard.

With tears welling, I nod.

They almost topple when Rico shouts, "He was going to rape you, Blaire! Do you understand that?"

"Yes. I'm aware of that," I reply, gingerly nodding. "But he has a wife and three small children—"

"Children he doesn't deserve to have!" His angry roar startles me so much I jump.

After pushing his chair back from his desk, he stands with his fists clenched at his sides and his face lined with anger. Fear unlike anything I've ever felt races through my veins. It isn't because I believe he will hurt me. For some reason unbeknownst to me, I truly believe he means me no harm. My worry is for Timothy and his family.

"I'm not saying he doesn't deserve to be punished for what he did. He does. But not like this. Not unlawfully."

"You wouldn't be saying that if you knew what he was planning to do to you!" The bite of agony in his voice sets me on edge. "If you hadn't fallen into my lap, you would have fallen into a shallow ditch."

Dread clutches my throat, squeezing so hard, I can't inhale an entire breath. "What?"

Rico runs his hand across his scruffy chin before snatching papers off the printer on his desk. His dark, haunted eyes stare into mine for many seconds before he hands the printouts to me.

I hesitate, wary of the concern beaming from his eyes before I eventually drop my eyes to the photos I'm clasping for dear life. My spare hand shoots up to cover my mouth when my stomach lurches in protest of the ghastly images reflecting at me. Although each picture has a unique backdrop, the theme of the photographs is horrifyingly similar. They all contain the body of a woman in her early to mid-twenties lying lifeless in a shallow grave.

When I raise my eyes to Rico, I notice he is watching me cautiously. Although his face is lined with anger, I now realize his anger isn't directed at me. It's for the monster who did this heinous act to these poor defenseless women.

"Who did this?" I ask, my voice quieter than a hushed whisper.

"Timothy," Rico replies without pause, his voice deep and teemed with anger.

Refusing to acknowledge that a family man could ever be responsible for such atrocious acts, I shake my head. This is not something a married father of three would do. This is the deed of a horrible person with a black soul.

Rico crouches down in front of me then removes the papers and photographs from my hand. He lays the pictures out in a pattern similar to a timeline on the varnished wooden floors.

My heart breaks when my eyes roam over six beautiful ladies who lost their lives way too early.

"Annie Rogers was killed on May tenth last year." Rico points to a police image of a lady with long caramel hair buried in a shallow grave in front of a mountain landscape. "Timothy attended a conference in her hometown the same weekend." He taps on the second image.

"Clarissa Enrode was killed July thirtieth. Timothy was a guest speaker at her university the same weekend."

For each name he goes through, my heart cracks more.

"Could it be a coincidence?" I lock my moisture-filled eyes with his. "There has to be some explanation. Some..." My words drown out when I fail to find a legitimate reason as to why Timothy would be at each location on the exact dates the women were killed.

Panic roars through my veins when Rico says, "There are surveillance tapes matching yours for each girl in each town. He drugged them, raped them, then killed them." His dark eyes settle on mine. "If you didn't fall into my lap, he would have done the same thing to you."

My heart stings when the undeniable facts he has displayed crash into me. I sit on the floorboards, my stomach churning with fear and grief. I had danced with the devil and once again escaped with my life. These beautiful women weren't as lucky.

My throat tightens as I struggle to hold in the sob dying to break free. My efforts are fruitless. Nothing can keep in my despair. I thought life as I'd known it ended when I stumbled into Rico's lap. Little did I know it was only just beginning.

The instant the first whimper escapes my parched lips, Rico scoops me into his arms. I cling to his white dress shirt when he moves us to sit on the edge of the bed. Tears flood my cheeks as the disturbing images play on repeat in my mind. I know why Rico had to show me the photographs—I would have never believed him otherwise—but now I wish I'd never seen them. It's another set of memories I'd give anything to forget.

Rico doesn't speak a word over the next several minutes. He simply runs his hand over my back in a circular motion until I eventually give in to unconsciousness.

Several hours later, I wake up startled and confused, and for the first time in years, without the body-havocking effects of a nightmare. I'm lying in bed with my back pressed against the warmth of a body. Just from the spicy scent alone, I know it's Rico sleeping next to me, but the way every nerve in my body has sparked is another clear indication.

Unlike when I entered the room earlier, it's void of any light, natural or unnatural. Since the shutters on the windows are closed, I can't tell if it's night or if the plane is in a dark airport hangar.

After giving myself a few minutes to gather my bearings, I carefully roll onto my opposite hip, not wanting to wake Rico. A breathless squeal squeaks between my lips when I'm met with his dark and beautiful gaze. He's awake and staring straight at me.

"How long have you been awake?" My voice is scratchy from the rawness of my throat.

He brushes a bunch of unruly hairs off my face while replying, "I didn't sleep."

My brows furrow. "Then why are you lying in bed with me?"

A flare of emotion passes through his eyes, renewing my hope that I didn't lose all rational thoughts when I was drugged. Although I'm sure my laced drink impeded my usually astute brain, while peering into the eyes of the stranger lying across from me, I realize it wasn't just drugs ruling my decisions last week. Part of it was my heart.

What I said to him earlier was true. I don't know him, but my heart does.

Rico takes his time configuring a response to my question. Just when I think he isn't going to answer, he says, "You whimpered every time I moved."

I have no chance of holding in my grin, so I set it free. "You stayed with me so I wouldn't wake?" Disbelief and a small dash of glee are evident in my tone.

While peering into my eyes, he nods.

"How long?" When he looks at me, confused, I add, "How long did you stay with me?"

He checks the time before announcing, "A little over four hours."

My heart skips a beat. Dark Rico intimidates me, but knowing he stayed with me for four hours exposes a side to him I don't think many people have witnessed—the light side.

After a short beat, I ask, "Why does this feel so familiar?"

Rico smiles a vain grin. "Because it is," he replies before tugging on a strand of my hair.

Although hazy, the faintest memory creeps into my mind from his playfulness...

My heavy eyelids slowly flutter open before drifting around the opulent room to absorb the rich antique furniture and beautiful chandelier hanging from the ceiling rose. My observant gaze has me stumbling onto an even more beautiful sight—a pair of dark and alluring eyes.

"I fell asleep again, didn't I?" My words are lazy and hoarse.

Rico's lips tug into a grin as he nods. "Only for twenty minutes this time," he replies before pulling a strand of my hair playfully.

While stretching out, a glimmer of light captures my attention. Smiling, I lower my left hand to inspect my newly added accessory—a ruby and diamond platinum wedding band. "It's so beautiful."

Rico props himself onto his elbow and peers down into my light green eyes. "Not as beautiful as you."

Even with a broad smile stretched across my face, I can't stifle a big yawn. I'm exhausted.

"Sleep if you're tired, Kitten." Rico runs his hand down the side of my face, doubling the heaviness of my eyelids. "I'll be here when you wake..."

I prop my elbow onto the satin pillowcase and rest my weighted head on my open palm. "Did you sleep at all the night we got married?"

Rico smiles similarly to the one in my memory before shaking his head.

"Why not?" I grimace when my girly voice bounces around the quiet room.

"Because I didn't want to wake up to find out it was all a dream." His reply is so faint, I barely hear what he says.

Heat expands across my chest, filling some of the cracks that formed in my heart the past week. I want to say something to ease the confused look on Rico's face, but I can't think of a single phrase that would be appropriate in this situation. It's so odd. Although the man before me is technically a stranger, he also seems so familiar. *Is that even possible?*

"Other than the snippets of memories you unearthed tonight, how many others have you had?" Rico tries to hold in the eagerness of his words. He fails.

I slip my hand under the satin pillow and rest my inflamed cheek on the cool softness before killing his excitement with one short word. "None."

I'd like to elaborate on my response, but there's no need.

All my disappointment was expressed with that one paltry word.

"Why don't I have any memories?"

In less than a nanosecond, the smile on Rico's face vanishes, and a new expression settles in its place. It's the same unapproachable look he wore when deciding Timothy's fate. "Because Timothy gave you a drug known on the black market as 'club drug.' Because of its strong amnesia-based additive, most victims have limited recollection of their assault."

I twist my lips. "If he was planning to kill me, why would it matter if I had any memories?"

"The drug isn't just used as a date rape drug. It's also distributed as a party drug. Rohypnol is regularly taken by teens to get high. To some individuals, it has the same effect as heroin or cocaine. It's the reason you were more... *carefree* the weekend we married. Your insecurities vanished." His words are informative and clear until the end. His last two sentences come out heavily laced with confusion.

Since I am also confused, I seek clarification for part of it. "Can you see a difference between the Blaire you met last week and the one before you now?"

Rico's tongue delves out to replenish his lips before he murmurs, "No. But it's not a drug steering your decisions now. It's fear."

"I'm not scared of you, Rico," I splutter out, allowing my heart to overrule my head.

"You should be, Kitten." He's so quiet. If I didn't see his lips move, I wouldn't have known he'd spoken.

A stretch of silence crosses between us. I wouldn't say it's awkward, more necessary. The flight over this side of the country was only five hours long, but it feels like five months have passed. So many life-altering decisions have been made during our trip. But my biggest worry is that the most imperative one wasn't made by me. It was made *for* me.

"What will happen to Timothy's family?"

Rico's dark eyes stare directly into mine as he replies, "Nothing. As far as his family is concerned, Timothy will merely vanish without a trace."

My eyes burn as a new batch of tears well into my eyes. My tears are not for Timothy. They're for his wife and children who will be left wondering what happened to him. For some people, that can be more upsetting than learning the ill fate of their loved ones. When a life is lost, you never forget, but you get to grieve and try and move on. But not knowing what happened, you can't get closure. You spend your entire life scanning strangers' faces wondering if one day you will spot them in the crowd, or every time the phone rings, you ponder if it will be the call you've been waiting for the past ten years.

The people who are left wondering what happened have no chance of closure and no chance of healing.

"What about the victims' families?" I ask, incapable of reining in my desire to lessen their grief.

Rico's heavy brows stitch. He looks angry or perhaps even stumped by my question. "What about them?"

His tone is knee-shaking low, but it won't stop me from asking, "Don't they deserve to know justice was served?"

Rico's lips set into a firm, straight line before he shakes his head.

"Why not? They deserve to know. They have the right to know." My voice gets louder and angrier with every sentence I speak, and although I see the same amount of anger brewing in his dark eyes, it doesn't dampen my pleas the slightest. "Someone they loved was killed. They've suffered enough, so they shouldn't have to live their life wondering if they are walking amongst a killer. Give them peace, Rico. Give them closure."

"That's not the way it works in this industry, Kitten. It's not my job to—"

"Why? Because the mob doesn't have a heart? They don't understand compassion!"

"No, they don't." His loud roar vibrates my heart right out of my chest. "They'll slit your throat without a second thought and dump you in an acid bath before sitting down to enjoy a meal. Their stomachs won't twist. Their hearts won't feel pain. They will feel *nothing*. That's the type of men you're dealing with, Kitten, and believing any differently will only get you killed."

His chest heaves up and down so violently, it competes with mine with every breath he takes. "If you want any chance of coming out of this alive, you need to learn your place. Women are seen, not heard. Your body is a valuable commodity, not your mind, and you should *never* voice your opinion unless asked. And even then, your replies should echo your male counterpart." He stares into my eyes, ensuring I'm aware the words he speaks are nothing but gospel.

Once he's satisfied I've absorbed his warning, he rolls out of bed and puts on his suit jacket. In seconds, the man who spent hours comforting me is replaced with a cold-hearted, emotionless stranger. His eyes are bleak, his jaw clenched, and the stern mask he wears when surrounded by his crew has slipped back into place.

After fastening the button on his suit jacket, Rico nudges his head to the washroom. "Tidy yourself up before meeting me in the hangar," he instructs, his words clipped.

Not waiting for me to reply, he paces to the door, his steps fast and efficient. Before he exits, he cranks his neck back to peer at me. When his gaze zooms in on the moisture forming in my eyes, his stern mask slips for the slightest second, exposing an emotion I was certain he didn't know—fear.

Although regret is by far the highest emotion in his voice, his next set of words leave me on edge. "I'm trying to protect you, Blaire. Please don't make it harder on me."

11

After splashing cold water on my face and using a napkin to remove the mascara stains tracking down my cheeks, I roll my shoulders, lift my head high, then exit the bathroom.

My brisk strides falter when I sense a presence in the room. Unlike the weird buzzing sensation that fills me when Rico is close by, this isn't a rush of excitement.

It is unbridled fear.

With my heart dropped past my shoes, I spin on my feet to face my unwanted welcomer. Glacier blue eyes on a ruggedly handsome face reflect back at me. The backside of the unnamed man who confronted me last week is propped on my suitcase, and his eyes are trained on me.

Upon noticing he has gained my attention, he angles his head to the side and snickers, "One little bag for a week worth of packing." His voice is gritty and colored with a Russian accent.

My heart finds its way to my throat when he pushes off my suitcase and paces toward me. He walks with an air of authority, but his commanding swagger isn't as refined as Rico's. Wearing ripped jeans rising from black military boots and a buttoned-up dark navy shirt, his clothing showcases his body in eye-catching detail, not even the evilness beaming from his eyes can detract from. The blue-eyed stranger is a similar size to Rico, but I'm dwarfed by his height when he stands next to me.

When he circles me like a shark homing in on his prey, a vein in my neck thrums. During his slow trek, he drinks in every detail of my face before he eventually drops his eyes to my body.

Mere seconds pass, but it feels like hours.

You'd think my first thought would be to dart for the door mere feet from me, but I'm frozen in place, incapable of thinking, let alone fleeing.

When the mysterious stranger sniffs my hair, I balk. It isn't a quick, dignified whiff. He takes his time, soaking in every strand of my wavy blonde hair.

I breathe for the first time in almost a minute when he murmurs against my skin, "Rico has always had an eye for quality." His breath fans my sweat-beaded neck when he snickers about my whitening face. He moves into eyesight before muttering, "He knows what you haven't even worked out yet. That's why he married you before fucking you."

My eyes slit as a hiss ripples through my lips. I don't know the man standing before me, yet he believes he has the right to disrespect me.

Loving my feisty response, the stranger's eyes flare in excitement. "There it is. I knew it was hiding in there somewhere." He tilts in closer. "Oh, Ангел, you'll be a lot of fun... if only Rico would loosen your collar. A little kitty should be free, not restrained."

Even the most naïve person in the world couldn't miss the sexual innuendo in his reply, which prompts me to something Rico said earlier in the Escalade. "Rico doesn't share."

I snap my eyes to the stranger when he asks, "Not even with his little brother?"

As my eyes scan his face, I seek any similarities between Rico and him. Although they both have dark hair, tanned skin, and gorgeous facial features, there are no distinct similarities between them.

"You're Rico's brother?" I try to mask the shock with a friendly tone. I fail.

His lips curl into a smirk that sets my heart racing, but unlike Rico, it isn't a good heart flutter. "Yes. I am Nikolai. But you, my sweet *Ангел*, can call me *Сатана*."

Before I have the chance to ask what *Сатана* means, a new type of awareness prickles my skin. I feel as if I am being watched, and the recollection as to why I could be freezes both my feet and my heart. *'You can't trust anyone, Kitten. Even when they don't appear to be watching you, they are. Especially me.'*

The already insane beat of my heart kicks into overdrive when my eyes lift to the doorway and connect with a pair of eyes that are teeming with anger. Rico's head is tilted to the side, and his stern gaze is fixed on his little brother. His six-foot-plus frame swamps the room, and his edgy composure suffocates the room of air. Even seeing him standing behind his brother doesn't conjure any similarities between them to form in my muddled brain.

Either unaware of his brother's furious gaze or ignoring it, Nikolai leans into my side and whispers, "You're ninety-nine percent angel, but oh how I can't wait to unearth the other one percent. There are devilish thoughts in the most angelic minds. I can't wait to hear yours."

I'm torn between feeling safe and worried when Rico snaps out something in Russian. I settle on relieved. Even not understanding a word he's speaking could have me missing the authority in his words.

He's reminding his brother of the pecking order, and mercifully, Nikolai disclosed earlier that he is the younger of the two.

After flashing me a teasing grin, Nikolai spins around to face his brother. While rubbing his hands together, he rocks on the balls of his feet. "There's no need for rudeness, Rico. I was merely welcoming your *kitten* to the family."

He turns his gaze back to me, wordlessly requesting I back up his claims. I stand muted, not only refusing to acknowledge his demand but also unsure what our exchange was about. Although he intimidates me, he wasn't threatening or welcoming.

My frozen stance ends when Rico barks out, "Come, Kitten."

Like a dog being called by its owner, my feet leap into action before my brain can register its disgust. I could say my obedience is solely to smooth the thick grooves lining Rico's forehead, but, in all honesty, it isn't. I can barely breathe with how much testosterone is suffocating the air, so if jumping on cue for my husband is a way to escape the throat-clutching awkwardness plaguing the air, I'll take it.

My eyes dart to Rico when Nikolai starts singing a song as we exit the bedroom. From the flow of the words and the softness of his voice, it sounds like a nursery rhyme.

I double-guess myself when I catch sight of Rico's haughty expression.

He looks less than impressed.

"What is he singing?" I ask Rico as we merge onto the steps of the private jet. Even though it's late, humid Las Vegas air smacks into me, adding to my swirling stomach.

While he guides me down the small steel steps, Rico advises, "It's a rhyme our father recited to us when we were younger."

So my original assumption was correct. It is a nursery rhyme.

Then why did it cause such an adverse reaction from Rico?

Too curious for my own good, I ask, "What nursery rhyme is it?"

Rico drops his dark eyes to me. "Not now, Kitten."

Not speaking another word, he directs me toward a long motorcade lined up outside the hangar. A gentleman with silver hair and a kind smile dips his head in greeting while opening the back passenger door of a four-wheel drive.

Other than advising the driver to take us to the Popov compound, Rico doesn't mutter a syllable the thirty minutes of our trip. I don't mind. It gives me time to run the foreign words Nikolai sang through my head. Although it was in a foreign language, it has an addictive rhythm I can't help but repeat.

Отправить ангел в дьявола кровать, удерживайте ее, ценить ее, затем отрежьте ее головки блока цилиндров. Она дебютировала с сатаны и в настоящее время она является мертвой точки для всех лежа в дьявола кровать.

It only dawns that I'm humming the words out loud when Rico roars, "Enough!"

When my eyes snap to him, I swallow the brick his demand lodged into my throat. His nostrils are flaring, and his chest heaves. "You're singing a song about sending an angel to her death."

Shock ripples through me. "What? You said it was a nursery rhyme. They don't include death."

"They do when the devil sings them," Rico fires back, his tone deep and knee-quaking. "Send the angel to the devil's bed, hold her, cherish her, then cut off her head. She danced with Satan, and now she's dead, all for lying in the devil's bed." He sings the song in the same low tone Nikolai used on the plane but hearing it in a language I understand doesn't lessen its impact. It's just as spine-tingling.

"Why would a father sing a song like that to his children?"

"Because to him, all *Ahrens* must pass Satan's test."

"*Ahren*?" I query, recalling Nikolai calling me that.

My heart stops beating when Rico replies, "*Ahren* is Nikolai's version of angel. He couldn't pronounce *Ангел* when he was a child, so he said it how it was spelled instead of how it sounded. For some reason, it stuck."

Although his story is cute, I can't settle the nerves twisting in my stomach. "What does *Сатана* mean?"

My breathing shallows as I wait for Rico to reply. Considering *Сатана* was only used once in the nursery rhyme Nikolai sang, I'm reasonably sure I know what it means, but I still want Rico to spell it out for me. I don't want to get worked up over a simple childish rhyme. I've got enough on my plate with an unknown husband, barely escaping a murder attempt, mob-like activities, and unearthing my lost memories to add an immature threat into the mix.

Any chance of sweeping Nikolai's taunt under the rug slips away when Rico says, "*Сатана* is Satan, Kitten."

Everything blurs when the last part of the rhyme runs through my head—*She danced with Satan, and now she's dead, all for lying in the devil's bed.*

I sound as tormented as I feel while asking, "Aren't Satan and the devil the same person?"

Dark strands of hair fall into Rico's eye when he shakes his head.

"Not in this rhyme. Satan sends his angel to the devil's bed to test her. If she fails, Satan cuts off her head."

"How does the angel fail?"

He runs his index finger across his top brow, removing a bead of sweat formed there. "By sleeping with the devil."

"Who's the devil then?" I snap out so fast I startle the driver.

Rico shrugs. "Whoever Satan decides to test his angel with."

After sinking deep in my seat, I take a moment to work through the information I've been bombarded with. Why would Nikolai request that I call him Satan after calling me angel? It doesn't make any sense. Unless he thinks I'm going to sleep with the devil?

My pupils widen. *Was that Nikolai's way of warning me that I am sleeping with the devil?*

The cruel twist on my heart weakens when I turn my eyes to Rico. He's watching me with the same tenderness he did when he comforted me on the plane hours ago. Even shrouded by darkness, there's something in his eyes that exposes he isn't the devil I need to be wary of. He's the man who saved me from the devil, not the one testing me.

Confident in my assessment of the situation, I advise, "Nikolai called me *Ангел*."

Rico's jaw tightens, but he doesn't appear totally shocked by my admission. "Nikolai calls all beautiful women *Ангел*." Even with his composure not altering, his tone is low, exposing that my disclosure still agitated him.

And that angst doubles when I blubber out, "He also told me to call him *Сатана*."

Now he looks shocked.

Actually, it's more like fury is beaming out of him.

After removing his seat belt, he slides across the small section of leather between us then gathers my hands in his. "Stay away from Nikolai, Kitten. Do you understand me?"

Although I could construe his words as aggressive, his eyes aren't relaying that.

All I see is genuine concern.

Relief empties his lungs with a big sigh when I say, "I understand."

The remaining ten minutes of our trip are made in silence. Rico held my hand the entire time, and it said more than any words ever could, but I'd be a liar if I said dread didn't wash over me when the six-car motorcade pulls into the ginormous mansion I fled from only a week ago.

I truly thought my long walk of shame through this residence would be the last time I stepped foot onto this property.

How wrong was I?

After opening the back passenger door and sliding out, Rico dips down to offer me a hand. Tension hangs thick in the air as we climb the stairs leading to the main entrance of the house. A tall gentleman with slicked-back hair, cold blank eyes, and an evil smirk blocks the entry into the mansion. I can tell the instant Rico notices him as his grip on my hand tightens and an expressionless mask slips over his face.

"Maya, come," Rico demands, his tone deep and brusque.

A young woman with long brown hair tied back in a ponytail peeks her head out from a group of women on our right. She bows her head at the gentleman hogging the entrance before locking her dark eyes with Rico.

"Take Blaire into her room and get her settled," Rico instructs.

After dipping her head again, Maya waves her hand to the elegant staircase behind her.

Although desperate to escape the awkwardness cracking in the air, I'd rather not walk the gallows alone. "Are you not coming with me?" I ask Rico, my voice panicked.

His pendulum-swinging moods startle me, but I'd choose to be attached to his hip than be left to defend myself in a house of horror with a lady who is so waif thin, a slight breeze could blow her away.

"I'll be up in a few, Kitten." Before I can plead with him, he peers past my shoulder to Maya and says, "Take her now." Unlike his earlier tone, this time his request comes out with the nasty bite of demand.

I'm not the only one noticing Rico's new superiority. Maya jumps to his command by intertwining her arm with mine and lugging me toward the stairwell. For a girl who has twigs for arms and legs, she has a lot of gusto in her core. She drags me through the lobby as if I'm the one missing twenty pounds on her frame.

As we climb the first step, I crank my neck back to Rico. He's standing toe-to-toe with the gentleman everyone seems frightened of.

Everyone except Rico.

He looks him directly in the eyes as they speak in Russian, not the slightest bit intimidated that their exchange has caught the attention of over a dozen pairs of eyes. It's a scary yet riveting confrontation.

When we reach the landing of the stairs, I shift my focus to Maya. "Maya, who is the man Rico is speaking with?"

Her throat works hard to swallow before she whispers, "Father."

My head rockets back to Rico so fast, my neck screams in protest. "That's Rico's father?" My question comes out tainted with disbelief. Fathers are meant to nurture and protect their children, but that man emulates the traits of a tyrant.

Maya doesn't need to answer my question, but I reach my own conclusion when Rico's eyes lock with mine for a fleeting second. Even though his lips don't move, I hear his silent plea. "Go, Kitten, before you once again dance with the devil."

Maya accompanies me to the room I woke in last week, supplies me with a hearty Russian dinner of a Reuben sandwich, and attempts to teach me how to play a Russian card game, Durak. Three hours have ticked by on the clock, and I haven't seen hide nor hair of Rico.

Although Maya's English is best described as poor, it isn't her lack of vocabulary that has our girly night ending. It is my heavy eyelids.

After bidding farewell to Maya, I head to the bathroom. Upon entering, I stare at the gorgeous clawfoot bath, hoping it will garner me the energy to draw it. A few hours soaking in a tub sound like heaven.

Although the temptation is strong, I don't think my eyelids will remain open long enough to enjoy it, so instead, I turn on the double shower at the side of the tub then shed my clothes, leaving them where they fall.

Have you ever been so tired, you wonder if you're awake or dreaming? That's how I feel right now.

I am beyond exhausted.

Once my clothing is removed, I step into the steam-filled space. Hot water bombards my body, waking me from my sleeping state. When I lean further into the spray, water pours down my cheeks and rolls over my heavy breasts, triggering a hidden memory to rush to the surface of my muddled brain...

With a lavender-colored shower puff, I lather my body with soapsuds, being extra cautious not to touch my newly inked skin. When I step into the spray, blissfully hot water heats my front at the same time a warm body molds my back. My heart doubles in size when a large hand with a ruby and diamond wedding band wrapped around the third finger curls around my stomach. Even with the shower filled with muggy dampness, goose bumps follow the trail the hand makes when it slithers up the smooth planes of my stomach to cup my desire-heavy breast.

"I thought you didn't want a shower?" My voice comes out throatier than normal, giving it a sexy edge.

"I didn't..." His Russian accentuated voice does even more wicked things to my insides. "Until I realized it was ten more minutes I could spend with you."

A ghost of a smile stretches across my face as I lean into him deeper. It turns into a full-toothed grin when his erection presses into my back. He's thick and long, swelling halfway up my spine.

"Only ten minutes," I jest, my tone a unique mix of playfulness and seduction. "Feels like a whole lot more than ten minutes."

The deep richness of his laugh quickly fills the room. It's a beautiful chuckle that sees my head following my body's desires for a change.

I spin around...

"No!" I slant into the water, hoping it will bring back my memory. "You can't end it there."

Even knowing in my heart that the man in the shower was Rico, I want to see it, recall it, and cherish it. It doesn't matter if I'm unearthing two seconds of memories with him or two minutes, a range of emotions wallop into me with every one I discover. And no, they aren't all solely based on my libido. Unveiling my memories is like working on a Rubik's cube. It seems like a complicated waste of time, but once I achieve the seemingly impossible, I'll have a better understanding of the square box with the six unique colors.

Rico is my Rubik's cube. I didn't marry him because I was drugged, so I want to discover what else drew me to him that night. Behind his cloaked-in-danger façade, Rico is insanely gorgeous, but deep down inside, I know his looks alone wouldn't have made me agree to marrying a stranger. Until I discover the other reasons, I won't stop hunting until every lost memory is unearthed.

After switching off the shower, I curl a fluffy towel around my body then use another to secure my wet hair in place. Because I forgot to turn on the exhaust fan, the floor-to-ceiling mirror attached to the double vanity is covered with steam.

It's probably for the best. I don't need to see myself to know how wretched I look.

I can feel it.

My lazy steps stop halfway out the door, closely followed by my heart when an awareness of being watched smacks into me. My heart rate—although agile—returns when I discover a pair of dark eyes peering at me from across the room. Rico is sitting on a high-backed chair. His suit jacket has been removed, and the sleeves of his dress shirt are rolled up to his elbows.

After his eyes finish raking over my body, he locks his heavy-hooded gaze with mine. Unnerved by the darkness of his eyes, I take a retreating step. They are the blackest I've seen them.

"Come here, Kitten." His voice is throaty and spine-tingling deep.

With my heart flipping, I shake my head, denying his request.

Rico strengthens his glare before repeating, "Come here, Kitten," for the second time.

His authoritative tone has me pushing off my feet before my brain can register a complaint. I've never been a confrontational person, and tonight is clearly no different.

Even though I'm following his command to a T, every step I take alters the power between us. Not only do Rico's eyes reveal I'm not the only one confused by our weird kinship—he's just as baffled as me—they also show there was something more than a laced drink guiding my decisions last week.

I'm in a house that makes the burliest men quake in their boots, but with Rico looking at me like he is now, all my insecurities fade into the horizon. It's just me and him—the stranger I married.

When I stand in front of him, he grips my towel and pries it open.

My hands shoot down, endeavoring to maintain my modesty the best I can in a skimpy towel, but my abrupt movements halt when I realize he only opened the towel far enough to uncover his name inked on my hip.

Although there's still a scandalous amount of my skin exposed, it isn't sufficient enough to warrant an overreaction.

"Is it itchy?" Rico questions with his eyes fixed on the flaky skin on my hip bone.

I shrug. "A little." When his truth-absorbing eyes connect with mine, wordlessly demanding an honest answer, I mumble, "A lot."

I followed the advice posted online about caring for newly-inked skin, but no matter how stringently I adhere to the guidelines, my tattoo is blotchy, scaly, and painstakingly itchy. I try my hardest to ignore the desire to scratch, but just like my ability to deny Rico's attention, I have the occasional slip-up.

My chances of having another relapse grow when Rico secures a tube of hydrocortisone cream from the drawer beside him. He unscrews the cap, squirts a small portion of lotion onto two fingers, then carefully applies it to my hip.

I stare at him, utterly dumbfounded. He is dutifully attending to me like a caring husband would his wife. I won't lie, my nose is tingling, and sentimental tears are pricking my eyes. It's a sweet thing for him to do even with it seeming out of character.

"If you keep it well-moisturized, the itching sensation will lessen." Rico screws the cap back onto the tube then lifts his eyes to me. "But no matter how uncomfortable it gets, don't pick at it."

I nod before handing him the towel wrapped around my drenched hair so he can dry his slicked fingers. Upon noticing my wound is already less itchy, I say, "Thank you."

His dark eyes glance into mine before his chin balances on his chest. "Maybe next time you'll heed my warning on an impromptu tattoo session."

My mouth gapes, shocked and blinking. "Me? Wasn't my tattoo your idea?"

When he throws his head back and laughs, my shock intensifies. He has a beautiful laugh, the type that shreds through my body and warms my heart.

It also makes my stomach do a stupid fluttery thing, but we will keep that between us.

Once Rico's laughter settles down, he answers, "No, Kitten. The tattoo was all *your* doing."

"But... *are you sure...* I thought it was some ownership slash branding kind of thing."

The laughter lining his face vanishes, replaced with an emotion I find a little hard to decipher. "Hmm... is that why you chose my chest?"

My eyes bug, then they almost bulge out of my head when Rico unfastens the top three buttons on his shirt. I swallow harshly to relieve my burning throat when he pulls open his shirt to expose my name in thick black ink swirled on his left pectoral muscle.

It isn't solely the six letters of my name raising my body temperature but also being awarded the visual of his smooth, muscular torso.

From his build alone, I knew he'd have an impressive body, but seeing it up close... *Jesus.*

Now I wish even more that my flashback of our time together in the shower went a few seconds longer.

My heart threatens to break out of my chest when Rico seizes my wrist to run my fingers over his chest. His pecs contract when he runs my fingertips over the peeling ink. Although his tattoo doesn't look as scaly as mine, there's no doubt it's fresh ink.

Talking through the lump in my throat, I mutter, "I branded you." Disbelief, and if I'm not mistaken, a little bit of honor dangle off my vocal cords.

"You can't brand someone unwilling, Kitten," Rico replies, staring up at me. "Memory?"

The hope in his eyes dampens when I shake my head. "I had a flashback earlier, though."

His heavy brow cocks as he waits for me to continue.

"It was in the shower."

He smiles at the flustered state my confession causes my cheeks before asking, "Was it a good memory, Kitten?"

"It was a little short," I blubber out, honestly.

Now it's my turn to smile at his shocked expression.

"My memory, not your..." I stop talking as heat floods my cheeks.

I don't want to be, but disappointment clouds me when Rico removes my hand from his chest. "You look tired, Kitten. Let me shower, then you can go to bed."

"Okay." I catch my eye roll halfway from the neediness of my voice. I've never been a clingy type of girl, but for some unknown reason, Rico incites a side of me I didn't know existed.

Maybe it is because I've always been the girl who plays it safe? Marrying Rico added an edge of danger to my life I've never been brave enough to explore. Meeting him forced me out of the safe box I have been living in the past ten years. He isn't just a challenge for me to unravel, he challenges me as well.

"Your sleeping clothes are on the bed." Rico nudges his head to the ginormous bed on my left.

A smile etches onto my weary face when I follow his head nudge and notice he has laid out my pajamas—a satin slip and a three-quarter length silk negligee. When I shoot my eyes around the room, the warmth spreading across my chest flourishes. Not only did he remove my sleeping garments from my suitcase, but he also unpacked my bag.

Suddenly, my happiness evaporates. *Does that mean he intends for my stay to be a long one?*

My heart rate hits an all-time high, but if I were honest, I'd admit I don't know if it's beating faster in exhilaration or alarm.

After pressing a quick kiss to my temple, Rico ambles into the bathroom. Once he slips behind the door, I hurriedly get dressed and hop into bed, vainly trying to disregard the breakneck speed of events.

Seconds have never felt like hours until I'm in Rico's presence.

13

I've been tossing and turning for approximately fifteen minutes when the creak of a door screeches through my ears. Although I'm beyond tired, sleep is evading me after my exchange with Rico. The entire day has been nothing but a blur of confusion. In a matter of hours, I went from being surrounded by twenty-three grubby faces to trying to ignore the affections of a man who equally intrigues and intimidates me.

Any chance of ignorance is lost when I twist my head to the side and spot Rico entering the room wearing nothing but a pair of skimpy boxer shorts. His hair is wet and flat, his naked torso is shimmering with droplets of water I'm suddenly envious of, and his plain blue cotton boxers have no chance in hell of hiding his yummy six-pack or the defined cut of his oblique muscles.

When he spins around to face the dresser, my mouth falls open. A large tattoo covers a majority of his left shoulder blade and twists halfway down his back. It's an intricate design that weaves through muscles I didn't even know existed. And his ass... *oh*... there should be rules against a man having an ass that fine.

Failing to notice my ogling stare, Rico undoes the latch on his gold watch, places it on a tray on top of the dresser, then turns to face the mirror on the dressing table. He runs his fingers through his gloriously thick hair, giving it that sexed-up look usually achieved through bedroom antics.

Like the first time I viewed an original Monet painting, I can't stop staring at him, both riveted and confused. His body is truly spectacular —a fine piece of art.

After tussling his unruly hair into place, Rico throws a plain shirt over his head then spins to face me. In silence, I watch him stride across the room. Just the way he moves his body with such fluidity and ease, I know he'd be extraordinary in bed. Sheet-clenching, I'll-never-forget-being-claimed-by-him, mind-hazing sex.

The heat in my cheeks doubles when my mind wanders to the time I discovered a three-pack of empty condom wrappers under this very bed.

That was a mere week ago.

Seems more like a lifetime.

The fiery warmth clogging my veins diverts to another region when Rico pulls back the sheets. Not saying a word, he slips into bed next to me.

While springboarding into a half-seated position, I stammer out, "W-what are you doing?"

He adjusts two pillows behind him before connecting his dark eyes with mine. "Getting ready for bed."

"In *my* bed?" I splutter, my voice high and cringeworthy.

"Kitten," Rico draws out in a long, husky moan that causes the hairs on my arms to stupidly bristle. "This is not *your* bed."

I peer around the room, confused. This is the room Maya brought me to. Doesn't that automatically make it mine?

My eyes stop aimlessly floating when Rico continues, "It is *our* bed."

I speak slowly, still shocked. "*Our* bed?"

He smiles a lazy grin that sets my pulse racing. "Yes. *Our* bed."

Annoyed at my body's reaction to his playful grin more than the way he says 'our,' I mutter, "And how many other women have you slept with in *our* bed?"

I'm not going to lie. A stabbing pain hits my chest just from thinking about him with anyone but me.

Is that inconceivable for me to say? I don't know him—he's practically a stranger—but I'm jealous about any prior relationships he may have had.

Yeah, that's inconceivable.

My shock multiplies tenfold when Rico answers, "Not one."

I arch a brow, demanding further explanation. There's no way a man with looks like his wouldn't have women falling at his feet, so I find it extremely doubtful no one has slept in his bed before me.

Upon noticing my skeptical gaze, Rico explains, "We purchased this bed an hour after being married. At your request, it was delivered before we arrived here."

I release a long-winded breath. "*Ohhh.*"

He smiles at my ambiguous reaction before tilting in close to my side. "I've never had so much fun breaking in a bed." His breath on my ear causes goose bumps to race to the surface of my skin.

That isn't the only response his closeness instigates, though. It also causes a new memory to rush to the forefront of my mind...

Not the slightest bit embarrassed, I yank down the zipper of my floral skirt, step out of it, then charge for a monstrous bed in the middle of the room. A girly giggle explodes from my mouth when the softness of new sheets engulfs me.

"Oh my goodness, it's huge!" I squeal before fanning my arms and legs out like I'm making a snow angel in the high thread count sheets.

My nostrils flare, relishing the scent of new bedding, but that isn't the sole cause for my quickening pulse. It is the distinct aroma of spices on sweat-slicked skin.

My darling husband is close by.

Immature laughter switches to a needy purr when Rico presses a kiss on the edge of my ankle, closely followed by one on the back of my knee. I squirm when his beard scrapes the skin high on my inner thigh. Fighting my body's desire to pull my knees inward, I loosen my thigh muscles and sweep them open.

I'm on the bed my husband purchased for us to christen on our wedding night. Now is not the time for modesty.

My breathing pans out when the softest pair of lips graze past my pussy. I gasp, incredibly turned on when Rico places a gentle peck on the middle of my satin panties. Acting purely on instinct, my hips swivel, soundlessly pleading for more direct contact. I only just hold in my disappointed moan when Rico's sinful lips continue their journey, denying my body's silent pleas.

Every kiss placed on my skin as he leisurely travels from my ankles to my torso has my excitement growing. I'm incredibly aroused while also reveling in his tenderness. I've never had a man treat me with so much compassion before. Every kiss he gives is filled with silent promises that he will always love and protect me, keep me safe, and never break my heart.

My heart swells, incapable of accommodating the massive surge of blood pumping into it when a final peck is pressed on the dip in my collarbone. It isn't the softness of the kiss that has my heart defying logic. It's the beautiful pair of dark eyes staring down at me.

Rico's hair has fallen into his face, framing his chiseled cheekbones and shaped brows. His lips are swollen from our kisses shared in the back of the car during our travels, but his most exquisite feature is the look beaming from his eyes. Nothing but admiration reflects back at me, abundantly proving I'm not the only one who has fallen head over heels in a matter of hours.

He loves me too.

Rico presses a kiss to the edge of my mouth, drawing my sole devotion back to him. "Are you sure this is what you want, Blaire?" he asks with his gorgeous dark eyes dancing between mine. "This is your last chance to back away. Once this happens, I'll never give you up, so I need you to be sure."

I cup his jaw and return his devoted watch. "I've never been more sure of anything in my life," I reply, only just concealing my smile at the way his jaw twitches under my touch. "I love you, Enrique. From the tips of your toes to the top of your gorgeous head."

Blood surges to my heart, making it swell even more when the most captivating smile stretches across Rico's handsome face...

As I merge out of my memory, I gasp in a quick breath, shell-shocked by my admission in my flashback. I've never spoken those three words to another man before, but I gave them willingly to Rico within hours of meeting him.

What type of drug was I given that it knocked down my walls so quickly?

My eyes stray to the side when a cold hand gives relief to my flaming cheeks. Rico's dark eyes are rapt on me. His gaze is primal, dominating, and strong, and it adds to the heat hueing my skin.

"You remembered."

Although he appears to be asking a question, his powerful gaze isn't reflecting that. He seems to know me well enough to know where my thoughts strayed to.

That adds even more astonishment to the giddiness clustered in my brain.

When I nod, the first splash of a tear spills from my eye. Rico intakes a sharp breath before the backs of his fingers slides across my cheek, catching my tears in one swift motion.

"If you remember, Kitten, why are you crying?" His voice is gravelly and crammed with worry.

When I notice his eyes are wearing the same tender look they had in my memory, my worry fades for hope. Even digging through the mountain load of darkness suffocating his beautiful eyes, I can tell he cares for me.

I'd be lying if I said he was the only one harboring unexplainable feelings.

Even knowing Rico isn't a man I should fall in love with, I can't deny the weird sensation my heart gets every time he is near. I've tried to ignore it. It isn't possible. Although he is technically a stranger, in my heart, I feel like I've known him half my life.

While I'm being forthright, I'll admit the idea of falling in love with a man who equally thrills and terrifies is a truly petrifying notion. When I'm with Rico, it feels like I'm at the crest of a large waterfall. It's beautiful from the high vantage point, but if I jump off the edge, what's hidden beneath the water waiting for me? Am I plunging into a sea of blackness? Or something magical?

A stormy cloud forms in Rico's tempestuous gaze when I fail to answer his question. I try to get my mouth to cooperate with my brain, to say something to ease the hurt in his eyes, but nothing comes out. I'm stunned into silence.

When more stupid tears unwillingly spill from my eyes, Rico scoops me into his arms and pulls me into his chest. "Shh, Kitten, shh. You're okay." His deep tone is as rickety as my composure.

I'm balancing precariously on the crest of a steep waterfall, but I nuzzle into Rico's chest to accept his comfort without protest, throwing my wariness to the side for a few moments with the hope of gathering my scattered composure.

We sit in silence for several moments. I feel like my world has been upended. It might seem a little dramatic to outsiders, but that doesn't mean it isn't true. In a matter of a week, everything I knew about my life changed—my career, my marital status, my heart. In the blink of an eye, I went from a kindergarten teacher to mob wife—two vastly contrasting roles.

While wallowing about being forced into a family I would have never chosen to become a part of, a new reality dawns.

Rico never had a choice, either. He was born into his role.

I had a normal upbringing with two loving parents nurturing me.

Rico was raised by a monster.

My pupils widen when the veracity of my statement smacks into me. I've heard those exact words before, and no, I'm not referring to the time Rico said it in the Escalade after signing our annulment papers.

As my brain labors over the last time I heard that statement, I close my eyes.

When another memory smashes into me, I inhale a quick, jagged breath...

"No, Blaire, you do not belong in this lifestyle. I will not drag you into the darkness."

I tighten my grip on Rico's hand before digging my heels into the carpet. Even though a man of Rico's size could easily yank me across the pristine marble floors, he stops walking and spins around to face me. Excitement mingled with anxiety lines his face.

"You're not a monster, Enrique. You were just raised by one," I mutter as my glistening eyes dance between his.

"We've only known each other for three hours. You're not qualified to make that assumption," he replies. Although his tone is aiming for stern, it comes out with more sentiment than he is aiming for.

"I only needed thirty seconds to see the real you." I peer into the eyes that captured my soul in under a minute. "Now I want a lifetime to show you what I already know."

After taking a few moments to register his shocked expression, I drift my eyes to the chapel on my right. I feel Rico's gaze slide over my face before he too shifts on his feet to face the chapel. "If we do this, Blaire, I can't promise you a lifetime of sunshine, but I can promise to always protect and cherish you."

I don't even need to look at him to know what he's saying is factual. The truth is evident in his voice.

"I can't promise to always protect you, but I promise you a lifetime of sunshine." I drift my loved-up gaze back to Rico. "I'll be your light in a life full of darkness."

We recited similar vows to each other when we wed in that very chapel an hour later...

My overworked heart slicks my skin with sweat as my newly discovered memory plays on repeat. No matter which way I play it—backward, forward, or in reverse—the facts never alter. A drug wasn't leading my decisions last week. Although I acted a little riskier than normal in my flashback, I was lucid and capable of making my own decisions. I'm not slurring my words, and I don't seem intoxicated. I was merely the carefree version of me that usually comes out when Lacey and I share too many glasses of wine. I also seemed happy—truly and utterly happy.

After swallowing down the bile tarnishing the back of my throat, I pop my head off Rico's chest and peer into his eyes. "It was all me," I mumble, still shocked by my audacity in my flashback. "Our tattoos, our wedding, everything was my idea." I bounce my eyes between his while asking, "Why did you go along with it? I was a stranger to you mere hours before."

He scrubs the back of his hand across my cheeks, removing the last of my tears before saying, "When an angel falls into your lap, you don't make her wait. You grant her every wish."

Even in the awkwardness of the moment, he reassures me it wasn't the drugs in my system steering my moral compass last week. It was him.

He's a stranger, and at times, he scares me more than any man before him, but there's something about him I'm drawn to. I don't know if it's love like I declared last week or because I have the urge to protect him as he guards me, but deep in my soul, I know there's something greater between us than a drunken mistake.

Snubbing my shaking hands, I cup his jaw and align our eyes. "I wish for us to leave this lifestyle," I say, allowing my heart to talk for the first time in a week.

The quickest flare of emotion brightens Rico's dark gaze before he snuffs it. "If that were possible, Kitten, you wouldn't be here. But I can only grant wishes, not miracles."

My shoulders slump as a new upwelling of tears flood my already swamped eyes. The only thing that holds them at bay is when the entirety of his reply replays through my muddled mind. "Me or us?"

He locks his hard-set eyes with me. "You, Kitten. I can't leave until I get answers."

I fall backward until my backside is resting on the balls of my feet. "When you get the answers you're seeking, will you leave then?"

Fear curls around my throat when he shakes his head, then it almost asphyxiates me when he says, "There's only one way I can leave this family, Kitten. I wouldn't be breathing."

14

My groggy head lifts from the pillow when the creak of a door sounds through my ears. My half-asleep eyes widen when I scan the unfamiliar room. Unlike last week, it doesn't take me long to gather my bearings. It isn't the familiarity of the room or the fact I've once again woken with a thumping skull, it's the smell of a delicious spicy scent lingering in the air.

When the distinct noise of a shower turning on sounds through my ears, I crank my neck back and peer toward the bathroom. Not surprisingly, the door is closed. My lips quirk when my eyes catch the time on the bedside clock. It's a little after six.

I didn't realize Rico was such an early riser.

After our heart-strangling discussion last night, Rico gathered me in his arms and held me until I fell asleep. His thumbs caught my tears, and his warm body soothed the shakes impeding mine.

I'm not going to lie. I liked being wrapped in his strong arms. On the surface, Rico seems like a complicated man, but when I look past the hard shell he wears in front of others, I understand the desire to marry him on sight. The man I was with last night was heartfelt and enduring, a complete contradiction to the man I met the previous week.

Hoping a few more hours of sleep will dull the furious thump of my skull, I flop my head back onto my pillow. I jump out of my skin when a final sweep of the room detects another presence. The lady who entered my room last week is standing by the door, scowling at me. Just like our first confrontation, her hard-hearted eyes set my pulse racing.

"Hello," I greet, my voice apprehensive. It's only a little after six, so I'm surprised she's entering my room so early, let alone unannounced.

"You. Take." She thrusts two folded towels balancing on her open palms my way.

While rubbing my tired eyes with my palm, I slip out of bed and pad toward her. My steps are slow and shaky. Not just because I'm tired but because I'm wary of the anger pumping out of her in invisible waves. I'm unsure why she doesn't like me, but it doesn't take a rocket scientist to read her signals. It's clear this lady is not a fan of mine.

I accept the lavender-scented towels from her grasp while mumbling, "Thank you."

"You. Take," she grunts again, her voice heavily slurred by a thick Russian accent.

I draw the towels into my chest. "Yes, I take."

Even with her eyes narrowed into tiny slits, I can't miss their roll. "Not you take. You. Take."

I stare at her, utterly confused. "I did take." I swallow the brick lodged in my throat when my words come out stronger than I'm anticipating.

Returning my glare—except with more viciousness—she says, "Not you take. You. Take. Rico." She gestures her hand to the closed bathroom door.

"Oh." *Ohh.*

I shake my head so fast I make myself dizzy. "He's in the shower." *Naked.*

A silent squeal bubbles up my chest when she shoves me toward the door. Just like Maya, she has a lot of gusto hidden in her small frame. Her push is so strong, I cross the expansive bedroom in three heart-pounding seconds. "You. Take. Rico."

"I can't go in there. He's naked. You. Take. Rico." My heart stops beating when I impersonate her accent to perfection—throaty gargle and all.

My mouth gapes, shell-shocked by my rudeness. Even not being able to see her, I feel her anger growing from the pit of her stomach to her face. She's so mad, her hands scorch my back when she continues shoving me toward the bathroom.

After rolling my shoulders and wiping the fear from my face, I spin around to face her. My attempt to pretend I'm not intimidated by her furious composure is left for dust when her livid gaze spears me in place.

"Sorry." My tone is as weak as my pathetic apology.

The hair on her chin wobbles when she sneers, "You. Take. Rico. You. Wife!"

With my heart clutched with worry, I nod. "Okay. I'll take these to Rico." I take two measly steps toward the bathroom before turning back around to face her. "I don't have to hand them to him? Right?" I query, my voice quivering. "I can just leave them on the vanity?"

She looks at me like I'm an imbecile. "You. Take. Rico."

"Okay." I breathe out slowly. "I can do this." *I hope.*

I swear I'm on the verge of hyperventilating when I push down the door handle. Steam seeps through the gap in the door when I swing it open, but my breathing pattern returns to a safe level when I remember how badly fogged the mirrored wall was when I showered last night. Add that to the bathroom's configuration, and I should be able to place the towels onto the vanity without incident.

Keeping my gaze lowered on the floor, I step deeper into the bathroom. I think I'm in the clear, then the stupid door shuts loudly, announcing my arrival.

I almost make a run for it when Rico instructs sternly, "Anna, leave the towels on the vanity."

Grimacing, I squeak out, "Okay."

I stomp my feet like a five-year-old when my attempt to impersonate Anna's accent this time around comes out sounding like I'm a twelve-year-old boy in the midst of puberty.

While releasing a deep breath, I scuffle across the tiled floor as quickly as my quaking legs will carry me, only lifting my eyes when the empty wastebasket enters my peripheral vision. Holding my hands out in front of me to gauge the distance, I place the towels on the vanity without peeking at the mirrored wall.

I'm not going to lie. It's a tortuous feat.

A silent squeal bubbles up my chest when the towels slip off the vanity and flop to my feet. Grumbling, I bend down to gather them back up. My clit throbs when my crouched position awards me with a mind-hazing visual. Although the top half of the mirror is covered with a dense layer of steam, the bottom half is void of any vision-impeding fog, meaning I'm graced with the reverent view of a completely naked Rico.

Oh, for the love of god, the man is a masterpiece.

My eyes gobbled up every inch of his torso last night, but they run over it again like they're assessing the authenticity of a priceless painting. Water is sloshing down the side of his face, flattening his dark hair around his temples, and his body is carved with rock-hard muscles hidden under creamy smooth skin. He's dark and dangerous rolled into an undoubtedly beautiful package.

My lips part to draw in ragged breaths when the scene switches from awe-inspiring to scandalous. After adjusting his position so the heavy flow of water can remove the suds coating his back, Rico commences *cleaning* another region of his perfect physique.

After spacing his feet to the width of his shoulders, he wraps his manly hand around his fat cock and pumps it in long, controlled strokes. My ethically motivated brain screams at me to respect his privacy by leaving the bathroom, but my lust-driven heart keeps my feet firmly planted on the floor.

When the tempo of his thrusts increases, any possibility of me leaving is a lost cause. I'm too busy studying how every muscle in his body constricts with each pump he does to consider leaving. I'm riveted and insanely turned on watching such a beautiful man in a raw and carnal position.

It's a sight I'd line up to witness time and time again.

A pleasurable jolt rockets through my body when Rico closes his eyes and his lips separate. My nipples are budded and aching, my pussy is slicked with dampness, and my morals are wavering so considerably it's taking all my strength to remain hidden. I want to enter the shower like Rico did in my flashback last night.

A familiar tingle runs the length of my spine when my eyes lock in on the wide head of Rico's cock sliding in and out of his hand. I know you shouldn't call a penis beautiful, but his is. It's beautiful, manly, and large.

I squeeze my thighs together when a hot trickle of desire puddles between them. I never thought I could climax just from watching a man please himself, but Rico is unearthing many sides I didn't know existed. The moral, upstanding kindergarten teacher I was yesterday would have never entered the bathroom, where my Vegas morally-lost self can't tear my eyes away from the womb-clenching visual playing out in front of me.

As the minutes tick by, his race to climax speeds up. I've never seen anything so captivatingly raw as a man bringing himself to ecstasy. This man is a machine, his body built solely to give pleasure. He's so wondrous, he doesn't even need to touch me, and my orgasm is begging to be released.

His thrusts into his suds-covered fist quicken, forcing the muscles in his stomach to flex with every grind. A soft groan whizzes through my gaped mouth when his teeth drag over his bottom lip. His face shows his race to release is intensifying as much as mine. The glistening bead on the end of his knob increases along with his pants of breath.

I pant right alongside him, unable to hold in my excitement. My body is coated with a dense layer of sweat, my eyes are wide and heavily dilated, and an orgasm is lingering deep in my core, dying to break free.

Several strokes later, the most animalistic growl I've ever heard tears from Rico's parted lips at the same time a stream of cum rockets out of his knob.

My hands dart up to secure a death-tight grip on the vanity as I struggle to contain my excited moans. Even battling to keep my crouched position unknown, my eyes remain focused on Rico. Considering he is the sole cause of the pleasurable shimmer revitalizing my body with renewed hope, he deserves my dedicated devotion.

Rico continues stroking his cock until every drop of his cum is released while I fight to keep my pleasurable groans to a hum. It's one of the hardest battles I've ever fought.

My grip on the vanity loosens when his pumps slow from manic to a gradual pace. When he releases his still-firm cock from his grasp, reality smacks into me. I just hid in the corner of a bathroom to watch a man bring himself to ecstasy.

Oh. My. Lord. I'm a horrible person.

Beyond embarrassed about my appalling behavior, I scamper off the floor and charge across the room as quickly as my shaking legs can take me. My heart wildly beats, matching the pulse surging through my pussy, and blood rushes to my skin, coating every inch with a vibrant red hue.

I've barely slipped out the door when the shower being switched off sounds through my ears.

I lean against the door and gasp in quick breaths, grateful that it was only a close call.

15

After taking a moment to calm my racing heart, I push off the door and amble to the chair in front of the dressing mirror. My steps are heavy, weighed down by the guilt maiming my heart. I can't believe I did that. I've never been so bold... *or disturbing.*

Vegas should come with a warning label.

"Life as you know it will become nonexistent," I mumble while waving my hand in the air dramatically.

When I plop into the chair, I catch my reflection in the mirror. My eyes are wide and bright since my natural beige coloring is accentuated with rosy cheeks, and my lips are plump from my teeth dragging over them.

I'd like to say my rouged appearance is solely based on the stifling Las Vegas heat already pumping into the room, but that would be a lie. Even a stranger could read the signs my body is relaying. I'm the most sexually aroused I've ever been.

Who wouldn't be after witnessing an event like that?

Ignoring the gnawing pit in my chest for invading Rico's privacy, I snag a concealer stick out of my makeup bag and set to work on hiding the bags plaguing my drooping eyes. Nothing but a few hours between the sheets will fix the flustered look on my face, so I may as well start at the least complicated part of my unsightliness.

Within seconds of applying the first layer of concealer, Rico enters the room. I continue with my mission, pretending I haven't noticed his presence.

My ignorance lasts only seconds when I spot his reflection in the mirror.

His *stark-naked* reflection.

The concealer stick drops to the dresser with a clatter as my eyes drink in every inch of his gloriously naked frame. I try to tear my perverted gaze away, but just like in the bathroom, my morals have been left for dust. It would be like taking a girl to Tiffany's and telling her to only look at the earrings. That will *never* happen. When there's something beautiful to admire, you devour every inch of it, giving equal devotion to each admirable asset.

And that's what I do to Rico's body as he gathers clothing from the walk-in closet and commences getting dressed. By the way my eyes refuse to blink for fear of missing something, anyone would swear he was doing something more riveting than getting dressed. But like everything he does, he dresses with a sense of confidence and stature. He moves with such gracefulness you can't help but be entranced.

Even though I've seen him shirtless numerous times in the past twenty-four hours, my eyes roam over every spectacular ridge and dip of his muscular physique. His biceps aren't brawny like weightlifters, but they're thick and veiny and clearly show he works out, and the six bumps in his stomach constrict when he bends over to step into a pair of blue boxer shorts.

Not wanting to miss the opportunity to see his spectacular package once again, I slowly drop my eyes to the lower half of his body. A trail of dark hair flows from his flat inner belly button to a small patch of curly hair. Just like his facial hair, his pubic hair is trimmed, but it still has an edge of manly roughness to it.

The throb of my pussy overtakes the pounding of my head when my eyes drop to his glorious cock. Even flaccid, his penis is thick, long, and mouth-wateringly beautiful.

When his cock twitches, a dash of desire thickens my blood, and my eyes rocket to his. The tingling of my pussy intensifies when my dilated eyes meet with his heavy-hooded gaze. He clearly noticed my avid assessment of his body. His grin is smug, and his eyes are blazing with lust. He is the cockiest I've ever seen him, which is saying something for a man with as much confidence as Rico.

With a cheeky wink, he slips his cotton boxer shorts up his thighs, covering the core-clenching visual from my devious eyes. Not the slightest bit annoyed that I'm ogling him from across the room, he throws a plain white cotton tee over his head and tugs a pair of dark blue jeans up his legs before pushing off his feet and heading my way. My clit thrums with every prowling step he takes, but like a deer trapped in headlights, I remain frozen and muted, rendered immobile by the massive surge of euphoria pumping through my veins.

He locks his dark gaze with mine in the mirror before muttering, "Good morning, Kitten." His raspy voice adds to the warm slickness coating my panties.

"M-m-morning."

When he stands behind me to run his fingers through his hair in the mirror, the heat of his elongated cock scorches my shoulder blade. My breathing increases to rapid-fire pants as I struggle to ignore the pleas of my body.

Once his fingers have wrangled his dark locks into the sexed-up look he regularly wears, he locks his eyes back to me.

I dart my gaze away, pretending I wasn't daydreaming about replacing his hands with my own.

"Did you sleep well?"

"Uh-huh," I mumble through the lump in my throat, the huskiness of my voice exposing my excitement at his closeness.

He leans over my shoulder to snag his watch from the dresser, bringing his lips super closer to mine when he asks, "Why are you up so early?"

Air traps halfway to my lungs when my senses are bombarded with the delicious smell of his body wash. It's unique, virile, and adds a sweet aroma to his spicy scent. "Couldn't sleep. You?"

After fastening his flashy-looking watch on his wrist, Rico returns his eyes to mine reflecting in the mirror and says, "I needed to work off some restlessness, so I went for a run."

Heat creeps across my cheeks as the image of him in the shower plays through my mind.

Obviously his run didn't have the outcome he was aiming for.

Rico glides the back of his hand down my flushed cheeks, the same hand that was earlier wrapped around his cock.

Every fine hair on my body bristles as excitement sparks through my throbbing sex. If I weren't frozen in place with desire, I'd beg for an encore of his performance in the shower, but since my eagerness has muted me into silence, I merely return his lust-filled stare.

After placing his hand on my shoulder, Rico spins me around to face him. "Are you okay, Kitten? You still look a little restless yourself. Flustered even."

I lick my dry lips before forcing out through the dryness, "I'm fine. Nothing a hot shower won't cure." My lips part as my pupils widen. *Could I have chosen a more pathetic set of words?*

The corners of Rico's plump lips twitch as he struggles to hold in his smile. "A hot shower is a wonderful cure for any edginess, but I don't know if it will be enough for you. You seem like you need something more. Something *deeper*." The low tone of his voice sends a thrill of pleasure through my body. It rockets through every inch of my skin before clustering deep in my aching-with-need pussy.

Incapable of going down without a fight, I turn back to face the mirror, needing to look at anything but his deliriously handsome face before I lose all rational thoughts. My efforts to act unaffected are fruitless. I look even more aroused now than I did when I fled the bathroom.

Ignoring my shaky hands, I lift the concealer stick to my face and get back to work on tackling the black rings under my eyes while wishing there was a way I could remove the lust-filled glint in my eyes just as quickly.

Rico stands behind me in silence for several minutes, watching me work my magic on the tiredness even the world's most perfect shower wouldn't have the chance of erasing. Even though he doesn't speak, my awareness of his closeness is paramount. Just the scent of his body wash ensures my wicked mind never strays too far from him.

Happy I've camouflaged a night of restless sleep and ignoring the fact I've put on my makeup before showering, I return my makeup to my cosmetic bag, then stand from my seat.

Thirty minutes have passed since Rico's fire-sparking display in the bathroom, but the intoxicating scent of lust is still thick in the air.

"I'm going to grab a quick shower," I mumble before making a beeline for the bathroom door. I don't know why I felt the need to update him on my happenings, it just naturally flowed out of my mouth.

My quick steps to the bathroom slow when the deep rumble of "Kitten" comes out of a voice with an edge of invincibility. Rico's tone is so smooth and sexy, I think I could come just from listening to him recite the phone book.

After rolling my shoulders, I turn around to face him on a wobbly pair of legs. My knees curve inward when I meet his blazing-with-lust eyes. He watches me for a few seconds, categorizing every feature of my face before he says, "I forgot to thank you."

My brows squeeze together in confusion. "For what?"

Sweat coats my palms when he paces toward me, his grin smug, his eyes firing. I can barely breathe when he tilts in close and whispers, "For the towels."

I freeze, panicked at how he'll react to me invading his privacy. Panic is a waste of time. When I shift my gaze sideways, I catch the impish gleam brightening his dark eyes, undoubtedly proving he knew I was watching every scandalous minute of his performance.

My panic recedes more when his lips curve into a heart-fluttering smirk. He knew I was watching. That's why he thoroughly *cleaned* that region of his body. His performance was a show. A pussy-tingling show I'll never forget.

My knees clash together when Rico says, "Enjoy your shower, Kitten. I'll be waiting for you when you've finished."

16

*A*llowing my vicious heart-versus-mind battle to run the gauntlet of my tired brain, I take my time in the shower. My body is begging me to give Rico a chance to prove how good he could make me feel, but my head is telling me there's too much murkiness lurking behind his eyes to trust him.

My heart—that's an entirely different story altogether.

After switching off the shower, I wrap a heavenly soft towel around my body and slowly trudge toward the bathroom door. My steps are heavy, not just weighed down by the dilemma muddling my tired brain but also from the climax clustering in my core, begging to be released.

Even the world's most scalding shower couldn't dampen my excitement the slightest. I'm so wound up I can't think straight. I'm sure it would only take the meekest touch from Rico to send my climax sprinting past the finish line. I just have to decide if I'm willing to give myself fully to the stranger I married because, for some reason unfamiliar to me, it isn't just my body up for barter with Rico. It's all of me—heart, body, and soul.

When I exit the bathroom, my lazy steps stop. Just like he said he'd be, Rico is on the same chair he was in last night, waiting for me. His hair is still damp from his shower, but the rivulets of water that soaked into his shirt have dried.

Though I'm still fighting confusion, his steely eyes show he isn't waging the same battle. He knows what he wants, and he is determined to get it.

After snagging the hydrocortisone cream from the drawers next to him, Rico connects his dark eyes with mine. He doesn't need to speak to issue his request. His candid eyes tell the whole story. He wants me. Wholeheartedly.

Deciding I'm running a race I will never win, I push off my feet and amble toward him. With every step I take, the air shifts between us. There's no doubt I have a sexual connection with Rico. It's as obvious as the sun hanging in the sky, but there's something greater than my libido that has me sidestepping the massive obstacles placed between us. He truly intrigues me, more than any man before him, and to such a degree, I appear to have lost all my common sense.

The thrum of my pulse intensifies when my leisured strides stop in the exact spot they did last night. Just like the last time we danced this intricate two-step routine only hours ago, Rico clasps the edge of my towel and pries it open. The only difference this time around is I don't protest.

My heart squeezes when he rubs cream into his name inked on my skin in careful, devoted strokes. The air is fired with lust. It's so electric it sets my pulse racing.

A moan topples from my lips when his finger dips a little lower on my hip. His simplest touch can cause a feverish heat to scorch my veins.

My lips part to accommodate more needy gasps of air when he lifts his eyes to me and asks, "Did you take care of your restlessness in the shower, Kitten?"

Even blinded by lust, I can't miss the hidden innuendo in his question.

Unable to speak through my dry, parched throat, I shake my head.

A flash of gratitude passes through his eyes. "Do you want me to take care of you? To make you feel better?"

Before any words can spill from my lips, his long index finger runs over another erogenous zone in my body—the area just above the heated ache between my legs.

I open my mouth to protest, but in all honesty, it's just a ploy to convince myself that unbridled hankering isn't clouding all my shrewdness. Considering my lips parted, I'd say my theory has been proven. It isn't lust keeping me here. It's him, Rico—the stranger I married.

When he lowers his finger down my quivering pussy, objections roll out of my mouth hard and fast. They aren't what you're thinking. They are disgruntled protests when his finger fails to stop at my pulsating clit.

"Shh, Kitten, I'll take care of you."

Any hostility lingering in the back of my mind becomes a distant memory when he locks his heavy-hooded gaze with me. His eyes are dominating and forceful, and they make my pussy pulse with desire. He stares at me for several moments as if waiting for permission.

When I nod, allowing my body to win this round in the debilitating mind versus heart debate, Rico slowly inches his finger inside my shuddering core in a long, mouthwatering thrust. My pussy grows wetter when he says, "Ah, my naughty little Kitten. I've only just touched you, and you're already wet for me."

A whimpering groan flows from my gaped mouth when he withdraws his finger at the same tortuous pace he entered it. The walls of my vagina quiver around him, begging him to stay, to make me come, but their pleas are left unanswered.

I groan when he fully withdraws his finger. It switches to a moan when he pops his glistening digit into his mouth. A flicker of light fires through his dark gaze, closely followed by a carnal growl. "You taste exactly how I remember."

When his arms curl around me, I arch into his embrace, surrendering to the power he holds over me. As he steps toward the bed, he seals his lips over mine and spears his tongue into my mouth. Just like our kiss in the Escalade, he explores my mouth in slow and controlled strokes. He savors every inch of me like he's afraid I may soon vanish.

I float into the softness of high thread count linens when he lays me down in the middle of the bed. I'm splayed before him naked, quivering, and wet while he is fully clothed, but not the slightest twinge of modesty swamps me. I don't have time to be modest when I'm battling a ferocious out-of-control wildfire in the pit of my stomach.

He cups my breast in his large hand, kneading and caressing it with gentle squeezes while I rock against him, wanting to feel him on every inch of me.

"Enrique…"

"Shh, Kitten. I've got you."

My teeth comb my bottom lip when he lowers his mouth to my aching-with-need breasts and tugs my nipple with his teeth. It sends a jolt of pleasure through my soaked pussy. My nipples are usually not an erogenous zone, but every tug of his teeth tightens my coil more.

Inaudible purrs ripple through my lips when his long, dexterous fingers work one of my nipples into a hard bud while his mouth bites, licks, and sucks the other. When he lifts his head and looks at me, I'm confronted with the same set of eyes that blessed my dreams every night the past week. They are beautiful and innocent, causing my heart to swell.

Prickles sprout on my skin when he places a trail of kisses down my misted-with-sweat stomach. My legs squeeze together, vainly trying to lessen the insane throb between them when his tongue delves out to lick the salty substance slicking my skin with moisture. I watch him, panting and incredibly turned on as he makes his way to a region of my body, paying careful attention to every move he makes.

He kneels beside me, still fully clothed. "I've never seen a pussy as pretty as yours."

When he brushes his hand down my vagina, a tinge of vulnerability clouds my perception. This man who obviously has extensive knowledge of the female anatomy eyes me, but when he thrusts his finger back inside me, I push my weakness to the side, deciding now is not the time to evaluate my husband's sexual conquests.

My pussy ripples around him greedily, sucking him in deeper when he switches from one finger to two. I arch my back as a needy moan purrs through my lips. My brain is mindless, stuck in a trance of chasing an orgasm.

Rico sucks my throbbing clit into his mouth, boosting my race to climax. I dart my hands down to entwine my fingers through his hair, needing something to tether me down as I begin floating toward orgasmic bliss.

He rolls his tongue around my clit as my pants become labored and breathless. "Oh... God... Enrique."

Every muscle in my body tightens as his tongue works on my clit while his fingers pump in and out of me in precise, effortless thrusts. My back arches further off the bed with every flick of his tongue. I can feel my orgasm building, but something is holding it back, stopping it from being released.

"Stop fighting me, Kitten. Give me what I want, then I'll give you the same."

When the tension scorching through my body becomes too much to handle, I slump into the mattress and let out a long, throaty purr, surrendering not just my body to the man kneeling before me but my heart as well.

"Good girl," Rico murmurs against the quaking lips of my pussy. "Now you'll get what you need."

He increases the pressure of his tongue on my clit, and the pumps of his fingers become unyielding, switching my sprint to climax from a leisured walk to a hundred-yard dash. Sweat slicks my skin as a massive rush of euphoria blazes through every nerve of my body.

While gripping the sheets in a white-knuckled hold, I climax while whispering "Enrique" into the early morning air on repeat. I shudder and shake beneath him, not the slightest bit ashamed that he brought me to climax without removing an article of his clothing.

He gradually brings me down from orgasmic bliss by using a gentler approach than he used to take me there. He slows the thrust of his fingers while keeping pressure on my throbbing clit with his teeth. His bite is firm enough I'll never forget he was there but soft enough to guide me down from the haze of climax.

Once every orgasmic shudder has been exhausted, Rico presses a kiss on my right inner thigh before locking his eyes with my weary gaze. From the exulted gleam in his eyes, anyone would swear it was him who just endured the strongest climax of his life, not me. He looks smug, cocky, and, if I'm not mistaken, pleased, whereas my earth-shattering climax took the last portion of energy I had left in my body, making me limp, incoherent, and drained—mentally and physically.

When my blinks grow longer, Rico rolls onto his side and gathers me into his arms. His thick, hard body heats my back and spreads warmth across my chest, adding to the breakneck speed of events that are already tethering my heart to him.

After pulling the blankets out from beneath me, he covers me with their heavenly softness before muttering, "Sleep, Kitten. I'll be here when you wake."

17

"Run, Katie, run!" I scream through the sheet of tears streaming down my cheeks.

My stomach lurches when a stained white handkerchief narrows in on my face, protesting the strong waft of chemicals lingering from it. I kick the shin of the person whose arm is wrapped around my torso, fighting to break free. Even in my endeavors to escape the clutches of the person dragging me across the cracked concrete sidewalk, my eyes remained locked on Katie, my next-door neighbor and best friend since kindergarten. She wouldn't have been in this predicament if I hadn't convinced her to walk to the corner store against our parents' wishes on a late Friday afternoon.

"Nooo!" I cry in a blood-curdling scream when Katie's lifeless body is thrown into the back of an unmarked white van. Her pleated skirt bunches around her waist when she's pulled deeper into the van by a set of hairy, tattoo-covered hands...

I wake up in Rico's bed screaming. As my lungs heave for oxygen, my wide eyes scan the room. Sweat beads on my temples as tears slosh down my cheeks. I flinch when an arm wraps around my shoulders and drags me backward. Just like in my dream, I fight with all my might, kicking and screaming.

"Blaire, it's me. You're okay."

Even recognizing Rico's voice doesn't dampen my panic in the slightest. I lurch away from him so violently I fall onto the floor with an almighty thud. After kicking off the sheets entwined around my legs, I scamper across the highly polished wooden floor on my hands and knees.

My attempt to reach the wastebasket in the corner of the room before the contents of my stomach see daylight is bolstered when Rico climbs out of bed and brings it to me. He holds back my hair as the memories I've tried to keep buried for ten years resurface in the most ghastliest way.

"Shh, Kitten. You're okay. You're safe." He runs his hand down my spine as I heave into the bin.

Once every portion of slosh in my stomach has been expelled, he aids me in getting dressed before he pulls me into his arms and rocks me in his chest. Even during the middle of summer in a disgustingly hot climate, shivers havoc my body. I try to get my mouth to cooperate so I can offer some type of explanation to Rico as to why I've awoken screaming like a lunatic in the middle of the day, but nothing but painful sobs spill from my lips.

Over time, the warmth of Rico's body curled around mine dampens my shudders, and the rhythmic beat of his heart has my eyelids growing heavy...

The roughness of a concrete sidewalk scratches my knees as I crawl away from the man I kicked hard enough in the shins he threw me to the ground. When my ankle is seized, my chin hits the ground with so much force I freeze momentarily, dazed and disoriented. The blood from my grazed knees lines the sidewalk in vibrant red streaks when I'm dragged toward a van parked in an alleyway.

I lie lifeless on the concrete, no longer having the strength to continue my vicious fight. My vision is blurry, hindered by the massive number of tears, but it isn't blurry enough that I fail to notice an unresponsive Katie lying inside the van. She looks like she's sleeping with her head lolled to the side and her lips slightly parted.

My heart snaps in two when my bleary eyes lock in on a man seated behind her. His evil gaze alone is enough to make my skin crawl.

"I'm sorry, Katie," I mumble through a sheet of tears flowing down my face.

I don't know if I've reached hysteria or if Katie is conscious, but an upwelling of energy pumps into me when the faintest whisper of, "Don't give up, Blaire," sounds through my ears.

Fighting against the pain roaring through my body, I roll onto my side, crawl onto my knees, then stand on a pair of shaky legs. I barely make it three steps out of the alleyway when my body is pinned to a chain-link fence on my left. My lungs heave when my attacker's clutch on my throat becomes so firm, I can no longer breathe.

Not even two seconds later, the brute of a man holding me against the fence is tackled from the side. He and another unknown man land on the concrete path with a sickening thud. I stand frozen, rendered motionless with fear as my savior throws his clenched fist into my attacker's face, momentarily dazing him.

I snap out of my tranced state when my dark-haired savior turns his eyes to me and says, "Run! Blaire! Run!"

I ran and ran until my legs gave out.

Katie was never seen again...

"Wake up, Blaire!"

The authoritativeness in the deep male voice has me snapping to his demand. My eyes pop open to scan the room as I gasp for air, struggling to replenish my heaving lungs. Although the setting of the room is familiar, it takes me several moments to gather my bearings since I'm absorbing it from a different vantage point. My frantic breaths pan out when I grasp that I'm still on the floor of my bedroom in the Popov compound, nestled in Rico's strong arms.

"You're okay, Kitten. I promise you're okay," assures Rico, his voice raspy.

The aftereffects of my nightmare dampen when my eyes swing to the window, and I notice the sun has shifted from east to west. Heat blooms across my chest, filling some of the cracks formed there. Rico stayed on the floor with me for hours solely to comfort me.

I knew there was more to this man than just darkness.

After lifting my groggy head off his chest, I peer into Rico's eyes.

Even though his backside must be hurting from sitting on the hard wooden floor for hours, nothing but genuine concern beams from his eyes.

"I'm sorry—"

"Shh." He places his index finger on my lip. "Don't ever apologize for having a nightmare. You can't help what happened to you."

My brows knit in confusion. "You know what happened to me?"

A flicker of hesitation flares through his eyes before he nods.

"I told you what happened?" I squeal in surprise, shock evident in my voice.

Guilt has stopped me from sharing my story with anyone not in my inner circle. Even Lacey doesn't know the entirety of what happened that day, so I'm somewhat surprised I voluntarily shared it with Rico. Either the drug Timothy laced my drink with was stronger than anyone could have predicted, or the power Rico has over me is substantial.

When I peer into his remorseful eyes, I'm fairly sure the latter is a more accurate assumption.

Rico stands, taking me with him. From the agility of his movements, no one would suspect he'd spent the last three hours sitting on a rock-hard surface. He holds me close to his body as he walks toward the bathroom.

His long strides have us reaching the edge of the double shower at a record-setting pace.

My wide eyes dart to his when he says, "Let me look after you, Blaire. Let me wash away your pain."

When I peer into his worried eyes, there's no possibility my mind will ever win this battle, so I nod with my teeth grazing my bottom lip.

The hotness of his breath tickles the strands of hair clinging to my sweat-drenched forehead when he releases a relieved breath. After switching on the shower, he flicks off his black polished dress shoes before setting to work on the belt wrapped around his waist. I stand muted, grateful his riveting striptease is pushing my haunted memories to the back of my mind.

I follow the trail his fingers make as he undoes the buttons on his dress shirt before slinging it off his shoulders. My eyes absorb and categorize every inch of his torso. His muscles are so well-defined that his skin is pulled tautly over them, but he isn't overly musclebound in a bulky bodybuilder type of way.

When he slides his trousers down his thighs, I'm not at all surprised to see that his penis is flaccid. This isn't about relieving sexual tension. He's comforting me as the aftershocks of my nightmare cling to my sweat-slicked skin.

Kicking his trousers to the side, he curls his arms around my neck to unlatch the fastener of my dress. Scenes from my nightmare rush to the forefront of my mind when his hand brushes past my neckline. He's barely touching me, but I swear I can feel my assailant's hand wrapped around my throat, strangling me.

"No one will ever hurt you, Blaire. Not while you're with me," Rico assures me as he lowers the zipper on my dress.

Once the zipper has been pulled down to the two dimples in my lower back, my dress slips off my hips and puddles around my feet.

Steam curls around us when we enter the shower. As the heavenly hot water sluices down the front of me, Rico's body heats my back. His fingers lace together around my stomach as his stubble scratches my neck.

He doesn't speak. He just comforts me by solely using his body. I close my eyes, allowing the water and Rico to chase away the remnants of a nightmare still playing havoc with my body.

When the violent shudders tormenting me have eased, Rico steps away from me. I inwardly sigh. My disappointment doesn't last long when he snags a shower puff from the tiled shelf and loads it up with body wash. My nostrils flare when the spicy, intoxicating scent graces my senses. The smell is virile and manly, and it pushes the ghastly odor of blood and sweat to the background of my mind.

Remaining quiet, Rico lathers my skin with suds. His dutifulness causes new tears to form. I should relish being so loyally cared for, but my mind continually wanders to Katie and her present situation. Is she being taken care of by the man she married, or is she...

A sob tears from my throat, my body choosing its own response to the life Katie is most likely living.

"Kitten." Rico sounds as pained as my heart feels.

He slings his arms around my torso and draws me into his chest. Salty blobs flow from my eyes as steadily as the water pumps out of the showerhead.

"I should have never begged her to come with me. She didn't want to go. She said it was nearly dusk. But I pushed and pushed," I sob, my voice a quiver. "It's all my fault."

Rico pulls me back by my shoulders and glances into my eyes. "It was not your fault. None of it was your fault." When I shake my head, his fingers flex on my shoulders as his demeanor switches from consoling to stern. "Nothing that happened that day was your fault." He stares me straight in the eyes as I did during our tussle in the Escalade last week and quotes, "Nothing."

When he reaches for the shampoo, I close my eyes and let the words he spoke play on repeat in my head. I've been told the same phrase time and time again for the past ten years, but for some reason, hearing them from Rico has a much greater impact.

I was only a child the day I begged Katie to walk to the corner store with me to get an ice cream, but it doesn't lessen my guilt. When she said she didn't want to go, I should have respected her decision. Instead, I insisted. I was a teenager, and I didn't want to be strangled by my overbearing parents for a minute longer.

I was wrong.

So very *very* wrong.

My thumping head lessens under the magic of Rico's fingers as he washes my hair without a peep spilling from his lips. Once all the suds have gurgled down the drain, he shuts down the water and steps out of the shower, carefully taking me with him. He pays the same dedicated attention to drying my hair as he did washing it before he steps to the vanity. My brows furrow when a fluffy bathrobe magically appears.

"Maya brought them in while you were sleeping," he informs my shocked expression.

He wraps me up in the heavenly softness of cashmere before scooping me into his arms. I'll be honest, even in the heart-strangling situation we are immersed in, I love the way he can carry me with such ease. He makes me feel guarded and safe.

"Bed or food?" he asks when we enter the main area of our bedroom.

I bounce my eyes between the silver serving tray stacked with breakfast delights on my left and our bed on my right several times before answering, "Bed."

I'm not tired. My tummy is just too swishy to handle any food right now.

Rico pulls down the bed covers and places me inside before heading to the drawers to dress in a pair of boxer shorts and a short-sleeve shirt. After running his fingers through his hair to remove the excess droplets of water, he slips into the bed beside me, then gathers me in his arms.

18

We've been lying in bed for nearly twenty minutes before Rico breaks the silence. "Have you been suffering nightmares this whole time?"

Usually, this type of question fills me with shame, but because it's coming from him while he's looking at me with nothing but remorse in his eyes, I don't feel as embarrassed admitting I'm an adult who suffers from debilitating nightmares.

I nod. "Yes. They aren't normally as bad as the one today. This one felt as if I was back in the alleyway. It was one of the most realistic dreams I've had in over ten years."

He runs his index finger under my eyes as if he's preparing to catch my tears before they have the chance to fall. Mercifully, his finger leaves my cheek unscathed. "Is it because of the *situation* you've been thrown into?"

"I don't know..." I shrug. "Maybe?"

Another stretch of silence crosses between us. It's long enough that the color of the sky slowly switches to the color of his eyes, but the silence isn't awkward. It strangely feels right.

A possible reason for the silence makes my lips dry, so I lick them before asking, "Did I have a nightmare the night we got married?"

Rico smiles before shaking his head. "No, but we didn't get much sleep that night." He may have been aiming for an informative tone, but it comes out witty.

His deep chuckle rumbles through my body when I punch him in the chest. "I gathered that when I found the strip of condoms hidden under the bed last week."

The heart-fluttering smile stretching across his face grows. "I was wondering where those went."

I roll my eyes, pretending I'm not a fan of his playfulness, where in reality, I'm loving it. Although the aftermath of a nightmare is still clinging to my skin, his cheekiness is easing the pain crippling my heart.

"Who keeps a strip of condoms joined anyway? That's just weird." My mouth gapes, shell-shocked I mumbled my inner dialogue out loud.

Rico doesn't seem to mind. "Not as weird as my wife showing me her balloon twisting skills while she's lying next to me naked."

I stare at him, slack-jawed and blinking. "I showed you my balloon-twisting skills?"

Smiling, he nods.

I inwardly die a thousand deaths. "With *condoms*?"

"You take what you can get and run with it." His smirks does wicked things to my insides. "Although I wouldn't recommend showing the same trick to your students."

I playfully punch him again. "And here I was the whole time thinking we'd done the..." I stop talking to swallow away a lump in my throat, "... *deed* three times in a night."

"Oh, we *did* that." He scoots closer so we share the same breaths. "And so much more."

My eyes light with excitement, and I swear the panties I'm not wearing combust. The mood shifts. It's quick and resolute. Gone are the debilitating effects of a nightmare replaced with nothing but unbridled lust. Nothing else matters but unearthing those lost memories of our wedding night and recreating them.

I don't need to speak for Rico to notice the change in my demeanor. He can see it beaming from my hankering gaze.

Like he could lessen the space between us more, he scoots even closer. My heart hammers my ribs as my palms sweat, but I meet his stare while feeling the most desired I've ever felt. Rico's eyes are sleepy, his hair is a tousled, sexed-up mess, and his lips are curved into a mouthwatering smirk, but the optimism beaming from his eyes makes him the most handsome I've ever seen him.

His carefree look alone is worth the sacrifice of having my heart broken. I'd give anything to see that gleam in his eyes time and time again.

Desperate to hide my stupid sentimental tears, I burrow my head in Rico's chest. When my lips press against his pecs, his heartbeat goes from a leisured pace to a wild thump. A grin curls on my lips. Even knowing I shouldn't admit this, I love the way his body responds to my touch. So much so, I can't stop my hand from sneaking under his shirt to caress the skin on his lower back.

The lazy smile stretched across my face enlarges when his muscles constrict under my faintest touch. They bunch more with every slither of my fingertips.

Upon feeling the incline of my cheeks, Rico places his hand under my chin and lifts my head. I bite the inside of my cheek, trying to hold in my immature smile, but nothing works. I shouldn't enjoy being wrapped in his warmth, but nothing can take away a woman's feelings when she's caressed in a pair of strong arms. I feel protected nestled against his big body. Like no one could ever hurt me. Which is utterly ridiculous considering the man caressing me is the same man who causes my greatest worries. He is the sole reason I'm living in an unknown environment, but he's also the reason my heart is beating so fast.

I've never felt more alive than I do right now.

The heat creeping across my chest amplifies when Rico murmurs groggily, "There's my Blaire."

"Blaire, what happened to Kitten?" I jest, my tone witty.

With a mind-hazing orgasm still surging through my blood and the disappearance of the headache that's been riddling me the past week, my attitude has taken a swing toward the positive.

My eyelids twitch when Rico runs his index finger over my curved brow. "This set of eyes belongs to Blaire."

My breathing quickens when his index finger leisurely travels down my body, only stopping when it hits a snippet of my breasts peeking out from my bathrobe. When his thumb brushes over my nipple before his index finger joins the party, I draw in a shaky breath. His talented hand soon works me into a frenzy by doing nothing more than tweaking my now sensitive nipples. It shows his skills in the bedroom, a natural dominance I've only just scratched the surface of. Pair that with the confidence he exudes in bucketloads, and he has an aggressive set of skills that wildly turn me on.

I only just hold in my disappointed groan when he moves his hand from my breast to run his index finger over my beaded-with-sweat brow once again. "These eyes belong to Kitten," he says while staring into my dilated eyes.

"But why Kitten? It doesn't make any sense."

Before I have the chance to react, Rico pounces. My back is consumed by the softness of a cloud, and my front is assaulted by ripped muscles belonging to a tall brute of a man.

When he rocks his hips, the crown of his thickened cock rubs my pulsating clit. Shockwaves dart through my body at the same time a purr escapes my O-formed lips. Beyond mortified by the erotic groan that just rumbled through my lips, I straighten my spine and snap my mouth shut.

I've never moaned like that before.

Not once.

My eyes snap to Rico when he croons, "That's why I call you Kitten."

The deep timbre of his voice spurs goose bumps to prickle my forearms. He stares down at me as he did in my flashbacks, his hair falling around his chiseled face, his lips slightly parted, and his delicious scent filling every inch of my aching-with-desire core. He's breathtakingly beautiful and thigh-shakingly dangerous at the same time.

"Who are you?" I whisper before my brain can cite an objection.

The corners of his lips curl into a heart-fluttering smirk. "You already know. You just need to remember." He stares down at me with the same eyes that stole my heart in less than a minute while demanding, "Kiss me, Blaire."

Ignoring the dangerous beat of my heart, I cup his jaw with my shaky hands and kiss him.

For a man with a rough exterior, his kisses are nothing but gentle. I sink into the mattress when he slides his tongue into my mouth in long, tempting strokes. He rocks his hips in a rhythm matching the pace of our kiss, allowing me to feel the effect our kiss is having on him. He's hard—*very* hard.

After weaving my fingers through his hair, I pull his head nearer to mine, not only deepening our kiss but strengthening our odd relationship. Rico growls at my assertiveness, then switches the intensity of our embrace, shifting it from soft and gentle to needy and urgent.

We kiss for several long minutes, sending the room's temperature from comfortable to roasting.

Just like every kiss we've shared, when Rico pulls away, I'm completely and utterly breathless. His eyes stole my heart in under a minute, but his kisses are capturing my soul.

I keep my fingers knitted through his hair, not willing to let go just yet. I've only just come to terms with the expeditious speed of our relationship, so I need a few more minutes to bask in this beautiful surreality before tiptoeing back into the Amityville Horror House.

The reasoning behind Rico's sudden withdrawal becomes clear when a loud knock bellows on our bedroom door. My bottom lip drops into a pout, disappointed my trip to Pleasantville didn't last as long as I was hoping.

I won't lie. When Rico rolls over—unpinning me from his heavenly warmth—my body screams in protest. Although my every want, desire, and need weren't fulfilled, one thing crystallized.

I do know this man.

I just need to remember him.

My heart continues swelling when Rico ensures I'm covered before he walks to the door. I tuck the sheets under my chin when the door swings open, and I spot Erik, Rico's lawyer, on the other side. Erik is a handsome man, but just like Rico, his true intentions are a little hard to read. Today, his expression looks both torn and passive.

After handing Rico a flat sheet of paper, Erik shifts his gaze to me. I hesitantly smile. I'm sure I look like an utter wreck. I've always been an ugly crier, and I doubt even the brilliance of a mind-altering orgasm could hide the puffiness my eyes get after a good dose of crying.

My heartbeat kicks up a gear when the mask Rico wears in front of his crew slips onto his face before my very eyes. My concern grows about his swift shift in demeanor when the carefree glint in his eyes fades into the blackness of his dark and dangerous gaze. Just like the man I confronted in the gloomy basement room last week, the Rico standing in front of me is once again a stranger.

After shaking hands with Erik, Rico closes the door and spins to face me. I freeze when I catch the quickest flare of emotion passing through his eyes as he walks back to bed. Like a man with two heads, his eyes relay two very contradicting emotions—tenderness and anger.

I throw off the sheets and crawl across the mattress when he sits on the edge and pats the bed beside him. Although I'm behaving like an obedient dog, my desire to unravel the mystery standing before me is guiding my decisions. It may make me seem submissive, but from the memories I've unearthed the past twenty-four hours, I know this hasn't always been the case in our whirlwind relationship.

Remaining quiet, Rico passes the sheet of paper Erik handed him to me. After bouncing my eyes between his unreadable gaze, I drop them to the document. Only six small words are printed in plain black ink, but they cause a significant impact to my faltering heart.

Timothy Jamison was arrested this morning.

I snap my eyes to Rico, searching his truth-bearing eyes for the confirmation he gives me with words. "Someone slipped the local authorities the information I obtained on Timothy before the Popov crew could *attend* to the matter. If the justice system prevails, I'll consider the matter closed."

Blood surges into my heart as a smile stretches across my face.

I knew there was more to this man than just darkness.

A small snippet of my happiness is sideswiped when he says, "Don't become complacent, Kitten. There's a long way to go before this is over. If I feel appropriate justice isn't served, I'll have no other choice but to become reinvolved in his case."

"I understand," I reply with a concise nod. "But that doesn't mean we can't celebrate the small victories. The victims' families will be so grateful you did this, Enrique. They will now have closure."

A spark of sentiment flickers through his eyes. "I didn't do it for their families, Blaire. I did it for you. To prove I am the man in your memories."

I smile through my tears threatening to spill down my face. "Thank you." Those two small words don't seem enough to express the surge of emotions pumping through me, but they are all I have to offer, so they are all I can give.

My eyes lift from the paper to Rico when he says, "Now I need you to do me a favor, Kitten."

I search his eyes, seeking any indication that he only did this for me for a favor in return. Failing to find any deceit in his eyes, I mutter. "Anything."

He appears relieved. "I need you to call off your friend before she stumbles into a life she doesn't belong in."

19

Utterly dumbfounded, I stare at Rico before my lungs lose the ability to fill with air. "Lacey isn't taking the news of your departure from Ravenshoe well. She's creating ripples. Ripples my family will soon discover. If you want your friend to stay safe, you need to force her to back away from her inquiries."

Bile twists its way from my stomach to my throat, but even feeling sick, I nod, agreeing with his terms. Lacey is my best friend, so I'll do everything in my power to protect her. I failed once before protecting Katie. I refuse to let it happen again.

Pretending there aren't tears praying to streak my cheeks, I lock my eyes with Rico and say, "What do you need me to do?"

He steps to a set of drawers on his right. After pulling out a plain black phone, he moves to stand in front of me. The torment in his eyes is even more compelling than it was earlier. "Call Lacey and ask her to back off."

My eyes dart between his, my confusion growing by the second. "Why can't I use my phone?"

"Lacey called in the authorities. There's a team of detectives stationed at your apartment. They will be tracing the call."

My heart slithers into my gut. "So I have to make my call quick?

Like they do in the movies?"

Rico smiles. It doesn't match the despair in his dark gaze. "No, Kitten. That's nothing but a Hollywood ploy. Maybe back in the eighties they took sixty seconds to trace a call, but with technology today, it can be done instantaneously. Lucky for us, the compound has numerous signal jammers installed, but for extra caution, I'd prefer you use a dump phone. They'll have a hard time tracking it when it's buried under a pile of rubble."

Ignoring my trembling hands, I stand from the bed and accept the cell phone he's holding out. Thankfully, even in a day of modern technology, I have a knack for remembering phone numbers.

After dialing Lacey's cell into the outdated phone, I press it close to my ear.

She answers not even a full ring later.

"Hello?" The concern in her tone makes her greeting come out sounding more like a question than a greeting.

I exhale a deep breath. "Lac—"

"Blaire! Oh my god. Are you okay? Where are you? Are you safe?" she blubbers out in quick succession.

"Lacey, calm down. I need you to listen... I don't have long." I shift my eyes to Rico, who is watching me with caution from the side of the room. "Did you call the police?"

"Yes, of course I did! Colt said you were dragged out of here by a man claiming to be your husband." She stops talking and inhales a big breath. She's obviously rattled as I can hear the shaking of her ribcage through the phone. "He also said two of the men flanking you were carrying guns."

The truth of Rico's statement rings true when Lacey's confession causes a flurry of activity to sound down the line. The most obvious evidence is the inclusion of two male voices I don't recognize.

"Blaire, are you there?" Lacey asks when a stretch of silence passes between us.

"Yes, I am here." I breathe out.

My heart is a twisted mess of confusion. Half of me hates that Lacey is upset while the other half wants to do everything in my power to protect Rico from the authorities. Don't ask me why. I wouldn't be able to answer. If I'd been held captive for longer than twenty-four hours, I could have used the defense of Stockholm Syndrome, but deep down, I know that isn't the case.

I'm truly not scared of Rico.

Startled, yes.

Scared, definitely not.

"What's going on, Blaire? Was it your husband?" Lacey asks, drawing my attention back to the present.

"Yes," I mutter faintly.

Lacey gasps in a ragged breath, shocked by my reply. "I thought your marriage was annulled?"

"I thought it was too, but the papers were never filed. We're still legally married."

"So you thought you'd just up and leave with him on a whim? Your Vegas experience was as cookie cutter as they come for Vegas, but that craziness is supposed to stop the instant you step foot in the plane." Her words come out in a flurry, her tone a mixture of anger and bewilderment. "You don't continue with the idiocy once you return home."

Pain strikes my heart when her quiet sniffles resonate down the line. "This isn't you, Care Blaire. You've always been the safe, smart friend. You wouldn't have just packed up and left of your own free will. He's hurting you, isn't he? Holding you against your will?"

I shake my head, soundlessly denying her accusations. My brisk movements cause tears to trickle down my ashen cheeks. Spotting my upset composure, Rico pushes off his feet and ambles toward me. The concern beaming from his eyes adds to the restrictive hold strangling my heart.

"Is he threatening you? Are you in danger?" Lacey asks through a barrage of hiccups.

"No, Lacey, he'd never hurt me."

My confession clears away the painful haze in Rico's dark gaze. He stands behind me and slings his arms around my torso, the heat of his body easing my shuddering shakes.

"Lacey, I'm begging you, please drop this."

"I can't." Her heartache is unable to be hidden by those two little words. "You're my best friend, Blaire. I won't sit back and watch you make a stupid mistake you can't take back."

My heart squeezes painfully. "I'm not asking you to sit back and watch me fail. I just want you to give me a chance to make my own decisions. Please don't make me feel guilty for finally living my life how I want. I don't want to be the *safe friend* anymore. I want to live. Please let me live."

Most of my statement is to keep Lacey safe—if she believes I'm here of my own free will, she will drop this—but part of it comes from deep within my soul. I've always been the *safe friend*. I never went to college parties, never stepped over the line that balances precariously between tipsy and drunk, and I never did anything that had an edge of danger or adventure attached to it. Although I wouldn't recommend waking up married to a mob boss with no recollection of your time together. My heart has never beaten so fast.

"Lacey?" I mutter into the phone when I'm greeted with nothing but silence. "Are you still there?"

"Yes," she replies, her voice jittery and weak.

"Please don't hate me," I mumble, sickened by the thought I've hurt her feelings.

A door sliding open sounds down the line, closely followed by the faint hum of the traffic that always impedes the streets of Ravenshoe. She must have stepped out onto the patio attached to the living room of our apartment. "I'd never hate you, Care Blaire. I just want to make sure you're safe."

Even though she can't see me, I nod. "I am."

A length of silence stretches between us, crammed with stifling heaviness. If it weren't for Lacey's panicked breaths sounding down the line, I would have assumed she had hung up on me.

"Why did it have to be a suit-wearing thug who *finally* cracked your shell?" Lacey jests a short time later, her tone not as pained as it was. "I've been chipping away at it for years, but I didn't even cause a hairline crack. You spent a day with him, and all your insecurities crumbled."

Rico must hear her as he stiffens during the 'suit-wearing thug' part and tightens his grip around my torso during her last sentence.

"Promise me you're safe," Lacey pleads into the phone. "If you can, I'll tell the detectives in our living room that this was all a big misunderstanding. And don't even think about lying to me, Blaire. Even over the phone, I'll tell."

A smile stretches across my face. What she's saying is true. She knows me better than anyone.

While exhaling a deep breath, I spin on my heels the best I can in the protective cocoon Rico has wrapped around me. When I lift my eyes to his face, my breathing sharpens. The same set of beautiful eyes from my memories stare down at me. Gone is the haunted, bleak look his eyes generally wear, replaced with the eyes of a boy lost in a world full of monsters.

I freeze as another lost memory is found...

"I'm not a good man, Blaire. I've done terrible, horrible things... way more than I can count. I don't deserve a woman like you. I don't deserve an angel."

I peer into Rico's eyes, seeing nothing but remorse reflecting back at me. We both know his words are true, but when I look deeper, past the guilt blackening his eyes, all I see is a little boy who grew up unloved. He's flawed and damaged but has one of the most beautiful souls I've ever seen. He simply needs to be shown how to look past the blackness. To be taught how to love.

"I'm not here to save you, Enrique. We are here to save each other..."

Now some of my decisions last week make sense. Rico wasn't a man I feared. He was the man I swore to protect. The vulnerability that flashed in his eyes the thirty seconds following my tumble into his lap had me pledging I'd stop at nothing until he walked through the darkness unscathed.

He truly did capture my soul in less than a minute.

I turn my attention back to the phone pressed against my ear before locking my eyes with Rico. "I'm safe. I promise you. I'm the safest I've ever been," I declare to both Lacey and Rico.

When a broad grin etches on Rico's face, I'm tempted to add, *physically, not mentally.*

20

"Are you ready?"

After flattening down the front of my cotton dress, I nod. My heart is thrashing against my chest, and nervous sweat is slicking my skin, but I am ready, nonetheless.

"Remember what I told you, Kitten. Stay by my side at all times and don't trust anybody." From the way Rico's words are laced with warning, anyone would swear we are about to meet Jack the Ripper, not have brunch with his family.

As I prepared for our outing, Rico gave me a brief rundown on how things in the Popov compound work. Usually, the women of the house serve the men, but since I hold the prestigious role of his wife, I'll be seated beside him during brunch.

Although shocked at the inequality of women in this faction, I'm not completely blindsided by it. The fact Rico's father sold his daughter on the black market is all the evidence I require that the Popov clan is a group of callous and cold-hearted men.

No further explanation needed.

After applying a dusting of blush to my already rosy cheeks, Rico wraps his hand over mine and we exit our bedroom. Things between us have been oddly normal the past five days. Our routine hasn't altered from the day I arrived. I spend my days holed up in our room like a prisoner in a minimum-security facility, reading and playing card games with Maya while Rico 'works.'

It doesn't matter if I go for a shower at eleven in the morning or ten at night, Rico is always waiting in the high-backed chair to apply cream to his name inked on my hip. When his 'working' day is over, he showers, then we spend the rest of our night together in bed, where thankfully, Rico's protective cocoon keeps my nightmares to a bare minimum.

We are like an everyday couple, our coexistence melding together surprisingly quick. The only difference between us and every other newlywed couple is our conversations aren't based on how his day at 'work' went or what china we'd like to purchase for our new house. The entirety of our discussions are if any of my hidden memories were unearthed and if I've had any more nightmares.

Unfortunately, other than the flurry of memories that were unleashed my first twenty-four hours here, I've not had any fresh memories revealed since.

I'll be honest. Even being held captive in a mansion full of gun-toting men, I'll happily pledge that the man I see in my flashbacks is the same man I wake up curled around every morning.

Away from others, Rico is attentive and sweet. A man I could whole-heartedly marry on sight. It's just the air of danger surrounding him that causes my greatest worry.

While I'm being totally forthright, I'll disclose another powerful point separating us from other newlywed couples—our lack of sexual contact. Don't construe my statement the wrong way. I'm not at all expecting the band on my finger to come with the agreed stipulation of sexy time. I'm just surprised I've spent the past five nights in bed with a man who appears sexually ambitious but have not once been propositioned. Lust is no doubt firing between us, but nothing more than an affectionate cuddle has been shared the last five nights.

I won't lie. My ego is suffering the brutal sting of rejection.

My grip on Rico's hand tightens when our brisk stride down the corridor has us reaching two burly-looking men at the end. Just like last week, their conversation ends the instant they catch sight of me. They don't speak. They just eye us with caution as we saunter by.

I lean into Rico's side when a group of suit-clad men at the end of the stairwell rake their sullied eyes down my body. Considering they are several years older than me and have partners attached to their hips, I find their gaze demoralizing and nauseating.

"*Отвернись сейчас же!*" Rico growls at them, his words vibrating right through my body.

Their eyes snap to Rico in sync. "*Она не шлюха?*"

Rico's pulse pulverizes my hand. "*Нет, она моя жена.*"

The men's eyes widen before they drop to their shoes.

"What was that about?" I ask Rico as he guides me across the opulent entry of his home.

"Nothing."

With every step I take, my legs quake, but I play my part as wife accordingly. I smile greetings at the curious stares of women eyeing me with wonder, and I redirect my eyes from the men whose avid gazes make my skin crawl.

"Who are all these people?" I query, shocked by the vast number of people mingling throughout the residence.

"Most are family members... brothers, sisters, cousins." Rico gestures his head to the group associated with each title. "The rest are *associates* of the Popov entity." Just from the way he says 'associates' indicates they're people I should avoid.

"What about the women in the den?" I nudge my head to the sunken lounge we are gliding by that's filled to the brim with attractive ladies.

Rico stiffens for the quickest second before he answers, "They are mistresses?" The unsureness of his voice makes what should be a statement come out sounding like a question.

My heart falls out of my ribcage. "Mistresses? Whose mistresses?" I grimace when my question is delivered louder than I intend.

He releases my hand from his grasp and places it on my lower back while answering, "Once Vladimir is finished with them, anyone who wants them."

My first reaction is disgust. Most of the women in the den would be in their mid-twenties to early thirties, way too young to sleep with a man Vladimir's age. My second reaction is jealousy—sick, twisted jealousy.

After taking a moment to settle my swishing stomach, I ask matter-of-factly, "Do you have mistresses?" This time, my voice comes out level and calm, even though I'm anything but.

After dipping his chin at a man standing guard near a concealed door, Rico guides me down an incredibly long dining table. Just like our room, this space is decorated with priceless paintings and opulent antique furnishings, but it isn't enough to dampen the queasiness passing through me.

Even with no knowledge of mob-related activities, I know Rico is moving us to the higher-ranked seating. It isn't merely the fact that the hum of conversation dulled the instant we entered the room, it is also the fact every set of eyes in the room is centered on Rico and me—even with them sneakily peering up from the floor. But even being eyed like I'm a circus act and having a queasy stomach, I can't harbor the jealousy heating my blood.

"Do you?" I ask again, ensuring I keep my tone as low as possible.

Rico drops his eyes to me. "Do I what?"

I snarl, baring teeth. The gleam in his eyes exposes he knows what I'm referring to. He's just choosing to be ignorant.

My scowl deepens, leaving a heavy set of wrinkles on my forehead. Spotting my angry snarl, Rico's lips curl into a panty-wetting smirk. "Are you jealous, Kitten?" He leans in close, gaining us the curious glance of a dozen people surrounding us. "Does my little kitty have her claws out, ready to pounce on any woman who dares get close to her man?"

His words jolt through me like I've sustained a physical blow while also adding to my worry that there's been no sexual contact between us since my first morning waking up in this compound. It's inanely ridiculous for me to be jealous, but I can't help it. Drugged mistake or not, Rico is my husband. Just thinking about him with another woman triggers merciless jealousy to sear through me.

Sensing my usually carefree composure slipping, Rico murmurs, "You have nothing to be jealous of, Kitten."

His words don't offer me any reassurance. If anything, they make me even more irate. If he has nothing to hide, why skirt my question? Why not just be honest?

My irritation switches to trepidation when he pulls out a chair second from the end and gestures for me to sit.

"Exactly what rank are you in this industry?" I stammer out before I can stop my words.

Before Rico can answer, his father enters the room from a concealed entrance on my left. He walks with a sense of arrogance like Rico, but his demeanor doesn't merely invite inquisitive stares of rapacious women. It demands resolute silence.

For his age, Vladimir is a fit-looking gentleman of tall height and average build. His hair is dark brown and slicked back, and his face is void of the wrinkles most men his age have. If I could look past his cold-hearted eyes and unapproachable demeanor, I'd say he is handsome.

When Vladimir saunters deeper into the room, the attendees react similarly as they did when Rico entered. Half stare at him in awe while the other half—the mainly female half—bow their heads.

Following the vibe of the room, I tuck my chin into my neck and stray my eyes to the tabletop. "No, Kitten," Rico growls before pinching my chin and lifting my head back to its original position. "You do not bow to him."

Ignoring the fact I'm shivering like a bag of nerves, I lift my chin and swing my eyes to Vladimir. I'm taken aback when I discover the cold, depraved gaze running over my body isn't from Vladimir. It's from the elegantly dressed lady beside him. Even with her eyes thinly slit, she has flawless facial features, plump lips, and a straight nose. Her dark hair is pulled back in a low ponytail, and her petite frame is draped in priceless silk and jewels. If I had to guess her age, I'd say she was early to mid-forties.

Dropping her green gaze to me, the unnamed female asks, "*Почему шлюха сидит за столом?*" Although I don't understand Russian, I can't miss the callousness of her tone.

"If you wish to address Blaire, you need to speak English." Rico shifts his eyes sideways to the unnamed lady. "She doesn't understand Russian."

"And yet you still married her," the dark-haired beauty retorts. "Spitting on your father's grave before he's even stepped foot in there."

Rico's jaw gains a tick, but he remains tight-lipped. After reassuringly squeezing my hand, he gestures for me to sit. When I do, he secures a white napkin onto my lap. I twist it in knots, needing something to settle the sick feeling in my stomach.

I swallow away a horrible bitterness in my throat when Vladimir affixes his gaze with mine. His face is impassive, his eyes from the devil himself. He watches me for several uncomfortable moments, assessing me from the inside out. My stomach churns with both fear and grief. Fear for Rico striving to be just like him. Grief for Rico being raised by him. It must have been horrible, worse than the deepest pit of hell.

I jump when Rico unexpectedly places his hand on mine, stopping my fidgeting. I've twisted the napkin so tightly around my fingers, it's cutting off my blood supply.

With Rico breaking our horrifying connection, Vladimir takes a seat at the head of the table, then gestures for the dark-haired woman to sit. No words are needed to issue his request. His stern gaze is demanding enough for her to jump to his command.

I only just hold in my surprised gasp when she takes the chair opposite me. I assumed she'd sit beside Vladimir, considering they are husband and wife. How do I know they're married? They have matching wedding bands like Rico and me.

"*шлюхи* don't belong at this end of the table," she snarls at me.

My eyes shoot to Rico, seeking translation. His nostrils flare as his face lines with anger, but he maintains a quiet approach. Before I can ask what *шлюха* means, the reasoning behind the dark-haired lady being seated away from Vladimir becomes apparent. Just like our meeting last week, Nikolai swaggers into the room with both an air of authority and a snip of fear. But unlike Rico and Vladimir, the female eyes in the room don't drop to the floor when graced with his presence. I don't know if that's because they see him as more approachable than his predecessors or because he has not yet earned their reputation. Either way, my eyes immediately dart down to the table when he issues me a cocky wink.

"Ah. My beautiful Ангел blushes too. If only you had fallen into my lap instead of Rico's," Nikolai jests before sitting on the chair across from Rico.

The heat on my cheeks grows as does the grip of Rico's hand curled around my thigh. Snubbing his brother's furious glare, Nikolai smiles a smug grin before he lifts his fingers to his lips, pretending to lock his mouth.

After slouching into his chair, he turns his eyes to his father on his left. From Vladimir's untroubled look, it appears this type of bickering is nothing new for Rico and Nikolai.

Or perhaps he doesn't know how to change his deadpan expression?

With a wave, Vladimir demands his staff to commence serving brunch. Unable to tolerate the evilness beaming out of numerous pairs of eyes in the room, I drop my gaze to my empty plate and concentrate on keeping my breathing patterns level.

Within minutes, my plate is loaded with a vast variety of food. Bread, sausages, eggs, Russian pancakes, and tea are plentiful. It smells delicious, but my stomach is too twisted to risk sampling any of it, so instead, I push my food around my plate with a fork while sneakily scanning the room.

While sipping a glass of sweetened tea, my eyes anchor on a familiar face entering the dining room from the other end—Erik, Rico's lawyer. The women pay him the same amount of attention as Rico, but they don't hide it beneath lowered lashes.

I can understand their fascination. When he isn't cloaked in darkness, Erik is a handsome man. Not as handsome as Rico, but that would be a hard feat for any man to conquer.

After taking his seat three places up from Nikolai, Erik addresses my gawking stare with a hesitant smirk before accepting a plate of food from Maya. After returning his greeting, I return my devotion to sneakily assessing the room.

Over the next forty minutes, the tension in the air never leaves, and the flow of conversation increases. Although most of the discussions are in Russian, I've noticed one word being used on repeat—*шлюха*. If the sneer of their tone isn't enough of an indication it's a derogative word, the fact numerous pairs of eyes glare at me while saying it is a surefire sign.

Unable to harbor my curiosity any longer, I turn my gaze to Rico. The stubble on his jaw cannot hide its relentless tick, and his eyes are narrowed into thin slits.

Obviously, I'm not the only one noticing the thick stench of hostility in the room.

I keep my tone low, ensuring no one within earshot will hear my inquiry. "What does *шлюха* mean?"

Rico stiffens for the quickest second before wiping his mouth with a white napkin. "Nothing. Finish your breakfast, Kitten."

Anger unlike anything I've ever felt boils my blood. He didn't even look at me while speaking. He just dismissed me without so much as a sideways glance.

Strangers' ignorance I can tolerate, but from my husband? No, that's something I will not stand for.

Gritting my teeth, I stand from my seat and excuse myself from the table.

I've reached my quota of dealing with ill-mannered men for one day.

Before I push away from the table, my wrist is seized, and I'm yanked back into my seat.

My unladylike topple ends with a bang, not just to my backside but my pride as well.

"Sit down and eat." Rico's angry sneer shudders through my chest.

I stare at him, dazed and confused. Although the maliciousness of his words doesn't match the remorse beaming from his eyes, anger still bombards me. Who is this man? He isn't the man I've awoken to the past five mornings, and he most definitely isn't a man I'd marry on sight.

Battling against threatening tears, I direct my eyes away from the cold-hearted stranger next to me. While diverting my eyes, I catch the leering grin of the unnamed lady across from me. Humor lines her heavily made-up face, and her eyes are brimmed with amusement.

Noticing she has captured my attention, her evil grin enlarges. "Do you want to know what *шлюха* means?" she asks me, her words laced with vindictiveness.

Not willing to participate in the belittling games of this corrupt family, I shake my head before lowering my eyes to my barely touched plate of food. With my stomach swirling from the tension in the air, my usually robust appetite is waning.

Any chance of easing my squishy stomach falters when Nikolai remarks, "*шлюха* means whore, *Ангел*."

My heart drops into my stomach as my eyes rocket to Nikolai. I don't need him to repeat his explanation. All the evidence I need projects from the amused gaze of every set of eyes gawking at me. They're mocking and full of torment.

"If you had fallen into my lap instead of Rico's, I would have cut out the tongue of every man who dared speak of you with such disrespect," Nikolai states before drifting his narrowed eyes to his brother. "I wouldn't sit by and watch my wife be called a whore without reprimand."

"*Закрой свой рот*," Rico spits off his tongue, his eyes fixed on his brother. "*Или я закрою его для тебя*."

Rico's words are obviously vicious as the room falls into silence. It's thick and tangible and has my pulse quickening.

The smug grin Nikolai has been wearing all morning enlarges, clearly pleased he has sparked a reaction from his brother. After kissing the cheek of the lady seated beside him, he excuses himself from the table and walks out of the room with his cocky swagger on full display.

Ignoring the pain stabbing my chest, I wait for the hum of chatter to once again fill the room before shifting my eyes to Rico. "You knew they were calling me a whore, but you said nothing?" My words come out in a hiss, strained through a sob sitting at the back of my throat. "Why didn't you stand up for me?"

"Now is not the time," Rico replies, his words abrupt.

"They called me a whore, Rico. When is that ever appropriate?" My voice gets louder as I battle to leash my anger, but even knowing I'm attracting stares, I can't stop my onslaught. I'm hurt that the only person who defended my honor was the man who wants me to call him Satan. "Why would you let them call me that?"

His ticking jaw gains momentum. "We'll discuss this later."

"No! Tell me now," I shout, gaining me the attention of every pair of eyes in the room.

I balk like I've been physically slapped when Rico snarls, "Because that's what all women are. Whores."

21

Before I can comprehend the repercussions of my actions, I slap Rico across the face. The callousness of my hit forces his head to sling sideways and for my palm to set on fire.

While nursing my injured hand, I push back from my seat and make a beeline for the double doors at the end of the room. My heart wallops my ribcage, and tears loom, but I refuse to let them fall. I will not give anyone in this room the satisfaction of thinking they've made me upset.

My quick exit is halted when two large men block my path. When I try to sidestep them, they move back into my way.

After exhaling a nerve-cleansing breath, I raise my eyes from their boot-covered feet to their faces. I gulp harshly when I see their furious scowls, then bile creeps up my windpipe as the severity of the situation smacks into me.

I just slapped a head honcho in a Russian mob in front of his goons.

Can I be any more stupid?

When one of the wide-shouldered goons grabs the tops of my arms, I grimace. His hold is so rough, panic zips through me as fragments of my past clash with my present.

Flashes of being grabbed in the alleyway momentarily daze me, but when the goon shakes me—knocking my back molars together—my fighter instincts kick in. I claw at him viciously and thrash out my legs, not willing to go down without a fight for the second time.

My battle seems to irritate him more. He firms his clutch, and the redness lining his face intensifies, but his fingers stop digging into my bicep when a deep voice from behind me growls, "Let her go."

Rico's voice is so gravelly it shakes my heart right out of my chest.

Cranking my neck back, I watch him urgently stride toward me. His gaze is fierce, and it sets my pulse racing. When the goon fails to acknowledge his request, he snarls, "This is your last warning. Get your hands off my wife before I slit your throat and watch your body shiver as you take your last breath."

I barely hear the collective gasps of the guests seated at the dining table over the ringing of my pulse in my ears. Rico's eyes display his threat is not idle. He intends on following through with his pledge if the goon doesn't adhere to his warning. His composure is dangerous and menacing, and it sends my heart rate skyrocketing.

His gaze is so toxic, the henchman drops his hands and takes a retreating step, his pupils large, his eyes wide. He looks even more frightened than I do.

After speaking to the two gentlemen accosting me in a deep Russian tone, Rico curls his arm around my sweat-slicked back and guides me out of the room. Friction plagues the air, making it hard for me to breathe while also adding nicks to my already damaged heart.

I suck in deep breaths as I tell myself on repeat that I'm safe and no one can hurt me. I'm stronger than I was ten years ago. I've got this. *I hope.*

By the time we reach the landing of the stairs, I've gathered back a small sense of normality. I'm still quivering like a bag of nerves, and hot, salty tears are threatening to roll down my cheeks, but my survival mode mechanism has kicked in.

Spotting the tears dying to stream down my face, Rico murmurs, "Kitten."

Paying no attention to the lurking glares from the two men stationed at the end of the hallway, I pull away from Rico and angrily stride to our room. As my normal composure emerges from the thick cloud of despair, the events leading up to my frightened state steamroll back into me, particularly the part when Rico allowed me to be humiliated in front of dozens of spectators.

"Keep the corridor clear," Rico instructs the men before increasing the length of his steps to catch up with me.

When he reaches me, he places his hand on the crook of my elbow.

I yank away from him.

"Kitten—"

"Don't Kitten me," I interrupt, standing up for myself for the first time ever. "You lost the right to call me a nickname when you let people call me a whore!"

His eyes drift around our surroundings before he murmurs, "I did that for you."

I stare up at him, shocked and disgusted. "Do I look like an idiot?"

My chest is heaving, and wetness is bombarding my eyes, but I hold his gaze, trying to display I'm not as weak as he thinks I am.

Rico scowls but maintains the quiet approach he exhausted during brunch.

It angers me further, drying my tears. "How could letting people call me a whore be for my own benefit?"

When Rico steps toward me, I hold my hand out in front of me, demanding for him to stay away. I need to keep a safe distance between us because even teeming with anger, an excited tingle ran the length of my spine when he grasped my elbow earlier.

Clenching my teeth, I glare into Rico's eyes, not only disgusted he let people belittle me in front of him but also at myself. What type of sick, twisted person gets turned on by the same man stabbing a knife into her chest?

I blamed Vegas for my foolhardiness last week. But it wasn't Vegas.

It was me. I am just as sick and twisted as the man standing before me.

Noticing my irate gaze, Rico growls, "Goddammit, Blaire, don't look at me like that."

"Like what? How am I looking at you? Like you're a monster? Because that's what you are!"

Overlooking the way my callous words caused a brutal pain to hit my chest, I fling open our bedroom door and storm inside. I wait until I hear Rico enter before I spin around to face him. My fists are clenched at my side, my body poised to fight.

He attempts to speak, but I beat him to it. "What type of man are you if you allow your wife to be ridiculed directly in front of you?"

Anger lines his face. "When the time is right, they'll suffer the consequences of their actions. Their stupidity will not go unrebuked. Their punishment alone will ensure no man will dare speak of you with such vulgarity again."

His anger makes his words come out with a heavy Russian accent. They also have an edge of danger to them that sends a shiver through me.

"It isn't about punishment, Rico. It's about decency. They belittled me as if I were nothing but a worthless whore right in front of you. That means you agree with what they were saying. I thought I meant more to you than that?"

"You do!"

My brows knit into a frown. "Well, you have a very funny way of showing it." I cross my arms over my chest, my heart heavy, my pulse escalating. "I stupidly told myself that it wasn't the drugs in my system last week that made me agree to marry you. But I was wrong, so very, *very* wrong."

The expressionless mask Rico wore throughout brunch slips, momentarily revealing a blaze of emotions. Regret, sorrow, guilt all radiate from his beautiful eyes. But the biggest one—the one that causes the most impact to my heart—is the look of hope.

"You were not wrong, Blaire." He steps closer to me, his tone less heated, his eyes less pained. "It was not the drugs influencing your decisions. It was you. It was us. Together."

The brief shake of my head forces a tear to tumble from my eye. I angrily swipe my hand across my cheek, loathing that it makes me look weak. "That man out there..." I point to the door leading to the corridor, "... I would have never agreed to marry that man."

"You didn't marry that man." He pounds his fist on his heaving chest. "You married me, Blaire. You married Enrique."

"It's the same man," I yell, my voice cracking with emotions.

Rico shakes his head. "No! They're not the same. Rico is an act, a role I must play. The man here, the one standing in front of you, this is Enrique, the man you married. Me. You married me." My pulse quickens when he pushes off his feet and spans the distance between us. "You know this, Blaire, you just need to remember."

I shake my head, sending tears rolling down my face. "I don't know you. You're a stranger."

My chin quivers from the torrent of pain surging through his beautiful eyes. "No, Kitten. You know me. The real me."

I try to shake my head to deny his claims, but no matter how hard I fight, my heart refuses to acknowledge the pleas of my logical brain. Even though I realize I've only known him for two short weeks, my heart disagrees.

"You know me," he says again, staring me straight in the eyes. "You just need to remember." His hands curve my jaw, and he stares into my eyes as he painfully whispers, "Remember me."

The pain crippling my heart triples when his lips kiss away my tears. The sorrow in his eyes as he battles to clear away the evidence of my disappointment in him causes more tears to well in mine. These tears are sentimental ones, not anguished.

The reasoning behind my sudden change of heart becomes apparent when Rico drops his lips to the shell of my ear and whispers, "Remember, it's the darkness, Kitten, not me," ever so quietly.

Just hearing the repentance in his voice tells me what he is saying is true. It doesn't ease the sting my ego copped, nor soothe the ache tingling in my chest, but it silences the screaming protests of my brain telling me to run away from him before I lose all my scruples.

After his thumbs ensure his lips didn't miss a tear, he pulls back and glances into my eyes. I return his benevolent stare in utter shock. I'm not surprised by his sudden shift in demeanor—he can switch from night to day in an instant—I'm surprised at myself. How is it possible I've gone from steaming with anger to riddled with guilt from just one glance into his dark and dangerous yet innocent eyes?

"Trust me, Blaire. I was trying to protect you," he says with his sorrow-filled eyes boring into mine. "If they discovered you are my weakness, they would use it to their advantage, which would put you in harm's way. By them believing you are nothing more than a drunken mistake, I could have protected you better." The darkness in his eyes deepens. "But it's too late now. Our cards have been shown."

"They're your family, Rico, so why would they want to hurt either of us?"

His eyes grow wider. "They're not my family. This may be the life I was born into, but that does not make them my family."

He runs the back of his hand down my face, removing a rogue tear that spilled from his statement. My heart is pained, hating that he grew up in such an unloved environment. The children in my class are so young—they are only babies. Rico was younger than them when his mother died, leaving him no other choice than to be raised by a monster in a house of horrors.

"I couldn't promise you a life of sunshine, Blaire, but I promised to always protect you." He quotes part of the vows we recited to each other two weeks ago. "That was what I was trying to do today. I wanted to protect you."

I stare into his forthright eyes, seeking any untruth in them.

I fail to find any.

My lips quiver when I begin to speak, "I understand, but just like you promised to protect me, I promised to *always* be your light in a life full of darkness. I can't do that if you shut me out."

My cheeks twitch when he runs his thumbs over them. "I know, Kitten." His tone is less distressed. "I'm not purposely trying to shut you out. There are just... *aspects* of my life I can't disclose to you."

My brow arches. "Can't or don't want to?"

He takes his time configuring a response before he answers, "Both."

Not letting me reply, he presses his lips to mine and slides his tongue along my gaped mouth. I stand muted for several seconds, knowing he is exploiting my sexual attraction to him but unable to fight it.

I'll never be strong enough to deny his advances.

I'm not the only one helpless in this relationship, though. From the memories I've unearthed and the past five days we've spent together, I know Rico is as smitten as I am in this tumultuous relationship we've created. I never used to believe in love at first sight, but truly, when you look deeply, we are surrounded by it every day. You fall instantly in love with a child when he is born. Who's to say the same thing can't happen with a stranger? It may seem instant and extreme, but ultimately, it could be a long-lasting attraction that spans a lifetime. Should I ignore what could be the greatest love of my life just because it's happening in the blink of an eye?

Giving in to my heart's desire, I return Rico's kiss with as much passion as he's bestowing. I rake my fingers through his hair and stroke my tongue into his decadent mouth.

His kiss sparks a carnal desire in me I've never felt before. A desire I'm willing to do anything to unleash—heart, body, and soul.

Within seconds, my hands are all over him—stroking the girth growing in his trousers, running along the bumps of his six-pack, and fiddling with his shirt buttons.

Rico's hands are just as adventurous. One of his hands cups my breast, squeezing it until it's aching with desire while the other one places feathery touches to numerous erogenous zones of my body.

In no time, I'm panting, wet, and more than eager.

When my hands wander to the belt of his trousers, Rico abruptly pulls away. I stare at him, wide-eyed and confused. It's only when I see a black cloud filter over his shimmering eyes do I realize why he has reacted so fiercely.

We're not alone.

Vladimir is standing in the doorway of our room with his evil eyes fixed on me and a mean, unapproachable demeanor. A sick feeling twists into my stomach like something awful is about to happen. It intensifies when Rico snatches my wrists and pulls me behind his big, protective body.

He must also feel the change in the air.

A callous smile carves onto Vladimir's face as the evil gleam in his eyes brightens, thrilled he forced Rico to respond.

While Rico and Vladimir speak to each other in Russian, I send a prayer to God, praying that the consequences of my actions during brunch aren't too severe. Rico only warned me hours ago about the inequality of women in this compound, and I went and stupidly struck him in front of the very man who sanctions the formidable rules.

Any hope I'm holding for a reduced penalty vanishes when Vladimir leaves the room, and Rico drops his dark gaze to me. His eyes are crammed with uncertainty, and his usual confidence is subdued. "I need to go sort some things out."

Unable to speak for fear of sobbing, I shake my head and tighten my grip on his hand. My eyes plead with him, expressing all the things my mouth can't.

"I don't have a choice," he murmurs, his voice growing raspier.

Acting like he can't smell the dread permeating from my pores, he loosens my grip and enters the walk-in closet.

I hold my breath for several terrifying seconds when he emerges not even two seconds later with a suit bag in one hand and a semi-automatic pistol in the other. Fear consumes me, adding to my swirling stomach.

Not trusting my legs to keep me upright, I sit on the edge of the bed and lower my eyes to the floor. I refuse to watch Rico's evolution from day to night, especially since I'm the reason he's transitioning. I've told myself numerous times that he has a double-sided façade, so why did I foolishly forget about it during the most imperative moment?

Once he's dressed, Rico crouches down in front of me and lifts my downcast head. Panic holds me captive when I notice the darkness of his narrowed gaze. His eyes are as black as his tailored suit and relay his every intention.

Bile swarms the back of my throat.

I did this. I caused him to switch back to his cloak-and-dagger lifestyle.

"Lock the door behind me, Kitten, and don't open it for anyone but

Maya," he commands, his low tone ensuring I understand this is not a request.

"Please," I barely whisper, falling onto my knees so I can meet him eye to eye. "This isn't you, Enrique. My heart knows this isn't you."

My pleas fall on deaf ears when his impenetrable mask slips over his face. "I don't have a choice. It's the only way I can keep you safe," he replies, his tone a mix of remorse and anger.

Tears form when he stands from his crouched position and exits the room without a backward glance.

22

After wrapping a towel around my body, I exit the steam-filled bathroom. My steps are slow, weighed down by the guilt hanging heavily on my shoulders. I've been sick out of my mind with worry all day. I paced the floors for hours, ate more chocolate than I'd consumed my entire childhood, and begged Maya to disclose if she knew of Rico's whereabouts.

Nothing worked to calm the uncertainty twisting my stomach.

Not even the world's hottest shower.

My breath catches halfway between my lungs and throat when I step out of the bathroom. Rico is in the same high-backed chair where he's always waiting for me. A potent rush of yearning slams into me just from the sight of him, and the desire to cry overwhelms me, but I manage to hold it in. *Barely.*

When he lifts his eyes from the tube of moisturizer in his hand to me, I rush to him before he has the chance to dip his chin.

My frantic speed slows when the quickest flash of a smirk has me stumbling over my feet. Rico's smile enlarges over my clumsiness, which only makes my movements falter even more.

As I slowly saunter toward him—hips swinging, heart rate surging

—my eyes run over him, seeking any indication of the repercussions of my foolish actions.

Thankfully, none are found. He appears as he did before he left. The only difference is his suit jacket has been removed and slung over the back of the dressing table chair, his gold watch has been placed on a crystal dish on the antique dresser, and the smell of cheap floral perfume is permeating off him.

Huh?

My speed slows even more, closely followed by my heart. When I stop in front of him, Rico's hands move to my towel to pry it open, whereas my eyes scan every inch of him. I'm no longer searching for evidence of my stupidity. I'm seeking signs of betrayal.

Panicked is switched to enraged remarkably quick, completed in under a second, when my eyes zoom in on a red smear on the collar of his dress shirt. If I'm not mistaken, it's the vibrant smear of lipstick.

Blood roars to my ears, and my back molars smash together.

"What?" I stammer when Rico's deep voice breaks me out of the jealous trance the red mark on his shirt forced me into.

He lifts his eyes from my tattoo to me. "It's looking much better today. Is it still itchy?"

Catching my lower lip between my teeth, I shake my head. I've lost the ability to talk as our interaction this morning regarding the Popov mistresses runs through my blinded-with-jealousy mind. Rico neither denied nor agreed that he had mistresses. He merely skirted my questions like any criminal mastermind would.

The room spins as the swirling of my stomach amplifies.

Rico once again smiles at my wobbly composure.

It doesn't have the same effect on me as it did earlier.

"We'll give it a few more treatments with the hydrocortisone cream before switching to a standard moisturizer."

After closing my towel, he stands. Upon noticing the switch in my composure, he eyes me curiously, his eyelids growing heavy as he scans my face. I roll my shoulders and force an expressionless look to mask my furious appearance. Until I've had time to assess the situation properly, I can't jump to conclusions, no matter how much my brain cites my reasons to. Accuse now, ask questions later is the tactic it wants to use.

Not buying my attempts to veil my anger, but apparently not wanting to push the issue, Rico presses a kiss to my temple and ambles into the bathroom. "I'll be out in a few."

His usual alluring composure still beams out of him in invisible waves, but his shoulders are slumped a little lower, and his cockiness isn't as paramount.

Even with his demeanor askew, I go looking for trouble, unable to harness the voice in my head telling me it isn't just his composure that's changed.

I smell a rat from a mile away.

After waiting for the shower door to open, I carefully pry open the bathroom door. Wanting to ensure it doesn't announce my arrival, I embrace its closure, meaning it only gives out the slightest click when it shuts. With my heart walloping, I slant my head to the side and prick my ears. Once I'm happy I haven't attracted Rico's attention, I quickly span the distance between the door and the linen basket at the side of the double vanity.

Just like every other time I've showered in this room, the mirrored wall is thick with steam, but it isn't dense enough to fully conceal the visual of Rico in the shower. He's standing with his feet planted the width of his shoulders and his head hanging low. Water is pelting out of the showerhead, squashing his normally tousled locks into smooth wisps of hair.

With his palms flattened on the white marble tiles, he steps further into the spray, allowing the steaming hot water to run down the length of his spine. His posture looks defeated, but it doesn't stop the vehement jealousy pumping through my body.

When I snatch his dress shirt out of the basket, fiery rage adds to the pink hue blemishing my cheeks. There's no doubt the red mark smeared across the cuff on his collar is lipstick. It's as obvious as the sun hanging in the sky.

Pain twists my heart and swirls my stomach.

Dropping the shirt onto the floor, I stumble out of the bathroom, my steps wobbly and unsure. My brain is telling me not to be so dramatic. It's just a little bit of lipstick on the collar of a stranger's shirt. My heart, though. It's not even functioning right now to articulate a response to my soul-shattering discovery.

Fighting through the tears pricking in my eyes, I throw one of my short-sleeve shirts over my head and yank a pair of cotton panties up my quivering legs. Numerous scenarios explaining how the mark could have gotten on Rico's shirt run through my mind as I'm dressing, but not one acceptable reason is found as to why there would be a pair of female lips sitting intimately close to his neck.

Unless he was...

I slap my hand over my mouth to stop my stomach's vicious heaves. I thought Rico was waiting for me to feel comfortable around him, and that was why he hadn't put any moves on me the past five nights.

Obviously, I was wrong.

When the creak of a door sounds through my ears, I drag my hand over my cheeks, ensuring no sneaky tears have trickled from my eyes before climbing into bed. I hear Rico moving around the space, but since my stomach is so queasy, I refuse to look at him.

I don't think I could stand the sight of him right now.

When he slips into the bed and curls his arms around my waist, I stiffen like a board. Just like he has done every night we've been together, he draws me into his chest, surrounding me with his scent and warmth, a smell still doused in rich floral perfume.

Incapable of battling the jealousy eating away at me, I push away from him and scamper to the furthest edge of the bed. I'm dangling so dangerously on the edge that one more inch would have me sleeping on the floor.

The mattress dips when he moves over to my side of the bed and gathers me back in his arms. "Don't fight me, Kitten. Not tonight."

I kick and wail against him, devastated and inconsolable. My fight is so vicious, one of my wildly flung legs kicks him in the shin while breaking free.

The deep growl torn from his mouth puts a stop to my wailing. I freeze absurdly in equal parts fear and arousal. I've never heard such a provocative noise.

"I need my light. I need to hold you."

His words pain my heart, but it doesn't ease my anger.

Pretending he hasn't noticed my cold demeanor, he caresses me like he does every night. His hand runs down my forearm, and his warm breath tickles my neck. The only difference tonight is I don't melt into his embrace.

I repel from it.

After a few minutes of stiffened silence, Rico releases a deep exhalation of air. It expresses way more than any words ever could.

He's hurting as much as I am.

"It's not what you think." His tone is flat and brimming with uncertainty.

I scowl. "How do you even know what I'm referring to? Unless guilt is on your conscience."

When he growls again, it rumbles straight through my body before clustering in my stupidly excited core. "You left my shirt on the floor, Kitten. I'm well aware of your reason for being angry."

He moves back to his side of the bed before pulling on my shoulders, forcing me to roll over. Even with the room shrouded in darkness, the moonlight shining through the cracks of the curtain is bright enough I can see all the fine details of his face. His eyes are full of torment and shadowed in darkness.

He stares me straight in the eyes before muttering, "It isn't what you're thinking."

Seeing the hurt in his eyes doesn't lessen mine. "Don't insult me, Enrique. How else could lipstick get on the collar of your shirt unless it was put there by female lips?"

My anger accelerates to never-before-reached levels when he throws back his head and laughs. "You think I cheated on you?" he chokes out between bouts of laughter. "I thought you were angry because..." I can't hear anything he's saying over his hearty chuckle.

Gritting my teeth, I throw my clenched fist into his chest. "It's not funny, Rico. Stop laughing."

He laughs even harder. "I can't help it. I love seeing my little kitten with her claws out," he says, still laughing.

The only thing that simmers his body-shuddering laughter is when he spots wetness welling in my eyes. He scrubs his face as he struggles to regain his composure.

His efforts are fruitless. Nothing can wipe the glint of happiness sparkling in his glistening eyes.

"Let's see who is laughing when I return the favor," I sneer under my breath, my tone callous. "In a house full of men, I'm sure I can find a suitor for the night."

All the laughter on his face vanishes in an instant as does my ability to breathe when his body pins me to the mattress.

His pulse rages through his body as he stares down at me with his nostrils flaring and his eyes blazing with anger. "I don't share, Kitten."

"Well... *neither do I!*"

I move my fists to pound his chest, only to have them snatched and clamped to my side.

Normally, his hold would frighten me, but even dealing with the wrath of jealousy, I know he'd never harm me. My heart? That's an entirely different story.

No longer able to hold in my devastation, I scream my anger into the silent night. My heart is beyond shattered, my body inconsolable.

Upon being alerted of my devastation, the fire raging in Rico's eyes switches from angry to remorseful. He stares at me, seemingly at a loss on how to handle my weeping.

"Kiss me, Blaire," he requests a short time later, his tone less angry, his eyes shimmering with hope.

I inhale a ragged breath, beyond shocked. "What? Are you insane? No!"

When he smiles a seductive smirk that sets my heart racing, I twist my head to the side, needing to look at anything but his sinfully handsome face. I'm not strong enough to deny his advances with his cock pressing against my aching core, let alone when he smiles at me like that.

My nape prickles with goose bumps when his stubble scratches my jawline as he demands again, "Kiss me, Blaire."

When his teeth graze my earlobe, an erotic purr topples from my lips, and my walls crumble. Giving in to the fact I'll never be strong enough to reject his attention, I lick my lips, preparing for our kiss. Like he can sense my submissiveness, he slants his head to the side so our lips are better aligned.

With my arms pinned to the side of my head and his body gloriously pressed into mine, I kiss him with everything I have, showing him what he has lost by playing me for a fool. Although his hold is rough, his kiss is nothing but gentle. He kisses me with so much passion that when he pulls away, I can barely remember my own name, let alone what we were fighting about.

A tightness spreads across my chest when he stares down at me with lust-filled eyes. The tightness has nothing to do with him pinning me to the bed—he's holding his weight with his elbows—it's the peace in his dark and stormy eyes that causes my heart to stutter.

After releasing one of my wrists, he runs the back of his hand down my blemished cheek. "Perfect, Kitten. Why would I settle for anything less?"

Even though I can see the truth in his eyes, I can't leash the pain slicing my heart in two. "Then why is there lipstick on your collar?" My breathlessness is unable to hide the pain laced in my words. I am devastated.

A flash of hesitation sparks through Rico's dark gaze before he murmurs, "It isn't lipstick."

All the anger his heartfelt kiss washed away returns in an instant. "Don't treat me like an idiot, Rico! I know a lipstick stain when I see it," I fire back, my loud voice gaining momentum.

An involuntary moan ripples through my lips when he rocks his hips forward before he reconfirms, "It isn't lipstick."

While snarling at him for using my sexual attraction to him to his advantage, I kick and buck against him, endeavoring to get free. Stupid tears well in my eyes, hating that he can make me feel special and worthless within seconds of each other.

Not the slightest bit intimidated by my vicious fight, Rico leans harder against me, leaving not even an ounce of air between us. My squirming comes to a shrieking halt when I feel the heat of his solid cock halfway up my belly. Even with my heart cut open and bleeding, if he mauled me right now, I wouldn't put up a fight. I'm defenseless to his touch.

The damp mess between my legs eases when he confesses, "It's not lipstick, Kitten. It's blood. The red smears on my shirt are bloodstains."

I freeze, certain I haven't heard him right.

It's only when I see the truth in his remorseful eyes do I realize my hearing didn't fail me.

"But you smell like women's perfume."

His pupils grow so large they fill his entire cornea. "Our industry doesn't discriminate between genders."

I glare at him, knowing he's lying.

"Not when handing out punishments."

My stomach churns as my mind tries to contemplate how he could get blood on the collar of his perfume-scented shirt in a humane way.

Unable to find a reasonable explanation, dread overwhelms me.

"Did you..." I can't force the words out of my mouth. Even my brain agrees that the man who comforted me after my nightmare and has awoken in my bed the past five nights couldn't be so callous. He would never harm a woman.

"No," Rico replies sullenly.

I suck in a relieved breath.

It's quickly redrawn when he confesses, "But I didn't stop the man who did."

My heart shatters as horror floods my eyes.

Rico releases a deep breath before he rolls off me. "This is why I didn't want to tell you about my industry. I didn't want you to look at me differently."

"I'm not looking at you any differently." My words are weak and pathetic, matching the sluggish beat of my heart.

My slow heart rate gets a boost when I catch sight of his livid gaze.

His narrowed eyes call me out on my deceit without a word needing to spill from his lips.

I swallow the lump in my throat before confessing, "I'm not looking at you differently. I just don't want the darkness to win. This isn't you, Enrique. My heart knows this isn't you."

"You don't understand, Kitten. I was raised in this lifestyle. I don't know any better."

I roll onto my side and glance into his eyes. "Don't know any better or don't *want* to know any better? As those are two completely separate entities. You might have been raised by a monster, but you don't have to live like one."

An indecisive storm builds in his eyes. "In this industry, your value is measured by your callousness, not your morality. The more ruthless you are, the more respect you gain."

"Fear is not respect, Rico. They're not even close to being the same thing."

He scrubs the stubble on his chin. "I know. But I have a reputation to live up to. I'm Vladimir's son. His firstborn son. That title comes with expectations. Expectations I was filling. I was a terrible man, Kitten. A parodist of my father." He locks his beautiful eyes with me. "Until I met you. Then I realized what I was craving wasn't power or respect. It was you. I wanted you."

Heart hammering, I cup his jaw and peer into his eyes. "You can have me." I scoot closer to him so our hot pants of breath intermingle. "You just need to fight through the darkness."

A flare of emotion brightens his gaze for the tiniest second before it once again becomes swamped by blackness. "I can't."

"Why?" I shout through a sob. "Why can't you?"

"You don't understand how things in this industry work, Blaire, so you're not qualified to pass judgment. This is the only way I can protect you. They know you're my weakness, and they're using it against me." Anxiety strangles my heart when he says, "They'll kill you the instant I step out of line."

He scoots up the bed and rests his back on the headboard before running his hand down his face. Just like earlier, his posture is slumped, and he looks genuinely defeated.

From his stance alone, I know my concerns about him fading completely into blackness will never reach fruition.

A soulless man doesn't feel regret.

They don't feel anything.

For the first time in over a week, I act on the instincts of both my heart and mind. After pulling Enrique's hand away from his tired face, I crawl into his lap and stare into his remorseful eyes.

The murky cloud in his gaze clears away when I say, "Let me be your light." I rock my hips forward, dragging my soaked vagina along the length of his stiffened shaft. "I may not understand this industry, but that doesn't mean I can't guide you through the darkness."

23

eavy sentiment fills the air when I grasp the hem of my shirt and pull it over my head. The mood is so thick it's almost palpable. As my breasts fall gently to my chest, Rico devours me with passionate dark eyes. I arch toward him, my aching breasts thrusting out in offering.

A shiver bolts down my spine when the back of Rico's hand runs over my inflamed cheeks before tracing the curve of my heaving chest. "Are you sure this is what you want? I've been waiting for you to be sure."

I sigh in relief before a broad grin stretches across my face. "And here I was thinking you didn't want me."

"I've never wanted anything more in my life." He locks his entrancing eyes with mine. "You're my light in a world full of blackness."

A faint purr topples from my O-formed mouth when he runs his finger across my pebbled nipple, sending a zing of pleasure straight to my pussy. "Are you sure?" he asks again.

When I see the darkness in his eyes fading, I nod. I've never been more sure of anything in my life.

He grows heavy beneath me, getting thicker and wider as my belly flutters with butterflies.

"Please, Enrique," I shamelessly beg when his hands remain fisted at his sides. "I need you. Please."

"That sounds more like someone who is sure than a simple nod," he replies to my shameful plea.

When he shifts his hips upward, I quiver above him, wild and free of any doubt. "I'm sure. Very, very sure," I purr.

My words turn into a gargle when his tongue circles my nipple before he sucks it into his warm, inviting mouth. I draw him in closer, my aching core tightening with every swirl of his tongue. As he licks my nipples, my hands are all over him, unable to resist feeling the softness of his skin pulled taut over his brawny muscles. His stubble adds to the excitement clustering in my pussy when he devours my breast with long licks, playful bites, and teasing gropes. As my pussy grows wetter, I rock against him, needing something to quench the insane throb between my legs.

Every thrust of my hips has my mind spiraling, incapable of thinking of anything but the hard ridge in his cotton boxers. I need to taste him. Desperately. My nipple pulls out of his mouth with a pop when I draw my chest away from him. I don't need to speak to announce what I want to happen next. The hankering in my eyes relays the whole story.

With a seductive smirk, Rico says, "Be my guest, Kitten."

A groan tears from his throat when I run my hand along the length protruding from his boxer shorts. As I work him through his undergarments, he places his hands on the side of his hips before lifting his glorious backside off the bed so I can slide the cotton material down his thighs.

When his cock pops free, I freeze for a moment, giving my eyes time to absorb the enormity of his glorious package. His cock is jutted and hard as stone, the tip glistening with evidence of his arousal. Desperate to taste him, I circle my hand around the base of his fat cock before adding another, unsure if one hand will be adequate to handle so much man.

Rico chuckles at my unsureness. Normally, any hint of amusement in a bedroom would have me cowering, but his laughter spurs on my pursuit. It isn't malicious or vindictive. It's heartwarming and kind.

Any humor left lingering on his mouth is swiped straight off his face when I run my tongue over the crest of his cock, eagerly gathering up his drop of pre-cum.

While I stroke his heated flesh with my hand, my mouth and tongue work his swollen knob. I take him deep in my mouth, all the way to the back of my throat as guttural hisses escape his lips.

"Don't choke yourself, Kitten. Only take as much as you can," Rico murmurs through a groan.

Fighting through my gag reflex, I take him even deeper, goaded by the raspy moans rumbling up his chest and the lust brightening his eyes. His thumbs stroke the grooves in my cheeks from my greedy sucks as I devour him. It aids in soothing the ache of my muscles as I give it my all.

I work the velvet crest of his cock in and out of my swollen lips over the next several long minutes, loving the weight of his cock in my mouth.

His hands move to my hair when I run my tongue down the vein nourishing his glorious penis. A ghost of a smile creeps onto my lips, relishing in discovering one of his weak spots.

It's a rare treat to find vulnerability in a man as controlled as Rico.

"The desires of my cock aren't my weakness, Kitten. You are," Rico says, once again reading my inner dialogue.

Still pumping his silky-smooth shaft, I lift my hanker-filled eyes to his. "Show me."

Not needing any more encouragement, he bands his arms around me and pulls me toward him. With one hand on my neck and the other on my back, he kisses with so much passion my libido soars to never-before-reached levels. It is primal and urgent and shreds any chance of walking away from our relationship with my heart intact.

I melt into his embrace, fully surrendering to the man who can wipe away every insecurity I've ever had with a simple kiss.

By the time his lips move to my neck, I'm totally lost in the desire burning through me. "Enrique..."

"Shh, Kitten."

He adjusts our position so my back is resting against the softness of the mattress while he is kneeling. The damp mess between my legs grows when he snaps my panties off my body before pinning my wrists above my head. When he trails his beard across my silky skin, marking every inch of me with his spicy scent, I squirm beneath him, both ticklish and turned on.

His natural dominance oozes out of him in bucketloads, but I'm too caught up in the thrill of chasing a climax to care, and in all honesty, his strength and assuredness calm me. He will never intentionally hurt me, so I feel safe with him even while being held aggressively.

When Rico's scratchy beard reaches my aching-with-need core, he stops and stares unashamedly at my bare mound. "Pretty and pink and dripping with wetness. My little kitten is ravishing."

He presses an intimate kiss on my clit, forcing me to call out and arch my back. My legs instinctively pull together, unable to stay still when a surge of desire puddles between them.

I watch him, beyond enchanted, when his dark eyes bore into mine as he slowly inches his finger into my quivering pussy.

"So tight."

I clench around him, begging for more.

"And greedy."

I throw my head back and snap my eyes closed when his beard scrapes the most sensitive area of my body. Inaudible words tumble from my throat when his tongue rolls over the lines of my pussy before it spears inside me. It feels insanely good, and in a short period of time, I'm lost in the throes of ecstasy.

My orgasm hits me by surprise, steamrolling me into an incoherent, blubbering mess. I writhe against Rico's tongue and mouth, blindsided by the strength of my mind-hazing climax.

With his smile felt by my thighs clamped around his head, his fingers stroke the sensitive spot inside me, drawing out the length of my orgasm while his tongue flicks my throbbing clit. His speed is relentless, unwilling to give me a moment of reprieve until I come for the second time.

A familiar tightening builds deep in my core, but I fight against it, not believing it's possible to have two earth-shattering climaxes so close together.

"Stop fighting me, Kitten," Rico says against my drenched lips.

The deep timbre of his voice pushes me over the edge for the second time. I close my eyes and yield to the brilliance of ecstasy, shouting Rico's name in a long, guttural groan as I take everything he's willing to give me.

My fall is blessed and long.

I've only just finished riding the crest of orgasmic bliss when a packet being torn open sounds through my ears. My excitement builds again when I watch Rico roll a condom down his thick cock. Even stuck in a trance only two mind-blowing orgasms can incite, nothing can dampen my readiness to be claimed by him again.

Rico runs his hand down my flushed cheeks. "Fuck... I love seeing you flushed... you're so beautiful. So, so beautiful."

I have no chance of holding in my smile, so I set it free.

Mimicking my giddy expression, Rico's hands slide over the wetness slicking my skin when he curls his arms around my back and draws me to his overheated body. Warmth blooms across my chest when he rests his sweat-drenched forehead against mine and stares into my eyes. The heat of his thickened rod sits hard and ready between us, but it isn't the only reason lust sparks through every inch of me. It's the look of content in his beautiful dark eyes.

"Are you sure, Blaire?" he asks again, his warm breath fluttering my hungry lips.

My heart swells as I cup the edge of his jaw. "I'm sure, Enrique. I've never been more sure of anything in my life," I quote, speaking directly from my heart.

The rest of the sentence I quoted to him the night we married is sitting on the edge of my tongue, but my mouth refuses to relinquish the words.

One step at a time, Blaire, my brain pleads to my heart.

Rico's thumbs clear away the sweat careening down my cheeks before he adjusts our position so the tip of his engorged penis rests against the entrance of my soaked vagina.

With his eyes arrested on mine, he sheaths me one glorious inch at a time.

"Ah, Jesus, Kitten, so tight."

I swivel my hips, my body naturally trying to ease the uncomfortable intrusion. Pain rockets through my core from taking a man as well-endowed as Rico all the way to the root, but it is also pleasurable.

Rico keeps his movements still, giving my body the chance to adjust to his girth as his lips kiss away my pain. I taste myself on his lips as he strokes his tongue in my mouth in slow, dedicated licks, and my pussy grows wetter with every caress of his tongue.

Once the sting of invasion has eased, I squeeze the walls of my vagina around him, advising I'm ready for him to move.

"I'll go slow for as long as I can—"

"Don't hold back, Enrique. Take what you need. Give me your all."

"I won't hurt you, Kitten. I can't."

I stare straight into his eyes so he can't miss their honesty when I say, "I know. You'll never hurt me, so there's no reason to hold back."

The words I couldn't force out earlier nearly topple from my mouth when the most heartfelt smile I've ever seen graces Rico's sinfully handsome face. I bite the inside of my cheek, swallowing my absurd declaration of love for a man I'm only starting to know when he slowly rocks back out of me.

Any ludicrous thoughts in my mind vanish when he thrusts back in.

His movements start at a slow and controlled pace, but with every stroke, he slowly increases his speed. I sling my arms around his sweat-slicked neck and hold on for the ride of my life when his pounds become unforgiving. His cock pummels into my soaked pussy, thrusting another climax to the forefront of my mind. When he spreads his knees wider, opening my hips more, I purr an erotic moan. He takes me even deeper, pumping every glorious inch of his thickened shaft into me.

The veins in his neck throb nearly as furiously as the one feeding his cock as he pounds into me at a frenzied yet precise pace. My coil tightens as my sprint to climax gains momentum. The buildup is frantic—almost blinding.

"Give it to me, Kitten," Rico growls, his voice vibrating all the way through my drenched pussy. "You're fighting a battle you'll never win."

Sweat rolls down his cheeks as he strengthens his pumps, ensuring every stroke hits the tender spot inside me. He fucks me like an out-of-control animal, unwilling to give me an inch of leniency until I give him my all—until I give him everything.

I become lost in the blessedness of an orgasm for the third time when Rico runs his thumb over the erogenous zone of my collarbone. I choke his name with a string of incoherent garbage as a surge of passion sparks through my exhausted body.

I'm barely lucid from the devastating effects of three life-altering orgasms, but there's one statement during my blinded-by-lust rant I hear loud and clear—my declaration of love.

Rico's dark eyes blaze into mine as the thickness of his cock increases. Not removing his beautiful eyes from mine, he slows the brutal pounds of his cock, slowly bringing me down from the haze of climax.

When every pleasurable shudder shimmering through my body has been exhausted, Rico locks his heavy-hooded gaze with me. All the indecisiveness in his eyes has vanished, replaced with nothing but optimism.

"Say it again." His deep voice is husky with his arousal strangling it.

My nose tingles when I mutter, "I love you, Enrique," in the faintest whisper.

A throaty purr rumbles through my lips when Rico's cock throbs inside me, my declaration of love alone enough to make him come.

24

My lazy steps to the bathroom stop when a knock rattles through the wooden door of my bedroom. I freeze, mindful of Rico's regular warnings about not opening my door for anyone but Maya.

Considering Maya only left here ten minutes ago, I'm doubtful it's her.

My assumptions are left for dust when Maya's voice projects through the thick door. My steps to let her in are slow as my body is still reveling in the orgasms Rico awarded me with last night.

Shockingly, I've been on a high the past five days. I thought once the aftershocks of our intimate gathering wore off, I would have backpedaled on my declaration of love, using my blurry state as a plausible defense, but not once has uncertainty entered my mind for the past five days.

I feel the most content I've ever felt in the midst of a loved-up haze.

Rico and I have spent the last five nights in bed kissing and fondling each other for hours before our lightning-paced union joins in the most earth-shattering way. I never thought sexual contact would be a way I'd feel comfortable expressing myself, but everything about me is different when I'm with Rico. He brings out parts of me I didn't even know existed.

He truly does make me wild with desire.

There isn't a shadow of doubt in my mind that the man I wake up with every morning is the same man I married nearly three weeks ago. Rico is attentive and sweet—a man I wouldn't hesitate to marry on sight. And thankfully, as our oddly compelling union grows strong, the more the blackness in Rico's eyes recedes.

I never thought I'd be strong enough to guide him through the darkness plaguing his life like I promised in our wedding vows. Now, I'm thinking differently. If things keep following this path, I have no doubt I'll always be the light in his life.

Ignoring the sentimental butterflies taking flight in my stomach, I pull open the heavily weighted door and greet Maya with a smile. Although Maya barely speaks a word of English, we've become close since I arrived here over ten days ago. She's the only female confidant I have in this house, so I relish the hours we spend together.

The happiness making my stomach a jittery mess eases when I notice a cloud of concern filtering over her usually expressive eyes. "Maya, are you okay?"

I run my hand along her forearm. My concern grows when I feel the clamminess of her skin. Maya is a small-framed lady, but she has the heart of a dragon. Normally, nothing frightens her.

Keeping quiet, she hands me a slip of paper I didn't realize she was holding until now. After bouncing my eyes between her evocative gaze, I drop them to the folded-up piece of paper. The tremble of my hand rattles the cream-colored document when I unfold it. Since there's only a one-line sentence on the paper, it doesn't take me long to recite the message.

Kitten, meet me in the servants' quarters. Rico.

My heart rate soars. Rico mentioned earlier today that he had a surprise for me, but no matter how much I pleaded with him for a hint, he remained tight-lipped, only disclosing that I'd find out more when he returned later this evening.

This is obviously part of his surprise.

I return my eyes to Maya. "Where are the servants' quarters located?"

My head slings to the side when she stretches her arm and points to a door marked with *'sluzhashchiy'* halfway down the hall.

"Okay. Thank you."

Maya bows her head then spins on her heels and walks down the hall.

Her head flings back to me when I ask, "Did Rico say what time?"

Her pupils widen before she shakes her head. I wait until she reaches the crest of the stairs before shutting the door. Although I'm concerned about Maya's odd reaction, I can't hold in my excitement about Rico's note.

I rush to the mirror to check my hair and makeup. My cheeks are rosy from the stifling Las Vegas heat that graced my face when I sat in the window seat for hours reading this afternoon, and my eyes are full and bright.

Deciding to wear my aroused look with pride, I place Rico's note on the dressing table before exiting the room. My knees clash together with every step I take down the long hall. I've only walked this corridor once. It was when I attended my disastrous brunch with Rico.

It's amazing to think how much has changed between us in so little time. But I guess time has no place when I'm with Rico. It just stands still.

My heart rate speeds the further I move away from my room. Although this side of the Popov compound is elaborately decorated, nothing can take away the ghastliness plaguing the air. Just like a cemetery, no amount of potted color can hide the ugliness of death.

I stop frozen halfway down the hall and gasp in a quick breath when I spot the same two men from last week guarding the stairwell. Since they are engaged in a deep conversation, they fail to notice my quiet approach.

Not wanting to place myself on their radar, I carefully open the servants' quarters door and slip inside the narrow stairwell. The muggy Las Vegas air adds to the giddiness swishing in my stomach as I wind down a set of rickety spiral stairs. My eyes shoot in all directions, taking in what would have been a servants' quarters back in the day. White and yellow wallpaper covers the antique corniced walls, and gorgeous cedar hardwood lines the floors.

I'm so immersed in staring at an old set of service bells hanging in the middle of the room I don't notice another presence sneaking up on me until it's too late.

Pain sears across my cheek when a man backhands me with so much force, my head flings to the side. The taste of copper engulfs my taste buds as I fall to the floor with a sickening thud, my wrist jarring painfully when it hits the hardwood floor.

Blood trickles from the side of my mouth as I lift my frightened eyes to my attacker. A large brute of a man who would easily be the height of Rico and two times wider sneers an abhorrent grin as he takes a step toward me.

I shake my head, then scramble backward, ignoring the screaming protests of my limp wrist. Pleas for help sit on the tip of my tongue, but my frightened composure has once again frozen me into stiffness.

My temples scream when the stranger fists my hair and yanks me off the floor, his roughness causing the roots of my hair to pull away from my scalp. After gritting my teeth to ignore the tortuous pain rocketing through my skull, my hands dart up to claw him. I dig my nails into his hands and scratch him hard enough I draw blood.

My battle angers him more. He pushes me backward until my back is splayed against the wallpaper I was admiring minutes ago. He glares at me with a set of malevolent, morally bankrupt eyes as he lowers one of his hands to clutch my throat. My mind spirals, unable to separate the past from the present.

When images of my attack in the alleyway flash before my eyes, I shift my gaze sideways, expecting to see my savior running toward me.

My heart rate kicks into overdrive when I discover no one is within eyesight.

I drift my frightened gaze back to the man pinning me to the wall.

He keeps one hand wrapped around my throat while the other painfully squeezes my breast through my dress. My lungs heave as violently as my stomach, sickened at the glint of lust forming in his eyes.

Not willing to lay down without a fight, I kick my legs out wildly, fighting with all my might. When one of my kicks hits him with enough force to loosen his grip around my neck, I suck in lung-filling gulps of air.

Using his stumbling composure to my advantage, I crash my knee into his groin, then push him hard in the chest. His hand darts down to protect his crotch from another vicious attack as he takes a fumbling step backward. "You fucking bitch," he sneers in a thick Russian accent.

I slip under his arm and race to the rickety stairwell on my right. Tears flood my cheeks as I fight to keep my hidden memories from ten years ago buried in the back of my mind.

My fast speed to the stairs comes to a halt when my ankle is snagged, and I'm yanked backward. I land on my knees, and a harsh puff of air parts my lips. My mind is frantic, drifting between the present and future, but I kick my way out of my attacker's grasp, then scamper across the wooden floor.

I put up a similar fight the last time I was attacked, but this time is different.

This time, I'm not at the mercy of a dark-eyed stranger.

I throw out my leg, kicking my assailant in his despicable face. I may not weigh half what he weighs, but I'm not a fourteen-year-old girl unable to defend myself anymore. I'm a strong woman who refuses to lie down willingly.

Any life left in my assailant's hollow eyes vanishes the instant the heel of my sandal smashes into his crooked nose. Red hot anger lines his face when a trickle of blood dribbles out of his nose.

"Now you will pay," he snarls viciously.

The back of my head hits the bottom step of the stairwell hard, temporarily dazing me when my legs are pulled out from underneath me. My vision blurs, melting the images that frequently haunt my nights with my newest nightmare.

My confused state only lasts as long as it takes for my brain to register my attacker's filthy hands roaming over my body.

"No!" I scream, grateful my scared state has finally lifted when his hand slides under my skirt and inches toward my panty-covered pussy.

My head rockets to the side when the faintest, "Blaire," comes sounding from the top of the stairs.

Before I can respond, just like in my memories, my attacker is brutally hit from the side.

I crawl backward, pushing down the hem of my shirt as Rico and my attacker slam into the wooden floor with bone-crushing force.

The hard impact does nothing to lessen Rico's fury. He pummels his fists into my attacker's face repeatedly until his knuckles are covered in the same vibrant red coloring lining his face.

"Stop, Rico," I mumble when the man he's beating stops fighting against him.

I scramble onto my knees and crawl across the floor when his manic onslaught continues on the lifeless man. Just like in the bedroom, he's a machine, frighteningly unstoppable, designed to issue punishment.

Unable to inflict any more damage to the man's bloody face, Rico lowers his fists to his body, where he strikes him with blow after devastating blow.

I squeal and stumble backward when my hand touching his shoulder causes him to yank away from me violently.

Like he can recognize my touch, he stops swinging his fists and cranks his neck to the side. The fury in his eyes vanishes the instant he sees me cowering on the floor beside him. His eyes roam around the room. He looks frightened and confused. He runs his hand down his face, removing a stream of sweat pouring down his cheek.

When he returns his eyes to me, the swirling of my stomach gains intensity. The same set of eyes from my nightmares are staring back at me.

I stagger backward, my whole body shaking. "You're... you're..."

Panicked shock overwhelms me when Rico dismounts the man he's beaten into unconsciousness and slowly approaches me. Blood drips from his hands more quickly than remorse fills his eyes.

I stare at him, more confused than ever.

"Shh, Kitten, shh," he croons, his voice cracking with emotion.

Speaking through the sob in the back of my throat, I stutter, "Y-you're the man... th-th-the man from the alley."

Rico's eyes blaze into me, full of emotion and turmoil as he says, "Yes, Kitten. That was me."

Then my entire world crumbles.

25

ENRIQUE

Blaire stares at me in shock, her pupils wide, her beautiful light green eyes gloss over. Her whole body is shaking, mimicking mine to a T. I'm generally fearless, but seeing the way Blaire is looking at me now, frightened and timid, I'm truly scared. I've once again become the four-year-old boy lying next to my deceased mother for three days waiting for my 'uncle' to discover her death.

When I reach out to touch her, my heart stops, praying she doesn't pull away from me.

My prayers remain unanswered when she shakes her head, begging for me not to touch her.

I can't, though. I'll never stop. I love her. I have from the moment I laid my eyes on her.

I've lived my life at a speed double the rate of everyone surrounding me. After my mother's death, I lost contact with my sister and was thrown into a makeshift family of servants and Popov whores. Everyone in the Popov compound hated me. At first, I thought it was because I'd shown weakness by crying when they laid my mother's body to rest with only three people by her graveside—me, the priest, and my father, who stood three steps back from the unmarked grave her coffin was being lowered in. But as the years moved on, I realized my assumptions were wrong.

I wasn't hated.

I was feared.

I, Enrique Julies Popov, am the firstborn descendant of the world's most ruthless empire.

Although my father's mistresses have birthed many children over the years, I'm Vladimir's firstborn son, meaning I'm the sole heir to the Popov empire. My father's values are traditional, based on principles that stretch back as far as the seventeen hundreds when the Popov empire was created by a short, stout man named Anatoly Popov. He started the Popov empire as a cloak-and-dagger business—killing for hire. As his reputation grew, so did his ruthlessness and his crew.

Over the centuries, the Popovs' beliefs have rarely altered—men are powerful, women are weak.

Most kids my age grew up in households that encouraged their children to have their own beliefs. My upbringing was far from that. Discipline became a game to me. How many lashings did it take until the sting of the whip was no longer felt? How many droplets of my blood would spill onto the floor over the thirty minutes of my punishment? And how many ways could I exact my revenge on the man wielding the whip marking my skin?

To others, it may seem cruel.

To me, it was my life.

I knew nothing different.

By the time I was fourteen, I'd already lived most of my life. In this industry, you barely make it past your teens. I'd done countless hideous things, stuff I'll never mention again until I meet with my creator. I was ruthless, believing nothing could stop me until I saw her, my little kitten...

We were driving through a small town a few hours out of Florida. I couldn't say where as I'd spent the last seven weeks on the road, and my bearings were slightly adrift. My attention diverted from the scenery streaming past the heavily-tinted window when I noticed a beautiful teen walking on the cracked sidewalk, laughing and talking with her redheaded friend.

The late afternoon sun bounced off her hair, shrouding her in a golden halo. She had the kind of beauty that captured you and didn't let go. The face of an angel, lightly tanned skin with the smallest gathering of freckles on the bridge of her nose, and a body more mature than her years.

Even the way she skipped down the path had me in a trance. I watched her for only seconds, but it felt like the moon had circled the globe numerous times.

My eyes only left the entrancing blonde when a deep Russian voice at my side snapped me out of my imaginative state. "You like, Rico? You want to get out your tackle and have some fun with the little girlies?"

I lifted my narrowed eyes to Sergei, my cousin and goon. His mocking grin irritated me. I stared at him and sniffed, purposely goading him. Sergei was double my age, but we were of similar size and build. For what he lacked in stature, he made up for in arrogance. He too was raised in the Popov compound, but since he failed to have the legacy of the Popov last name, he was nothing more than a paid goon.

Sergei slapped the chest of Timur, sitting on his left. "Наверное, не знает, как этим пользоваться!" he mocked.

"You won't be able to use your cock again when I cut it off," I snarled back, lowering my stern gaze to the crotch of his pants.

Sergei swallowed away a lump, then stared at me in surprise, shocked I understood what he said. To start with, I don't know if it was stubbornness or reverence to my English-speaking mother, but I rarely spoke a word of Russian. As the years went on, I discovered there's an immense amount of power being seated in a room with a group of men who don't realize you're bilingual.

As the seconds ticked by on the clock, the look in Sergei's eyes changed, going from scared to a gleam I'd only seen in his eyes a rare handful of times.

"Stop," he demanded the driver of the Escalade we were traveling in. He banged his hand on the privacy partition to add strength to his request.

I turned my eyes to my brother, Nikolai. His icy-blue eyes drifted between Sergei and me for several seconds before he shrugged his shoulders. In the reflection of the mirrored privacy partition, I saw the dirty white van that had been following us most of the day pull in behind our stationary vehicle. The men inside I hadn't met. All I knew was that they were from another Russian entity that was run by a counterpart of the Popov empire. After we aided them in a business transaction taking place in a small town called Hopeton, they were to return to their station, and we were to travel back to Vegas.

My heart rate surged when Sergei pulled a two-way radio out of his pocket and said three short words. "Secure the assets."

I sat motionless with my heart thumping against my ribcage when two large Russian men curled out of the van and approached the blonde I had been admiring.

My stomach lurched in silence when one of the men wrapped his arm around the blonde's friend and placed a white cloth over her mouth. Even though the fabric muffled her words, one distinct word was clear—Blaire.

I moved to the edge of my seat when the second man with a snake tattoo wrapped around his wrist and halfway up his forearm approached the blonde. My hand moved to the door handle, my mind running purely on instinct. The only thing that stopped me was when Nikolai placed his hand on my shoulder and squeezed.

Drifting my eyes away from an immoral act I'd seen played out time and time again in my fourteen years, I peered into my brother's eyes. He shook his head, advising me not to respond. He knew Sergei was testing me, ensuring my loyalty remained to the Popov empire.

I continued watching the scene with my gut twisted in a knot. I didn't understand why my reaction was so fierce. I had witnessed that and far worse things numerous times in my short life, but there was something different about me that day.

Something inside me snapped.

When Blaire laid lifeless on the concrete sidewalk, her body bloody and bruised, I whispered into the air, "Don't give up, Blaire."

Like she could hear my pleas, she rolled onto her side and leaped to her feet. She had more strength than any man I'd ever punished.

My back molars smashed together when her dash down the alleyway was stopped by the Russian who had thrown her unconscious friend in the back of the van minutes earlier. Blood roared in my ears when he pinned Blaire to a steel fence by her throat.

Before I could contemplate the severity of my punishment, I threw open the Escalade door and charged at the man double my weight. My speed was unchecked as I rammed into the side of him with all my might. He let out a loud "oomph" when we smashed into the concrete with a sickening thud. I felt no pain. All I felt was fury.

I threw my fists into his face, dazing him long enough that I could turn my eyes back to Blaire. She stood motionless against a steel-chained fence, her knees bloody, her eyes wide.

"Run! Blaire! Run!" I screamed at her.

She stared into my eyes for a fleeting second before she ran down the alleyway as fast as her trembling legs could take her. When her original attacker hot-footed after her, I scrambled off the man lying half unconscious on the cracked asphalt and threw my arms around his ankles.

As he plummeted to the ground, I saw the quickest flash of blonde running into a busy street.

Relief engulfed me.

That was the last time I saw Blaire until she fell on my lap weeks ago...

Ignoring the shake that has encroached my hands, I undo the buttons of my dress shirt. The creak of the rickety stairwell at my side gains my attention. Maya is standing at the foot of the stairs, her eyes rocketing between a shocked Blaire and me.

"*Извини,*" she whispers, issuing her apologies in Russian.

She moves to a stack of shelves in the corner of the room to gather a bunch of towels as she mumbles under her breath. Although her rant is a mixture of Russian and French, it follows a similar path. That she knew something wasn't right, and she should have trusted her intuition.

After removing my dress shirt covered with specks of blood, I yank my white undershirt over my head. Blaire stares up at me, clearly in shock as I place the shirt over her head before pulling her blood-streaked hair out of the collar. Tears roll down her cheeks unchecked as her entire body quakes.

Her tears I can handle, but the vacant look in her eyes—I don't even know where to begin.

After wiping off the smears of blood covering my hands with a towel Maya gave me, I crouch closer to Blaire. With my heart walloping against my ribs, I once again raise my hand to her face. She blinks several times in a row but, thankfully, doesn't repel from my touch.

Glancing into her eyes so she knows I mean her no harm, I brush away a bunch of unruly hairs clinging to her sweat-drenched neck. Her skin prickles with goose bumps when my soft touch runs over the sensitive skin on her collarbone.

My eyes shift sideways when the man I beat to an inch of his life makes a gagging noise as he chokes on his own blood. He should be grateful he's still breathing. If Blaire's welfare weren't my utmost priority, he'd have a bullet wound between his eyes.

Deciding Blaire doesn't need anything added to her shocked state, I return my gaze to her. She's still staring at me, wide-eyed and quiet. Her pupils are massive, filling her entire cornea, making her eyes the darkest I've ever seen.

I peer into her eyes with the same amount of sincerity she usually awards me with. "Let me take care of you, Blaire. Let me wash away your pain."

There's no greater gift than the one I'm given when she nods, accepting my assistance.

Careful not to touch the scrape marks marring her beautiful skin, I band my arms around her body and pull her to my bare chest. She whimpers into my neck as she clutches onto me for dear life.

Her nails digging into the scarred skin of my back is a cruel reminder of the world I forced her into when I failed to give her up a second time.

I knew who Blaire was from the moment she tumbled into my lap hours after I'd returned from Russia. Blaire's beautiful golden hair, angelic face, and seductive body are features any man would have a hard time forgetting. But it was her light green eyes peering up at me that unveiled her. It was the same set of eyes that blessed my dreams every night for the past ten years, and the same eyes that weathered me through my darkest storms.

When she walked away from me that night in Vegas, slightly stumbling, I tried to let her go, but just like my desire to protect her ten years earlier, something greater had me pushing away from the poker table and walking toward her.

One sideways glance was all it took. She recognized me too. Although, three weeks ago, she handled the discovery of my real identity in a much calmer fashion. It was only when I discovered she'd been drugged did the reasoning behind her serene approach make sense.

We sat in a VIP booth in Omnia Nightclub for nearly three hours talking. I told her everything, disclosing things I've never shared with anyone. The murder of my mother. How I killed a man to protect my sister. Every bad thing I'd done in my life was laid out for her to see. In all honesty, half of my confession was to ease the burden I'd been carrying on my shoulders for the past twenty-four years, but the other half, the bigger half, was because I was trying to scare her. I wanted to show her the man she was staring at in awe was nothing but a monster. But the more I shared, the greater her wonderment grew.

She wasn't the only one entranced.

I was addicted to her.

She was my light in a world full of blackness.

She is my light in a world full of blackness.

As I walk through the Popov compound with a quivering Blaire in my arms, the usually robust atmosphere is smothered with despair. The elderly women who transitioned from whores to maids stare at me with concern while a snick of fear sets in the eyes of the men wary of what my reaction will be.

When I enter the foyer, my stern gaze connects with Erik, who is exiting the den. His pupils widen as his eyes drift between Blaire and me.

"The servants' quarters," I inform his questioning eyes. Erik nods when I continue, "Make sure he pays his penance, or I'll return and do it myself."

26

—————

BLAIRE

My eyelids slowly flutter open when the smell of fresh-cut flowers lingers through my nostrils. The silkiness of high thread count sheets caresses the weary muscles of my naked body when I pull my arms out of the comforter and have a leisured stretch.

When my tongue delves out to replenish my parched lips, a pinch of pain throbs in the corner of my mouth. My brows stitch in confusion when the tangy flavor of copper engulfs my taste buds. I jackknife into a half-seated position as memories of my attack two nights ago trickle back into my mind.

The events after the attack are nearly as hazy as my recollection of my Vegas trip three weeks ago, but there are portions I remember as clear as day—the way Rico carried me through the residence to an Escalade parked at the front of the stairs of the Popov residence, how he held my hair out of my face when my haunted memories became too much for me to bear, and how he wiped away every tear that fell from my eyes with nothing but remorse reflecting from his beautifully tormented gaze.

He guided me through my darkest days—when the blackness tried to swallow my life whole.

Now I need to do the same thing for him.

I've awoken in an empty room, but I don't need to feel Rico's presence to know he is close by.

I can sense him.

Gathering the bedsheets around my body, I walk through the large residence. As my feet pad down the long corridor with floor-to-ceiling windows, my eyes absorb the spectacular views I was too shocked to appreciate when we first arrived at this penthouse two nights ago. The dazzling view of the Las Vegas strip stretches as far as the eye can see. It looks so beautiful from this vantage point, concealing the cesspool of crime and inhumanity that occurs there every minute of every day.

Although I'm still shocked from the aftereffects of my attack and discovering that Rico once again saved my life, I feel the calmest I've ever felt. My heart has always known he was a good man, and now that my mind wholeheartedly agrees with it, the tiresome mind-versus-heart battle I've been enduring the past three weeks has vanished, leaving me free to pursue a relationship with Rico without fear of repercussion.

It's an invigorating feeling.

I walk past a ten-seater wooden dining table located next to a small but functional kitchen. The furnishings show this apartment is owned by a man with substantial wealth, but it still has a homey feel to it with a small range of potted greens and hand-selected artwork accenting the opulent decor.

With the rawness of my throat, I'm tempted to stop by the kitchen for a refreshing glass of water, but I continue walking past the double-door refrigerator without a break in my stride. My desire to find Rico is more fervent than the requests of my thirst.

My brisk pace only slows when I reach a high-glossed door on my left. Even though the door is closed, my intuition is telling me to stop. Trusting my gut, I place my hand on the door handle and push down. My perception of Rico's presence is proven dead on point when the deep timbre of his voice sounds through my ears the instant the door cracks open.

Mimicking the time I interrupted him in the private jet, he's sitting behind a wooden desk with a cell phone attached to his ear. His tone is clipped and authoritative until he notices me leaning in the doorjamb.

"*Kitten.*"

The urge to cry overwhelms me from the pain displayed in his one simple word. He shuts down his phone, shoves his chair away from his desk, then stands. I push off the doorjamb and race toward him. He catches me in his arms as the first lot of wetness splashes my cheeks.

"Shh, Kitten. You're okay. No one will ever hurt you," he promises, reciting the words he said to me on repeat the last forty-eight hours.

He tightens his grip around my shoulders, adding more of his spicy scent to the bedsheets curled around my shaking body. I push into him harder, needing more direct contact, wanting the warmth of his body to take away the shakes impeding mine.

My thigh muscles bunch when he tucks his hands under my knees, and he hoists me off the floor. He moves to a double-seated sofa in the corner of the room and sits down. The cotton material of his shirt catches my tears his thumbs miss. He holds me close to his chest and confirms his promise over and over again.

Once my tears have settled to a slight trickle, I lift my head off his chest and peer into his remorseful eyes. "What happened to Katie?" My voice is croaky but full of hope. I've barely been lucid the past two days as Rico guided me through my shock, so I've only just realized he could have answers to questions I've been asking for the last ten years.

Panic squeezes my heart when Rico shakes his head. "I don't know, Kitten. She was still in the van when it shot out of the alleyway shortly after you." He cups my jaw and stares into my eyes. "Just like you, I've been looking for her every day. I'll find her for you, Blaire. I'll never give up."

Call it blind faith, hysteria, or insta-love, but I know what he's saying is true. My heart knows it, and so does my mind. Just like me, Rico won't give up until he discovers what happened to Katie.

We sit huddled together in his office for what feels like hours, but it's more like minutes as I play the events of my life over the past ten years. Having Rico's arms around me makes me feel safe as if no one will ever hurt me again, not even him. It's a feeling I've craved for years but never thought I'd achieve.

He makes me feel invincible.

I draw myself closer to his chest and slip my hands under his shirt. I flatten against him, trying to mold us into one person. I need more, so much more of him, it makes it hard for me to breathe.

"What do you need, Kitten? Tell me what you want."

"You, Enrique. I need you," I reply in an instant.

He hesitates for a fleeting second with his confused eyes bouncing between mine, assessing my face for any signs of distress. I made a similar demand the past two nights, but with my mind still trapped in shock, he refused to oblige me.

That made me fall in love with him even more.

Upon failing to find a morsel of anguish on my face, he jumps to my command. I listen to the mad beat of his heart as his long strides follow the path I took thirty minutes ago. With every step he takes, the turmoil in his eyes changes, switching from tormented to yearning, not just to protect me but to satisfy me as well. A tingle of excitement rushes down my spine, stirring the heated ache between my legs.

When he places me on the bed, I lace my fingers through his hair and pull him down with me. He growls, concerned his weight falling on me may have added to the small collection of bruises mottled across my skin.

"You didn't hurt me. You never would."

The groan of concern rumbling up his chest is swallowed by my mouth when I seal my lips over his. I kiss him tenderly, expressing my gratitude for everything he did and still does for me. He returns my kiss with the same amount of rawness, accepting my thanks while also issuing his own. My chest puffs high, creating room for my swollen heart.

As we kiss, lick, and fondle each other, my fingers make quick work of Rico's clothes. I gasp in delight when I feel his warm skin on mine. The muscles in his back twitch when I run my nails down the length of his spine, tracing the swirly pattern of his tattoo. Then a squeal topples from my mouth when he flips us over, so I'm straddled on top of him—his seemingly favorite position.

Small white lights flicker in front of my eyes when his cock nestles at the opening of my vagina. I grind against him three times before resealing our lips.

The temperature in the room increases with every rock of my hips and stroke of my tongue. He suckles my bottom lip into his mouth before he playfully bites it.

I yelp and pull away from him, laughing. "No biting. What are you, an animal?"

He cocks his head to the side and arches a brow. "A tiger playing with his little kitten." His words come out so rough, they sound like a growl, and they send an electric current straight to my core.

The heated ache between my legs grows so exponentially, I'm tempted to scissor them together to ease the pain. I'm hot, wet, and needy.

A flare of excitement crosses Rico's heavy-hooded gaze as he watches me squirming above him, but he does nothing to ease the discomfort his seven little words created.

"Please..." I aim for my pleading word to come out strong. My effort is borderline.

A purr escapes my parted lips when Rico thrusts his hips upward, dipping the first inch of his heated cock into my aching core. I arch my back and snap my eyes shut, giving my body time to adjust to the spark scorching through my veins only his touch can produce.

When he notches in another inch, my pussy contracts around him, urging him deeper.

With his hands on my hips, carefully guiding me, Rico takes his time, delivering every inch of his cock in painstakingly slow installments.

By the time he fully sheaths me, my first orgasm is already lingering deep in my womb. Seemingly sensing my climax is close, Rico lowers his thumb to my clit, then flexes his cock.

With his thumb placing the perfect pressure on my clit and the devoted look in his eyes, my climax hits fruition.

I hold the gaze of the man who has saved me time and time again as the blessedness of an orgasm revitalizes my drained body. My pussy clamps around him as a cold sweat coats my skin.

My orgasm isn't the strongest I've had, but mentally, it's the most powerful.

"This. I don't want to see any other look on your face but this." He runs his spare hand across my pink-hued cheeks.

Once my pleasurable quivers ease, he moves his hand from my clit and places it back onto my hip. He adjusts my position so I am more open to him before slowly withdrawing his cock. The wetness of my climax soothes the sting from taking a man as wide-girthed as him.

I cry out in pleasure when he thrusts back inside me in one fluid stroke. He goes so deep, he bottoms out at my cervix.

After flattening my palms on his sweat-slicked pecs, I meet his thrusts pump for pump. My heart rate surges when my spread hand cannot hide my name swirled across his chest. Just like every time my eyes scan his name on my hip, a smile stretches across my face.

If any name belongs marked on my body, it's his—my savior.

When he ups the tempo of his thrusts, I gyrate my hips and contract the walls of my vagina.

"Again," Rico demands, his words breathless.

He screws me in a rhythm fast enough that my chase to climax matures with every thrust he makes but slow enough there's no chance he will hurt me.

That will never happen—physically or mentally.

Every grind of his cock increases the pressure building low in my pussy. As my coil tightens, so does my grip on his pecs. When he adds a flick to his pumps, I claw his chest, accidentally drawing blood.

Regret clutches my throat when a droplet of vibrant red blood follows the rivulets of sweat sliding down his torso. I snatch my hands away, mortified that I've maimed him. Rico seizes my wrist and places them back onto his chest before he continues pummeling inside me, seemingly unaware of the injury I inflicted on him.

Tears prick my eyes as the heaviness on my chest outweighs the climax brewing in my belly.

"No!" Rico shouts, startling me when a sly tear escapes my eye and trickles down my flushed cheek.

He glares into my eyes unyieldingly, his gaze so scorching, it dries my tears before they have the chance to fall.

Remaining hilted in me, he rolls us over so he is now on top of me. The weight of his body adds to the heaviness on my chest but in a soothing way. He stares down at me with sweat-damp hair falling around his face like a dark curtain before he slowly thrusts inside me. His pace is more controlled as is the storm clouding his beautiful eyes.

He gathers my hands with his and runs them over the little indents my nails made on his skin.

"These scars I'll wear with pride," he says, his truthful eyes adding to the strength of his statement.

He places my hand on his left shoulder, and while maintaining eye contact, he runs my hand down the side of his back, following the pattern of his tattoo.

My lips quiver when my fingertips run over a jagged surface hidden beneath his dark swirls of ink.

"Just like these," Rico continues, peering into my moisture-filled eyes. "Every scar holds a story, Kitten. As long as that story includes you, I'll wear them with pride."

27

———

ENRIQUE

Silk running across my tattoo, tracing the scars marking half of my back wake me. Usually, I repel from anyone touching the marks that converted me from a boy to a man, but this person isn't anyone. It's Blaire—my little kitten.

"I did this, didn't I?" Her voice is so soft it matches the beauty of her angelic face.

I remain quiet as her fingertips follow the grooves hidden by a tattoo designed specifically to conceal the mottled skin on the left half of my back. It isn't that I don't want to answer her question, but the story behind my scars has never been shared because it's simply that— a story. The scars define me as a man. They made me a man. A better man. Others see them as weakness, but I don't. They are my ally, a reminder of when an angel fell from the sky and brightened my miserably bleak life.

Ever since that day in the alleyway ten years ago, I changed. I stopped being the ruthless man who could claim a life without an ounce of remorse passing through me. I evaluated scenarios and formulated my own response, ensuring I was only instilling punishment to men who deserved to be punished. Cowards like the men who attacked Blaire and her friend.

I'm not saying what I've done over the past ten years has been lawful, it's far from it. I was raised in a life cloaked in darkness, yet my actions have been tamer than my counterparts.

Well, until it comes to protecting Blaire. I'll stop at nothing to ensure she is safe. Even throwing myself into the line of fire, I'll protect her until my very last breath.

"Did you get those scars from protecting me?"

"No, Kitten." My voice is low as I struggle to mask my deceit. "They were given as a reminder of my journey. A life I chose to live."

When she sniffles, I roll onto my hip, letting the bedsheet fall away from my body in the process. If I can use the unmarked side of my body to distract her, I will. I hate seeing her cry. I saw enough tears spill from her eyes last week to last me a lifetime. I don't want to see any more.

She peers into my eyes, her beautiful face looking tired and worn before her gaze suddenly drops. My cock goes from flaccid to painfully hard in an instant when a hue of pink adorns her cheeks. Even tired, nothing can take away from her natural beauty—plump pink lips, an angelic face, and eyes that imprinted my soul with just one glance.

Like I have every night we've shared a bed, I pull her into my arms and run my hand down her forearm. As much as my cock would love to spend a few more hours wrapped in her warmth, she needs rest. Although the small injuries she sustained in her attack have healed well the past week, she still looks exhausted.

Her tiredness is understandable. Struggling out of the depths of hell is a brutal fight for any person to battle. It was one of the cruelest battles I've ever endured.

Over time, her breathing levels out and the tightness in her shoulders relaxes. I wait a few more minutes to ensure she's sound asleep before pulling back. I like to watch her when she's sleeping. She truly looks like an angel trapped in the depths of hell. A place she doesn't belong.

I should have heeded the warnings screaming in my brain three weeks ago when we stood at the foot of the chapel we married in. I should have walked away from her without a backward glance. But I was stuck, stupidly believing that fate had brought Blaire to me, and she was a gift for changing my life full-circle. I was reckless, and now Blaire is suffering the consequences of my stupidity.

Although I love Blaire, I'd give anything to go back to that day and save her from this lifestyle. An angel doesn't belong living in the blackness of hell, no matter how much I want to keep her.

When my endeavor to sleep becomes unachievable, I slip out of bed, careful not to disturb Blaire. Sleep has never been an ally of mine. I'm lucky to get three to four hours a night. Usually, I'd stay awake for as long as possible before crashing days at a time, but I can't do that with Blaire here. I need to be on guard and alert. Luckily, when she is in my arms, my quest for sleep is more successful. That might have more to do with sexual exertion than anything.

After pulling a pair of trousers up my legs and throwing my shirt over my head, I exit my bedroom, carefully closing the door behind me.

<hr>

I've been working on some developments in my industry for nearly two hours when my awareness of Blaire's closeness activates. I lift my eyes from my youngest sister's kindergarten enrollment forms to the door of my office. Blaire has her shoulder propped against the doorway. Her face still looks restless, but unlike hours ago, the torment in her eyes has vanished. She's wearing a knee-length floral skirt and a three-quarter sleeve shirt I laid out for her earlier. She looks innocent and fuckable at the same time. Two complete contradictions.

When I push my chair away from my desk, a smile slowly creeps across her flushed face before she pads toward me. Completely unaware of her appeal, every step she takes naturally seduces me. I'm sure that over the years, other men have overlooked Blaire's natural beauty as they preferred women who dressed more scantily.

They were foolish men.

I relish Blaire's choice of clothing. It means only those privileged get the opportunity to see the skin her modest clothing hides. I just wish it wasn't fear that altered her clothing selection.

Blaire wasn't attacked in the alleyway because of her short, pleated skirt and midriff top she was wearing. She was attacked because she caught the eye of a man who shouldn't have been looking, a man who should have known better. Her clothing wouldn't have changed anything that happened that day. I know it, but Blaire hasn't worked that part out yet.

When Blaire reaches the end of my desk, I catch her by the waist and pull her to sit on my lap. Her faint giggle is replaced with a throaty purr when she discovers how her closeness soothed my hesitation and traded it for desire. The scruff on my chin scratches the silky-smooth skin on her neck when I nuzzle in close to savor her refreshing scent. Her smell reminds me of daisies on a dewy winter morning. Don't ask me how I know what that smells like, as I wouldn't be able to answer you, but that's what Blaire smells like, I'm certain of it.

"Why aren't you sleeping?"

She lifts her eyes from the paperwork on my desk and locks them with me. "I couldn't sleep without you."

My chest puffs high, beyond smug. Like my entire life, my relationship with Blaire has matured at breakneck speed. Although the expeditiousness of our relationship is daunting, I wouldn't change a single thing that has happened in the past five days. It has been perfect. *Almost too perfect.*

"I had a few things I had to take care of, but it can wait. You need your sleep." I brush a few stray hairs away from the pillow crinkle mark on the side of her face.

She screws up her nose. "I'm not tired." She drops her eyes to my desk. "What are you working on?" Her eyes suddenly rocket to the side as she gasps in a quick breath. "Is that..."

She doesn't finish her sentence. She just slides off my lap and pads over to a free-floating bookshelf on our left. My chest grows tight when she gathers the mandatory Las Vegas quickie wedding photo off the shelf and stares down at it.

I inwardly smile when she says, "Darn it. I was kind of hoping we had an Elvis impersonator as our celebrant." From the lowness of her tone, I can't tell if she's being serious or witty.

I stand from my chair and amble to stand next to her. As I peer over her shoulder at the photo, reality dawns on me. I should have known she was drugged that night. Her outward appearance is an exact replica as she stands before me now, but the sparkle of life in her eyes that held me captive from the moment she glanced at me ten years ago is missing. Her eyes are still bright and full of life, but they just aren't as vibrant as they are now. With how carefree her eyes look now, it has me wondering if I ask her to marry me again right now, would she?

"Hmm?" I ask when Blaire's soft voice breaks me out of my daydream.

"Who's this?" She hands me a faded Polaroid picture in a wrought iron frame.

I accept the photo from her grasp and roam my eyes over the lady I only remember in hazy memories. "That's my mom."

My mother's death is the main reason I returned from Russia three weeks ago. For years, I was told my mom died of a drug overdose. The older I got, the more rumors circulated throughout the compound that her death wasn't an accident, that a man took her life. A man well-known to the Popov entity. My father is an abhorrent man—a reincarnation of the devil himself—but he loved my mother. She was his Ангел, his gift from heaven.

When the rumors about the uncertainty of my mother's death reached the pillar of the Popov entity—my father—he awarded me free rein. I could use any means necessary to find out if the rumors were true. I used them, and I discovered the truth. My mother was murdered right under my father's nose. It was the ultimate betrayal.

People assumed that when I killed the man who strangled my mother to death, the story would end there. It didn't. Before his death, Col Petretti disclosed that members within the Popov compound knew of my mother's murder and hid it from my father. Spineless snitches who needed to be punished before they met with their creator. That's why I came home. To serve justice for the people who aided in my mother's death.

Well, I thought that was the case until Blaire fell into my lap. Just like ten years ago, our chance meeting ended with me saving her life for the second time, before I ultimately claimed it.

"She's very beautiful." Blaire runs her index finger over the frame to clear away the dust that settled on the glass during the six months I was in Russia.

I purchased this apartment months before I was sent to Russia by an associate of my sister's fiancé. Contractors related to the Popov entity have been remodeling the main living areas over the past six months. I was planning on surprising Blaire with news that the renovations had been finished the night she was attacked. I had planned on us moving in this weekend. I knew Blaire living in the Popov compound was dangerous, but I assumed my reputation would have been sufficient enough to protect her. Obviously, I was wrong. *Terribly wrong.*

"She looks a lot like your sister," Blaire murmurs, dragging me away from my thoughts. She nudges her head to a photo I placed on the mantel the day I drove her to the airport.

I'd never expected my investigations into my mother's death to lead me to my sister. With the number of mistresses my father has, I have many siblings, more than I could count, but Isabelle is my only true sibling. We share the same blood. Just like my memories of my mother, my memories of Isabelle as a child are best described as cryptic. But the instant I saw her, I knew she was my sister. She's identical to our mother in every way, except for her eyes.

I hated using Isabelle to seek the answers to our mother's death, but she was the only leverage I had. Although frightened, she was never in any danger when I kidnapped her to lure Col Petretti out of hiding, despite what Isaac claims.

Blaire places Isabelle's photo back onto the bookshelf before shifting on her feet to face me. "The picture of the little girl on your desk. Is she your sister... or your..."

A smirk etches on my face from the uncertainty in her voice.

She's even more beautiful when she's ruffled by jealousy.

"She isn't my daughter. That's my sister, Callie."

Relief fills Blaire's impressive eyes. "I wasn't sure. Her eyes are identical to yours."

A smirk etches onto my mouth. "All the Popov children have Vladimir's eyes. Scorched from the ashes of hell we were born in."

She screws up her nose. "Not all of you. Nikolai doesn't have dark eyes."

Jealousy slashes me open just from her mentioning Nikolai's name. Nikolai and I were close when we were younger, but after the incident in the alleyway, things changed between us. He became a shadow of our father—a ruthless and coldhearted man—where I strived to become my father's opposite.

"Who does Nikolai get his blue eyes from?" The confusion on her face grows. "I'm assuming the lady who called me a whore at brunch is Nikolai's mother?"

Knuckles popping is the only outward appearance of my anger at Blaire being taunted. It still kills me that I didn't stand up for her that day, but I was truly trying to protect her. Lessons were taught that day —no man will ever speak of Blaire with such disrespect again—not if they have a fondness for breathing.

"Yes, Oskana is Nikolai's mother," I confirm with a precise nod.

"And Vladimir is his father?"

I nod again.

"Are you sure?" Her voice is full of uncertainty.

She shifts her eyes to the photos on the mantel piece. "You said it yourself. All Vladimir's children have the same eyes." Her gaze drifts back to me, her demeanor more askew. "Nikolai doesn't. His eyes are icy blue."

I peer into Blaire's eyes and shrug, unsure what she is referring to.

"Oskana's eyes are green. Vladimir's are brown. The chances of them having a blue-eyed child are low, Enrique."

My heart rate kicks into overdrive as a million rumors I've heard over the years run through my head. "How low?"

Blaire holds my gaze, ensuring I can see the truth in her eyes. "Not impossible, but very unlikely. Both parents would need to hold a recessive blue-eyed gene."

Our conversation ends when a doorbell ringing shrills into my office. My head rockets to the side as my urge to protect Blaire kicks into overdrive. Only those in my inner circle know this apartment exists, so I find it surprising that someone is knocking on my door a little after six in the morning.

Blaire remains quiet as I gather my pistol from the hidden drawer in my desk. Although there are numerous ways you can kill a man without a weapon, a bullet is a lot less messy.

"Stay here," I instruct her before moving into the corridor.

Frozen in fear, she nods. My steps down the corridor are soundless. Not even Wolverine would hear me coming.

I release the breath I'm holding in when the faint voice of Maya squeaks through the door. Housing my gun into the back of my trousers, I unlatch the numerous deadlocks on my door and swing it open. Blaire must have recognized Maya's voice as well, as she arrives at my side not even two seconds later.

Blaire releases a deep sigh as she rushes to Maya's side. "Oh Maya, what happened?"

Fury blackens my blood when I discover what caused Blaire's skittish response. A nasty bruise circles one of Maya's brown eyes, her lip is busted open, and her wrists have welts only rope burns create.

As Blaire continues to fuss over Maya, I step into the hallway of my apartment building and run my eyes down the length of the hall. The exact set of eyes I'm expecting to see greet me from the end of the corridor. Erik.

Erik is my one and only confidant in the Popov compound. I trust him with my life. He shares the same sentiment. I duck my head back into my apartment to make sure Blaire and Maya are occupied before closing the front door behind me.

Erik meets me halfway down the hall.

"What was Maya punished for?" I question, recognizing the injuries Maya has suffered. I've seen them numerous times the past twenty-four years on Vladimir's mistresses. I'm just shocked to see them on Maya, considering she is his daughter.

Erik hands me a folded-up piece of paper. "Confronting the man responsible for this."

I dart my eyes between Erik's before lowering them to the piece of paper. My veins turn black when my eyes roam over the document.

"They orchestrated Blaire's attack?" I ask, already knowing his reply.

He nods.

I didn't even consider why Blaire was in the servants' quarters the night she was attacked. I just assumed her curiosity got the best of her. I never fathomed she was set up.

"Who did this?" My words come out strained, strangled through the fury pumping in my veins.

Erik hesitates before muttering, "Nikolai."

28

BLAIRE

As I pass Maya a handful of ice wrapped in a tea towel, a door slamming bellows through my ears. Rico moves down the corridor so quickly he's nothing but a blur of black. After placing Maya's half-drunk glass of water and a bottle of pain medication on the coffee table, I tell her I'll be back in a minute, then take off after Rico.

I find him five minutes later in the walk-in-closet of the spare bedroom. I can barely breathe when my eyes lock in on a black mat he has rolled out on the floor. Knives, tweezers, clamps, and other stainless-steel instruments I can't stomach to mention are stuffed into the pockets lining the leather material. It looks like an ideal setup for the creator of Frankenstein.

Sensing my presence, Rico lifts his head from the ghastly set of instruments in front of him to me. Tears pool when I see the blackness swamping him. I hold my hands out in front of my body and take a step closer, hesitant to approach him while he's stuck in the depths of despair.

Rico angrily shakes his head, urging me to stay away.

"Don't do whatever you're thinking of doing, Enrique. It isn't worth it. Maya wouldn't want you—"

"He set you up, Blaire," he interrupts, the pain in his eyes growing. "He sent you down to the dungeon so that monster could kill you."

I gasp in shock. "Who?" I ask through the bile lodged in the back of my throat, my stomach as squishy as my mind.

My stomach lurches when he replies, "Nikolai. He sent you the note to meet me in the servants' quarters. He orchestrated your death."

After rolling the mat up in front of him, he stands from his crouched position. I move closer to him, ignoring the threatening glare he is issuing me, cautioning me to stay away.

"He may have organized it, but it didn't happen, Enrique. You saved me."

"What happens if he tries again, and I don't hear your cries? What happens if I'm too late?" he roars, startling me.

I shake my head, sending strands of hair into my eyes. "That will never happen. You will *always* be there to save me, Enrique. You will *never* let anyone hurt me."

Fear greater than anything I've ever felt blazes through my veins when I see the pain in his eyes. My fear isn't for Nikolai or myself. It's for Enrique. He has walked so far into the blackness I don't know if I can drag him back out.

Ignoring my shaky hands, I curve them around his jaw, which ticks so furiously, it pounds against my palm. "Let me be your light," I plea, staring into his dark eyes.

He stares at me impassively, his whole demeanor off kilter.

"I need you, Enrique." I tilt my lips closer to his. "I love you."

My heart shatters when he murmurs against my lips, "Then you understand why I need to do this."

After pressing a brief peck to the side of my mouth, he stalks out of the room without a backward glance.

29

BLAIRE

I sense Rico's presence before I feel him.

The stranglehold that's been clutching my heart the last two days loosens when he slides into our bed and gathers me into his arms. I've been sick with worry the last forty-eight hours, but when I saw the grim look on Erik's face when he collected Maya this morning, my anxiety grew. I was barely functioning as it was, but the concern lining Erik's face activated a self-preservation mode I haven't used in years.

I've spent the entire day operating on autopilot. I haven't cried. I haven't spoken a word. I just sent numerous prayers to God for Rico to be returned home safe and uninjured.

Thankfully, my prayers appear to have been answered.

Blood rushes to my heart when Rico whispers in my ear, "Be my light, Kitten. I need my light." His deep voice is low and brimmed with uncertainty.

As I roll onto my opposite hip, the air is forcefully removed from my lungs when my eyes are met with his beautifully tormented gaze. His pupils are wide, his eyes the blackest I've ever seen them.

They look utterly soulless.

My shaky hands cup the edge of his jaw as I move my lips closer to his. My mouth swallows the deep sigh expelled from his lips when I seal it over his. He kisses me like he never has before—a heart-tethering kiss that soothes the nick in my bleeding heart. He savors every inch of my mouth in long, controlled strokes like I am truly his savior.

Within minutes, I go from the depths of despair to wildly turned on. Nothing is on my mind but enjoying every precious moment with the man in front of me—the stranger I married.

Only Rico's kiss can do that.

Only his touch can make me fully forget.

When his strong hands move up my back, a gathering of goose bumps follows their trail. As his tongue slides around my mouth, he hauls me so close to him that not even air exists between us. I gasp, incredibly aroused when the heat of his thick cock presses against my aching core. When his spicy scent lingers in my nostrils, the movements of my hands become needy. They are all over him, touching, stroking, and groping.

I can't get enough.

I'll never get enough.

When Rico grips my ass tightly, I purr, loving the bite of his fingers on my skin.

He stills my movements when I buck against him, soundlessly urging for him to do it again. "No, Kitten." His words are clipped and dangerous, adding to the excitement raging in the pit of my stomach.

"Please," I beg unashamedly. "You'll never hurt me, but I want to feel you, Enrique. I need to feel you. On me. In me. Everywhere."

Two lithe movements have my position switched from lying on my side to balancing on my knees. My bare ass is thrust high in the air, and the coolness of the air conditioning blows on the heated ache between my legs.

"You want to feel me?"

I nod a little overeagerly.

"Everywhere?"

"Yes," I beg with excitement evident in my voice. "Everywhere."

He slaps my ass—hard. I cry out as my knees slide across the crisp sheets, trying to lessen the furious throb between my legs.

Rico stops my efforts by cupping his hand over my pussy. "Ah, my naughty kitten. Saturated." His tone is lower than I've ever heard. "You like to be punished? You enjoy the roughness?"

I don't answer his questions. I've lost the ability to do anything but surrender to the man stroking my throbbing clit.

Blood rushes to the surface of my skin as the heat of desire blazes through my veins when Rico inflicts another perfect smack to my tingly backside.

"Not yet, Kitten. When you come, it will be on my cock," he demands, sensing the upwelling of desire scorching my blood.

The arrogance in his low tone bolsters my eagerness. Although he's always been a dominant lover, this morning, he has a blood-pumping edge of unbridled assertiveness attached to his natural dominance.

He adjusts the tilt of my hips, erotically exposing me even more. My race to climax speeds up when he runs his thumb up and down the folds of my pussy, coating it in my juices. His meekest touch has my orgasm precariously balancing on the edge of a very steep cliff.

When he removes his thumb from my pussy, he slides it across the puckered hole of my rear. I stiffen and crank my neck back to peer at him.

"You said everywhere, Kitten." He stares at me with a set of eyes I don't recognize as he adds pressure to his thumb circling my back entrance. My body puts up a protest to the intrusion. Although I've experienced a vast range of sexual positions with Rico the past few days, I've never participated in *this* type of situation.

Sensing my body's reluctance, Rico moves his spare hand away from my hip and strokes my clit with perfectly precise flicks. His thumbs roll in sync, stimulating both entrances in slow tantalizing swirls.

In no time at all, I once again become lost in the chase of a climax.

My eyes snap shut, and a jolt of pleasure and pain rockets through my body when Rico's thumb slowly slips into an area no man has been before. I press my damp face into the pillow to muffle the erotic purrs rumbling up my chest. While perched on the crest of orgasmic bliss, I wait for Rico's next move.

He does nothing.

He remains completely still.

I want to scream in frustration. Every muscle in my body is pulled taut, waiting for release. My skin is slicked with sweat, and his thumb is in an area I never considered an erogenous zone, but surprisingly is, yet he remains completely motionless.

Unable to stand the heavy tension weighing down my pussy, I push back and grind against Rico. My legs quiver when my movements cause his thumb to slip deeper inside me. I moan, then rock my hips again. My pussy grows slicker, loving the feeling of him in my back entrance while also knowing this is something I'll only ever experience with him.

"Good girl, Kitten. Now that you've stopped fighting, you'll enjoy it more."

I jerk violently when he slowly withdraws his thumb before slipping back inside. I've always thought this region was a no-go zone, but it's driving me wild. So much so, I rock back and forth, meeting the thrusts of his thumb stroke for stroke. My toes curl as the furious fire in my stomach becomes uncontrollable.

"Wait," Rico commands when the muscles in my rear clamp around his thumb.

"Please. Oh, god. Please," I sob, my voice exposing how close my orgasm is.

While keeping his thumb inside me, Rico mounts me from behind. I scream into my pillow when he slams his cock into my drenched pussy in one quick thrust. My nails dig into the sheets as I try to crawl across the sweat-damp mattress, needing to get away from the man pounding into me with brutal force.

It's too much.

I'm too full.

I can't handle both holes being assaulted at once.

"You wanted to feel me, Kitten. Feel me!" Rico grunts, his strokes quickening. "Take all of me. Everything I'm giving. Then you'll never forget what it feels like to be claimed by me."

I scream without shame as the most ferocious orgasm I've ever endured crashes into me. Rico's name is torn from my throat as my legs buckle from its brutal force. My earth-shattering climax steals all the strength from my muscles, causing me to sink deeper into the mattress with every vicious quiver my body does.

Rico uses his knees to spread my legs wider, so he can take me even deeper as I slump against the mattress, utterly exhausted. I don't notice the removal of his thumb from my rear until the sting of his fingers hits both sides of my waist.

He grips on to me before continuing with his furious pace.

"Can you feel me, Kitten?" He growls, his deep, vibrating tone adding to the tingling of my pussy.

A bead of sweat runs down from my drenched hair when I nod. "Yes. Everywhere. I can feel you everywhere."

He increases his thrusts, claiming every inch of me. "Don't forget what this feels like. Don't ever forget."

Distress grips me from the pain laced in his words.

"Never," I mumble through a sob. "I'll never forget."

I don't know why, but it feels like he's saying goodbye.

When I lift my head from the pillow and look back at him, pain shreds through my heart.

I'm too late.

He's already gone.

He has walked too far into the blackness, and I can't lure him back out.

30

While admiring how the fake diamonds sparkle in the bright lights of the vanity mirror, I run my hand down my silver drop earring while praying the fake smile I'll be wearing tonight will have the same effect. The Rico who screwed me into oblivion until the wee hours of this morning is the same Rico taking me out to dinner tonight.

I don't know why I agreed to go. I've spent most of my day in a trance, trying to work out where I'd gone wrong. Nothing Rico did to me this morning hurt me, but from the way he's been cold and distant, anyone would swear he stabbed a knife into my heart.

Rico walks out of a closet on my right, stealing my focus. "Are you ready?"

After ensuring the clasps on my earrings are fastened properly, I nod. A faint smile unwillingly sneaks onto my mouth when my eyes absorb the fitted dress Rico laid out for me in the vanity mirror. It's a beautiful mint green color, matching my eyes perfectly. The knee-length skirt ensures my modesty is kept, but the V-drop neckline adds a dash of sexiness I'm comfortable with.

When I spin around to face Rico, the heaviness on my chest doubles. He's wearing his usual attire of a black suit and light dress shirt, but he has paired it up with a tie that has green stripes in it—stripes that match my dress to perfection.

To outsiders, we look like an unbreakable couple. It's only the crippling pain in my heart stopping me from believing the same thing.

Rico holds my hand as we walk out of his apartment and down the corridor, but he's still distant. Even his hand is ice cold. Lust fires the elevator with electricity as we travel down multiple floors, but it isn't enough to ease the ache in my heart.

When the elevator car stops at the lobby, Rico places his hand on my back and guides me through the bustling space. People stop to stare, delighted at seeing such a beautiful man up close.

Ignoring the fascinated stares of numerous women, Rico walks us to an Escalade parked at the curb.

"Thank you," I mutter when he opens the door and gestures with his head for me to enter before him.

My breathing turns labored when my eyes lock in on a man seated in the seat across from me. Erik—Rico's lawyer.

"Why is Erik here?" I mumble to Rico, my voice unable to hide the sob sitting in the back of my throat.

As the events of the last time the three of us rode together play through my mind, sick gloom spreads across my stomach.

Rico remains quiet, acting as if he didn't hear a word I spoke.

Thankfully, the drive to the restaurant is short, but it's long enough for Rico's eyes to be completely swamped by blackness. His stern mask has slipped into place, and his composure is brutish and reserved.

Bulbs flash when I exit the Escalade and walk into the restaurant on Rico's arm. My knees clash together with every step I take as he guides me to the back of the bustling space. It is full to the brim with the same people who attended brunch last week. A lump forms in my throat when he strides down a very long table and pulls out the second chair at the end for me.

I cough, clearing the nervousness from my throat before whispering, "What's going on, Rico? I thought we were dining alone."

Before he can reply, the chatter in the room dulls to a faint hum. I don't need to look up to know Vladimir has entered. The ice-cold fear sliding through my veins is the only indication I need to know the devil is walking the gallows.

My brows knit in confusion when Rico stands from his chair and greets his father with a kiss on each of his cheeks. Then dread clutches my throat when Vladimir peers down at me and says, "Hello, Blaire."

Who knew two words could sound so threatening?

When I turn my gaze away, refusing to peer into the eyes of a monster, Rico retakes his seat, then intertwines our fingers together. With a wave, Vladimir gestures for the remaining attendees left standing to take their seats.

My chest rises and falls when I notice the two seats opposite Rico and me remain vacant, the seats that belong to Nikolai and his mother, Oskana.

Oh my Lord. What did he do?

My regular breathing pattern returns when a commotion at the front of the restaurant secures my devotion. Nikolai and Oskana are pushing their way through a gauntlet of paparazzi guarding the restaurant doors.

After slinging off her lightweight coat, Oskana saunters into the room with a vibrant smile stretched across her face. She places a kiss on the edge of Vladimir's mouth before taking the seat across from me.

My stomach winds up to my throat when I notice a range of fresh bruises on Nikolai's face. But even battered and bruised, his cockiness is still paramount.

After giving me a sneaky wink, he takes his seat next to his mother.

"*Shyulakas* don't belong here," Oskana snarls at me, glaring.

"Neither do old *sukis*," I fire back.

Nikolai coughs, only just holding in his laughter. Rico's response isn't as reserved. His beautiful laugh fills the silence when he throws his head back and laughs.

Oskana's furious gaze scorches into me before she shifts her eyes to Vladimir, soundlessly demanding justice for me calling her an old bitch, but Vladimir's expression remains unchanged. He looks as hideous as he always does.

Rico leans into my side. "Maya?" he asks so only I will hear.

I nod. It took me hours to explain the term I wanted to say to Maya, but we eventually got there.

A lazy smirk stretches across Rico's mouth as his glistening eyes stare into mine. His new carefree approach fills me with hope that he hasn't fully succumbed to the darkness surrounding him.

Sparks of the man I've fallen in love with shines bright when he places a kiss on the edge of my mouth. They combust low in my stomach when he says, "Never forget me, Kitten," against my lips.

Before I can respond, Rico stands from his chair, produces a gun from the back of his trousers and points the barrel at the small portion of skin between Oskana's green eyes.

Fear overwhelms me when over half a dozen men push back from the table and aim their weapons at Rico. I shake like a leaf, and my lips twitch, but not a peep escapes my mouth as I watch a series of stomach-churning events unfold before my very eyes.

My eyes bounce between Oskana and Rico when Rico sneers, "First, you murdered my mother, then you tried to kill my wife."

Oskana viciously shakes her head, sending tears rolling down her cheeks.

Rico's jaw tightens. "You can deny it all you like, but don't underestimate me. I know more than I say, think more than I speak, and notice more than you realize. It's usually the people you least suspect who are your biggest enemy."

Oskana's eyes rocket to Nikolai. Shock and disbelief are tainting her face. Nikolai keeps his gaze planted straight ahead, refusing to even acknowledge her presence.

When she returns her gaze to Rico, he demands, "Tell Vladimir what you did. Tell him how you scheduled my mother to meet with a monster because you knew she wouldn't give herself to him."

Vladimir sinks deeper into his chair as he drifts his eyes between Rico and Oskana. His eyes show his interest, but his composure remains calm.

"Tell him how you set her up!" Rico startles me with his loud voice. "You may not have strangled my mother, but you still *murdered* her. You knew she was Vladimir's *Ангел* and that he would never love you like he loved her."

Oskana's pupils widen, and the veins in her neck thrum, abundantly proving Rico's accusations are true.

"You killed my mother so he wouldn't leave you for her. Then you tried to do the same thing to my wife because you knew she would take your place!"

When Oskana shakes her head, Rico's index finger squeezes the trigger of his gun. My chin quivers when dots shimmer on the black material covering Rico's chest—the same area my name is inked on.

"Tell him!" Rico roars, not the slightest bit intimidated by all the guns pointed at him. "Tell him you killed his *Ангел*."

My eyes shoot in all directions when the men with their guns drawn step away from the table and move in on Rico. I'm full of fear but frozen, my brain incapable of formulating a way Rico and I can get out of this situation still breathing.

When Oskana's lips remain tightly shut, Rico says, "Tell him, or I'll kill your son." His voice is dangerously low—a stark contradiction to the one he was using ten seconds ago.

Oskana gasps when Rico turns his gun to Nikolai.

Unnerved, Nikolai holds his brother's gaze, his stature composed, his facial expression deadpan.

"Three... two... one," Rico counts down in a tone I've never heard before.

"Okay," Oskana shouts, her voice jittery. "Okay. I'll tell him. I'll tell him everything, but please, Rico, don't hurt Nikolai. Don't kill my son."

I pant, unable to secure a full breath when Rico ignores her pleas and squeezes the trigger of his gun even more.

"No!" Oskana shouts. "Have a heart, Rico. You have to understand. I had four late miscarriages. All boys. Then Felicia had you. A son. Vladimir's firstborn son." She shifts her eyes to Vladimir, who is still seated at the table, seemingly unmoved by the devastating events happening around him. "Felicia ruined everything. I wasn't going to let her take my place as well. I earned it. It belonged to me. I loved you. I still love you. But you only cared about her. Even when she wasn't with you, I could tell you were thinking about her. If that weren't bad enough, *her* son took the title *our* son deserves to have. Nikolai deserves to rule the Popov empire. Nikolai deserves—"

"Nikolai is not my son!" Vladimir's low tone sends a chill down my spine.

A collective sigh sounds around the room as my eyes rocket to Nikolai. He appears as unmoved as Vladimir was earlier.

Clearly, today is not the first time he's been confronted with this news.

My massively dilated eyes shift back to Vladimir when he stands from his chair and signals for his men to stand down. I inhale my first full breath in over ten minutes when the red dots shimmering on Rico's chest disappear.

"You knew?" Rico's voice is as shocked as his facial expression. My heart starts beating again when he lowers his gun to the side of his body.

Vladimir smiles a vindictive grin before muttering, "Yes."

A chair scraping across the wooden floor booms into my ears when Nikolai stands abruptly from his chair. "You knew? This whole time you knew?"

Vladimir doesn't need to answer his questions.

His callous grin tells the whole story.

"Then why did you pretend I was your son?" My heart squeezes painfully from the hurt projected in Nikolai's voice.

"Because you were the ultimate pawn," Vladimir snarls. "My plan was to nurture you into a born killer, then I was going to make you kill your father. It would have been the sweetest revenge for your mother's betrayal." Vladimir turns his lifeless eyes to Rico. "But Rico beat you to it."

Another collective gasp bellows around the room, the majority of it from me. I know Rico was forced to do some terrible things in his life, but hearing it firsthand is still shocking.

Taking advantage of Vladimir's honesty, Rico questions, "Then why did you sell Isabelle? If you loved my mother so much, why sell her daughter?"

My jaw muscle slackens when Vladimir's impenetrable mask momentarily slips, exposing a flare of emotion I was certain he didn't have. Remorse.

"Because I couldn't look at her without seeing your mother's betrayal," Vladimir spits out in disgust, his stern mask firmly back in place.

Rico shakes his head. "She never betrayed you! That's why Col killed her," he replies, his anger rising. He turns his eyes to Oskana. "Tell him how Col strangled my mother because she refused to give herself to him. Then tell him how you helped Col cover it up."

Oskana's throat works hard to swallow, but she doesn't attempt to refute Rico's claims.

Fear unlike anything I've ever felt blazes through my blood when I catch sight of the threatening glare Vladimir issues Oskana. "You said Felicia betrayed me! You said you saw it with your own two eyes."

"She played you for a fool," Rico sneers before drifting his eyes back to Vladimir. "Everything she ever told you was a lie."

Oskana's vow of silence continues, proving what Rico is saying is true.

"I did what you asked," Rico says, speaking to his father. "I brought you the person responsible for killing your Ангел. Now you need to keep your side of our agreement."

Time comes to a standstill when Vladimir and Rico undertake a heart-strangling staredown. It's steaming and full of palpable tension.

The red-hot anger lining Rico's face softens when Vladimir nods. "One wish," Vladimir says while holding his index finger in the air.

"Let Blaire go," Rico responds immediately, not even taking a second to deliberate. "Full sanction. She can't be touched."

I jump to my feet, my body responding before my brain has the chance to register an objection. I slip my hand into Rico's sweaty half-clenched fist and turn my eyes to Vladimir. "*Us*. Let *us* go. Rico meant to say *us*," I mumble, my shallow words barely heard in a room quieter than a graveyard at midnight.

I tilt into Rico's side when Vladimir swings his barren eyes to me. "That would be granting two wishes, Kitten, not one. Besides, Rico and

I discussed the terms of our arrangement. No mention of his pardon was ever debated."

Rico's hand tightened around mine when Vladimir called me "Kitten."

It firms even more when Vladimir steps closer to us, his demeanor frightening, his eyes lifeless.

After he finishes assessing every inch of my face in skin-crawling detail, Vladimir turns his desolate eyes to Rico. "I'll let your kitten go, full sanction, if you agree to the terms we discussed last night. You stop this nonsense of equity and go back to the man you were before your Ангел misguided you. Become a true Popov. One worthy of the name." Vladimir's eyes flick to me for a fleeting second when he sneers, "Ангел." When Rico remains quiet, Vladimir asks, "Do we have an agreement, Rico? Your soul to set your kitten free?"

I squeeze Rico's hand, begging him to deny Vladimir's demands. My heart falls from my ribcage when the conceited grin on Vladimir's face tells me he already knows Rico's answer.

He's going to accept his offer.

The thick stench of panic leeches from my pores when Rico does a single nod as he answers, "Yes. We have an agreement."

Fear spreads through me like brittle ice, shredding my heart with tiny, invisible nicks, then it suffers more damage when Vladimir smiles a grin no woman should ever have to witness.

It's the smile nightmares were created from.

"Good. Start with her." Vladimir jerks his head at Oskana. "If you handle this *situation*, your kitten will be given full sanction. You have my word, no one will ever touch her." A chill runs down my spine when Vladimir turns his evil eyes to Oskana and sings the rhyme Nikolai sang in the plane two weeks ago. "Send the angel to the devil's bed, hold her, cherish her, then cut off her head. She danced with Satan, and now she's dead, all for lying in the devil's bed."

Anxiety paralyzes me when Oskana remains quiet, absorbing Vladimir's cruel taunt without the smallest switch in her composure. I glare at her, urging her to fight, begging for her shocked state to lift, but no matter how much I stare, she maintains a dignified approach, either accepting her fate with quiet poise or stuck in the trance of denial.

After clearing the room with a wave of his hand, Vladimir turns to face Nikolai. "Are you coming, *son*?"

My astonishment grows when Nikolai dances his eyes between Vladimir and his mother before he stands from his chair and follows Vladimir out of the room.

Oskana appears as mortified as me.

My pupils widen to the size of dinner plates when Rico lifts his gun dangling at his side and points the barrel at Oskana. The veins in his neck are bulging, and his lips are set into a hard, determined line.

"Enrique, don't, please," I plead, my voice weak.

He glances over my shoulder for the quickest second, his eyes dark and bleak. "Erik, take Blaire back to Ravenshoe," he demands, his voice as lifeless as his narrowed gaze.

"No!" I scream when Erik attempts to pull me away from Rico's side. "This isn't you, Enrique. Don't do this."

"Take her now!" Rico roars, the vein in his neck protruding.

When Erik wraps his arms around my torso, I kick and thrash against him. Dread scorches my veins, but I fight with all my might, unwilling to give up. If Rico does this, I'll never bring him back. He will merge too far into the blackness.

"This isn't you, Enrique," I scream at the top of my lungs as Erik drags me across the restaurant floor. "You're not a monster. You were just raised by one."

The refreshing wind from the air conditioning does nothing to settle the sick fear creeping up my windpipe when Erik swings open the restaurant doors and drags me outside.

"Don't, Enrique! Don't do this," I yell with tears streaming down my cheeks.

"Don't forget me, Kitten," is the last thing I hear before the restaurant doors slam shut.

Then my heart shatters into a million pieces when a bullet being dislodged from a gun booms into my ears, proving there is no noise more devastating than the crippling sound of death.

31

One Month Later...

"Hey, you look nice," Lacey greets me when I walk into the kitchen of our modest two-bedroom apartment.

"Thanks." Smiling, I run my hands down my floral knee-length skirt, clearing away the invisible wrinkles I believe are in the dead-straight material.

Lacey puts an extra dash of vodka into the dirty martini she's mixing before pouring half of the contents into two salt-rimmed glasses. "You've got this, Blaire."

When she hands a full-to-the-brim martini glass to me, I nod, even though my heart is screaming *no she doesn't.*

"To getting my life back on track." I clink my glass against Lacey's.

She returns my gesture before running her hand down my arm in a comforting manner. "Two weeks doesn't equal a lifetime, Care Blaire," she replies, reiterating what she has said to me numerous times over the past month. "But even if it did, you've got this. Just remember what Dr. Avery taught you. One step at a time."

I try to issue her a genuine smile, but my heart isn't into it. Not yet. It's still struggling to piece itself back together after it was shattered into a million pieces last month. I thought I missed Rico the days following our Vegas quickie wedding, but it's nothing compared to my yearning for him the past month.

My heart is barely functioning, it's been so distraught. Like all people in mourning, my emotions have been put through the wringer. First, I couldn't stop crying. Then, I got angry, not just at Rico but also at myself for not being strong enough to pull him out of the darkness. Now, I'm carefully wading through the final stage of my grief —acceptance.

I only reached the acceptance stage half an hour ago. It's been such a longwinded process as my heart is trapped between a rock and a hard place. Half of it is yearning for Rico while the other half is stuck in debilitating confusion. My heart was certain it knew the real Rico—the man behind the veil he wore in front of others. But when news of Oskana's death circulated on every news channel in the country the days following my return to Ravenshoe, my heart began to wonder if it was duped by Rico's charm as badly as my astute brain. Did I misread him completely? Or is he more cunning than I ever predicted?

When I first arrived home, I vowed to keep myself occupied so I wouldn't stew over every nanosecond of the two weeks before our disastrous dinner date, searching for clues on where it had all gone so terribly wrong, but with Mr. Rodchester refusing to let me return to my teaching job until after the stipulated time Rico's men requested, I had no choice but to evaluate every second I spent with Rico.

Even after weeks of deliberation, I'm genuinely at a loss as to what happened.

The Rico who risked his life to save me ten years ago wasn't the same Rico I was torn away from last month. I know he can switch from night to day with a flick of his fingers, but I thought the days we spent together changed him. He felt responsible for my attack, but I truly thought we'd moved past that. I thought it made us stronger as a couple.

Obviously, I was wrong.

Lacey slings her arm around my shoulders and draws me in close to her side. "Come on, Blaire, just one night with no tears," she murmurs against my temple.

I nuzzle into her neck and inhale a large breath of her freshly washed hair. Lacey has been my savior this last month. Understandably, I arrived home a blubbering mess. Lacey said nothing. No reprimand, no lecture on my stupidity, she just held me while I cried until I had no more tears left to shed.

Most people don't understand the unique bond Rico and I formed in the two weeks we were together. They don't believe such a strong relationship could be achieved in a matter of days. I normally would have agreed with them until I met Rico. He has proven time and time again what I think I know isn't always the case. He made me see the bigger picture.

At times, it was beautiful.

Other times, it was hideously ugly.

That night in the restaurant was a combination of both.

I've encountered a riot of emotions the past month. It's been a truly challenging time, both physically and mentally, but Lacey is determined to guide me through the tumultuous storm battering my life. She's so strong-willed, she has forced me out of holey, food-stained pajamas for the first time in a month.

After ordering my heart into lockdown, I lift the martini glass to my mouth. My sole focus tonight is to push myself out of survival mode. Because as much as it kills me to admit this, Lacey is right. I need to start living again. I need to move on to the next stage of my life.

That would be a whole lot easier to do if I didn't have so many unanswered questions.

I chug down the entire martini in one hit, more than eager to get our girls' night off to a roaring start. Lacey arches her brow and eyes me curiously when I help myself to a second serving of the delicious drink.

"Taxi?" she queries with raised brows.

The smile I award her with this time is genuine. Normally, I'm the designated driver for our monthly dance-like-the-floor-is-on-fire get-togethers, but tonight, I need to let my hair down. I'm not saying I'm planning to get drunk, I just don't need to stress about whether two martinis would put me over the legal limit to drive.

It's lucky Lacey called a taxi.

Even with most of the alcohol in my system being pumped out onto the dance floor, there's no doubt I'm intoxicated. My words are slurred, my skin is a sticky mess, and I feel the most carefree I've been in the past month. If I'd known alcohol was the cure for the world's worst heartache, I would have started drinking the instant Erik dumped me onto the very plane that delivered Rico and me to Vegas only two weeks earlier. I don't know if that private jet is Popov-owned, but it was a cruel joke on a demented and twisted day.

After lifting my sweat-drenched hair off my neckline, I close my eyes and let the music overtake my body. There are attractive men as far as the eye can see, but I'm not interested. I'm here solely to wash away what's been one of the worst months of my life using nothing but great music and the vibrancy of a bustling environment.

Over the next forty minutes, that's exactly what I do. The pain inside my heart is still there, it just isn't as paramount as it is when I'm lying in bed with nothing but time on my hands.

Several songs later, the hairs on my arm prickle to attention. I flutter open my eyes and swing them around the space. It takes three long blinks for my eyes to adjust to the blinding strobe lights bouncing around the decadent space.

A smile curls on my lips when my heavy-lidded eyes absorb the area surrounding me. There's nothing as captivating as a group of cheerful faces having an enjoyable time.

Well, except one thing.

Nothing in the world is as captivating as Rico's beautiful dark eyes.

When the song pumping out of the speakers switches from a heart-thumping beat to a slow and steady pace, I head to the bar. On my way, I spot Lacey on my left, grinding her backside on a handsome dark-haired gentleman. Sensing my snooping stare, her dilated eyes lift to mine. I flash her a smirk, grateful I succumbed to her relentless nagging the past six days. She was right, dancing won't cure my heartache, but it's a great way to relieve tension.

When Lacey cocks her brow in silent questioning, I gesture that I'm going to grab a bottle of water. I wait for her to nod before continuing with my endeavor.

The smell of sweat on heated skin lingers in my nose as I weave in and out of the densely populated dance floor. With the club's popularity and it being a Saturday night, the floor space is crowded with sweaty patrons.

Just as my flat-soled sandal steps off the mahogany floor, my long strides freeze, closely followed by my heart. Although it was quick, I swear I saw a profile a thousand whiskeys couldn't erase from my mind. *Rico.*

Disregarding the twinge of pain hitting the middle of my chest, I push through the throng of sweaty bodies in the direction I saw him. When I hit the end of the bar I swore he was standing at, I stretch onto my tippy-toes and swing my head to the right before slowly drifting it to the left. The sweat slicking my skin amplifies when I spot a flurry of black ducking down the hallway where the restrooms are located.

Adrenaline surges my heart rate to a never-before-reached level.

The blaring music booming out of the speakers dulls to a hum when I enter the hallway. Due to the club being at capacity, the hall is lined with patrons waiting to use the restroom.

After wiping my sweaty hands on my skirt, I pace further down the hall. Once I've walked past the long lines, the vibrancy in the air shifts. My heart is still pumping, but it's more from fear than exhilaration.

I barely hold in a swear word when a clearly intoxicated couple stumbles out of a supply closet. They giggle loudly while smoothing their crumpled clothing. My wide-eyed expression watches them as they stagger down the hall. Once they become lost in the crowd, I gather my heart off the floor and continue my endeavor. I could be completely off the mark, but I'm operating purely on instincts, allowing my intuition about Rico's presence to guide my steps.

The further I saunter down the hall, the greater my perception of

Rico grows. Just as I take a sharp left at the end, my wrists are seized, and I'm yanked into a hidden nook on my right. The window-shattering squeal rumbling up my chest is suffocated by a hand when it splays over my mouth. I suck in deep breaths as I fight through a torrent of emotions bombarding me at once.

Joy.

Despair.

Hope.

It all smacks into me.

The tightness spreading across my chest weakens when I lift and lock my frightened gaze with a pair of eyes I recognize.

Colt.

"Jeez, Colt, you scared the living *hell* out of me." I breathe out heavily when he removes his hand from my mouth. He scared me so badly, the curse word screaming through my head nearly came out of my mouth.

The regret in his eyes grows. "Sorry, baby girl. I thought you saw me." He glances into my eyes curiously. "You were following me down here, weren't you?" Add his slurred words to the scent of alcohol on his breath, and it appears I'm not the only one who's been drinking tonight.

"No. I thought I saw someone I knew."

I lean out of the nook and peer down the corridor.

The hope thickening my blood thins. Other than a fire exit door at the end, the hallway is empty.

"You know me," Colt states matter-of-factly, dragging my attention back to him. The playfulness in his tone causes a smile to stretch across my face.

"Yes, I do know you, but I thought you were someone else. Did you see anyone come down here before me?"

Disappointment dampens my alcohol-fueled good mood when Colt shakes his head. "Only you." He taps his index finger on the tip of my nose. After dropping his finger to run it over my top lip, he murmurs, "You look good tonight, baby girl. You look happy."

Arching a brow, I retort, "I look drunk." *And heartbroken.*

"Then you should get drunk more often," he jests, his smile enlarging so his dimples become exposed. "Drunks a good look for you."

My brow arches higher. "Drunks?"

My heart rate I've only just settled down beats a little faster when he stammers, "I may be a little drunks myself. We're a couple of good-looking drunks. Especially you. You're a real pretty drunks."

Even though he's under the influence, Colt's compliment gives me back some of the confidence I lost while seeking Rico in a crowd. I can't believe the first time I've left my apartment in a month had me going on a wild goose chase. If that isn't already disturbing enough, finding out my perception of Rico's presence isn't as stellar as I first thought is another low blow to my already crippled ego.

Not wanting my foolhardiness to end my night on a sour note, I loop my arms around Colt's elbow and step back into the hall. "How about us two drunks go and get some water?" I pull him into the packed corridor.

"Water? Oh, no, is Ms. Cardigan-Wearing Williams back? I kinda liked the naughty Blaire better."

I elbow him in the ribs, pretending his snide comment didn't dent my pride. "I didn't say we would *only* drink water. We'll do shot for shot."

"Yeah! Shots!" He cheers, startling a group of girls in line for the bathroom.

As I guide a stumbling Colt down the packed hall, I ignore the pleas of my heart to peer over my shoulder. My heart truly believes it can distinguish the closeness of its mate in a crowded space, but I can't risk disappointing it. With how many cracks my heart has sustained the past month, that little nick of disappointment may completely shatter it.

32

When I stumble out of my bedroom a little after noon on Sunday I have a vicious hangover. It serves me right. I lost count of the number of shots Colt and I did by two o'clock this morning. As instructed, we did a shot of water for every shot of liquor we had.

For future reference, it doesn't have the same effect as glass for glass.

Lacey giggles into her coffee mug when she notices my disheveled appearance staggering into the kitchen. My heavy steps aren't just weighed down by the furious thump of my skull but also from the guilt I'm feeling. When I'm hiding in my room, eating crap and sleeping way too much, I never feel guilty. But waking up with overly exerted muscles from hours of dancing and my finger void of the heaviness of my platinum wedding band, guilt has made itself comfortable in the place my heart used to belong.

Last night, I pretended to be someone who wasn't heartbroken.

Today, I'm back to the miserable Blaire I've been the past month.

Lacey props her hip onto the kitchen counter then asks, "Coffee?"

"Please." I cringe when my tongue hits the roof of my mouth. It tastes like I ate roadkill for breakfast.

Lacey hands me a double-strength coffee before running her hand down my forearm. "You think you feel bad now, imagine what you'll feel like after Colt's self-defense class this afternoon."

I wince when the coffee burns my mouth. "Defense class?"

"Oh, no, does Care Blaire have a case of drunkenitis?" She laughs with a waggle of her brows.

While nursing my mug of coffee, I rack my throbbing head for the events that occurred last night. Although nothing is overly vivid to me, small fragments of Colt giving me an impromptu self-defense lesson in the lobby of our building crashes into my blurry mind.

"Twelve lessons?" I squeak out when the entirety of our night filters through my brain. "I agreed to twelve lessons?" The pounding in my head intensifies when my overly nasal voice bounces off the kitchen cabinets and shrills into my ears.

Lacey's broad smile expands. "Yep! And you were so eager you paid up-front." She nudges her head to the now empty swear container housed on top of our refrigerator.

With her fondness for profanity over the past two years, the swear jar was overflowing.

Now, only a few nickels remain.

After finishing my coffee, I shower and get changed. Three headache tablets have eased the furious pounding of my skull, but the niggling pain in my heart remains. The smile Lacey has been wearing most of the morning grows when I walk into the living room of our apartment wearing a pair of borrowed gym shorts and a crop top.

"How can you work out in these?" I mumble while digging the tiny shorts out of my backside and attempting to yank them down my thighs. "I can't even walk in them, let alone bend over."

Lacey laughs but maintains a quiet front.

Since my father raised me to be responsible about money and commitments, I will attend my self-defense class this afternoon. My dad's rules are simple. Don't ever buy something unless you intend to use it more than ten times a year, don't fall for quick money-making schemes, and never make a commitment you aren't planning to keep.

If I hadn't already paid for the self-defense lessons at Colt's gym, I might have attempted to back out of our agreement, but since my hard-earned money has already been handed over, I'll honor my commitment.

And if I'm being honest, I'm willing to give anything a shot if it will help ease the constant dull ache in my chest.

"Blaire!" Lacey snickers when I throw a super baggy shirt over my head, swamping the scandalously skimpy gym attire.

"I don't want to get arrested for public indecency," I argue before snagging my car keys off the coffee table.

She laughs but doesn't refute my claim. She knows as well as I do this outfit can't really be called an outfit. I swear my swimsuit has more material in it.

"Wish me luck," I plead before pressing a kiss to Lacey's cheek.

She returns my gesture. "You won't need it."

Nervous butterflies take flight in my stomach the instant I pull open the heavy glass door of M.S. Gym. The smell of sweat mingles through my nose as blood-pumping music filters into my ears. There's so much testosterone thickening the air, the environment has an invigorating feel to it.

A small smile cracks on my lips when I spot Colt in the corner of the room. He waves a greeting before finalizing his conversation with a blond gentleman working out on a leg press machine. I swing my eyes around the space, taking in the state-of-the-art gym. It's over two levels, and nearly every piece of equipment has a body attached to it. Whoever owns this gym must be pleased by the high attendance rate on a late Sunday afternoon.

My hand automatically darts up to smooth the frazzled pieces of my hair when Colt steps toward me. Colt is no doubt attractive—*not as appealing as Rico, but who is*—but that's not why I'm fluffing my hair like a woman fishing for a compliment. I've seen Colt shirtless numerous times, but not normally when I'm suffering the severe effects of a hangover.

I look like I've been dragged a quarter-mile under a bus.

Colt looks like he's just returned from being photographed for the cover of *Men's Fitness Magazine*.

I snort. He probably has.

"Hey, baby girl, you ready?"

Colt swoops down to place a kiss on my cheek. Even his breath smells fresh.

Not wanting to kill him with my skanky roadkill breath, I nod. "All right, let's get this show started."

With his hand on my lower back, he guides me through the gym. Numerous women's eyes track his every move, no doubt admiring the way the muscles in his cut arms flex with every stride he takes.

My disheveled appearance becomes even more apparent when I take in my female counterparts gawking at me in surprise. They are working out in body-hugging gym clothes, perfectly up-swept hair, and a full face of makeup. I don't have a speck of makeup on my face, my shirt is three sizes too big, and my hair is limp since it's still carrying the effects of the sweat-infused club last night. I look as wretched on the outside as I feel on the inside.

When he walks us into a room at the side of the gym, my heart rate kicks into overdrive. "Where is everyone?"

Colt closes the thick glass door, blocking the endorphin-pumping music blaring through the gym before shifting on his feet to face me. "Everyone?"

"For the defense class." My voice is as unsure as my facial expression.

He smiles a boyish grin that makes my pulse surge a little faster. My reaction can't be helped. Even hungover and nursing a broken heart, he has a wonderful smile.

"Everyone who needs to be here is here, baby girl."

I swallow harshly. "Umm... are you sure? There are only two people here. Me and you." I roll my eyes at the dimness of my voice. After squaring my shoulders, I straighten my spine and stand taller. "I thought I agreed to a self-defense class?"

"You did," Colt confirms. I wave my hand over the vacant room that's clearly void of any other gym patrons. My hand gesture freezes halfway when he says, "You requested one-on-one defense classes, Blaire."

I drop my hand to my side. "I did?"

"Yes, you did." He moves to a set of protective mats housed on shelves near the glass-paned window at the front of the gym. "And since you're a good *friend* of mine, I wanted to ensure you got the best instructor." He puts on a set of square black pads before spinning around to face me. "That means you get me all to yourself, baby girl, for an hour, three times a week, for a whole month."

My mouth falls open. I should have listened to the pleas of my brain. Shots are never a good idea. No matter how heartbroken you are.

As Colt walks back toward me, his eyes absorb my baggy shirt hanging halfway to my knee. "Didn't have any gym clothes to wear?"

Gritting my teeth, I shake my head. I hate lying, but with the way his eyes are beaming into mine like he wants to ravish me, I'll let my little white lie slide. It's funny. Before Rico, I would have done anything to have Colt looking at me like that. Whereas now, I want to go back to us being friends.

I wonder if my logic will change as the months continue to fly by.

Or will I never move on from Rico?

My heart squeezes. *I'll never forget him.*

Colt directs me to a section of floor that's covered with a bouncy material similar to a gymnastics mat. It's squishy and reminds me of a trampoline, and forces a genuine smile onto my face. I loved gymnastics when I was younger. Katie and I practiced our routines on the trampoline in her backyard for hours every weekend. That was what we were doing before our attack in the alleyway. Understandably, I haven't done gymnastics since that day.

Trying to keep my focus on the task at hand and not the burning hole in middle of my chest, I yank a hair tie off my wrist and secure my hair into a ponytail. "All right, let's do this."

Colt smiles a full-toothed grin while waggling his brows. I flinch and stumble backward when one of the pads covering his hands whizzes past the tip of my nose. Although the pad didn't connect with any region of my face, my first response is to drop to the floor and cower. Thankfully, I hold my ground even with ice-cold fear lacing my veins.

Panic wells in my stomach as the memory of my attack in the servants' quarters races to the forefront of my mind. I shift my eyes to the side, anticipating seeing Rico magically appear.

The pain shredding my heart in two amplifies when I fail to locate anyone next to me, let alone the man who promised to always protect me.

"Blaire." Colt's voice sounds distant. I blink three times in a row when he yanks off one of his pads and touches my cheek, drawing me back to the present.

When I see the confusion marring his face, I pretend my knees aren't clanging together. "Sorry, my reflexes are a little slow today. Probably shouldn't have drunk so much last night."

I can tell by the concern clouding his usually mischievous gaze that he isn't buying my explanation, but mercifully, he doesn't push the matter further. Colt is one of the people who doesn't understand my unique bond with Rico. To him, I was the naughty school teacher having a two-week bender in Vegas. He doesn't comprehend that I can barely breathe without Rico in my life.

"When the pads move in front of you, Blaire, you need to block them. Strike. Block. Strike. Block." Colt sweeps the pads across the front of me but at a slower pace than he used earlier.

"Okay." I breathe out slowly, my one word shaky.

Over the next hour, Colt teaches me basic self-defense moves. How to block a direct hit, how to execute an open-hand punch, and how even someone with my small stature has enough strength to throw a man Colt's size over my shoulder.

The last part of our training was theory, not practical. Since I had to fight the urge to flinch every time he grabbed me, he said we'd slowly build up to that level of training.

Although I was apprehensive when I first arrived, I did enjoy our one-on-one training session. Actually, I really enjoyed it. Colt took his time, never pushing me further than I felt comfortable, and for the past hour, my mind moved away from my heartache. That, in itself, is worth the burning ache of my weary muscles.

"I'll see you on Tuesday?" Colt asks while guiding me to the gym's main entrance door.

I swallow down half a bottle of water before nodding. "Wouldn't miss it. Thanks."

Forgetting we are at his place of employment, I kiss his cheek.

When a collection of wolf-whistling and catcalls sounds through my ears, my cheeks turn a hue of pink.

"See you Tuesday," I mumble before spinning on my heels and fleeing the gym.

Lacey's head lifts from her laptop balancing on her knees when our front door gives out a creak, announcing my arrival. "Hey, how'd you do?"

She shuts her laptop screen as I throw my keys onto the entry table. "Good. Although I think my muscles might have a different opinion tomorrow."

"As my father would say, 'at least you know you're alive.'" She places her laptop on the coffee table and stands from her seat. "There's a registered letter on the kitchen counter for you."

My lips quirk. "On a Sunday?"

Lacey shrugs. "Might be important."

After grabbing a bottle of water from the refrigerator, I lift the envelope off the counter. The heaviness Colt's workout cleared off my chest comes steamrolling back in when I see the return address—The Office of Erik Monstrateo.

I dump my water bottle onto the counter so hard it falls over, sending water dribbling down the cabinets of our modest-size kitchen.

I don't bother cleaning up the mess. I'm too curious as to what is in the envelope to do anything.

This is the first contact I've had in a month from anyone associated with Rico.

Sensing my rattled composure, Lacey joins me in the kitchen. I register her lips moving, but I don't hear a word she's speaking as I tear open the envelope and scan my eyes over the heavily documented forms inside it.

Any pathetic attempts I made at healing my heart the past month come undone when I read the title of the forms—Petition for Dissolution of Marriage.

"He's divorcing me," I mumble through a sob. "Rico filed for divorce."

Just like the day I arrived home a little over a month ago, Lacey cradles me in her arms and holds me until I have no more tears left to shed.

33

When my back hits the mat with brutal force, I gasp in a shaky breath. Pain rockets through my body, but instead of cowering away from it, I embrace it.

Lacey's dad is right—feeling pain reminds me I am alive.

Ignoring my winded composure, I crawl onto my knees and lift myself from the floor on a shaky pair of legs.

Colt is standing across from me. His eyes are remorseful, but his grin is arrogant. "Get your head in the game, Blaire. We've done this routine every day for the past month, and you're still not doing it right. An attacker won't wait for you to get your balance. You have mere seconds to escape his clutch."

The words Colt speaks are way too familiar, but I nod anyway, pretending his knowledge is informative.

I know far too well that seconds can feel like hours when you're attempting to escape the clutches of an attacker.

"Let's do it again."

I run a towel over my face, removing the beads of sweat rolling down my cheeks before turning my back to Colt. We've continued our self-defense classes as agreed upon the past month, except I increased the number of lessons from three a week to seven. The burn my muscles felt the days following Colt's training session was the only thing reminding me I was alive.

Soon to be divorced, but alive, nonetheless.

If my muscles weren't burning from the exhaustive activities we did that afternoon, I may have never crawled out of bed to soothe them with a long soak in a tub.

Although I was served divorce papers a month ago, I still haven't signed them. Don't ask me why as I wouldn't be able to answer you. Lacey placed them on the denial shelf in my room the day I received them. I haven't touched them since. Avoidance isn't the solution for any issue, but when you're running on empty, you use anything you can.

My mind snaps back to the present when Colt suddenly grabs me from behind. Even though my first thoughts go to panic, my body reacts according to the lessons he's been teaching me for the past four weeks. I jam my heel into his toes before inflicting a brutal elbow to his ribcage. I throw my head back so it connects harshly with his nose before seizing his wrist with my shaking hands. A long, guttural moan tears from my throat when I pull down hard on his wrist and attempt to throw him over my shoulder.

My pupils widen when Colt lands on his back with a sickening thud.

Pushing aside the desire to scream out in victory, I straddle his hips and throw a set of fake jabs into his face. When he flops his head to the side, announcing defeat, I can no longer hold in my excitement.

"I did it!" I squeal loudly, throwing a fist pump into the air. It has taken me over a month to perfect that move, but Colt is one hundred percent muscle, so it's a feat I'll celebrate.

Colt pokes his index finger into my belly. Even it isn't as squishy as it was last month. "You did, baby girl. I'm so proud of you."

"I don't deserve all the credit." I roll off him. "I have a wonderful teacher."

My eyes squint when the overhead fluorescent lights blind my vision.

When I twist my head to the side, my nose screws up. The sky is completely black.

"Did our session run over?" I scan my eyes over the room, seeking any type of time-telling contraption. Normally, our sessions run until seven, but with the blackness of the sky, it seems a lot later than that.

"Yeah, around an hour. But I could tell you were close to mastering the move, so I didn't want to break your focus." Colt climbs onto his feet before extending his hand in offering.

"Only you could make an hour of torture sound like you're doing someone a favor."

Colt laughs. "Learning how to protect yourself isn't torturous, baby girl. Besides, other than one other strenuous activity, exercise is the best way to relieve tension."

"With how much I'm sweating, I'm seriously considering taking up the other option you're offering."

My pupils widen when the entirety of our combined statements smack into me.

Did I just flirt with him?

Although Colt and I have spent a lot of time together the past month, we've never flirted the way we did before my trip to Vegas. Colt has maintained a professional front during our lessons while I kept my heart in lockdown mode.

My theory is proven to be dead on point when Colt's eyes flare with excitement. The air is rife with muggy sweat, but a new scent slowly streams through my nose.

My pulse quickens when I realize what the smell is. It's the unmistakable aroma of lust.

I stand still, rendered motionless with alarm and excitement as Colt slowly prowls toward me. My heart is begging for my feet to move, to walk away before I lose the chance. My brain—it's completely switched off, deciding it's no longer strong enough to continue the vicious battle it's been fighting against my heart the past four months.

When Colt cups my face, I shockingly lean into his embrace. Even with my heart still debilitated from losing Rico, it wants Colt to take away its pain.

Maybe he can force me to forget memories that both haunt and excite me?

His lips catch my pant when he seals his mouth over mine. Just like I knew it would be, his kiss is enthralling and sets my pulse racing. He smells manly and tastes like the energy drink he was guzzling down earlier.

When he cups my thighs, my legs instinctively lift and wrap around his waist. A husky moan seeps from my lips when the hard ridge of his cock rubs the ache between my legs. Although my outfit is more modest than the clothes Lacey lent me last month, they still expose a scandalous amount of skin.

As he walks us toward the locker rooms, I grind myself along the long length of his stiffened shaft. From what I can feel between two layers of gym pants, I can happily testify that his nickname is very fitting.

With the late hour, the gym is empty. Not that I'd care either way. I'm too entranced by the way Colt's skillful kiss is breaking through the negativity surrounding me to care if we have an audience.

When Colt reaches the locker rooms, he places me on my feet. I rest my back against the steel lockers that line the walls of the modern space as I gasp in shocked breaths.

The coolness of the steel gives relief to my overheated skin while the intoxicating scent of manly body wash adds to my excitement.

"Fuck, baby girl, I knew your mouth would taste good, but I had no idea," Colt murmurs while rubbing his thumb along my top lip.

I slant my head to the side, exposing my neck to his mouth when he trails his lips along my jaw. As he suckles on the sensitive skin, my hand drift across his midsection.

His throaty groans send a thrill of excitement down my spine, so I increase the exploration of my hands.

When he squeezes my breast through my shirt, a purr rumbles through my parted lips.

My eyes snap open at the same time my heart constricts. Gloom spreads through me when the memory of why Rico called me Kitten slams into my hazy mind.

I snatch my hands away from Colt as guilt overwhelms me.

Sensing the sudden shift in my demeanor, he stops lathering my neck and inches back.

"I can't," I barely mumble when his confused eyes bounce between mine. "I'm sorry for leading you on, but I can't do this."

I adjust my disarrayed clothing while making a beeline for the door.

"Blaire, wait!" Colt shouts, his voice rattled with anxiety.

I pretend like I can't hear him as I charge onto the packed sidewalk.

People eye me with curiosity as I weave past them, but thankfully, they don't approach me. I don't know how I'd react if they did. I've never behaved so erratically before, but since I married Rico, my emotions have become a devastating rollercoaster ride with awe-inspiring highs and life-altering lows.

A logical reason for my pendulous moods becomes evident when my brisk strides down the sidewalk have me scrambling past a drugstore. My frantic pace slows to the speed of a tortoise when a sign blowing in the refreshing fall wind catches my eye.

Are you trying to get pregnant?
Talk to one of our specialists about the latest range of prenatal vitamins.

"No," I mumble to myself as my brain frantically tries to recall the last time I had my period.

My heart rate speeds up, and my palms grow damp when I fail to recall having a period since my trip to Vegas.

In a trance, I stumble into the drugstore and buy one of each pregnancy test on the shelf.

"No," I mutter for a second time when the test strip I've just peed on in the public restroom turns the color of Nikolai's eyes, ensuring there's no way I can deny the results.

Oh. My. Lord.

I'm pregnant.

34

"I'm good, thanks, Dad. How are you guys doing? Are you enjoying your trip?"

My dad sighs happily. "It's wonderful, darling. You should consider traveling yourself. Do it while you're young enough to enjoy it."

Smiling, I accept my order of a rye-crusted peanut butter and jelly sandwich from a pretty lady serving behind the counter of my local bakery.

"You're sixty, Dad. You're not even close to being too old to travel." I issue a silent thank you to the bakery employee before walking outside.

My dad chuckles. "True. Probably best to get as much traveling in as we can now before we get laddered down with grandbabies."

Pain strikes the middle of my chest. "Yeah, sounds like a good idea," I push out through the tightness wrapped around my throat.

My dad has made similar jokes over the past three years. They never hurt until today. The handful of positive pregnancy tests I collected two weeks ago have been placed on the denial shelf in my room right alongside the divorce papers I still haven't garnered the strength to sign.

If I'm being honest, I'll admit I've been sitting on the denial shelf myself for the past two weeks.

When I first went home from the drugstore, dazed and confused, I had every intention of sitting down and working out what I was going to do about my *situation*. My good intentions were left for dust when I realized I didn't have a way of contacting Rico. I don't have his cell phone number, private address, or any personal information whatsoever.

So, like all good exes, I stalked him on social media.

I found nothing.

Rico Popov is practically a ghost.

I've called the number supplied with our divorce documentation a minimum of three times a day for the past two weeks. Either Erik is avoiding me as skillfully as Rico, or his voicemail service provider isn't passing on my messages.

After exhausting all avenues, I went about my day-to-day life. I've been forcing myself to pretend everything is fine. I've started teaching again. I went to the movies with Lacey twice last week, and I even apologized to Colt for running out on him two weeks ago.

To everyone surrounding me, I seem to have resumed my normal pre-Rico existence. It's just the empty feeling in my chest stopping me from believing the same thing.

Exhaling a deep breath, I push my phone closer to my ear. "Listen, Dad, I have something important I need to tell you and Mom."

"I'm listening, honey," my dad replies.

I swallow away a lump in my throat. "I'm..." My brows stitch when my eyes lift from the ground and I see a profile I'd never forget in a million years.

"I'll have to call you back," I stammer out to my dad.

Not giving him the chance to reply, I disconnect my call and step closer to the gathering of people mingling around a dark-colored SUV. My heart is walloping against my ribcage, and nervousness slicks my skin with sweat, but I keep moving forward, more determined than ever.

"Katie?" My one word is unable to hide the hope in my voice.

When the lady with hair as molten as lava cranks her neck to the side for the quickest second, I take a step backward. *It's her.* I know it is.

It wouldn't matter how many decades slip by, I'd never forget her steely blue eyes and turned-up nose.

When I attempt to close the distance between Katie and me, two burly men wearing stained jeans and misbuttoned shirts step into my path. Even frightened at their standoffish composure, nothing can dampen my eagerness. I stomp on one of the brute's feet and sidestep the second man before rushing to Katie. My movements are so agile, I slip by the two men before they have the chance to formulate a reaction.

"Katie!" I call out again when a man with platinum blond hair and a wonky nose hurriedly guides her into the back of an SUV idled at the curb.

Dust kicked up from the roadside burns my eyes when the driver of the SUV slams his foot on the accelerator and dangerously merges into the heavy flow of traffic surrounding us.

Ignoring the fear spurring on my furious pulse, I dart into the street and signal for a taxi. Thankfully, with it being midafternoon, my request is filled remarkably quick.

I crawl into the back seat of the cab and instruct the driver to follow the dark SUV. As I fasten my seat belt, I turn my eyes back to the two men who accosted me on the sidewalk. The crazy beat of my heart weakens to a gallop when I fail to notice them anywhere.

Over the next ten minutes, the taxi driver follows the SUV through the streets of Ravenshoe, going from the newly built-up areas to a side of town that isn't as well maintained.

"Don't get too close," I instruct the driver while touching his shoulder. My shaky hand ruffles the collar on his crisp white dress shirt. "I watched reruns of a seventies-era cop show with my dad for years. Even back then, the biggest mistake the person tailing made was announcing their interest."

The taxi driver tightens his grip on the steering wheel before nodding. His eyes are as wide as mine, but he has an edgy grin stretched across his face like he appreciates the unexpected action I've forced into his life.

"Pull over here," I request the taxi driver when the SUV stops in front of a poorly lit nightclub.

After scanning my eyes around the less-than-stellar surroundings, I shift my dilated gaze to the cab driver. "Can you keep the meter running?"

Relief engulfs me when he nods without a moment of hesitation.

After handing him a selection of bills from my purse to express my appreciation, I exit the cab and walk toward the club I saw Katie and the blond-haired man entering. My legs wobble with every step I take, but my poise is determined.

As I walk past a group of men eyeing me with zeal, I give myself a mental pep talk that I'm stronger than I've ever been and that I've got this. *I hope.*

I clutch my purse close to my chest when my goody-two-shoes outfit gains me the attention of a large beast of a man guarding the nightclub doors. He takes a few moments running his eyes over my body before he lifts his hardhearted gaze to my massively dilated eyes.

With a belligerent grin, he opens the cracked wooden door for me. I force a neutral expression onto my face before walking into the premises like I've always belonged here.

Clearly, I don't belong here.

Considering my clothing has ten times more material than every scantily dressed woman mingling in the dingy club, I stand out like a sore thumb. I look like a kindergarten teacher walking into a biker's bar.

I get eyeballed by people with every step I take, but I continue with my mission, not willing to wait until I've built up enough courage to tackle this task head-on.

It's taken ten years to find Katie, so I can't give up now.

My steps become shaky when a dark-haired man in a booth on my right lifts his chin, inviting me to join him. I shake my head before changing the course of my direction. My wobbly steps come to a dead halt when the strobe lighting shackled to the roof bounces off Katie's vibrant hair.

Tucking my clutch under my arm, I rush toward the fiery redhead.

"Katie," I call out, fighting hard to raise my voice above the horrid techno music booming out of the speakers.

When I reach the redhead, I grab her by the shoulder. Disappointment smashes into me when she turns around to face me. Her eyes are brown in color, and her face lacks Katie's turned-up nose.

"Sorry," I apologize to her annoyed expression.

When the unnamed redhead returns to dancing with her friends, I roam my eyes around the space, seeking any indication of which direction Katie went.

I freeze when my eyes lock in on a figure moving quickly toward me. Then blood roars to my ears as the man whose foot I stomped on thirty minutes ago briskly strides toward me. His steps are unhindered as everyone surrounding him moves out of his path when they see him coming. His lips are set in a hard line, and his nostrils are flaring.

My brain screams at me to run, but I instinctively loosen my muscles as my body prepares to assert the maneuvers Colt has been teaching me for the past six weeks.

Just as the large brute grabs ahold of my forearm, a gun being fired shrills through the filled-to-capacity club. Panic overwhelms me as patrons of the club scramble, pushing and shoving past me as they scamper to get out of the firing zone. I stand frozen, unable to move out of fear. Flying fists I've learned to dodge. Bullets, though, I don't stand a chance against them, and neither does my baby.

My fear switches to confusion when my eyes lock in on my attacker lying in the middle of the now-isolated dance floor. His face is scrunched. His eyes are tightly shut. While muttering obscenities under his breath, he holds his right knee with both his hands. From his squirming movements alone, I can tell he's in an immense amount of pain.

The thump of my heart turns wild when I notice blood seeping between his interlocked fingers.

With my heart dropped out of my ribcage, I shift my eyes to the direction the smell of gunpowder is coming from. I gasp, beyond shocked, when I spot the cab driver near the club's entrance with a gun braced in front of his body. He lifts his right hand to his mouth and mumbles something into the sleeve of his white dress shirt before he houses his gun into a holster wrapped around his waist.

My eyes grow wider with every stride he takes toward me. "We need to leave before the authorities arrive." He slings his arm around my shoulders and drags me toward the exit. Panic rages in my stomach when I recognize his accent.

He's Russian.

"Who are you with?"

My eyes frantically shift in all directions, soundlessly requesting aid from the people gawking at me with a snick of fear in their eyes. When my silent pleas fail to secure any assistance, I lift my eyes back to the man beside me.

"I have full sanction." My words are hoarse, strangled by dread.

Acting like he can't hear a word I'm speaking, the unnamed man ushers me to his taxi idling at the curb in front of the club. After opening the back passenger door, he places his hand on top of my head and assists me inside. His eyes scan the premises as he slips behind the steering wheel and lurches the cab into the heavy flow of traffic.

My shocked state amplifies when I notice the taxi identification hanging on the glass partition doesn't match the man driving. The picture resembles a man in his mid-sixties with a receding hairline and a round tummy. The man driving has slicked-back black hair, a fit body shape, and couldn't be older than thirty.

"Who do you work for?"

When he fails to answer my question, I keep my eyes planted on the rearview mirror as I lift my shaky hand to the door handle. Upon discovering the door is locked, dread curls around my throat, but I refuse to succumb to it.

I've spent the last ten years of my life on high alert, always trying to spot the bad guy in a crowd, but the fear I've lived with the past ten years is nothing compared to the broken look Katie's eyes had when she glanced at me for a fleeting second.

I need to do this for her. I must fight through my fear if I want any chance of finding her.

When the taxi pulls into a derelict building on the outskirts of town, the driver exits the vehicle and walks around to my side of the car. Because he's too busy sheltering his eyes from the rapidly setting sun, he fails to notice me adjusting my position.

The instant he opens the back passenger door, I wildly kick out my leg, smashing my running shoe into his nose. When he stumbles backward, I scamper across the seat and lurch out of the taxi. I complete the maneuver Colt has demonstrated to me time and time again when the unnamed man wraps his hand around my ankle.

Adrenaline surges through my veins when I execute the move to perfection, not only disarming myself from my attacker but adding another kick to his already bruising face.

After scanning the area for a suitable location to hide, I charge toward the derelict building. It resembles a warehouse I've seen in many horror movies, but it's the only place that will shelter me while I work out my next move.

Gravel kicks up around my feet when I slide behind the rusted framework at the side of the warehouse to hide.

"Dammit!" I curse when I turn my eyes back to the taxi and notice my purse on the back seat. "There goes my chances of calling for help," I mumble to myself.

When my assailant gingerly rises from the dirty ground he's writhing on, I scuttle further into the shadows. My heart leaps out of my chest when I crash into something firm—something that feels distinctively like a broad set of thighs.

Using the adrenaline pumping into my veins to my advantage, I leap to my feet and take off running for a cracked-open door to the warehouse. I make it halfway across the leaf-riddled concrete before my wrist is seized, and I'm yanked backward.

Spinning around, I execute an open palm to the nose technique before bracing myself in preparation to knee my attacker in the balls.

I inhale a sharp breath when I lift my eyes from the cracked concrete to my attacker. With the sun setting behind a low-hanging cloud, most of my assailant's face is hidden, but there's enough light illuminating from the warehouse for me to recognize one distinct feature—a pair of dark and beautifully tormented eyes.

"Enrique?" I query, my mind spiraling, unable to differentiate between the past and the present.

I maintain my braced approach, prepared to strike at any moment when the shadowed figure takes a step closer to me.

My brave façade of the past two and a half months crumbles when the deep rumble of "Kitten" sounds through my ears from a voice I immediately recognize.

35

"Sorry," I apologize for the fourth time the past thirty minutes when I catch the curious stare of the man I kicked in the face—twice!

He continues holding a wad of tissues to his bloody nose as he talks to Erik in the corner of a dingy office in the back of the warehouse.

Ignoring the way every hair on my body is bristling, I move to stand next to Rico. He's shuffling through a range of surveillance photos of Katie displayed across a table. He's barely spoken to me for the past thirty minutes, but I've felt his heated gaze on me the entire time.

I've spent the past half an hour struggling to grasp the reality that the man in the taxi is an *associate* of the Popov entity and that he's been tailing me for the past two months to ensure Vladimir's request for full sanction was fulfilled.

I don't know if that means Rico is aware of the kiss Colt and I shared two weeks ago or not, but I'm not game to ask. And, in all honesty, it isn't an appropriate time to question if my soon-to-be ex-husband suffers from the same jealousy issues that plague me.

Even with my body acutely aware of every move Rico makes and my brain begging for the chance to have some of its unanswered questions resolved, my focus must remain on Katie. I've waited for this opportunity for ten years, and I can't risk another ten years passing because my heart yearns for an unobtainable man.

"It is her, isn't it?" I ask Rico as my eyes roam over the large selection of photos of Katie.

When Rico and I reach for the same photo, our fingers connect. I gasp in a sharp breath when his meekest touch sends a surge of electricity up my arm. Even after two months apart, nothing has changed. The vibrancy between us is so intense, it's electrifying. I know Rico can feel it too. The stern mask he wears in front of others is still in place, but I witness the quickest flare of emotion spark his eyes from our slight touch. He appears as helpless as I am in this volatile relationship.

After coughing to clear his throat, Rico lifts a surveillance image of Katie being clutched firmly by the blond-haired man I saw pushing her into the SUV earlier before nodding. "We've been tracking Katie the past month, waiting for an appropriate time to get her out. With the contacts I have in this area, it's an ideal time for my crew to move in."

Some of the little nicks on my heart heal when he locks his beautifully tormented eyes with me. "I promised I'd get Katie back for you, Blaire. I'm going to keep my promise."

I exhale a relieved breath, making the weight on my shoulders ten times lighter in an instant. "When can we do that?"

Rico's heavy brow slants. "There's no *we*, Kitten. You're *not* a part of this team."

I balk like I've been physically slapped. Although I could construe his statement as solely referring to Katie's situation, the raging storm in his eyes doesn't relay that.

"We..." Rico gestures his hand between Erik and himself, "... will get Katie out tonight. You're going home with Brent."

"No!" I shout, my reply quick and resolute. I cross my arms over my chest and lock my eyes with Rico. "Katie is my friend. I put her in this situation, so it's my responsibility to bring her home."

"No, it isn't." His loud voice bellows through the isolated warehouse, gaining him the attention of numerous members of his team gathered in the derelict space.

His throat works hard to swallow as he battles to contain his anger. I stare at him, shocked and muted. Just from looking in his eyes, I know the past two and a half months have been as torturous to him as they have been for me, but that doesn't stop me from standing my ground. I've waited for this day for years, and I'm not backing away without a fight.

"Katie wouldn't be in this situation if I hadn't forced her to come with me. She didn't want to go, Enrique, but I stupidly begged her to come."

Rico drops his hand from running along the scruff on his chin. "Katie is in this predicament because I was looking at someone I shouldn't have been looking at. If I'd just kept my mouth shut to Sergei's taunt, none of this would have happened. Not to you and not to Katie. It isn't your fault, Blaire. Nothing that happened that day was your fault."

"We both take blame for what happened that day. Then shouldn't we both have the chance to exonerate ourselves?"

He steps closer to me, surrounding me with his spicy scent. "I gave up everything I've ever wanted to save you from this lifestyle, and now you expect me to let you back in?"

I shake my head. "No. I'm not asking you to let me back in. I'm merely pleading for you to understand the guilt I harbor from that day. I feel responsible for what happened. This is the only way I can ease the guilt I've been carrying the past ten years. It will give me the chance to move on."

"To move on from this? Or us?" he sneers before he has the chance to stop his callous words.

From the anger projected in his voice, I know he's aware of the kiss Colt and I shared, but now is not the time to discuss the stupid mistakes we've both made in our tumultuous relationship. Katie needs to remain our utmost priority.

I hold his vehement stare, striving to display I've matured a lot over the past three months. I'm not the same Blaire he married within hours of meeting. I'm stronger and more determined.

When the silence becomes too great for me to ignore, I mumble, "I'm not the one who filed for divorce." I cringe, loathing that my voice comes out with a quiver. "I would have never given up on you like you did me." I keep my tone low, ensuring his crew won't hear my painstaking confession.

"I did that for you," Rico says. "Every terrible thing I've done the past three months, I did for you. But I *never* gave up on you. I *saved* you from a life of misery."

An ache hits my chest when a cloud of pain filters over his beautiful eyes, but it's nothing compared to the agony I've been harboring the past two and a half months. "We made promises to each other the night we got married. You never gave me the chance to uphold my vows."

Rico's eyes bounce between mine for several heart-clutching seconds. They're still the darkest I've seen, but I know the real Rico is hiding in there somewhere. A man can't walk the earth without a soul, and his beautiful eyes show his soul is just as remarkable as his outer shell.

"I loved you enough to save you from my lifestyle," he murmurs, his voice low and pained.

"And I *love* you enough I would have chosen to stay." My voice cracks with a range of emotions. "But you never gave me the chance to prove it. You took away my right to choose who I can or cannot love."

His stern mask slips, exposing a flare of emotion. Although his appearance makes him seem like an emotionally detached person, I know that isn't true. He's a deeply emotional man who would do anything to protect the people he loves.

"Please don't take this away from me as well, Enrique. I need closure for what happened to Katie. This will give me closure."

The dark cloud in his eyes fades as he considers my plea. Regret. Hope. Worry. They all blaze through his beautifully tormented eyes as he stands across from me muted in silence. When he takes a step closer to me, Erik attempts to speak, but Rico raises his hand into the air, cutting him off. Anxiety spurs on my furious pulse. It isn't just concern that he will deny my pleas that has my heart rate quickening, it's my body's reaction to the closeness of its mate. Even in the most heart-strangling situation, his closeness still incites a carnal desire to run ravenously through me.

The past three months of despair disappear in an instant when he places his hand on my jaw and locks his glistening eyes with mine. It won't matter if it's endured two months of heartache or two years, his touch will always heal my maimed heart.

"Please, Enrique," I beg, returning his ardent stare.

His smoldering eyes stare into mine as he finally gives in. "You're to stay in the car with Brent the entire time."

I sigh in relief before issuing him my gratitude with a smile.

His spicy scent adds to the giddiness in my stomach when he tilts into my side and growls, "But if you so much as touch your seat belt latch, that spanking I gave you the last time we slept together will be the least of your worries."

Ignoring the way his threat both scared and thrilled me, I nod a little overeagerly.

A little after midnight Monday morning, I'm seated in the front passenger seat of a black Escalade three doors up from the house where they believe Katie is being held captive. Over the past several hours, Rico and Erik gave me a general rundown of the conditions Katie has been living under.

I'm not going to lie, it was hard listening to all the details. After Katie was snatched from Ravenshoe ten years ago, she was to be placed on the black market. But when she caught the eye of one of the head honchos of the Bobrov crew, he decided to keep Katie as his pet. In all honesty, I haven't worked out yet if that was a good or bad thing for Katie.

The blond-haired man seems to have taken a fondness to Katie. He has kept her fed, clothed, and safe the past ten years, but if he truly cared for Katie, wouldn't he do everything in his power to get her out of his corrupt lifestyle as Rico had done for me?

It was only during my discussions with Rico and Erik did the reality for what Rico did for me finally dawn on my tired brain. I've been devastated the past two and a half months, believing Rico didn't love me. Where, in reality, he loved me so much he sacrificed his own happiness to save me.

Once Katie is safe, I'll find a way to do the same for him.

I jump out of my skin when my cell phone unexpectedly dings, announcing I have a new text message.

"Sorry," I apologize to Brent when my startled reaction alarms him. Once Brent swings his irate gaze back to scanning the street, I drop my eyes to my phone.

LACEY:

How's the date going? Need me to call in backup?

A grin curls onto my lips. The only way I could get Lacey off my back when I called to say I wouldn't be home tonight was by pretending I was going on an intimate date. I thought she would have heard the deceit in my voice, but with my emotions still running high from being in Rico's presence, no deceit could be found.

ME:

It's going well. Now, shush, I'm busy...

LACEY:

Don't forget protection!

Her text is aiming for playful, but it causes a stabbing pain to hit my chest. It's my own fault. No one is aware I'm pregnant—not even Rico. For some inane reason, I wanted to tell Rico in a non-volatile environment. Considering our last four hours had been spent surrounded by members of a dangerous mob, I kept my mouth shut tight.

After rubbing my knuckles over the tightness in my chest, I quickly type out a message.

ME:

I've got it covered.

LACEY:

Good girl. TTYL.

ME:

Bye.

I shut down my phone and shove it into my clutch purse thrown on the floor.

"How long do these things normally take?" I ask Brent, my words garbled with suspense.

He turns his eyes from the poorly lit street to me. "It would be a whole lot quicker if I wasn't stuck babysitting my boss's girlfriend."

Okay. Apparently, he isn't happy with Rico's decision.

Before I have the chance to respond to his snide comment—or correct him that I'm Rico's wife—the brightness of headlights illuminates the cabin of the Escalade.

My already agile heart rate kicks up a notch when the SUV with gun-wielding men hanging on the side mounts the curb and pulls into the front yard of the house where Katie is held.

Time comes to a standstill when Rico curls out of the passenger seat with two semi-automatic weapons clasped in his hands. He's wearing his regular attire I saw him leave for *work* in every day I was at the compound—a crisp black suit, but he's minus the tie he was wearing earlier.

Even with tension hanging thick in the air, the sight of Rico hampers my ability to secure a full breath. Tonight, he's the very definition of dark and dangerous rolled into one undoubtedly beautiful package.

Like I'm sitting front row at an action flick, the scene unfolds before my very eyes in slow motion. Guns flare, bullets are dislodged, and men fall to the ground. Normally, this type of incident would have my stomach twisted in knots, but tonight I feel different. I don't know if it's because revenge is finally being served to the men who hurt Katie and me ten years ago or because Vegas did truly screw with my mind. But since now is not an appropriate time to evaluate my sudden shift to the dark side, I leash my feelings for a more fitting time.

As Rico moves closer to the residence, I keep my eyes locked on him while the same prayer plays on repeat through my mind—that both he and Katie get out of this alive and in one piece.

The awful anxiety I felt when I first saw Katie returns the closer Rico gets to the heavily manned residence. I push aside the uneasiness swirling in my stomach, downplaying it as my pregnancy playing havoc with my emotions.

Seconds feel like hours when Rico and his men enter the derelict house. Although the scene is nowhere near as ghastly as it was when they first arrived, the air has an eerie feeling to it that makes my skin crawl.

Ignoring the niggling feeling in the back of my head that something bad is about to happen, I focus my attention on scanning the face of every man emerging from the house, seeking Rico amongst the group.

I inhale my first full breath when Rico walks out of the property moments later with a wide-eyed and clearly startled Katie in his arms.

Gratefulness swells my heart and tears well in my eyes.

Not thinking, I throw open the door of the Escalade and race toward them. My fast speed causes tears of happiness to trickle down my cheeks.

I hear Rico scream my name, but nothing can slow my brisk pace.

Nothing but a bullet...

ENRIQUE

"*B*laire!" I roar when I spot her racing down the cracked sidewalk.

Concern strikes my heart when the moonlight bounces off the tears rolling down her cheeks. A smile stretches across her face as she sprints toward me.

Clearly, her tears are tears of happiness not sadness, which eases my anxiety.

Although her breathtaking smile is something I've craved seeing for weeks, the area isn't secure enough for her to be out here yet. Normally, lurkers are lying in wait for a prime opportunity to take down a major player in our industry. That's the reason I made her stay with Brent. I shouldn't have let her come at all. It isn't safe, but I'm completely lost to this woman.

Even being separated from her for two and a half months didn't dampen my feelings the slightest. I love her, without a doubt, but that's the reason I gave her up. She doesn't belong in my industry, so I did everything in my power to save her from it. I sold my soul to the devil to ensure my *Ангел* didn't have to live in the depths of hell. I became a man by doing what I should have done the moment she landed in my lap three months ago.

I set her free.

It was only during our heart-strangling confrontation earlier tonight did I realize I hadn't fully saved Blaire from the pits of hell. I partly pushed her into it. I thought I was saving her from a life of misery when I accepted my father's offer of a full sanction for her. In reality, I made her life miserable.

The pain in her eyes when she told me I stole her right to choose who she can love felt like sustaining a direct hit to my heart. It gutted me even more than seeing her kiss Colt. But in my defense, the hurt Blaire has experienced the past two and a half months is nothing compared to the life she could have faced if I hadn't forced her decision.

I know she's hurting—so am I—but I'll never stop protecting her. I'll do everything in my power to keep her safe.

Even sacrificing my own happiness.

When I spot Brent coughing and wheezing as his three-packs-a-day lungs struggle to secure a full breath, I realize he doesn't have the speed to reach Blaire before she enters a world she doesn't belong in.

Cursing in the night air at Brent's incompetence, I hand our target, Katie, to Erik.

When I spin back around to face Blaire, the air in my lungs is forcefully removed. Her brisk sprint down the cracked sidewalk halts mid-stride when a bullet rockets through her stomach.

"Blaire!" I roar before executing the man who shot her with a direct hit between his eyes.

He drops to the ground, his eyes still open wide but void of any signs of life.

I run to Blaire, only just catching her in my arms before she hits the concrete sidewalk. Bile rises to my throat when the blood gushing from her wound covers my hands in under a second. Her breaths are wheezy and slow as she fights through a torrent of pain rocketing through her body.

When I lay her down on the dew-covered ground, I apply pressure on her stomach. Panic engulfs me when her warm blood gushes between my interlocked fingers. I know all too well that she's mere minutes away from bleeding out.

A gargled groan whimpers through her lips when I increase my pressure on her stomach while yelling, "Get a medic!" at the top of my lungs. "Where's the fucking ambulance?"

Blaire peers up at me with glistening, tear-filled eyes. Her lips twitch, but not a word leaves her blue-tinged mouth.

"Shh, Kitten. You're okay. I've got you," I murmur when she continues trying to speak.

I crank my neck to the right when a first responder breaks the eerie silence enveloping us. Relief washes through me when the visual of an ambulance gliding down the street greets me.

Returning my eyes to Blaire, I murmur, "Help is on the way. Just hold on."

Tears trickle down her temples as she continues moving her mouth. I slant my head and lean in close as my ears struggle to hear the faint word she's whispering on repeat.

Sirens wail, intermingled with whimpers of pain, but the most devastating thing I've ever heard shrills through my ears and issues my heart with another direct hit when Blaire murmurs, "Baby."

I pull back and glance into her eyes, certain I haven't heard her right.

Keeping her dilated gaze on me, she moves one of her shaky hands to the bottom of her flat stomach while her other hand covers my hands vainly trying to stop the blood gushing out of the open wound.

Dread engulfs me when I feel how cold her hands are.

They feel like ice.

Droplets of blood splatter her lips when she whispers, "Our baby."

"Baby? You're pregnant?"

My blood blackens and scorches my veins with furious heat when Blaire dimly nods. My chest heaves in turmoil as my eyes absorb the amount of blood that has seeped into her shirt. I don't know anything about pregnancy, but Blaire's life is already precariously dangling on the edge of a very steep cliff from the amount of blood she has lost, so I can't stomach what the odds are for our baby to survive such a trau-matic injury.

Any chance to ease the lingering fear that our baby has been harmed is lost when her blinks lengthen and her head lolls to the side.

"Blaire!" I shout through the nausea circling my windpipe. "Stay with me, Blaire. Fuck. Please. Stay with me."

I'm so focused on Blaire I don't notice the blackness creeping up on me until it's too late.

37

BLAIRE

$\mathcal{J}$ust like it had following my attack ten years ago, my brain has been operating in lockdown mode the past five days. I've drifted in and out of unconsciousness, confused between what is reality and what is a dream. I can't recall the events leading up to me lying in a hospital bed, but from the ghastly smell and the constant prodding I've endured, I know that's where I am.

Fighting against my body's pleas, I slowly flutter my eyes open. My assumptions are proven accurate when my blurry eyes lock in on an IV stand with one and a half bags of fluid dangling off it. The beeping of monitors filters through my ears, and the swirling of my stomach grows as I scan the sanitary-scented room. From my lowered position, I can see numerous floral arrangements covering every surface and the smallest tuff of inky dark hair resting near my right wrist.

"Rico." My word comes out hoarse, hampered by the scratchy rawness of my throat.

I cough to clear my throat before attempting to speak again. My brittle wheezing through my pained lungs announces my awakened status before another word can seep from my lips. The dark-haired man lifts his head off my bed and swings his eyes around my room. He appears dazed and confused.

Against my wishes, disappointment clouds me when the worldly eyes of my dad lock on my confused gaze.

I was hoping he was Rico.

"Blaire, honey. You're awake!" His loud voice adds to the giddiness clustering in my blurry mind.

He shoots out of his chair and races to the corridor more quickly than a sixty-year-old man should move. "Hurry! She's awake. Blaire's awake."

Not even two seconds later, my mom bursts into the room, infusing the ghastly smelling space with her rich wildflower scent. After dumping two vending machine coffees onto a side tray, she stops at the side of my bed. Lacey enters the room soon after my mom but respectfully gives my mom some space so she can issue her motherly smothering she does every time I'm in her presence.

"You've had us worried out of our mind," my mom mumbles into my hair as she curls her arms around my torso and squeezes me tightly.

I hide the grimace attempting to cross my face from her firm hold when she draws back to peer into my eyes. My confusion deepens when I roam my eyes over her face. I've not seen my mom for three months, but she looks like she aged three years in that time.

As tears form in her eyes, she runs her hand down the side of my face. When she glances into my eyes like she can't believe I'm in front of her, it takes all my strength to give her hand a reassuring squeeze.

Once my mom props her backside on the edge of my bed, I drift my eyes between the three sets of eyes staring at me with concern. "What happened?" I ask, my voice croaky.

My dad moves to the side table to pour me a glass of water. After sipping on enough chilled water to ease the scorching burn in my throat, I bounce my eyes between my parents and Lacey. My brows knit together. They all appear to have aged so much in a short time.

My confused eyes rocket to my hospital room door—adding to the giddiness in my head—when it suddenly swings open. An Asian-looking doctor with a kind smile and bright green eyes enters the room carrying a stainless steel clipboard.

"Hello, Blaire, my name is Jae," she greets me, her voice a unique mix of accents. "I'm the head of surgery at Ravenshoe Private Hospital. It's great to finally talk to you in person."

After returning her smile, I ask, "What happened?" I'm not meaning to be rude. I'm just seeking answers to my questions.

Lacey pushes off the door and stands next to Jae. "Blaire's having a little bit of difficulty with her memory."

Jae smiles a contrite grin. "That's understandable. We have had you heavily sedated the past five days."

Although shocked at her admission I've been in hospital for five days, I'm not completely astounded. I feel the most rested I've ever felt.

While removing a light from her crisp white doctor's jacket, Jae moves to the left side of my bed. When she flashes a bright light into my eyes, I inhale a sharp, ragged breath. My mouth falls open as all the events leading up to me being shot flash before my eyes.

Panic consumes me as my hands dart down to my stomach. "The baby. Is my baby okay?" I ask Jae, dread in my tone.

My parents stare at each other in shock. Their mouths wide, their brows stitched.

When her shock wears off, Lacey squeals, "You're pregnant?"

Tears almost dribble down my cheek when I nod at the three sets of eyes staring at me. Although their mouths don't utter a syllable, their eyes are questioning enough.

"Well, I was..." *Oh god. Please let my baby be okay.*

Dr. Jae places her small hand on my forearm, drawing my attention back to her. "Because you're only a little bit over three months along, the fetus is burrowed deep within your pelvis, happily nestled away from the area the bullet entered your stomach. Since the medics were advised of your condition on arrival, we ensured only pregnancy-approved drugs have been administered since you've been here. I'll schedule another scan in a few days, but everything appears to be following the path it should be."

I snap my eyes shut as sweet relief engulfs me.

My happiness is short-lived when the air shifts so dramatically, a shiver racks through me. Clutching my chest to ensure my wildly beating heart remains in my chest, I slowly open my eyes. A numbness spreads across my chest when I'm met with four sets of eyes staring at me in alarm.

"But..." I want to say more, but I can't force any more words out of my mouth. The tension suffocating the air of oxygen thickens as my concern grows exponentially.

"What aren't you telling me?" I force out through the painful lump in my throat.

Heaviness slams into my chest when Jae turns to face my parents. "I'll give you a few moments of privacy. Please be aware Blaire has just awoken after major trauma."

The beat of my heart merges into dangerous territory, sending the equipment on the side of my bed into alarm. They are the exact words spoken to my parents when they advised me Katie didn't escape our attackers' clutches the first time.

After switching off the wailing alarm, Jae exits the room, and I lock my eyes with my dad. "Katie?" My one word is rickety, coerced through a sob.

Keeping his eyes connected with my wide gaze, my dad moves to sit in the chair next to my bed. When he curls his hand around mine, the rattle of his hand vibrates all the way up my arm. His eyes glisten with unshed tears as he says, "Katie is okay. She's safe." I sigh in relief as tears of joy roll down my cheeks, but my breathing turns labored when my dad adds, "But Rico..."

My eyes rocket to my dad. "No... oh, god, please no," I beg when his eyes relay the entire story without another word needing to escape his lips.

My dad scoots to the edge of his chair and stares me straight in the eyes while saying, "He saved you, honey. Rico put himself in the line of fire to save you."

Pain shreds through my heart, tearing it in two. "No, Daddy, no." I sob, not wanting to believe the truth beaming from his truthful eyes.

Standing, he bands his arms around my shoulders. "I'm sorry, honey. I'm so sorry."

My heart shatters.
Not partly.
Not slightly.
Wholly.

38

BLAIRE

Four weeks later...

News of Rico's untimely death circulated on every news channel in the country the two weeks following his death. Hysteria broke out from the fear his murder would start the equivalent of World War III within the Russian mob. Even the governor urged calm. The only thing that eased the tempestuous waters was when the man who was arrested for killing Rico was found hanging in his jail cell the morning of his arraignment. Suspicions ran high that he too was murdered, but with the surveillance cameras in the local county jail on the fritz, they were only that. Rumors.

Just like the months following my return from Vegas, I've been slowly wading my way through the stages of grief. I cried. I got angry. Now, I'm in denial. I'm not just talking about Rico's death, I am talking about every part of my life that included him in it.

All I want to do is crawl into my bed and forget the world exists.

That would be a whole heap easier to do if I weren't lying in a hospital bed with an ultrasound wand gliding over the small curve in the bottom of my belly.

I've spent the last four weeks recovering in the hospital from my gunshot wound. The nursing staff and doctors have been wonderful. They didn't even bat an eyelid when my frightened screams in the middle of the night bellowed down the corridor or when they would find me huddled in the corner of the room crying like a blubbering mess. They took my drastic mood swings in stride, giving me space when needed and occasionally a shoulder to cry on.

They have been a godsend.

But with my injuries now manageable, I can go home—after they check on the little miracle nestled safely in my stomach.

Lacey's squeeze on my hand tightens when my baby's heartbeat fills the silence in the hospital room. It's a bittersweet sound.

Bitter, because Rico never got the chance to hear it.

Sweet, because a part of him will forever live on in his baby's memory.

"Do you want to know the sex?" the ultrasound technician, Jennifer, asks.

"Isn't it too early to tell?"

Jennifer smiles a tight grin. "Depends on the baby. Your baby is very obliging today." Her cheerful tone forces the first genuine smile onto my face in weeks.

"Okay. I want to know," I inform Jennifer, nodding.

I hold my breath as I wait for her to issue me the news I already know. It isn't because I can tell an arm from a leg in the images on the monitor at the side of my head, I can just feel it deep in my soul. I know I'm carrying Rico's son, a little boy who will have eyes as beautiful as his father's.

Jennifer clicks on the keyboard of her ultrasound machine before zooming in on the black and white image. "Can you see that?"

Blood surges into my heart as I nod. Even without having a degree in radiology, I can't miss the long dangling thing sitting between the baby's legs. *Rico's son's legs.*

After wiping the gel off my stomach, Jennifer helps me sit before handing me two black and white printouts. The weight on my chest doubles when I peer down at the images of the little miracle I created with Rico.

"After you empty your bladder, you're free to go." She wraps her arms around my torso. "Best of luck, Blaire. If you ever need anything, don't hesitate to call."

"Thank you." My voice is barely a whisper.

Throughout the day, the nurses and doctors who cared for me the past four weeks have expressed similar sentiments.

Putting on a brave front, I tell Lacey I'll be out in a minute before stepping into the bathroom. Although my injuries have healed quickly, a twinge of pain still rockets through my body with every step I take.

I manage to make it inside the bathroom before the first devastated sob tears from my throat. I bite on the side of my palm to ensure Lacey won't hear my heartbreaking howls as the final stage of my grief reaches fruition.

Acceptance.

I grip the edge of the vanity in a white-knuckled hold before crouching down, no longer trusting my legs to keep me upright. My cries are loud and gut-wrenchingly long. In these walls, I could hide away from reality and pretend nothing happened, but the instant I step foot out of this hospital, I'm being forced into a world where I have to start living again.

In a cruel, tormented world without Rico.

I don't know if I can do that.

The two and a half months following my return from Vegas was painful enough, but knowing I'll never see Rico again utterly destroys me.

After splashing water on my tear-stained cheeks, I exit the bathroom and shadow Lacey to her car. She can tell I've been crying, but thankfully, she pretends she can't. She's been great the past four weeks —the only person I could truly talk to—but I still don't think she fully understands the crippling pain I'm feeling. How can I explain that I lost the love of my life to a group of people who think Rico was nothing more than a drunken mistake? It's not possible. I've tried.

Remaining quiet, I keep my eyes planted on the scenery whizzing by as we make our ten-mile trip home. Just like the day Rico collected me from Ravenshoe, everything looks similar, but it feels different. The heavy clog of traffic is still on the roads, the sky is still blue, but something is missing.

Someone is missing.

Acting purely on instincts, I follow the same mundane routine I always do when I come home. I gather my mail off the floor and hit the button on the answering machine.

"I'll make coffee." Lacey stops halfway into the kitchen and spins around to face me. "Can pregnant ladies drink coffee?"

I laugh, but it's full of despair. "I don't know. This is all new to me too."

Lacey twists her lips. "I'll do tea just in case. Chamomile tea," she says with a slight nod of her head.

I force a fake smile onto my face, grateful she's taking my pregnancy in her stride. "None for me. I'm going to jump into bed. I'll see you tomorrow?"

Her bottom lip drops into a pout, and she looks like she wants to plead with me, but thankfully, she just nods. "One step at a time, Blaire. It will slowly get better."

After kicking off my shoes, I kiss her cheek and walk down the hallway to my room. Even though I've spent the past four weeks in bed, mine is still calling me. I don't know if it is my pregnancy making me sleepy or the heavy grief sitting in the middle of my chest.

Either way, I'm exhausted.

I stop halfway down the hall when my answering machine announces the timestamp of a message, one recorded within hours of Rico's death.

"Blaire, it's Katie..." She swallows before she continues, "Thank you. I know what happened, and I'm sorry, but I just wanted to say thank you for never giving up on me."

Pain twists through my chest. I've talked to Katie a few times over the past four weeks, but our conversations were quite brief. Understandably, we both have a lot of issues to work through. But, hopefully, one day, we'll both be strong enough to arrange a face-to-face meeting.

I run my hand across my cheeks, removing the tears tracking down my face before continuing with my mission. My steps are slow and sluggish. Although I faked a chipper personality throughout the hospital mandatory counseling for victims of violent crimes, I'm fairly certain I'm on the cusp of depression. I've lost weight, I constantly feel restless even doing nothing but sleeping, and no matter how hard I try to ignore it, I feel dead on the inside.

After flicking on the light in my room, I lower the dimmer so it's dark but not completely black.

I can't stand the thought of sleeping in a completely darkened room.

My sluggish steps to my bed stop—closely followed by the beat of my heart—when I detect I'm being watched. I blink several times to clear my blurry vision when my eyes lock in on a dark shadow at the side of my bed. My lips twitch, dying to spill the screams running through my brain, but my mouth fails to cooperate.

I'm once again rendered mute by fear.

Even frightened, my naturally engrained fighter instincts kick in.

It's not just me I'm protecting anymore. It's also my baby.

I'll protect him until I take my very last breath.

Any chance of leaving my room with my heart intact flies out the window when the shadowed figure steps out of the darkness and says, "Hello, Kitten."

Goose bumps rush over my skin as a dash of disbelief taints my blood. I shake my head, certain my eyes are playing tricks on me.

When the brisk shake of my head fails to clear the image in front of me, I take a step closer to the denim-clad man. With my composure balancing precariously between insanity and lucidity, my eyes scan every inch of Rico's body, seeking any type of morbid injury.

I fail to find any. Other than his hair being clipped close to his scalp, and his dark eyes concealed by a pair of thick-rimmed glasses, he looks the same as he always has—dark and dangerous rolled into one unbelievably handsome package.

"How?" I want to say more, but I've been rendered speechless. I can barely grasp what is and isn't reality, let alone speak.

When Rico removes his glasses and places them on my dresser, tears fill my eyes. "There was only one way I could leave my family, Kitten."

"Not breathing," we quote at the same time.

"But... it can't... you're..." Nothing I'm saying makes any sense. It can't be helped. I'm staring at a ghost.

When Rico moves closer to me, his spicy scent engulfs my senses, adding further confirmation that my imagination isn't playing tricks on me.

Rico is standing before me—alive and well.

You'd think my first reaction would be to throw my arms around his neck and never let him go.

It isn't.

My palm sets on fire when I strike him hard across the face.

"How could you do that to me?"

Unable to hold back the desires of my heart any longer, I throw my arms around his neck. I seek deeper contact, needing more, always wanting more when it comes to him. I bury my face in his neck and breathe in his scent, my mind spiraling, my heart shut down.

He scoops me into his arms and moves us to sit on my bed. I cling to his plain white shirt, certain he'll vanish at any moment. Holding my jaw in his shaking hands, his riddled-with-remorse eyes dance between mine, relaying his sympathies for the horror I've been living the past four weeks without a word needing to trickle from his lips.

"You broke my heart," I whimper with heartache in my brittle tone.

The pain in his beautiful eyes grows. "I know, Kitten, but we needed it to look real. We knew they'd be watching you. Your grief added to the belief of our story."

I frown in confusion. "Our?"

He brushes a tear off my cheek. "Erik and me. Erik isn't a lawyer. He works for the FBI." My confusion skyrockets when he adds, "So do I."

"What?" It's hard to get my words out with how tight my throat is.

He peers into my eyes so I can see the truth relayed in his. "I've been working alongside the FBI the past six years."

"You've been working *undercover* in the Popov compound for six years?" I ask through the bile sitting in the back of my throat.

I feel sick. My stomach is twisting so badly I feel physically ill.

When I attempt to scamper off Rico's lap, he holds on tight, refusing to let me go.

"You lied to me. This whole time you've been lying to me?"

I'm stuck halfway between angry and grateful.

Angry he never told me.

Grateful he can tell me now.

I freeze and gasp in a quick breath. "Is Vladimir even your father?"

Rico cups my jaw and glances into my eyes. Just seeing the torment in his gaze dampens the anger raging in my stomach. Only he can change my moods more quickly than he can convert from day to night.

"Everything you witnessed and heard about my life is true, Blaire. I've never lied to you. I'm Vladimir's son. His firstborn son. I may have been raised by a monster, but I'm not a monster myself. You know this, as you know the real me."

My brows stitch. "You've said that to me before, haven't you?"

The corner of his lips tugs high before he nods. "Yes, the night we got married. I told you every detail about my life. *Everything.*"

My mouth falls open. "I've known the entire time you're an FBI agent?"

His eyes dance between mine. "I'm not an agent... more of an *associate.*" His expression is as unsure as his words.

I take a few moments to let the information be absorbed by my exhausted brain.

The silence only creates more questions in my already overworked mind.

"Why did you wait so long? Why didn't you fake your death years ago?"

"After you were attacked in the alleyway ten years ago, my life changed in an instant. I wanted to be a better man," Rico replies before lifting and locking his dark eyes with me. "I wanted to be a better man for you. But Vladimir is very cautious. He knew he was being watched. The FBI has been undercover in the compound for years, but they had nothing on him. The information I obtained on him the past two years alone outweighs the last forty years of undercover work. I did more good from inside the compound than I ever could have from the outside because he never thought to suspect his own son."

He runs the backs of his fingers along my cheeks to gather my tears before dropping them to my mouth. The wetness of my tears relieves my dry lips. "I requested to leave when you were attacked in the servants' quarters, but the FBI wouldn't let me go. They needed more intel on Vladimir. That's what I did during our separation. I gathered as much evidence on Vladimir as I could."

His jaw gains a tick as he draws me in closer. He holds on to me like I'm truly the most valuable thing in his life. "When you got shot and told me about our baby, I knew I would never return to the Popov compound. I told Erik he either had to get me out or I'd find my own way out."

"How did Erik handle that?" I query, my rickety words unable to hide the mad beat of my heart.

Rico smirks. "Not very well, but he soon saw the benefit of it. My death means Erik is now ranked number three in the Popov empire. That's the deepest the FBI has infiltrated the compound."

"Except you," I mumble.

His smile enlarges. He looks part cocky, part smug.

After swallowing down the bitterness in the back of my throat, I ask the one question my heart wants immediately answered, "Oskana? What happened to her?"

His thighs tense beneath me as he clears his throat. "I had every intention of bringing her in. She killed herself before I had the chance." He stares into my eyes, ensuring I can see the truth conveyed by them. He's being honest.

I inwardly sigh. My heart knew he could never harm a woman. His soul is too beautiful to harbor a monster.

"Oskana knew her fate."

Rico nods. "She didn't know life outside the Popov compound. It was her entire world."

"Do you?" I interrupt. "Know life outside the Popov empire?"

"Yes," he replies without a pause for consideration. He connects his eyes with mine. "Especially when I'm with you."

His comment eases some of the nicks my heart has been beaten with the past three months. Don't construe my statement the wrong way. My heart still has a lot of healing to do, but I can see that process will be a whole lot easier now.

Although I still have many unanswered questions I want resolved, my brain is too overloaded with everything that has happened in the past thirty minutes to continue with our life-altering discussion. My heart? It only wants one thing. Him—Enrique—the stranger I married.

I run my hand over his clipped hair. "I like this," I mumble, my composure still halfway between insanity and reality.

Rico smiles. "Good. It was either clipped or blond."

He scoots us up the bed until his back is resting against the headboard. I nuzzle into his chest, loving his thumping heart booming into my ears. It was a noise I never thought I'd have the opportunity to hear again so I relish every precise beat.

We sit in silence for what feels like hours but is only mere minutes.

Once the silence becomes too great to ignore, I murmur, "Where do we go from here?"

I don't need to look at him to know he's smiling. I can feel it in my bones. "I've heard from a reliable source that Europe is nice this time of year. Although, he did warn me that I may need to take my wife out back to shoot her if it isn't planned well."

Lifting my head off his chest, I peer into his eyes. "Have you been talking to my dad?"

That's one of my dad's favorite sayings for when my mom's feathers get a little ruffled. Any time she gets flustered, he threatens to take her out back and shoot her. It's odd to think that in the family I grew up in, that type of bantering is perfectly acceptable, but for someone like Rico, he'd have to wonder if it was a simple joke or an actual threat.

That must have been a terrible environment to be raised in.

It makes me so grateful our son won't grow up in that atmosphere.

My pupils widen to the size of dinner plates. "Oh my God, I forgot to tell you. We're having—"

"A son," Rico fills in, smiling.

I stare at him, shocked and confused.

He tucks a strand of my hair behind my ear before locking his eyes with mine. "You can't trust anyone, Kitten. Even when they don't appear to be watching you, they are." He tilts his head closer so his minty fresh breath bounces off my lips before muttering, "Especially me."

Cringing, I sink deeper into the mattress. I'm already aware that he knows about the kiss Colt and I shared, but I don't have the energy to deal with that *situation* right now.

Another small stretch of silence passes between us. It's healing and most definitely required.

When Rico tightens his grip around my torso, I breathe him in, grateful we are getting a second chance in our tumultuous relationship. The past four months have been a teeth-clattering rollercoaster ride, but I'm sure now that the darkness has been vanquished, we will be unbreakable—a force to be reckoned with.

There's only one greater dynamic than a man protecting the woman he loves—a man protecting his family. So, although there's a niggle of doubt that this isn't the last we'll hear of the Popov empire, I have no doubt Rico will stop at nothing to keep our son and me safe. Just like I'll always be his light in a life full of blackness.

As the minutes tick by on the clock in silence, my eyelids grow heavy.

When I'm unable to stifle a yawn, Rico says, "Sleep if you're tired, Kitten. I'll be here when you wake."

He was.

That day.

And the next day.

And every day that followed.

BONUS CHAPTER

ENRIQUE

"We have a twenty-four-year-old pregnant Caucasian female with a gunshot wound to the upper right quadrant of her stomach, unresponsive on arrival but resuscitated on site. ETA to Ravenshoe Private is ten minutes," announces one of the paramedics into a radio strapped to his shoulder as his partner pushes an unconscious Blaire into the back of his ambulance.

I stumble backward when a third medic slams the ambulance doors shut before climbing into the driver's seat.

While running my fingers through my hair, my eyes scan the area. Dead bodies are sprawled across the compound of the recently reformed Petretti crew, and a few of my crew have sustained life-threatening injuries. But nothing compares to the lifeless look in Blaire's eyes when she peered up at me and told me she was pregnant. I've seen some bad shit in my life—stuff no man should ever have to witness—but her bleak eyes will forever haunt me.

I feel the blackness closing in on me, but I'm not strong enough to fight it anymore. I did everything I could to save Blaire from this lifestyle, yet she is still suffering the consequences of my actions ten years ago.

When is enough going to be enough?

I'm tired of this fucking life.

I'm tired of the game.

I'm tired of pretending to be someone I'm not.

Adrenaline surges through my body as I grab one of the many guns left lying on the blood-soaked lawn. I storm past the men in my crew, eyeing me with caution, my pace unchecked. Burning rubber lingers in the air when I dive into the black SUV mounted on the curb and shoot out into the street.

Ignoring the shake of my blood-covered hands, I check that my pistol is loaded and the safety is off as I make a short three-block trip.

I'm out of the SUV and storming toward a white surveillance van before the SUV comes to a complete stop. Numerous faces lift from the bank of monitors in front of them when I throw open the surveillance van's door and step inside. Their mouths gape open, and their eyes widen, clearly shocked at seeing the carnage they are witnessing firsthand on a computer screen, but they remain seated, either scared or unsure of what to do.

FBI agents jump from their seats when I move through the surveillance van, but I don't pay them any attention. There's only one man I came here to see—Agent Alex Rogers.

Because he's so immersed in evaluating the massacre that just occurred, he doesn't notice me sneaking up on him until my gun is pushed up against his right temple.

"You'll be dead before you even remove your pistol," I warn when his hand slides toward his gun holstered at his side.

"Rico—"

"I want out," I interrupt.

Like a man who has no concerns for his safety, Alex turns around to face me, pretending he can't feel my gun pinching the skin on his temple. "We still have so much information we need to get before I can approve that."

"I. Want. Out!" I roar again before pushing my gun to the small portion of skin between Alex's eyes.

I hear several guns being removed from their holsters to no doubt be pointed at me, but I don't back down. I've walked too far into the blackness for fear to stop me now. A soulless man can't feel anything, let alone something as weak as fear.

"Enrique," says a voice to my side. "We've discussed this. You know what we need."

I drift my eyes to Erik. "I've given your agency six fucking years of my life. Not anymore. I'm done."

I wasn't joking when I said my life changed full circle when Blaire was attacked in the alleyway. The FBI has been infiltrating the Popov empire for years, way before my mother was killed. The years following Blaire's attack, I tried to gain the trust of the men I believed were deep undercover in our compound, but none of them trusted me. They all thought I was hunting snitching rats. Erik was the only one who trusted me enough to fully disclose himself and his operation. He's been sheltering me under the FBI banner for the past six years.

"I've spent the past three months living in the deepest pits of hell. I became a man only a monster like my father would be proud of. I've given all I can fucking give. I'm done."

As Erik steps closer to me, his remorse-crammed eyes request that I lower my weapon without a word needing to seep from his lips. "Heads will roll," he warns when I refuse to lower my gun.

"Not as much as they will when I disclose every agent in the Popov compound to Vladimir." I swing my eyes back to Alex. "Starting with your brother."

Alex holds his ground, vainly trying to act unaffected by my threat. Little does he know, I know way more than he thinks I do. You don't spend years walking amongst the dead not to learn how they operate.

"I can arrest you right now, and you would never see daylight again," Alex snarls, his words vicious.

I laugh. It's a laugh that displays how far I've walked into the blackness that's been swallowing my life the past twenty-four years. "You really think four walls will stop me? Your agency was left scrambling when I was snatched right under your nose after I killed Col Petretti. This is way above your pay grade, Alex. It's time for you to step back and watch how the big boys play."

As much as it kills me to do, I lower my gun from Alex's head and turn my eyes to Erik. "I'm done. You either get me out, or I'll find my own way out."

With that, I turn on my heels and walk out of the surveillance van, trusting that Erik will have my back as he has for the past six years. He knows too well the hell I've endured the past ten years as he was standing right beside me. Erik was the one who sought medical attention when my back was burned with acid as punishment for helping Blaire. He was the one who helped me ensure my sister's fiancé was the winning bidder when my youngest sister, Callie, was auctioned on the black market, and he was the one who stopped me from killing Nikolai when I found out he orchestrated Blaire's attack.

Erik has guided me through some of my darkest days. And since today is the blackest day I've endured, I need to trust he will continue to have my back as I've had his these past six years.

———

Several hours later, I'm walking into a recovery room at Ravenshoe Private Hospital. The heaviness on my chest intensifies when my eyes lock in on Blaire lying in the middle of the bed. She looks so tiny and frail swamped by the medical equipment surrounding her.

"I'll keep the staff occupied for ten minutes, but I can't give you any more time than that." Jae runs her hand down my arm before gesturing for me to the enter the room.

Just before she exits, I call out, "The baby?"

Jae smiles. "They did a quick ultrasound during surgery. Everything looks okay."

The stranglehold clutching my throat weakens. "Thanks."

Jae nods before exiting the room.

I remove the cap hanging low on my head and place it on the side table attached to Blaire's bed before moving to stand next to her. Other than the medical equipment surrounding her, you wouldn't know she's injured. She just looks like she's sleeping. She has the same peaceful look on her face she was wearing when I saw her dancing at a nightclub six weeks ago.

The weeks following Blaire leaving Vegas, I tried to stay away from her. But just like my ability to deny her requests, I couldn't. I needed to know she was safe.

The night I followed Blaire to a bustling nightclub in Ravenshoe was a bittersweet night. I was glad she was safe and happy but also devastated she appeared to be moving on. Even though I wanted to save her from my life-style, I always hoped I'd be saved one day too and that we could be together.

Although seeing her enjoying life outside the compound hurt, it also rein-forced I had done the right thing. After everything she'd been through, she deserved to be happy.

That was why I filed for divorce. I thought it was what she wanted.

My mind snaps back to the present when Blaire mumbles something in her sleep. Her eyes are moving rapidly under her eyelids, and her face is scrunched up. When her hand creeps across the sheets to grab at the IV line inserted in her opposite wrist, I curl my hand around hers.

"Shh, Kitten, you're okay. I've got you," I mutter as I glide my thumb over her hand.

Over time, her jittery movements still, and the heavy grooves in her fore-head smooth. I sit with her for several minutes, comforting her in silence. Jae said Blaire's parents have been called, but with them in Europe, they won't be here for a few more hours. And since Lacey isn't related by blood, she can't see Blaire until she's wheeled out of recovery.

Several minutes later, when a door creaks, I shift my eyes to the side, expecting to see Jae.

I'm taken aback when I see Erik's six-foot frame filling the doorway.

He walks two steps into the room before saying, "If you want to do this, we need to do it now, and we need to do it right."

The heaviness on my chest clears away. It's time for me to finally go home.

I nod at Erik before kissing Blaire's cracked lips. "Don't forget me, Kitten," I whisper against her mouth. "I'll be home soon."

"Just do it already!" I shout, glaring at Erik.

His gun is pointed at me but he is failing to pull the trigger.

I take a step closer to him. "You said we need to do this right, so let's do it. You know the areas to avoid. Your aim is nearly perfect. Shoot me."

"Nearly perfect isn't fucking perfect," Erik replies, his words as uneasy as

his facial expression. "I could kill you, Enrique. One millimeter in the wrong direction can be the difference between life and death."

I shake my head. "That's not going to happen."

"How can you be so sure?" Erik's voice is laced with uncertainty.

"Because I trust you. You have my back like I've always had yours. Do it. Shoot me!"

Sensing Erik's hesitation, Alex hands the mobile device recording the incident of my 'death' to a blond-haired agent at his side. Without a moment of indecision, he yanks the gun out of Erik's grasp, points it at me, and fires three times.

Pain rockets through my right shoulder, my left thigh, and the upper right quadrant of my stomach. Bitter-tasting bile surges to the back of my throat as dizziness plagues me. I remain standing for mere seconds before the pain tearing through my body becomes too great for me to handle. I crash to the ground hard while clutching the wound in my stomach. Blood splatters my lips as I wheezily battle to fill my lungs with air.

The dew-covered ground cools my back when I roll over and face the stars scattered in a brilliant, dark sky. It reminds me of the shimmering in Blaire's eyes every time she's about to smile.

Looking into her eyes when she's happy is like staring up at a million stars brightening a pitch-black night.

It's so beautiful.

She's so beautiful.

My light.

My life.

My everything.

As the blackness slowly rolls in, my thoughts go to her—my little kitten.

THE END...

The next book in the Enigma series is about Hawke. Widower, soldier, and bodyguard of Rise Up. His book is called Second Shot

. . .

Did you know **Nikolai**, Enrique's brother, has his own series? It is called Nikolai: A Mafia Prince Romance

Facebook: facebook.com/authorshandi

Instagram: instagram.com/authorshandi

Email: authorshandi@gmail.com

Reader's Group: bit.ly/ShandiBookBabes

Website: authorshandi.com

Newsletter: https://www.subscribepage.com/AuthorShandi

Did you know **Nikolai**, Enrique's brother, has his own series? It is called Nikolai: A Mafia Prince Romance

ALSO BY SHANDI BOYES

Denotes Standalone Books

Perception Series

Saving Noah *

Fighting Jacob *

Taming Nick *

Redeeming Slater *

Saving Emily

Wrapped Up with Rise Up

Protecting Nicole *

Enigma

Enigma

Unraveling an Enigma

Enigma The Mystery Unmasked

Enigma: The Final Chapter

Beneath The Secrets

Beneath The Sheets

Spy Thy Neighbor *

The Opposite Effect *

I Married a Mob Boss *

Second Shot *

The Way We Are

The Way We Were

Sugar and Spice *

Lady In Waiting

Man in Queue

Couple on Hold

Enigma: The Wedding

Silent Vigilante

Hushed Guardian

Quiet Protector

Enigma: An Isaac Retelling

Twisted Lies *

Bound Series

Chains

Links

Bound

Restrain

The Misfits *

Nanny Dispute *

Russian Mob Chronicles

Nikolai: A Mafia Prince Romance

Nikolai: Taking Back What's Mine

Nikolai: What's Left of Me

Nikolai: Mine to Protect

Asher: My Russian Revenge *

Nikolai: Through the Devil's Eyes

Trey *

<u>The Italian Cartel</u>

Dimitri

Roxanne

Reign

Mafia Ties (Novella)

Maddox

Demi

Ox

Rocco *

Clover *

Smith *

<u>RomCom Standalones</u>

Just Playin' *

<u>Ain't Happenin'</u> *

<u>The Drop Zone</u> *

Very Unlikely *

False Start *

<u>Short Stories - Newsletter Downloads</u>

Christmas Trio *

Falling For A Stranger *

<u>One Night Only Series</u>

Hotshot Boss *

Hotshot Neighbor *

<u>The Bobrov Bratva Series</u>

Wicked Intentions *

Sinful Intentions *

Devious Intentions *

Deadly Intentions *

www.ingramcontent.com/pod-product-compliance
Lightning Source LLC
Chambersburg PA
CBHW071136180726
48291CB00007B/2195